Reviewers Say . . .

"A VIVID AND CONVINCING PICTURE"
King Features Syndicate, Parade of Books

"A BOOK TO BE READ WITH EAGERNESS AND TALKED ABOUT WITH ENTHUSIASM"
Atlanta Constitution-Journal

"A SINCERE AND PRAISEWORTHY WORK . . . DRAMATIC AND CONTROVERSIAL"
Minneapolis Tribune

"ONE OF THE MOST PALATABLE HELPINGS OF ROMAN POLITICAL HISTORY I HAVE ENCOUNTERED"
The Christian Century

"A BIOGRAPHY WITH FICTIONAL CHINKING THAT THE WORLD IS GOING TO BE READING AND TALKING ABOUT FOR A LONG TIME TO COME"
Indianapolis News

"AN INTRIGUING BIOGRAPHICAL NOVEL WELL WORTH THE READING. . . . FILLED WITH FAS-CINATING DETAILS OF IMPERIAL ROME, ITS CULTURE, RELIGION AND HISTORY. . . . AN IMPORTANT NEW PERSPECTIVE TO THE PASSION STORY WHICH IS CERTAIN TO AT-TRACT ATTENTION AND PROVE QUITE VAL-UABLE TO CHRISTIAN AND NON-CHRISTIAN ALIKE"
Moody Monthly

PONTIUS PILATE

A BIOGRAPHICAL NOVEL

Paul L. Maier

LIVING BOOKS
Tyndale House Publishers, Inc.
Wheaton, Illinois

Published by Tyndale House Publishers, Inc. by
arrangement with Doubleday & Company, Inc.

Library of Congress Catalog Card Number 68-10585
ISBN 0-8423-4852-2 Living Books edition

First printing, Living Books edition, January 1981
Printed in the United States of America

For
JOAN

Preface

The trial would become the central event in history. But for the judgment of one man, a faith shared by nearly a billion people today might not have been born. At least it would not have developed as we know it. The decision of the Roman prefect of Judea on the day called Good Friday may have stemmed from pressures of the moment, but it was conditioned by the turbulent politics of the Mediterranean world at that time. What really happened at that most famous of all trials? Was Pilate's judgment motivated by cowardice, expediency, or necessity? Where did he come from, and what became of him afterward—this man who unwittingly switched the flow of history into a new channel? This book proposes several answers.

There is too little source material on Pontius Pilate for a biography, yet too much for recourse to mere fiction. These pages attempt a compromise which might be called the documented historical novel. It seemed an appropriate genre for a case, such as Pilate's, in which much authentic data is available, yet with insurmountable gaps in the information.

In constructing this account, I first searched for all surviving bricks of fact, then cemented them together with regrettably fictional mortar into what I hope is something of an accurate restoration of the original structure of Pilate's career. As a documentary novel, it differs from regular historical fiction in that *no* liberties were taken with the facts: the bricks were used as discovered, without alteration. Reference notes on the most significant and controversial points of scholarship are provided at the end of the book. Most of these notes involve original sources, some of which provide new historical data.

To aim for accuracy, I adopted the following rules: 1) All persons named in this book are historical characters; no proper name has been invented—if it is not known, it is not given. 2) No portrayal of any personality, no description of any event, and no episode or even detail contradicts known historical fact (unless by author's error). 3) Only where all evidence is lacking is "constructed history," based on probabilities, used to fill in the gaps. Even here, as much use as possible is made of authentic historical data as ballast, also in dialogue. Important constructed segments have been identified as such in the "Historical Note" at the close of the book.

The role of the prosecution on Good Friday has, of course, been vigorously debated. I have largely followed the New Testament version of the trial because even Talmudic sources concerning Jesus substantially accord with it, as demonstrated in the Notes. But for later generations to draw anti-Semitic conclusions from Jewish involvement on Good Friday was an incredible blunder. The prosecution, acting in absolute good faith, still represented only a very small fraction of the Jews of the time, and its responsibility was never transferable. Indeed, to be anti-Semitic because of Good Friday is as ridiculous as hating Italians because Nero once threw Christians to the lions.

This portrayal has also tried to tell "the greatest story ever told" from its least-told vantage point, uncovering what may be one of the last aspects of that story which still needs telling. What happened in Palestine in the early first century is usually viewed from a Christian or Jewish—not Roman—perspective. Events in Judea are rarely linked to that larger complex which controlled the province: the Roman Empire. Yet the culmination of Jesus' career was not a story of one city, but a tale of two—Jerusalem *and Rome*. This, then, is the other part of the story.

P.L.M.

Western Michigan University
January 22, 1968

Chapter 1

A SALVO of trumpet blasts echoed across Rome, saluting the sunrise on the first of April, A.D. 26. It was the daily signal for synchronizing water clocks with the moment of the sun's appearance, a courtesy provided by men of the Praetorian Guard, billetted in their new camp at the edge of the city. Rome's day had begun at least an hour earlier with the first coral glimmer of dawn, when many of the merchants started opening their shops. By the time the sun peered over the hills east of Rome, the city was a raucous symphony of clattering carts, hammer blows, and screaming babies. Some in the leisure class allowed themselves the luxury of slumbering on till seven o'clock, but only those who had wined to excess would rise any later. The citizens of Rome took advantage of every daylight hour, because nights were dark, and illumination poor.

From the commanding heights of his palace terrace on the Palatine Hill, Tiberius Caesar Augustus looked out across his noisy capital with a lethargic stare, half-hoping that Rome would somehow vanish along with the morning mist, that all fourteen districts of the city might slowly dissolve into the Tiber and be disgorged into the Mediterranean like so much waste. Tiberius was well through his twelfth year as *princeps*, "first citizen" or emperor of Rome, that lofty office which he could not enjoy because of its demands, nor yet lay down without shattering precedent and inviting personal peril.

Unbiased voices in Rome agreed that Tiberius was governing surprisingly well, considering his unenviable role of having had to follow the glittering career of his stepfather, the now-Divine Augustus. And Tiberius had come to power under the most unflattering circumstances. Augustus had first appointed others to succeed him, naming Tiberius only after these had died. Now Tiberius nourished an obsessive resentment at having to be "emperor by default," listening too hard for the inevitable whispered comparisons and brooding too often over his bitter, corrosive memories of Augustus.

A tall, erect figure despite his sixty-six years, the princeps turned back into the palace for a breakfast of wine-soaked bread, pullet eggs, and a brimming cup of *mulsum,* a wine-and-honey mixture without which no Roman could face the day. Tiberius ate alone, fatedly alone. The joy of family life was denied him. When he was a boy of four, the first tragedy had occurred: his mother Livia divorced his father in order to marry Augustus, a bit of ambitious social-climbing common enough for that era. What scandalized Rome was the fact that on the day of her second wedding, Livia was six months pregnant—by her previous husband. That night, the Statue of Virtue supposedly fell on its face in the Forum, and had to be repurified at great expense. Not until his own happy marriage with Vipsania could Tiberius forget his complicated childhood.

But Augustus doomed that marriage, too. He insisted that Tiberius, as future successor, divorce his beloved wife Vipsania in order to marry his only offspring, Julia, instead —so desperately did Augustus want his personal bloodline to continue. Yet Julia soon became Rome's civic personification of vice, a woman so adulterous and vile that Augustus himself banished her for life to a Mediterranean island.

Only his son was left to Tiberius, Drusus, the promising heir apparent, but he had died of a strange illness three years earlier. Tiberius Caesar, sovereign of 70 million people in an empire extending from the English Channel to the gates of Mesopotamia, was a man quite alone.

He beckoned to a servant, pondered for a moment, and said, "Send word to Sejanus that I'll see him this afternoon at the eighth hour." The domestic delivered the message to one of the praetorian bodyguards, who hurried off eastward toward the mansion of Sejanus on the slopes of the Esquiline.

L. Aelius Sejanus was prefect, or commander, of the

Praetorian Guard, that corps of elite troops who protected the emperor and served as Rome's government police. A swarthy, muscular figure of large build, Sejanus was today flawlessly draped in a white woolen public toga. The prefect was middle-aged—though ageless in the eyes of the women of Rome—and he betrayed Etruscan ancestry in his non-aquiline features, so unlike the typical, high-bridged Roman face.

The inner Sejanus, his real loyalties and true political motives, was a storm center of controversy. Many claimed that Rome never had a more selfless and public-minded official, certainly never a more efficient one. But his opponents hinted darkly that Sejanus was a true Etruscan of old pre-Republic stock, and, as such, Rome's mortal enemy, a ghost of Tarquin risen up to haunt the Empire.

His rise had been meteoric. Though only of equestrian, or middle-class, status, Sejanus now possessed powers which made blue-blooded, patrician senators scurry to join his following, or sulk jealously outside it. Part of his attainment was inherited. Augustus had named his father, Seius Strabo, prefect of the Praetorian Guard, and Tiberius had appointed Sejanus to the same post, sending Strabo abroad to govern Egypt.

In the decade since that time, Sejanus had gradually enhanced his office; no longer was it merely a steppingstone to authority, but now represented poised, concentrated power itself. His brilliant reorganization of the praetorians had accomplished it. He had proposed to unite the nine praetorian cohorts, or battalions, scattered throughout Italy into one large barracks near Rome, where the elite home guard would be far more readily available to the emperor in any emergency. Tiberius had approved the idea, and a sprawling new *Castra Praetoria* was erected on the Viminal Hill, just outside the northeast city walls of Rome. But these troops were loyal to their prefect, and when Sejanus spoke, 9000 guardsmen listened and obeyed.

Too much power in the hands of one man? Tiberius thought not. He needed this instant security, and he had never detected in Sejanus a shred of disloyalty to himself or "the Senate and the Roman People," as the Empire officially designated itself. Tiberius judged that a man like Sejanus was indispensable at this stage of Rome's governmental evolution. No longer a republic, not yet a fully developed empire, Rome badly needed a strong administrative bureaucracy in place of her hodgepodge of commissions. Tiberius had this problem in mind when he urged Sejanus to serve also as his deputy in supervising the developing civil service of the Empire.

The message from the Palatine was delivered to Sejanus just as the two consuls for the year 26 A.D. were leaving his house. They had come to sound him out on rumors about Tiberius' plans for an extended vacation away from Rome. Characteristically, Sejanus would neither confirm nor deny the news. As the honor guard of ten lictors quickly shouldered their fasces and rattled to attention to escort the consuls through the streets of Rome, the two could be heard arguing over Sejanus, Calvisius whining his objections to the man, and Gaetulicus just as stubbornly defending him, a mirror in miniature of Rome's collective sentiments in the matter.

From the library where he conducted his official business, Sejanus looked into the atrium, or entrance court, of his mansion and saw the imperial messenger threading through the crowd of officials, clients, and functionaries, all waiting to see him. Upon reading the note from Tiberius, Sejanus rose quickly from his chair and took a few steps off to one side, turning his back to the noisy throng in the atrium in order to give himself a few moments of concentration. With shoulders hunched and chin to his chest, he remained motionless for perhaps half a minute, gathering together in his mind all the diverse factors bearing upon one of his latest political moves. Yes, he decided, the time was right to approach the emperor. But there was at least one step necessary before that. Grasping a stylus, he inscribed the following on a wax tablet:

L. Aelius Sejanus to Pontius Pilatus, greeting. I should like to see you early this afternoon, perhaps about the seventh hour. Had I not promised lunch to Domitius Afer, we could have dined together. Another time. Farewell.

The message written, he turned briskly to summon his next visitor.

A guardsman returning to the *Castra Praetoria* brought the note to the tribune of the first praetorian cohort, acting camp commander whenever Sejanus was absent, Pontius Pilatus. Pilate read the message and frowned slightly. Not that he disliked Sejanus—quite to the contrary—but he felt saturated with embarrassment over what had happened the previous night. At a party in honor of the praetorian officers' staff, when everyone had imbibed freely, Pilate had proposed a toast to "Biberius Caldius Mero" instead of "Tiberius Claudius Nero," a too-clever pun on the emperor's given name, which meant "Drinker of Hot Wine." Everyone roared with approving guffaws except Seianus, who merely stared at Pilate, a shivering, superior stare which the tribune spent much of the morning trying to forget.

If Tiberius got word of his indiscretion, he could lose more than his praetorian rank. Just the year before, he recalled with a shudder, a history published by Senator Cremutius Cordus had dared to eulogize the Caesar-slayers Brutus and Cassius as "the last of the Romans." Accused of treason, Cordus starved himself to death and his writings were burned. Speech was no longer so free as it had been in Rome's republican era. With an inner chill, Pilate prepared for the confrontation with Sejanus.

The message from Sejanus had been civil enough, but the time for the appointment was extraordinary, just after lunch when most Romans took a brief nap. This had to be important. After a quick—and wineless—meal, Pilate decided to change to civilian garb. His tunic sported the *angusticlavia,* a narrow bordering strip of purple running the length of the garment and indicating that the wearer was a member of the equestrian order, a class second only to the senatorial, which boasted the *laticlavia,* a wider purple strip. In public, the tunic was largely covered by a toga, and draping the toga was nearly an art. Every fold had to hang properly, gracefully, and just the right amount of purple had to show from the tunic: too much would be ostentatious, too little would betray false modesty. Pilate let several folds of purple appear near the shoulder, a compromise in good taste.

Accompanied by an aide, Pilate made his way down Patrician Street, a major axis leading southwest from the *Castra Praetoria* toward the heart of Rome. Except for his attire, he was not distinguishable from the milling Romans of all classes using that thoroughfare. Less than middle-aged and in the prime of his years, Pilate was of medium build, and his square-cut face was topped with curly dark hair duly pomaded with olive oil. He looked more typically Roman than Sejanus, but, like his superior, Pilate was also not of purely Roman stock. His clan, the Pontii, were originally Samnites, hill cousins of the Latin Romans, who lived along the Apennine mountain spine farther down the Italian peninsula, and who had almost conquered Rome in several fierce wars. The Pontii were of noble blood, but when Rome finally absorbed the Samnites, their aristocracy was demoted to the Roman equestrian order. Still, the Pontii had the consolation of ranking as *equites illustriores*, "more distinguished equestrians," and members of Pilate's clan had served Rome in numerous offices, both civil and military. Some had entered the business world, made fortunes, and even regained senatorial status in the Empire.

A sharp turn eastward up two winding lanes on the Esquiline brought them to the sprawling home of Sejanus. As Pilate was escorted into the atrium, the steward announced that Sejanus could see no one else that afternoon. A troop of disappointed clients, office-seekers, and hangers-on left the premises.

"Come in, Pilate," Sejanus invited, with unanticipated warmth. The two moved through an elegantly columned peristyle into the library. "I assume the garrison is running smoothly in my absence?"

On his guard, Pilate replied with the expected pleasantry.

"I have an appointment with the princeps in an hour," Sejanus said, his smile fading, "so we won't have as much time as I'd like."

"About last night, sir," Pilate faltered, cleared his throat, then resumed with just a trace of Oscan dialect in his Latin, "I regret how the wine must have addled my wits. My little joke was—"

"Oh . . . that," Sejanus broke in. "Yes. Clever, but dangerously clever. Better forget that pun. But we were among friends, so we can let it rest. Now, if that had been a public banquet, matters might have taken a different turn."

Vastly relieved, Pilate was promising to bridle his tongue in the future when Sejanus again interrupted. "As a high-ranking member of our equestrian order, you have an excellent education, Pilate, and you've nearly completed your military obligations with distinction. Now, what would you like to do after you've finished your stint with the praetorians? Resume your rise in the order of offices open to the 'equestrian career'—a civil service directorship, say, prefect of the grain supply? A foreign prefecture? Or, perhaps, stay on with the Guard and replace me as praetorian prefect some day?"

Pilate was not reassured by the smirk that accompanied Sejanus' last remark. A subtle man himself, and closer to the prefect than most Romans, he detected a patronizing ring to the question but did not rise to the bait. "Not your post—I think I'd collapse under the demands of the office," he responded dutifully. "But, while I've made no definite plans, I do prefer administration, so I hope to serve Rome in some kind of public office."

"Good. Too many promising members of our class are deserting politics for business—yet the Empire needs administrators now, not merchants."

The two men sat back easily in their chairs, to all outward appearances merely enjoying a casual conversation. But Pilate knew better and remained alert, having learned from experience that Sejanus was apt to circle his subject for quite some time, picking up bits of potentially useful information before settling on the real purpose of an interview. Rather than push the pace, Pilate offered measured responses.

Sejanus then turned the conversation in a more profitable direction. "Now, Pilate, let me ask you several random questions, and don't bother trying to fathom their significance, for the moment. First, what is the city saying about Sejanus?"

"The praetorians are loyal to you to a man. So is most of Rome. Tiberius seems distracted lately, if you'll pardon my presumption. He's aging, of course. And ever since the death of Drusus he seems a changed man—morose, suspicious, sullen. He's rarely seen in public. He doesn't get on well with the Senate. The general feeling is that for the good of Rome, a strong executive agent is needed to run the government for him, now more than ever. And you are—"

"Enough diplomacy, Pontius Pilatus. Be candid enough to show the other side of the coin."

"I was just coming to that," Pilate quickly responded, sensing that Sejanus was testing his integrity as well as his tact. "But you know best who your opponents are: Agrippina and her party, perhaps a third of the Senate—patricians who resent any equestrian in power—and a few stubborn republicans who feel you're holding together a government which should be allowed to collapse."

Agrippina, widow of Tiberius' popular nephew Germanicus, was an arch enemy of Sejanus. She resented his rising influence over the princeps at a time when her sons were next in line for the throne, while Tiberius equally resented her ardent campaigning in their behalf. Agrippina and Sejanus, then, constituted opposite poles in the highly charged party politics of Rome.

"Yes, that's an adequate catalogue of the opposition," Sejanus commented to Pilate, "but what about the commoners, the men on the street?"

"The plebeians have never been better off. Rome is at peace. The economy is prospering, and you are given credit for much of this. In candor, though, it's also known that you recently wrote to Tiberius, asking for Livilla's hand in marriage, and that he did *not* give you permission——"

"This is public knowledge?" Sejanus' eyes were widening.

"Some of the Guard heard it gossiped in the Forum. But it's also thought that you'll have your way—eventually. And the people see you as a patient man."

Livilla was the widow of Tiberius' son Drusus, and her affection for Sejanus so soon after her husband's death was a little below decorum. And since such a marriage would have driven Agrippina insane with jealousy, Tiberius had wisely disapproved it at this time.

"Yes, it was a bit premature. An error on my part, Pilate. Love sometimes interferes with intellect, as you must know! . . . Now, several other issues. Are you a religious man, Tribune?"

The query clearly caught Pilate by surprise. He shifted his position and cleared his throat. "Well . . . naturally I revere the official gods of the state——"

"Yes, of course. I'll wager you're a real fanatic," said Sejanus with a satirical smirk, since neither of them took Jupiter or Juno seriously, or any of the other Greek deities rebaptized under Latin names. Lately, it seemed, the gods were invoked only for proper emphasis in curses.

"Well, how about philosophy, then," Sejanus probed, "the intellectual's substitute for religion? Which school do you follow?"

Pilate reflected a moment. "I'd consider my view something of a cross between Skepticism and Stoicism. Searching for ultimate truth is fine exercise, but has anyone ever found it? If so, what *is* truth? Truth as taught by the Platonists or the Epicureans? By Aristotle or the Cynics? To that extent I suppose I'm a Skeptic. . . . On the other hand, Skepticism alone would seem inadequate for any rule of life. Here, I think, the Stoics, with their magnificent emphasis on duty, and the oneness of Providence, have something to teach the Roman state."

"Well, what about Jewish monotheism, then?"

"The Jews are supposed to believe in one divinity, but they're hardly Stoics!"

"Any other opinions on the Jews, as a people?"

"I think any Roman would agree that they're a hardworking but terribly in-bred and clannish sort of folk, always quarreling among themselves. Yet they bury their differences when it comes to competing with our businessmen! No, I don't think Jews make very good Romans, and you remember the Fulvia scandal, of course."

Several years earlier, four disreputable Jews had persuaded a Roman matron named Fulvia to send as an offering to the temple at Jerusalem a purple robe and some gold, which they promptly appropriated for themselves. When he learned of the swindle, Tiberius furiously banished the Jews from Rome, along with some foreign cultists and astrologers—the first such Roman persecution.

"I have to see the emperor soon," Sejnaus continued, "so allow me now to be brief. Valerius Gratus, the prefect of Judea, has been in office there eleven years, and the princeps and I think it's time for a change, an opinion, I'm glad to say, which Gratus also shares. In a word, I plan to suggest you as *praefectus Iudaeae* to succeed Gratus—if you approve." He paused. "Now, before you tell me otherwise, let me give you some of the background. At the moment, Judea is an especially important post, since there's no governor in the province of Syria during the current interim."

"What about Aelius Lamia?" objected Pilate.

"Lamia!" Sejanus laughed. "He's *legatus* of Syria all right—in title, but certainly not in fact. The princeps mistrusts him, and he has to serve his term of office here in Rome as absentee legate. So there's no brother governor just across the border in Syria to assist the Judean prefect if he runs into difficulty. Therefore we need one of our best men in that post. I thought of you for two reasons: a prefecture would be next in order for your equestrian career; and also your record—it's excellent; it speaks for itself."

"Thank you, Prefect! I'm honored that you thought of me in this connection," he managed to say smoothly.

Actually, Pilate was overwhelmed. A provincial governorship was a dramatic promotion for him, the largest step upward in that sequence of offices which the Romans called "the equestrian career." In assessing his future, Pilate had hoped eventually for a governorship, but had never anticipated Judea. Gratus had been such an able administrator that one simply never thought of replacing him.

"I'm rather curious, though, as to why you had me in mind *for Judea*," Pilate added, stalling for time in which to organize his reactions.

"Your experience in that quarter of the world, of course. You served, I seem to recall, as administrative military tribune with the Twelfth Legion. Correct?"

"Yes, but that was in Syria."

"Next door to Judea," said Sejanus, with a wave of his hand. "But perhaps you're not interested in governing a province?"

"Quite to the contrary! When do I sail?" Smiling, Pilate quickly ascribed his reticence simply to surprise.

"As you know, I'm sure," continued Sejanus, "your salary will be adequate—100,000 sesterces*—not to mention the perquisites. And if your performance warrants it, your stipend can be increased proportionately. The Jews are difficult to govern, of course, so you'll be earning your wage. But after your term in Judea, greater honors might await you in the government here, especially if you serve Rome well abroad."

Pilate was about to pose some questions when he was again interrupted, conversations with the praetorian prefect being notoriously one-sided. "But all of this is only conditional at the moment. Tiberius must first approve you, of course, and this afternoon I'll begin the process of winning that approval. I'll start by citing the needs of Judea, and then casually mention your name and background. Midway in our discussion I'll refer to you again, and once more at the close. By then you'll be something of an old friend to the princeps. This doesn't mean, of course, that he'll approve you today. Never. That would look as if he were acceding to me, and he's sensitive to criticism on that score.

---

* About $20,000 at current valuation, though see the Notes for further discussion.

Tiberius will 'decide' on you in a month or so, and that will be it."

"Do you think I should plan for the prefecture, or wait for Tiberius' approval?"

"Plan. I'm not going to suggest any other candidates, and I don't think the emperor has any in mind."

With that he escorted Pilate out to the atrium, and prepared for his own visit to the Palatine.

Pilate stepped out into an afternoon that had become unseasonably warm. A southwest wind was pouring down from the Aventine, carrying with it a fresh, wheaty smell from the large state granaries along the Tiber. Soon it would rain, but not till late in the afternoon.

While returning to the *Castra,* Pilate luxuriated in his transformed prospects. He had come expecting a reprimand, no, a cashiering; he had left with a Roman province. To govern Judea would be more than a challenge, of course. From all reports, it was an enormously complex task to keep the Jews satisfied under Rome's rule. He knew that Palestine had been restive and turbulent ever since Pompey conquered it nearly ninety years earlier. Rome had tried indirect government under King Herod and direct administration under her prefects, but a growing hostility between Roman and Jew in that sun-saturated land had still given birth to a series of riots and rebellions, each of which was put down in blood.

This was the prospect which troubled Pilate. He tried to analyze Sejanus' unexpressed motives for selecting him, and it soon became rather clear. Pilate had gained the reputation of being a tough commander ever since he had helped put down a mutiny in the Twelfth Legion by an adroit combination of oratory and force, applied in fairly equal parts. Word of Pilate's role reached Sejanus, and he had sent him a commendatory letter on that occasion. Maintaining control was the first commandment in Sejanus' decalog.

Suddenly, Pilate wondered if his prefect had a deeper motive. What about Lamia, the absentee governor-without-a-province? Was it only Tiberius who was suspicious of him and prevented his going to Syria? What about Sejanus? Several years earlier, Lamia had crossed swords with Sejanus in a public trial and since then had gone over to the party of Agrippina. And though quarantined to Rome, eastern affairs did pass over his desk. Someone, therefore, had to represent the party of Sejanus in the East, now that his father, who had been prefect of Egypt, was dead. Someone? Himself!

Well and good. For several years, he had staked his career to the fortunes of Sejanus, his fellow equestrian who was now second only to the emperor, and that calculated decision had paid off handsomely. Judea would be a formidable assignment, but if he succeeded, in Sejanus' words, "greater honors await you in the government here." It was a typical Sejanism—hyperbole with a dash of satire—but it gilded Pilate's prospects.

Chapter 2

A FEW days later, while reviewing the Guard at the praetorian camp, Sejanus told Pilate that the princeps had received his nomination with predicted favor and advised him to start briefing himself on Judean affairs by consulting scholars from the eastern Mediterranean who were teaching in Rome.

Above all else a prudent man, Pilate had not yet told his fiancée, Procula, about his new prospects. He thought it wise to remain silent until he learned how Tiberius had reacted to his candidacy. For a military man trained in the discipline of making quick, iron-clad decisions, Pilate was surprisingly gentle and patient with the young girl who would soon be his bride, and he had wanted to avoid raising hopes that could be dashed by a negative reaction from the emperor. Now he looked forward to that evening, when he would surprise her with news of the appointment.

Officially, their marathon engagement had not yet ripened into marriage, because Pilate needed time to complete the military commitment in his equestrian career. But he was beginning to wonder if that might have been a pretext. Like many of his contemporaries, Pilate had treasured bachelorhood, that blend of sovereign freedom and easy morality which had so captivated the men of Rome that marriage and birth rates were dwindling alarmingly. Pilate's family-arranged betrothal had formally engaged him to Procula when she was only in her early teens. This had allowed him several years before marriage would normally

21

take place, and he had taken advantage of the custom which allowed him a wide range of freedom.

Within the last year, however, Pilate had been drawn more and more to Procula and they had actually fallen in love, an unexpected and—by the standards of Rome—an unnecessary development. Procula was now little more than half his age—he in his upper thirties, she in her late teens—an average disparity, though friends were quipping that Procula might be getting a bit old for Pilate. Not a man to deceive himself, Pilate realized that the opposite was closer to the truth, and now resolved to marry as soon as possible so he and Procula could enjoy a full life together. He knew she would offer no resistance, since, in her own quiet way, Procula had been hinting at matrimony for the last two or three years.

After Sejanus' confirmative report, Pilate retired to his quarters to indulge in that premeditated assault on the human body which the Romans called their "bath." Cleanliness was only an incidental by-product of this elaborate process, which demanded a frigid plunge, then a parboiling in the hot bath, a roasting in the steam room, a parching on marble slabs in the dry-heat chamber, a scraping down with strigils, a thorough rubdown, and finally, an anointing with perfumed unguents to appease the violated skin. All this was genuinely relished probably only by masochists, but most Romans readily endured the bath: the sultry Mediterranean climate demanded it, and this was also prime time for the men of Rome to transact their professional and business affairs.

For his evening with Procula, Pilate chose a tunic-toga ensemble which was properly gleaming white. After entrusting the *Castra* to his officer of the day, he walked the short and familiar distance under the massive maroon arches of the Julian Aqueduct, through the lush Gardens of Maecenas, to the Proculeius mansion. The prospect of seeing Procula and announcing the news which would, hopefully, alter both their lives exhilarated Pilate. Today would be one of those hinge occasions, from which life would arc off in a new direction.

Her name was really Proculeia, the feminine of the gens name of the Proculeius family, but usage had shortened it to Procula, a familiar Roman given name. Society knew her as the girl who "had a grandfather, not a father." Actually she had both, to be sure, but her grandfather was *the*

Gaius Proculeius whose wit was so keen, whose career so colorful that he obscured his immediate descendants. A close companion of Augustus—he once saved his life in a naval battle—Proculeius had personally captured the Egyptian queen, Cleopatra, for Augustus, and after returning to Rome in glory had rejected political office to serve as patron of the arts instead.

Procula had been raised in her grandfather's shadow, for it was her father, the Younger Proculeius, who inherited the family residence near the Porta Tiburtina, overlooking the Gardens of Maecenas, and here she grew up in almost patrician luxury. The Pontii, near neighbors of the Proculeii in Rome's fashionable fifth district, were not so wealthy, but when the father of Pontius Pilate casually suggested the alliance of their families to Proculeius Junior, he was favorably inclined. The Proculeii and Pontii, after all, had much in common: both were highest-class equestrians; both had a military history; and both, lately, favored the party of Sejanus—except for Procula, who had a woman's sympathy for Agrippina.

Turning down Tibur Way, Pilate soon arrived at the two-story Proculeius mansion. Like many of the grand old houses of Rome, this one had an attractive, pillared portal, but very little else to commend it from the outside. It was the interior which harbored beauty in the Roman home, and the Proculeius mansion was popularly known as the "Tiburtine Art Museum" for its frescoes and the magnificent sculptures collected by the Elder Proculeius from across the Mediterranean. A servant admitted Pilate into the atrium, from which the entire pillared interior could be viewed as far as the garden, a tasteful composite of marble and mosaic, richly colored curtains, and fountains gently splashing into sunken pools.

"Please inform the Lady Procula of my arrival," Pilate told the domestic. While waiting, he sauntered over to the *impluvium* and put his foot to the edge of that rectangular basin, situated directly under an opening in the roof which admitted both sunlight and rain. Moments later he was caught by a shove from behind which nearly toppled him into the pool.

"I've been watching you the whole time from behind that column," Procula chirped.

"You lynx of Hecate!" he laughed, gathering her into his

arms. "Come out into the garden—I have a rare piece of news for you!"

"Oh? What is it? Surely not, at long last, the date of our wedding?"

"Perhaps. You'll see."

No conversation with Procula in recent months had been complete without her injecting some reference to marriage, and Pilate smiled to himself that this time she was not far wrong. They strolled through the peristyle, an even more elaborate inner court, and out into the garden. Procula was wearing a simple house tunic; not until marriage could she assume the formal *stola* of the Roman matron. She looked petite at Pilate's side, although a pile of luxuriant brown hair, combed up and held in place with jeweled pins, augmented her stature. The pronounced family features of the Proculeii had generously softened in her case to confer a serene loveliness, which was not lost on the aspiring young men of Rome. Only Pilate's nimble wooing of the last year and the security of the mutual family contract had preserved their courtship.

"Procula," Pilate asked as they reached the garden, "if I . . . if we had to live for a while outside of Rome—beyond Italy, in fact—where would you prefer to go?"

"Why? Are you being sent somewhere?"

"Answer my question first."

"Greece, of course. Now, not Athens necessarily. None of the cities. Just a sunny little island in the inky blue Aegean."

"Be serious, Procula."

"Oh, all right then," she pouted. "Egypt. The grandeur of Alexandria, the mystery of the Nile."

"Wrong again. Try in between."

She paused, then brightened. "Syria! Is it Syria, Pilate? Imagine living in luxurious Antioch."

"No, my romantic little magpie!" he laughed. Then, assuming a contrived pomposity, he announced, "Sejanus has formally recommended to Tiberius Caesar that I be appointed prefect of Judea."

"*Judea?*" She paused, looked out across a stand of pines into the darkening sky, and repeated, "Judea! . . . Well, the Jews *are* a fascinating people, I suppose. . . ."

Pilate sensed that this was a noble effort to conceal disappointment, so he quickly told her what the advancement meant to his career, and also of the sparkling hints for the future Sejanus had so broadly dropped. But Procula, more surprised than really disillusioned by the news, was already planning ahead in another category.

"The question of *where* you're appointed doesn't concern me nearly as much as whether or not you're going *alone*, Pilate." There was a smoldering determination in her hazel eyes that he had never noticed before.

Precisely here he made the capitulation which nature, society, and his inmost feelings demanded of him. "Procula," he hesitated momentarily, "are you prepared to go with me to Judea—as my wife? Are you ready to choose the day—"

"Ubi tu Gaius, ego Gaia," she whispered with a radiant smile, the formula she would repeat later at their wedding, "Where you are Gaius, there am I Gaia." Gaius represented any Roman name, since it was the most common.

After their exuberant embrace, Pilate said, "Do you real ize how lucky we are, *Carissima?* Several years ago, the Senate almost made it illegal for governors to take their wives along to their provinces. Caecina Severus stood up and proposed that the women be left behind, otherwise 'ambitious, domineering wives' would turn their husbands' heads and change Roman policy in the provinces."

"How cruel that would have been—to separate people in that fashion. Barbarous!"

"Well, you know who was behind the idea? Tiberius! It was actually his opening shot against Agrippina. When she was off in Syria with Germanicus and continually interfered with his gov—"

"That's your version of it," Procula glowered in reply. "Poor Agrippina is one of the most misunderstood, most slandered—"

"Don't *ever* say that in public, especially not in front of Sejanus," he snapped.

Until now, their bantering had been lighthearted, floating along on top of their joy, and Pilate tried to restore the mood. "Please, little one, let's not go over this again. Whatever you may think of Agrippina, just remember that her party is now regarded as hostile by both the emperor and his praetorian prefect, the two men on whom my future depends. So don't court disaster."

"Well, if Tiberius dislikes governors taking their wives along to provinces, do you still want to take me to Judea?"

"Of course! The princeps was only trying to embarrass

Agrippina. But when he saw how unfavorably the Senate reacted to the 'Wives Bill,' he quickly reversed tack, and the original motion was roundly defeated."

"All right . . . But I still don't understand why you get so snappish whenever I have a kind word for Agrippina."

"Procula, I'm not a consul, presiding over the Senate in 'The Case of Tiberius and Sejanus versus Agrippina.' For better or worse I'm in politics, and whether Agrippina is ultimately right or wrong isn't for me to decide. I have to honor loyalties that affect me directly. Now, Sejanus has treated me handsomely; I can only reciprocate. His enemies are my enemies. The only question I should ask myself is this: am I morally justified in following Sejanus? I think yes. The emperor himself reposes full confidence in him."

"But what if—"

"Did you know that images of Sejanus are honored among the standards of our legions? You've seen his bust next to that of Tiberius in the Forum . . . and his statue in the Theater of Pompey."

"But what if *all* of you are wrong and Agrippina is right?" Procula objected. Then she surrendered. "Oh, let's stop all this. That's why I hate politics—it's too difficult to know good from evil in your affairs of state." She looked at him with a new brightness. "But now, my ambitious Roman statesman, *when* are we to be married?"

"As soon as the calendar will allow," he laughed. "Tomorrow, if that were possible." Excitedly they returned inside for a family counsel with the rest of the Proculeii, who would have as much to say as they about setting the date.

Choosing a wedding day in ancient Rome was a very intricate matter. The object was to select a religiously favorable day to please the gods, but a non-holiday to favor relatives and friends, who would likely have other commitments during festival times. But since rituals, public games, and holidays had by this time reserved no less than 150 days of the calendar, nearly half the year was barred. Besides this, two days at the calends (1st), nones (5th or 7th), and ides (13th or 15th) of each month were deemed unlucky, as was the first half of March, all of May, and the first half of June. Since the remainder of April would not allow enough time to prepare for the wedding, the Proculeii decided on the fourth day after the ides of June (June 17).

The intervening weeks saw Procula shopping for their indeterminate stay in Judea, and preparing for the nuptials. Pilate was occupied with grooming his successor at the *Castra Praetoria,* consulting with Sejanus on Roman provincial policy, and learning as much as he could about Jews and Judea. Annius Rufus proved helpful here. He had been prefect of Judea from 12 to 15 A.D., just before the present incumbent, Valerius Gratus, and was now living in retirement at Rome.

"Three years was too short a time for me to accomplish much in Judea," Rufus apologized to Pilate, "but I don't think Gratus has done very much more in his eleven." The tone was that regularly used by predecessors who evaluate the work of successors.

"No, those were fairly quiet years—for Judea," he continued. "There had been a rebellion at the time the census was taken, but nothing much since then."

"So the people aren't really that hostile to Rome?" Pilate ventured.

"I didn't say that. They're always looking for a chance to shatter what they call the 'Roman yoke,' but don't give them that chance. First requirement for any governor of Judea will have to be firmness. Only after that comes justice and good government."

Rufus continued with a run-down on who supported Rome in Palestine: generally, some of the educated and ruling establishment, including priests. The common people could swing either way, while a group Rufus identified as the Zealots might, he happily assured Pilate, slip a knife between his ribs some dark night.

The former prefect alerted Pilate to other difficulties. "You'll be understaffed, undermanned, and undersupplied out there. Rome really should station a legion in Judea instead of those cursed local cohorts. Which is probably the reason you got the appointment, Pilate. The prefect of Judea must know his military tactics."

"Why *not* a legion, then? I could suggest it to Sejanus."

"No," the canny Rufus corrected him, "I doubt if Tiberius would spare a legion. Besides, legions are usually commanded by senatorial legates rather than equestrian prefects like yourself, so let things rest as they are. And I don't think Tiberius would like another senatorial legate in the East. Do you know why, young man?"

"Probably because he fears the Senate will interfere in

foreign policy. Even now the legate Lamia is detained in Rome instead of governing Syria."

"Exactly."

All Roman provinces beyond Italy were of two kinds: *senatorial* provinces, the older, pacified areas administered by the Senate, such as Sicily or Greece; and *imperial* provinces, lands which Rome had acquired comparatively recently, and which might require special military intervention, such as Egypt and smaller border territories like Judea. The latter were under the direct control of the emperor, who often sent equestrian rather than senatorial officials to govern them in order to balance the two upper classes off against each other. A senatorial legate governing Syria, for example, would find something of a modest counterpoise in the neighboring equestrian prefect of Judea. If one stepped out of line, the other would surely report it to the emperor.

"But any advice I give you is bound to be a little outdated by this time," Rufus admitted. "It's more than a decade since I was in Judea. Hardly seems possibly. . . . Gratus will give you a full briefing in Caesarea when you take command."

"Yes," Pilate acknowledged. "But one thing still worries me, Rufus. I served in Syria, so I know something of the country, and a little of the Near Eastern mind. But I've had hardly any contact with my future subjects—Jews. Well, I've run across them here in Rome—who hasn't?—but I have no friends of that persuasion."

"Naturally," snickered Rufus, with typical Roman prejudice.

"But if I went over to the Trans-Tiber, I could find some of the leaders of the Jewish community there. Do you think I'd gain anything by talking with them?"

"Not really, for several reasons. While the Roman Jew is related to the Jew of Judea, he may also be very different, depending on which faction he follows. Just an example: one of their synagogues here in Rome is called Congregation of the Herodians, in which they teach that King Herod was the Messiah promised in their scriptures. Messiah indeed!" he laughed. "Most Judeans would be revolted by such a thought. But don't worry, Pilate, you'll learn your Jews very quickly after you set foot in Judea."

"This talk of a Messiah. . . . What's it about?"

"Messiah is Hebrew for 'the Anointed One,' who is to be

a kind of religio-political Deliverer of his people—sent by their god, no less—to liberate the Jews from oppressions of every kind . . . and oppressors, by which they mean us. A new world monarchy under the Messiah-king is to replace the Roman Empire, and an era of peace and prosperity will descend on the earth. So if their Messiah appears, I suppose Rome would be obliged to disappear."

"I'll keep an eye out for him!" chuckled Pilate. "But a last question, Rufus. When you were in Jerusalem, did you ever get a glimpse into the forbidden recess of their temple?"

"You mean their Holy of Holies?"

"I think that's what they call it."

"No, and don't you try either. It would spark instant rebellion."

"Of course. I was only wondering if it were true—the rumor that there's a statue of a wild ass in there, or an ass's head, which supposedly represents their deity. Weren't the Hebrews fleeing from Egypt and dying of thirst in a desert when a herd of wild asses guided them to a spring of fresh water, and so they worship the ass image in their temple?"

"I've heard that story, but it must be false. At least there's no statue of an ass in the Holy of Holies. Pompey was the last Roman to look inside that sanctuary, after his conquest of Jerusalem, and he found it stark empty. And that does go along with Jewish belief that their god can't be represented in sculpture or painting of any kind."

Pilate took leave of Rufus with due thanks, even though he was under no delusions that his knowledge of Judea had been much enhanced by their discussion.

The month of May was a paradox. Though Italy was fragrant and bursting with spring, this was the time in the religious calendar for gloomy exorcisms of ghosts. But, like most Romans, Pilate and Procula gladly left this task to the priests while they made final preparations for their wedding. It would be one of the prominent equestrian events of the spring social season at Rome. In deference to the memory of the senior Gaius Proculeius, noted senatorial and patrician families had indicated they would attend. Sejanus and his numerous satellites promised to grace the occasion, along with the praetorian officers' staff, and even Pilate's relatives from Samnium would converge on the Proculeius mansion that June.

Pilate's father, a retired civil service official named Pontius, had shrewdly advised his son not to be timid when discussing dowry with Procula's father. This was a sticky point in Roman matrimony; weddings had actually been canceled when prospective in-laws could not come to terms on the size of the dowry. But such distasteful haggling proved unnecessary in Pilate's case, since Proculeius had vast holdings and the nuptial contract that he offered proved him a generous father-in-law-to-be.

On the day of the wedding, a chain of ceremonial was meticulously observed, some of it dating from the dawn of Rome. The night before, Procula had dedicated her childhood trinkets to the household *lares,* those good spirits of her old home whose protection she would abandon the next day. To ensure good fortune, she slept that night in a *tunica recta,* an expensive ivory-colored bridal tunic woven in one piece from the top down.

At early dawn, the same tunic was now secured to her waist by a girdle of wool, fastened with the "Knot of Hercules," a complicated hitch named for the guardian of wedded life. Only the new husband might untie it.

Dressing the bride was a mother's prerogative, and Procula knew that hers would make a ritual of it, since she was an only child. For weeks the mistress of the Proculeius household had been planning this wedding, but now that the day arrived, her well-chiseled features were drawn with worry that some important item had been overlooked. With exquisite care she applied several strands of silver jewelry, and finally took a spear to her daughter's head. Ancient custom, betraying the violence of tribal marriage by capture, demanded that the bride's hair be parted by a spear into six locks. A flowing gossamer veil of red-orange silk completed the ensemble, held in place by garlands of flowers. While her mother brushed aside a tear or two, Procula looked at herself in a mirror of highly polished metal and was frankly pleased.

Meanwhile, dressed in a gleaming new toga, Pilate was surrounded by comrades who crowned his head with a floral wreath. Then a glad troop of Pontii and their friends accompanied him for the short walk over to the Proculeius residence, which they found surrounded with rows of parked litters and waiting slaves. Wreathed with boughs of greenery and fairly sprouting with flowers, the mansion seemed more an arboretum. Incense and exotic perfumes hovered about the house, since the warm, breezeless June morning provided little diffusion.

Inside, Pilate was heralded with a glad shout from the great throng of guests, but all eyes quickly returned to the robed *auspex* who was busy taking the omens. He was an honored friend of the Proculeii who, acting as unofficial priestly augur, had a messy but necessary task to perform.

"Bring forth the consecrated ewe!" he sonorously intoned, for the ancient rite which inaugurated public functions in Rome was about to begin.

The assembly of guests hushed with anticipation as a beribboned sheep was led to an altar set up in the center of the atrium. It was important that the animal seem to approach willingly, so a little fodder had been strewn below the altar. The sheep saw it, bleated approvingly, and hurried in to its fate. The augur sprinkled a little incense, meal, and salt on the victim's forehead, offering a prayer in what was supposed to be Etruscan, a nearly dead language. Then he took a sacred mallet, cradled the head of the sheep in his arm, and smashed its skull with one blow. After cutting the throat of the dead creature, he caught the blood in a basin and sprinkled it on the altar. Finally, he carefully slit open its belly to inspect the liver, intestines, and gall bladder, which still quivered and twitched with departing life.

Absolute silence commanded the hall. If the entrails were in any way abnormal in such rites, armies could not go out to fight, the Senate would suspend its business, and certainly weddings would have to be postponed.

Since this was a dismal prospect after so much planning, Roman nuptials habitually had a second ewe in reserve in case the first ungenerously presented bad entrails. This gave way to an even more logical custom: the *auspex* at weddings was never to look *too closely* for abnormalities, and he never did.

After further probing and hesitation for due effect, the augur finally looked up. *"Exta . . . bona!"* he cried, with a smirk, "The viscera are *good!"*

"Bene! Bene!" shouted the guests. It was now proper for Procula, who never suspected anything could go wrong, to give a glad sigh of relief: the wedding could proceed after all. She and Pilate solemnly entered the atrium.

As a bachelor of long standing and a man of experience, Pilate had always assumed he would face his wedding cere-

mony with a certain cool detachment, if not resignation.
But now, watching his bride approach him, he was quite
unexpectedly overtaken by a flood of complex emotions.
Initially, but thankfully for only one terrifying instant, the
girl appeared to be a total stranger and Pilate could not
imagine what this young, rather silly-looking girl had to do
with him. Next, he was convinced that the whole ceremony
would degenerate into a long series of disastrous social
blunders, making himself and his bride the laughingstock
of Rome. First, he, or worse, Procula, would be unable to
remember the few simple procedures of the wedding ceremony. Then, instead of proposing the graceful toasts at
which he had had so much practice in his public career, he
would find himself tongue-tied at the crucial moment and
blurt out only a few incomprehensible words.

Mercifully, at the sight of Procula's sure and graceful
pace as she walked toward him, Pilate returned to normal,
felt secure in his love, and took a slight step forward to
meet his bride. Procula's *pronuba,* or matron of honor,
now led the bride over to the groom. The pair joined right
hands.

"Ubi tu Gaius, ego Gaia," said Procula, looking serenely
into Pilate's eyes.

A little lad called a *camillus* now presented a covered
basket, from which the couple took a cake of coarse wheat
bread and placed it upon an altar, offering prayers to Jupiter, Juno, and several gods of the countryside. Then a cry
erupted from the assembly of guests, *"Feliciter! Feliciter!*
Good luck! Happiness!" for the two were now man and
wife.

A lavish wedding banquet commenced, with festivities
lasting throughout the day. Proculeius was known to set a
superb table for even the commonest meals, and this nuptial feast for his only daughter was exactly the gourmand's
delight everyone had anticipated. Of the seven courses
which followed, roast boar was the principal dish, but there
were also more exotic viands, including Phrygian grouse,
Gallic chitterlings, roast peacock, Circeiian oysters, and—
the crowning delight—Corsican mullet. At a time when
Rome's vulgar rich were inflicting fifteen- and twenty-
course dinners on their friends, Proculeius, the guests
agreed, had shown remarkable restraint in his menu.

To wash down his delicacies, Proculeius had invaded his
deepest wine cellar and retrieved rich Chalybonium from

Damascus and other eastern vintages in honor of the new-lyweds' approaching journey, as well as Setinian and Faler-nian, the finest local wines. Some were chilled with snow, which several of Proculeius' slaves had carried down at great effort from Apennine mountain summits.

With the last course of the day-long feast came distribu-'ion of the wedding cake, traditionally served to guests on bay leaves. Then the darkening twilight reminded everyone that a final, important stage of the celebration had been reached.

"*Pompa! Pompa!* The Procession!" cried the guests. The time had come to escort the bride to her new husband's home. While a band of flute-players and torchbearers as-sembled at the door of the mansion, Procula embraced her mother and started sobbing. The groom walked over and brutally tore his bride out of her mother's arms, while she screamed all the louder. But all the guests were laughing and cheering, for the whole scene was just an act, the cus-tomary show of violence which etiquette required at Roman weddings ever since the Rape of the Sabine Women.

Procula quit struggling and broke into a radiant smile at her captor, kissing him happily before she took her place in the procession, which headed down the Via Tiburtina toward the heart of Rome. The fluteplayers led off, their music inviting any of the bystanding public to join the procession, as join they could and did. The torchbearers and younger wedding guests followed; next the bride her-self, attended by two boys holding her hand on either side, while a third carried a wedding torch of twisted hawthorn in front of her as a charm against magic. The little *camillus* pranced along proudly with his basket. Bridesmaids just behind Procula were carrying the symbols of her future domestic life, the distaff and spindle. Then, almost as an afterthought, came the groom, who threw walnuts to the street urchins of the city as symbols of fertility. Last in the procession marched the parent Proculeii and Pontii, their older friends and relatives, and finally, a roistering honor guard of praetorian officers.

Since he would be leaving Rome shortly, Pilate had not purchased a house for himself. Instead, a fine old friend of the Pontii, who had retired to his mountain villa for the summer, graciously allowed the newlyweds to use his town house during their remaining weeks in Rome. It was here that the noisy, lusty, flame-flickering cavalcade delivered the bridal couple.

Now Procula was lifted over the threshold, for a chance stumble at the door would have been the worst possible omen for her future married life. Inside, Pilate offered her a glowing fire brand and a small vase of water, symbols of life and worship together. Procula accepted these, repeating a final time the wedding formula, *"Ubi tu Gaius, ego Gaia,"* and then lit the fireplace with the torch which had preceded her. The hearth blazed up in soaring triangles of flame—a good omen.

After Procula prayed to the gods for a happy marriage, her *pronuba* led her to the nuptial couch, which was situated in the atrium. Then she left, closing the door behind her. Pilate's officer friends serenaded them just outside the door—a time-honored nuptial song. Then they too left.

Bride and groom looked at each other and smiled. It was the first silence and solitude they had experienced since dawn. He took off his now-wilted floral wreath. She did the same. He unwound himself from his suffocating toga, but she just stood there, shyly. Pilate pulled off her flaming red veil, gathered her in his arms, and kissed her tenderly. Then he lifted the lissome little figure off her feet and carried her over to the marital couch, which they would use that night and never again.

Chapter 3

SEVERAL WEEKS of post-nuptial events followed a large Roman wedding. On the evening after their marriage, Pilate and Procula hosted a second banquet, at which she offered her first sacrifice to the *penates,* another group of household deities who were first cousin to the *lares.* Procula still had some faith in these guardian gods, unlike her husband, who merely smiled indulgently whenever she discussed religion, or "superstition," as he styled it. Yet Pilate would have been reluctant to alter the traditional rituals and ceremonials. That would have been an affront to history, a violation of custom, even patriotism.

Additional dinner parties, given by various friends, consumed the rest of June. The adjustment to wedded life was particularly happy for Procula, since before her marriage she, like any Roman girl, had been closely guarded by her parents and only rarely appeared in public. Marriage was her literal emancipation. As *matrona,* she became a near-equal of men, completely in charge of the house, and free to come and go at will. Nowhere in the ancient world did women have so high a status as in Rome. Wrapped in her wifely garb, the ample and convoluted *stola,* Procula was now treated with deference throughout the city, be it dusty street or public theater, and no one, not even officers of the law, dared lay a hand on her.

Since Procula had inherited her grandfather's canny business sense, Pilate cheerfully surrendered to her the management of their household affairs. He also discussed mat-

35

ters of state with her, particularly those now affecting his future career. When close friends wondered how they were getting on as newlyweds, she retorted, "Splendidly. We agree on everything . . . except politics and religion." That regularly drew a chuckle, since the battle of the sexes in Rome was usually joined at these two arenas.

Surprised at the joy of married life, Pilate chided his bride, "Why didn't you liberate me sooner from those barracks at the *Castra Praetoria?*" But one undercurrent of concern was troubling him. Despite Sejanus' assurances that all was well with his overseas appointment, Pilate had not yet received word of a formal commission from Tiberius. Until he did, nothing could be regarded as settled, final.

A further complication was the absence of the princeps. For months he had kept announcing plans to take a long trip away from bothersome Rome, but had then canceled them so frequently that people began calling him "Callippides," the famed Greek clown whose big act was to imitate the motions of running without moving an inch. But now Tiberius startled Rome by actually leaving town. His stated purpose was to go down to Campania to dedicate as a temple the house in which Augustus had died, but astrologers were predicting he would never return to Rome.

Pilate did not need the stars to intuit what had happened. He knew that Sejanus had succeeded in his gentle campaign to lure Tiberius away from the city, perhaps to the isle of Capri. Not only would this provide the princeps a long-deserved vacation; just incidentally, it would also leave Sejanus in charge of Rome as Tiberius' deputy.

However, Sejanus' success in arranging the emperor's vacation apparently spelled Pilate's failure, since provincial offices were usually changed about the first of July, and unless his formal appointment came soon he might have to linger in Rome another year. Could Sejanus have forgotten to remind the princeps? It would all be a profound political embarrassment, also a social one for Procula, who had been busy shopping for items from a list provided by the wife of Annius Rufus.

Pilate could not contact Sejanus, since he had accompanied Tiberius to Campania, and their precise whereabouts were unknown at the moment. But in the second week of July, a praetorian messenger from the imperial party delivered a tablet sealed with Sejanus' unmistakable stamp. Pilate sliced through it with his dagger and read the following:

L. Aelius Sejanus to Pontius Pilatus, greeting. I wish I could report that the princeps has confirmed you as *praefectus Iudaeae,* but he insists he must first have a further interview with you. I had hoped that the time I presented you to him on the Palatine would have sufficed, but you recall how preoccupied he was that day with the Thracian insurrection.

After dedicating a temple to the Divine Augustus at Nola, we plan to go on to Capri. This week and the next we will be at the emperor's villa called "The Grotto." Tiberius requests that you see him here before we move on to Campania. Take the Appian Way till you reach the sea at Tarracina, then follow the shore road. Come the second day after you receive this, if possible. Farewell.

It took Pilate and his driver about twelve hours to reach the Mediterranean as they clattered away from Rome in their open *cisium,* a two-wheeled, two-horse carriage used for rapid trips. The morning had been magnificent, and the scenery just south of Rome never failed to inspire. Almost washing the highway was the jewel shaped Alban Lake; just beyond it towered the proud summit of Mount Albanus, which dominated the countryside. A millennium earlier it had been a grumbling volcano which kept the area uninhabited, but then it cooled, allowing people to settle beneath its slopes.

That afternoon, however, grew hostile. A smoldering Italian sun hung in the sky, untempered by any breezes from the sea. But what made the journey finally unbearable was the notorious Pontine Marsh, a vast, fever-breeding swamp which now bordered the highway. Caesar had planned to reclaim it for agricultural land, a project cut short by the daggers of the Ides of March.

A night in coastal Tarracina restored Pilate for his conference the next day, and he arrived at The Grotto by midmorning. The imperial villa was perched on a palisade above the Mediterranean coast. Below it lay the grotto proper, a huge natural cavern opening onto the seashore, which was used to good advantage as an outdoor dining room and recreation area. The coastline south of Tarracina

was perforated with large caves, and it was in the most
spectacular of these that Tiberius had fashioned his grotto.

Praetorian comrades at the entrance to the rambling villa
smiled and saluted as Pilate climbed down from his carriage and brushed the dust off his tunic. Sejanus appeared
in the vestibule. "A timely arrival, Pilate," he said. "We've
been discussing the eastern provinces. Refresh yourself and
then join us in the peristyle over there."

Entering the room a bit self-consciously a short time
later, Pilate found Tiberius sitting among the friends who
had accompanied him on the journey to Campania. They
served also as his advisers, a kind of unofficial imperial
cabinet.

"Gentlemen," announced Sejanus, "I present to you
Pontius Pilatus, Tribune of the First Praetorian Cohort."
Turning to Pilate, he continued, "I trust you recognize the
distinguished former consul, Cocceius Nerva." He nodded
toward a silver-haired patrician who was one of Rome's
finest jurists.

"And the eloquent Curtius Atticus—"

"*The* Atticus, who was such a close friend of Ovid?" inquired Pilate.

"The same," smiled Atticus a little nervously, pleased at
the recognition but embarrassed at the association, since
Augustus had banished the poet Ovid to the shores of the
Black Sea for his role in corrupting Julia. Too late Pilate
recognized his blunder.

"And Thrasyllus of Rhodes," Sejanus resumed, "scholar,
philosopher—"

"Court astrologer he is!" Tiberius interjected with a
chuckle, acknowledging the public paradox that, although
he had banished astrologers from Italy, he had kept one for
himself. Several Greek literati were then introduced.

But the focus of interest in the room remained Emperor
Tiberius, a tall, gaunt figure, dressed no more ostentatious-
ly than a senator. His was the head that virtually ruled the
world, and yet Pilate found it disappointingly, imperially,
and totally bald across its entire crown. The face, hollow-
cheeked and triangular in its flare downward from wide
temples, was rather pimpled and pockmarked from acne,
two of the larger eruptions covered with plasters. One
rumor had it that Tiberius left Rome because he was becoming sensitive to his physical appearance. Pilate stared at
the princeps—his first time at this close a range—and

thought the stories of the ulcerous and festering face somewhat exaggerated. Determination still showed in the broad
jaw and pressed mouth, though Tiberius did look every
month of his sixty-six years.

"Now Tribune," Tiberius shook Pilate out of his contem-
plation, "tell us why Rome should appoint one of its 'Samnite enemies' as prefect of Judea. Give us your background. Where were you born?"

"In Caudium, Princeps, a town again as far south on the
Via Appia as Tarracina."

"Caudium! You don't have to remind us where *Caudium* is. It was at the narrow pass just west of your home
town that our Roman forces were trapped by your Samnite
mountaineers and forced to surrender. Who was the Samnite general? Pontius . . . yes, Gaius Pontius. Any relation?"

"My great ancestor," Pilate admitted, with a little ill-dis-
guised pride. "But that was three and a half centuries ago."

"No apologies needed! Pontius was a great general. He
made our armies loosen up and learn mountain fighting."

Pilate chose to accept the compliment in silence. He was
fiercely proud of his ancestors' military record, but also
knew that Tiberius liked to think of himself as a serious
student of military history, and the last thing he wanted to
do was engage the emperor in a contest of historical recall.

"But wait a moment—you Pontii weren't always so
lucky," Tiberius persisted. "Does the name Pontius Telesinus
mean anything to you?"

"The brother of my great-grandfather, from Telesia. I
applaud your command of history, Princeps."

"Another brave and brilliant general who had the mis-
fortune of being on the wrong side. . . . Do you realize that
you Samnites *almost conquered* Rome just a century ago?"
Tiberius suddenly turned on Pilate with what seemed a
snarl. "Telesinus staged a surprise night attack on Rome,
which was all but unguarded. Never since Hannibal was
the city in such danger."

"But Princeps, the Samnites only wanted Roman citizenship," Pilate interjected, hoping to dislodge Tiberius' apparently swelling animosity.

But the emperor ignored his meager effort. *"Forty thousand* there were, and just before the battle it was *your*
great-granduncle, then, who went from rank to rank shouting: *"This is the last day for the Romans! These wolves*

who have ravaged Italian liberty will not be exterminated until we cut down the forest that shelters them."

In a low, almost oily tone which contrasted with the emperor's bellowing, Sejanus interposed, "But Sulla's forces arrived just in time to save Rome, and the head of Pontius Telesinus was cut off, shoved onto a spear point, and paraded outside the city walls." He paused for due effect. "And, as you pointed out, Princeps, that was more than a century ago. Now all Samnites are loyal Romans, equal citizens of the Empire."

"Yes, military history *is* my weakness," Tiberius conceded. "But now, Pilate, to the matter at hand. You have a good record so far. Sejanus tells me you've also been in touch with Annius Rufus. Fine. But I'm not overly concerned with the details of your preparation for Judea; these you can best learn from Gratus in Caesarea—if, that is, you succeed him. Let's rather talk about general provincial policy for Judea—and, mind you, don't try to bluff me. One of my tutors was the eminent Theodore of Gadara, who told me all about Palestine. . . . By the way, where is Gadara?" he asked abruptly, despite his stated disinterest in details.

"A city overlooking the Sea of Galilee, near its southeastern shore."

Tiberius glared, and in a trice Pilate corrected himself. "Or rather, the Sea of Tiberias." He flushed at his error in forgetting that the lake had been renamed.

"Now tell me this: just why is little Judea important to Rome?"

"It's the religious capital of the seven million Jews in the Empire, almost seven per cent of our total population. Judea itself commands trade routes and communications between Asia and Africa. This is particularly important for the defense and integrity of our eastern provinces, Syria and Egypt."

"And never forget it! If Rome weren't in charge of Palestine, Parthia would move in to block our access to Egypt, and that would be the end of the Pax Romana. Like it or not, Rome is now the police force of the Mediterranean, and police may not be universally popular, but they're necessary. . . . How do you propose to handle the Jews?"

"With firmness, Princeps. Weak governors only beget insurrection."

"True. But what if a general riot did develop? How would you deal with it?"

"Determine the cause. If changes were justified, make them. If not, have the auxiliaries put down the disturbance. If the troops failed, I'd call in the legions from Syria."

"That's a standard military answer, Tribune, and it's correct, of course. But one additional suggestion: why not try a little tact? Without it, you'd never succeed in governing the most ungovernable people on this earth. Pompey discovered the Jews for us, Caesar coddled them, Antony protected them, and Augustus favored them. Sometimes I wonder why. Sejanus has been urging severe measures against the Jewish community in Rome, and you may have to be severe also in Judea . . . if we send you there. But don't overdo it."

"No, Princeps," replied Pilate. "I have given the matter some thought, and I envision a fresh approach to the problem. Why not make an effort, at least, to Romanize the Jews? For almost a century Judea's been under Roman control. Other nationalities have been assimilated into Roman culture during this period of time—even in shorter times. Why not also the Jews? Is their culture immune to outside influences? I doubt it. Many of them have been Hellenized, and if a Jew can become half-Greek, we ought to be able to make a half-Roman of him."

Several advisers in the imperial circle nodded approvingly. Tiberius only shifted in his chair and observed, "Your proposal sounds reasonable, Tribune, but not practical. How would you ever bring it about?"

"Well, I've not yet thought this through completely," Pilate dodged, "but one means might be to educate sons of leading Jewish families in Rome."

"Pilate, do you hope to grow rich as governor of Judea?" blurted Tiberius.

"Certainly not, sir!" replied Pilate, with what he hoped was just enough pique to indicate what he thought of the insulting query, without antagonizing the princeps in the process.

"A nasty question, I admit. But too many provincial governors have left Rome in an aura of idealism, only to return in disgrace for condemnation by the extortion court. Take ex-Governor Capito, for example, the man who looted Asia Minor. Power corrupts, Tribune, and if appointed, you'd be the most powerful man in Palestine. Take care.

Now, suppose you were assigned a tribute quota of two million sesterces from Judea in a given taxing, but you were easily able to collect an extra half million and send it to Rome without the Jews knowing you had raised the surplus. Would you do it?"

Pilate pondered momentarily. Then he replied, "No."

"What? Not even for the greater financial benefit of the Empire?"

"No. Wouldn't it be unethical to—"

"You're absolutely right. Aemilius Rectus, my former prefect of Egypt, once sent in more taxes than his quota and expected commendation. Ha! I wrote him that I want my sheep *sheared*, not *fleeced.* . . . Suppose you leave us for now, Tribune, while we confer. Join us for lunch in the grotto."

With considerable relief, Pilate retired. The interview had drained him.

The grotto area was connected with the upper villa by several steep stairways. Framed by pines, this natural pleasure dome was embellished with pools, fountains, and exquisite statuary, some of it colossal in size. But Pilate barely noticed the beauty as he descended to the grotto in a cloud of exhilaration. The emperor had just formally commissioned him as prefect of Judea, and he was receiving congratulations from members of Tiberius' entourage.

The dinner party gathered around a table set in the middle of the grotto and then reclined on couches to a half-prone position for the meal, the usual languid pose which, Romans assumed, aided their digestion. While the Greek intellectuals in the imperial circle modestly chose the ends of the table, ranking advisers reclined near Tiberius, Sejanus, and Pilate at the center. Servants fluttered busily about them, serving up delectable viands and the rarest wines.

Pilate was satisfied that this was easily the most exotic place in which he had ever dined. At the mouth of the grotto was a circular fish pond of turquoise sea water, bordered with crystalline marble statues of fauns, satyrs, and demigods of mythology, little cupids and colossal deities, each fancifully executed in Rhodian baroque. But crowning the collection on a pedestal at the center of the pool was a magnificent Laocoön group, the familiar sculptured serpent-monsters strangling the priest of Troy and his two sons for warning against the wooden horse.

Thrasyllus, who was reclining next to Pilate, turned to him and asked bluntly, "When were you born, Prefect? I'd like to cast your horoscope."

Pilate, who had been mesmerized by the tortured sculpture dominating the pool, wrenched his eyes from the marble Laocoön to the living astrologer of Tiberius and cringed with astonishment. They had the same face!

"Look like him, don't I?" laughed Thrasyllus. "It's the beard that does it. But tell me the date of your birth."

"I . . . I really don't hold much stock in astrology," replied Pilate, with less tact than candor.

"That's all right. Your attitude won't affect the reliability of the horoscope. Wouldn't you like to know in advance what will happen to you, say, in Judea?"

"Perhaps. But your predictions probably have validity only in that they prepare someone to act unknowingly in fulfilling them, while otherwise—"

"Posh! You sound like a Greek Skeptic. You're actually afraid to tell me the date of your birth for fear I'll somehow tamper with your destiny. Well, don't bother then. I get paid handsomely for my predictions, which I offered you without charge."

Pilate was trying to apply the salve of diplomacy to the ruffled feelings of the astrologer when Thrasyllus ventured on a new tack. "When you get to Judea, Prefect, would you at least do me an important favor?"

"Certainly, Thrasyllus. What is it?"

"You know, of course, that the princeps spent almost seven years studying on the island of Rhodes? In fact, that's where he met me."

"Yes." Pilate thought sulking would have been a better term than studying, since this was the famous self-imposed exile of Tiberius, in resentment at Augustus.

"Well," continued Thrasyllus, "I was teaching the princeps astronomy, as well as its greater application, astrology, when my calculations were upset by a strange celestial phenomenon in the southeastern skies. A star . . . no, it was brighter than a star . . . a planet, perhaps, but larger than any we know . . . moved along the southeastern horizon somewhere south of Syria and north of Egypt, possibly Judea."

"Perhaps it was a comet."

"Yes, more like a comet than anything else, but its movements were more erratic. And it appeared just two years after the conjunction of Jupiter and Saturn in the Sign of Pisces, the Fish."

"Is that significant?"

"The planet Jupiter symbolizes the ruler of the universe. The constellation of the Fish represents the last days. And Saturn is the planet of Palestine. So Jupiter encountering Saturn in the Sign of the Fish means that a cosmic ruler will appear in Palestine at the culmination of history."

"Well, how does the comet fit in?" Pilate was doing his best to humor the astrologer.

"Comets signal important changes in the Roman state. What dominated the skies in the year Caesar was assassinated? A blood-red comet, so bright you could see it in the daytime. What preceded the battle of Philippi? A comet. What heralded the death of Augustus?"

"A comet?" Pilate ventured boldly.

"Exactly," smiled Thrasyllus. "So, on the basis of *both* the conjunction and the comet, this world ruler from Palestine should also cause great changes in the Roman state."

"A rather sweeping prediction. But what was the favor you wished of me?"

"When you get to Jerusalem, contact the college of priests and inquire whether some kind of astral event took place in the skies over Judea about thirty years ago. Then write me their reply and its description."

"Easily done."

The dinner progressed through a modest four courses. Pilate was rejoicing in the silence of Thrasyllus when he noticed Curtius Atticus fastening his beady brown eyes on him. "*Now* I know why the name Pontius struck me as so familiar," Atticus exclaimed. "The tribune Pontius Aquila —were you related to him, Prefect?"

Noticeably nervous, Pilate replied, "Just a distant cousin of my father."

"Oho! It was your relative Aquila, then, who wouldn't stand up to salute Julius Caesar in his triumphal parade," smirked Atticus. "And Caesar never forgot the insult. How did he conclude his speeches in the Senate? 'I will proceed in these matters . . . *if*, that is, Pontius Aqulia will permit.' "

The dinner party had stilled to an incongruous hush. The reference to Pilate's republican connection disturbed Tiberius, who stopped eating and now looked uneasily at his new appointee.

Unrelenting, Atticus continued, "And later on, your cousin Aquila helped stab Caesar to death."

Sejanus broke in angrily, "We *all* have some republican relatives, Atticus. Even the family of the princeps once opposed Caesar—"

"Thank you, Prefect, but even this is unnecessary," Pilate interrupted, now more angry than embarrassed. "Do you all remember how Aquila died? Fighting on Augustus' side. The Senate even voted a statue in his honor. Of all the conspirators against Caesar, Aquila was most honored in death."

"Enough, gentlemen!" commanded Tiberius. "You have our confidence, Pilate. Show as much loyalty to the Empire in Judea as Pontius Aquila, 'the Eagle,' did to the Republic. No one can ask for more."

Sejanus grabbed a goblet, raised it slowly, and said, "Then I propose a toast to Pontius Pilate. May he reform Judea as successfully as the javelin improved the Roman military!"

Pilate was delighted with the toast, for it had been a play on his name Pilatus, which meant "armed with a javelin." The *pilum* or javelin was a balanced missile six feet long, half wooden handle and half pointed iron shaft, which Roman legionaries hurled at their enemies with devastating effect. It was the *pilum*, in fact, which had made the Empire possible, Pilate proudly reflected.

Oblivious to the rise and fall of voices around him, Pilate happily anticipated Procula's excitement at hearing of his official appointment. He was too lost in thought to feel a slight tremor that shook the walls of the cave, nor did anyone else at the noisy dinner table.

Then he went on to explore several private doubts about his new post. Although his knowledge of Judea was far from complete, one consideration, which he suspected might be of prime importance, had already become clear to him. Force of arms alone would not ensure peace in Judea. A great deal of diplomacy would be required as well, and this was what worried him. Well aware of his own strengths and limitations, Pilate knew himself to be a more than competent military commander; but he wondered about his ability to understand these strange people, the Jews. How should one deal with subjects who, apparently, see little value in the Roman way of life and cling so tenaciously to their own laws and customs? Romanization? A fine proposal when discussed among Roman officials, but, he asked himself, how would the Jews react?

As Pilate came out of his reverie, he began to look with greater interest at the interior of the grotto. He now noticed that the walls of the cavern were not entirely stone as he had assumed, but appeared to consist of a good deal of clay as well. Another gentle vibration shook the cave, this time causing Pilate to bound to his feet. Then a much stronger tremor rocked the entire grotto, accompanied by a terrifying rumbling noise, as if the earth were splitting in two.

"Earthquake! Clear the grotto," roared Pilate, but his voice was lost in the ghastly creaking sound and the general confusion.

A huge, jagged boulder, smeared with foul-smelling clay, crashed onto the table, splattering Pilate and Thrasyllus with food and wine. Great sections of the ceiling of the cavern became dislodged and plummeted down on the panicked dining party. The pungent earth smell of the grotto grew intense, unbearably acrid, as more of the cavern caved in. Atticus, white as his toga, started screaming, and he was joined by a full shrieking chorus of terrified guests.

Accustomed to danger, but frozen with the fear of being helplessly trapped and squashed like an animal, Pilate hesitated for a crucial moment before gathering his wits and breaking toward the daylight of the grotto's entrance. But a razor-edged slab of stone broke off the ceiling and sent him sprawling to the floor of the cave. Oblivious to a serious gash in his left arm, he scrambled to his feet and now had to slosh through knee-deep water, since the fish pool was disgorging its water across the floor of the cavern. The Laocoön serpents seemed to come alive as the great statue lurched forward and crashed, amid the echoing clatter of shattering statuary throughout the cave.

When Pilate stumbled to safety on the open beach, he found Thrasyllus, quaking and crying, and could locate about half of the dinner party. But where was the emperor? And Sejanus? Pilate looked back into the murky darkness of the grotto and saw several figures trying to escape. At that moment, the huge upper lip at the mouth of the cavern parted from its matrix and came thundering down, completely blocking the entrance in a cloud of debris. The screams of those crushed beneath the masses of rock and earth echoed up and down the shore, while the Mediterranean started pouring in angrily through fissures which yawned open in the sands.

"The guards! The praetorians!" Pilate shouted. "Somebody get the guards!"

But the praetorians, who were ringing the villa to ensure Tiberius' privacy, had already started down the long stairways with the first sounds and tremors, and now they came rushing over to what was left of the grotto. With remarkable efficiency, they burrowed into the rubble and extracted the living, the wounded, and the dead. Pilate tried to assist them until a burly young praetorian pointed to the wound on his arm. Looking down, Pilate saw a great stain of spreading crimson and meekly surrendered to medical assistance. Casualties were soon set at five dead—two of the guests, Greek scholars, and three servants had been killed —with a score injured or bruised.

But where was Tiberius? In near hysteria, the praetorians resumed their grisly excavations. Since neither the emperor nor Sejanus had been found under the rubble around the entrance to the grotto, they were obviously trapped deeper in the interior, behind a wall of clay and rock—or under it. Tunneling deep inside, the guards kept shouting "Princeps!" "Princeps!" having little hope for the survival of either their emperor or commander. Clawing their way through moist earth and putting their shoulders to huge stones that blocked their path, the rescuers found that part of the ceiling had held, allowing passage into the grotto. With renewed hope, they inched their way into the darkness.

Finally they heard an anguished call for help from the very bowels of the cavern. Pulling away still more debris, they found Tiberius cringing near the floor, while Sejanus hovered over him, shielding him from falling rock with the trunk of his body. Sejanus himself had sustained several wounds and had to be helped out of the grotto, but a lusty cheer went up from the troops as they found their emperor distraught and dirty, but very much alive and physically unscathed.

The villa was transformed into an emergency hospital, as attending physicians did what they could for the injured. They promised Pilate and Sejanus that they would recover with no permanent disfiguration—barring complications.

Pilate was given the cheering information that had he been in only a slightly different spot in the grotto, the falling slab of stone would have crushed his head instead of only gashing his arm.

Later that evening, while his circle sat in the villa recovering from the afternoon's disaster, Tiberius was in a reflective mood. "It puzzles me," he said, "why so many at Rome presume to give the princeps advice . . . such *wrong* advice. How many senators during the past months have warned me of a danger to the state. There is an overambitious man, they say, who will stop at nothing to gain personal power for himself. Who? Sejanus. *The man who saved my life.* Sejanus is splitting the state, they whine. He is plotting against the princeps. His loyalties are only to himself. Who? The man who risked his life to save mine."

Frowning, Tiberius got up and stalked about the room. Then he stopped and spoke with marked emotion. "Know this, my friends, and see that Rome learns it too: today we have had the proof of blood. While all of you were scampering out of the grotto like so many mice from a foundering trireme, one man thought to serve his emperor. Let there be no further questioning of Lucius Aelius Sejanus. In loyalty and service, this man is the greatest in the Empire."

Chapter 4

DEPARTING IN August, Pilate had a choice between land or sea travel to Judea. Since the overland journey across Greece and Asia Minor was notoriously long and tedious, and since the Mediterranean was a predictable sea, offering safe, calm waters from May to September, Pilate chose the direct sea voyage.

With Rome dependent on Egypt for her wheat supply, Tiberius regarded the shuttle of grain ships from Alexandria to Puteoli as the lifeline of the Empire. These great, wide-beamed merchantmen, the largest ships afloat on the Mediterranean, unloaded their cargoes at Puteoli on the Bay of Naples, Italy's major port, and returned with plenty of space for passengers. Pilate booked passage for Palestine via Alexandria with a grain fleet that would sail the third week of August.

When he, Procula, and their personal staff left for Puteoli, a near-caravan of carriages trailed after them, loaded with gear and effects that could probably have been bought in Egypt or even Judea; but Procula, with her patrician tastes, did not want to take her chances in provincial marketplaces. Because it might be several years before they would return, they stopped over for a few days in Caudium so that Procula would have the chance to meet those of her husband's relatives who had not been able to attend their wedding.

Tiberius intentionally had not specified the length of Pilate's tenure, since he would want a free hand to remove

him after a short time in case he did not fulfill Sejanus'
promises. On the other hand, if he governed well, his term
of office might extend as long as a decade.

From Caudium it was only a short trip down to Puteoli.
The port was nestled in a northern corner of the Bay of
Naples, with the domineering Mount Vesuvius hovering
over the eastern shore. Pilate pointed out for Procula two
bustling towns near its base, Herculaneum and Pompeii,
and, just off the southern end of the bay, the fluted, gray-
white palisades of the isle of Capri.

The imperial harbor master had arranged for Pilate's
passage on the *Trident of Neptune,* a reliably large Alexandrian merchantman, about 180 feet long with 45-foot
beam. Its tall, central mainmast towered over a smaller
foremast, which slanted rakishly toward the bow. Hanging
from the single fat yard was a multicolored squarish main-
sail, rippling in the breezes as if impatient at being docked.

Surprisingly spacious passenger cabins were provided aft
below deck, and the best had been reserved for Pilate, Procula, and the modest company of three military aides and
four household servants who accompanied them. The captain made a special point of giving Pilate a gracious welcome on board, for although he was in charge of the maritime responsibilities of the voyage, the moment a Roman
magistrate stepped on board a vessel chartered for imperial
service, he, not the captain, was in supreme command of
the ship.

A fleet of eight merchantmen would make the voyage together—there was safety in numbers—and an extra day
was needed to load and synchronize the convoy. Just before sailing, an honor guard of praetorians marched onto
the wharf to bid Pilate farewell and present personal gifts
from the imperial party at Capri. Sejanus sent him a specially tailored governor's military standard with the image
of Tiberius in gold and the name "Pontius Pilatus" beautifully woven into the purple fabric. An even more significant gift came from Tiberius himself, a gold ring engraved
with his image, signifying that Pilate was now welcomed
into the inner circle of *amici Caesaris* or Caesar's friends,
an elite fraternity open only to senators and equestrians
high in imperial service. It all portended well indeed for the
new prefect of Judea.

Since Pilate was the highest-ranking officer in the flotilla,
the *Trident of Neptune* now set sail as the lead ship. While

rounding the promontory of Misenum, they passed several ships of the Roman navy. They were long, slender warships driven by oar, not sail, for maneuverability, each painted with a glaring eye near its bow and projecting ugly iron-clad beaks at water level for ramming enemy ships. Out across the bay, past Capri on their portside, and into the blue Tyrrhenian Sea glided their ships, aiming south-southeast for the Straits of Messina, the narrow channel between Italy and Sicily.

"If the Etesian winds hold out, we should make Alexandria in twenty days or less," the captain assured Pilate. "Every summer around the ides of July, the Etesians start blowing in from the northwest, and they keep at it for about forty days. We catch the wind at our backs and try to run before it all the way to Egypt."

In less than two days they were at the Straits, the presumed location for Homer's Scylla and Charybdis. As legendary navigational hazards, they failed to impress Pilate. The projecting rock from the Italian shore was hardly Scylla, the six-headed monster who dined on Ulysses' sailors; and the lazy whirlpool on the Sicilian side was a rather poor Charybdis, which supposedly had a vortex so fierce that even the sea god Neptune was powerless against it. And running aground on either side would require some very sloppy navigation, since at their narrowest the straits were still some two and one-half miles wide. Still, no sailor liked to run the passage in a storm.

Once past Sicily, the Etesian winds resumed with magnificent tempo, carrying the ships out of sight of land for the first time. Mariners loved these winds because they rarely blew before noon, allowing ship repairs and servicing to be done mornings, and giving time for the seasick passengers to recuperate.

A week passed without sighting land. Pilate strolled back to the *gubernator* or helmsman, who controlled the twin paddles that rode astride the stern to steer the ship, and asked, "How do you do it? Aim for Egypt when you can't see a thing?"

"Oh, but I can," the pilot replied. "See that red streamer flying ahead of us from the rigging? It shows our wind's direction, and we aim at just a slight bias from that."

"Are the Etesians that constant?"

"Usually. But we have ways of checking on them."

"How?"

"See this metal ring and pointer? We use it to gauge the height of the sun or stars, which helps fix our position." Then the helmsman smiled. "This isn't to say we never make mistakes. Notice that the other ships are strung out so far on both sides of us that we can't even see them all? That's intentional. If the *Pillars of Hercules* at the end of our port flank sights Crete, then they'll signal from ship to ship that we're too far north of course and we can correct accordingly. But if the *Medusa* to our starboard sights Africa, then we're too far south. Of course, that's not so bad, since then we can sail up to Alexandria without missing it."

Pilate only hoped the man was jesting. At any rate, no warnings were flashed from the other ships; evidently they were making a proper passage.

Procula was not a very good sailor—her maritime experience had been limited to a rowboat excursion on Lake Nemi near Rome—and she was having trouble riding up and down with the choppy Mediterranean rollers. Even before Sicily she had had a touch of nausea, but that was as nothing compared with the lingering siege of seasickness that set in at mid-sea. Pilate pleaded with the ship's officers for remedies, but every concoction from the galley confidently served to Procula she swallowed only temporarily and then surrendered to the Mediterranean. The one expedient which worked she discovered for herself. In the mornings, when the sea was calmer, she sat outside amidships and tried to imagine herself back in Rome.

On the evening of the eighteenth day came a glimmer of hope that her sufferings might end. The forewatch on the *Trident* called out, "Ho! Pharos ahead!"

Straining his eyes, Pilate could see only a tiny blemish of luminous orange on the southeastern horizon. But that speck grew in intensity and started flickering like the flame it was. Later on, many other lights came into view, all considerably lower than the original fireball, which now looked like the moon blazing out of control in some cosmic catastrophe.

"*A-ve Pha-ros! A-ve Pha-ros!*" the sailors reverently called out to the towering display of manmade pyrotechnics, which was the Pharos Lighthouse at Alexandria. The *Trident* assumed a steep list as passengers crowded the starboard rail to see one of the seven wonders of the world. But the good-natured helmsman claimed this list only assisted his sharp turn between the breakwaters into the Great Harbor of Alexandria.

The colossal lighthouse soared a staggering 400 feet into the Egyptian night. Since it was constructed throughout of milk-colored marble, Pilate and Procula had no trouble discerning its great square base rising from a harbor island, the octagonal mid-section, and its pillared upper stage. At the apex, a continual fire of pine logs blazed in front of highly polished metal mirrors to signal ships many miles at sea. Even more impressive than its obvious height was its age: by now the Pharos was 300 years old, yet in perfect repair.

Since it was too late in the evening to make other arrangements, Pilate and his staff decided to stay on board ship for the night. Early the next morning, a company of Roman soldiers, marching in their unmistakable cadence, clattered onto the creaking deck of the *Trident*. "Pontius Pilate, please identify yourself!" their centurion announced, his helmet pulled low over his forehead.

"I am he," replied Pilate, as he stepped out of the rear cabin.

"You, sir, are under arrest." The centurion spat out the words with frigid formality. "You have violated the emperor's specific orders that no Roman of senatorial or higher equestrian rank is to set foot in Egypt without his written consent. This regulation was first made by the Divine Augustus to safeguard the grain supply from interference by—"

"But I *have* such written permission, Centurion."

"Let me see it."

Pilate retrieved the document from his cabin quarters, and the centurion spent some time scrutinizing it. Pilate studied his face more closely, then reached over to push up his helmet.

"Gaius Galerius!" he shouted.

"Pilate!" laughed the pseudo-centurion, as the two clasped arms.

"And what might the Prefect of Upper and Lower Egypt be doing in the costume of a lowly centurion?"

"You don't sound appreciative, Pilate. I've been scheming for days in order to provide you this reception."

"Galerius, I've not had my nose tweaked so well since we served together with the Twelfth in Syria. And now you're at the summit of success . . . imagine . . . ruler of Egypt, successor to the Pharaohs!"

"Only as representative of Tiberius, or we'll haul you up for treason, too," Galerius chuckled. "And who is *this* incarnation of Venus? Perhaps Cleopatra, freshly revived, come to reclaim her Egypt?"

"Gaius, this is Procula, my bride of four months," said Pilate with quiet pride.

"May it go well with you," she smiled.

"And with you," Galerius bowed gracefully. "Now, Pilate, your ship for Judea doesn't leave until next week, so I'd be delighted to have you as my guests at the Palace of the Ptolemies just across the harbor there," he pointed. "Somewhere among its 150 rooms we just might be able to find enough space for your staff as well."

They cheerfully accepted Galerius' hospitality and spent a delightful week in the city that was second only to Rome, for Alexandria had replaced Athens as cultural capital of the East. In fact, in some respects Alexandria easily outdid Rome. Its grid-pattern streets were much wider, much straighter, and were illumined at night. Its magnificent civic buildings, parks, and gardens were better conceived; its hippodromes, gymnasia, and theaters more artistic. The great library at Alexandria was the finest in the world, boasting a half million papyrus scrolls, and the Museum adjacent to it was really a scholar's university, staffed by the most outstanding scientists of the day.

Galerius himself showed Pilate and Procula several of the city's prime sights, including the mausoleum of Alexander the Great, in which the waxlike body of the world conqueror could still be seen, embalmed in honey. Then there was the memorial to Pompey, the least the city could do to honor the man it had treacherously stabbed and decapitated in order to present his head, pickled in brine, to his rival, Julius Caesar.

But the monument which electrified Procula was the Mausoleum of Cleopatra. With all the suavity of a veteran guide, Galerius told them the story of how Augustus' friend Gaius Proculeius had climbed up the back of the mausoleum and dropped in through a window to seize Cleopatra after she had barricaded herself inside.

"Prefect," said Pilate grandly, "let me introduce to you

the Lady Proculeia, granddaughter of this selfsame Gaius Proculeius."

While Galerius was recovering from astonishment, Procula said, "Sorry to have made you go through the story. I was just checking on Grandfather's version of it, and it seems he didn't exaggerate."

Toward the close of their stay in Alexandria, Pilate casually hinted that they had seen all of the monuments but few of the people. Galerius responded by hauling them through the various ghettos of the city, and Pilate soon discovered that there was not one Alexandria, but at least eight.

"This city is an Egyptian-Greek-Roman-Jewish-Cyrenian-Anatolian-Syrian-Phoenician conglomeration," Galerius commented. "And trying to keep peace in this ethnic maelstrom is next to impossible. Small riots we have every year, but why no general insurrection has broken out only the great Father of the Gods knows."

"Is it true that there are more Jews in Alexandria than in Jerusalem?" Pilate asked.

"Easily. You see that section of the city over there?" He pointed southeastward to an area not far from the palace veranda. "That's the Jewish quarter of Alexandria, a city within a city."

"Any trouble from them?"

"Not really. Oh . . . some Alexandrians hate them, and it may come to bloodshed one of these years, but generally they've been a commercial and cultural success here. They have citizenship, and their own ethnarch to take care of internal affairs. . . . But why don't we drop over to visit the Jewish quarter? It's the only district we've missed. Besides, you can get a preview of your future subjects."

This was not Pilate's first contact with a Jewish community. Back in Rome, he had visited the Jewish colony across the Tiber in Ward XIV and been repelled by the bad living conditions and low economic level of the district, a ghetto of petty shopkeepers, peddlers, and prostitutes. But the Jewish quarter of Alexandria was a surprise. The section had attractive dwellings with pleasant gardens and even pools. After Pilate and Galerius had visited several synagogues, a rabbinical school, and the marketplace, the picture of a proud, well-organized, and thriving community was unmistakable.

"Alexandria would seem to prove, then, that Jews *can*

live happily under Roman administration," Pilate concluded.

"Of course. Rome's policy until Tiberius was even *pro-*Jewish," Galerius said. "Jew and Roman certainly started out as friends. It all began when a Syrian king, who modestly called himself Antiochus God-Manifest, tried to absorb Egypt and was ordered out by Popilius, our agent in Alexandria. The king said he'd have to think it over first. Popilius took his swagger stick, drew a circle in the sand around Antiochus' feet, and said, 'Decide before you step outside that circle.'—The God-Manifest was last seen running back north!—But he took his humiliation out on the Jews and tried to set up a pagan cult in the Jerusalem temple itself. That ignited a patriotic revolt led by a priestly family, the Maccabees, who beat off the Syrians. And who warned the Syrians to stay out of Palestine in the future? The Roman Senate."

He went on to explain that as early as 161 B.C., Rome even drew up an alliance with Judea, which actually held the Syrians at bay. Though it was part of Rome's usual policy in championing an underdog—Judea—to hold a potential rival—Syria—in check, the Judeans used the alliance to good advantage in winning diplomatic recognition and special privileges for Jews all over the Mediterranean, such as exemption from military service and freedom of worship on the Sabbath. Only when later Maccabean princes failed to renew the alliance did Judeo-Roman relations change from friendship to suspicion, to the kind of animosity which brought Pompey's invasion in 63 B.C.

"And even after Pompey conquered Judea," Galerius argued, "friendship between Rome and Jerusalem was still possible. Pompey took not one shekel from the temple treasury, but ordered the sanctuary cleansed and sacrifices resumed the next day."

"For that matter," said Pilate, "Julius Caesar himself proved Roman-Jewish friendship—"

"Oh, Caesar was *very* Judeophile! He had every reason to be, you know. Jews saved his life when he was here in Alexandria chasing down Pompey. The Egyptian army surrounded Caesar's pathetically small force of Romans, just near the harbor over there," Galerius pointed. "It was a nasty siege, the closest Caesar ever came to defeat. Only one man saved him, Antipater of Judea. Antipater helped relieving legions get through to Caesar, and he also had

Jewish communities in Egypt provision Caesar's forces during the siege, and this turned the tide in the decisive battle."

"This is the Antipater who was the father of Herod the Great?" Pilate inquired.

"Right."

"Small wonder that the Jews and the house of Antipater would stand high in Caesar's favor."

"Yes, Caesar conferred extraordinary privileges on the Jews. Judea was freed from Roman tribute, immunized from taxation, and no soldiers were to be raised or quartered in Judea, the highest favors accorded any state under Rome's control."

"Which explains the long lines of grieving Jews who visited Caesar's grave months after the Ides of March." Pilate reflected for several moments. Then he said, "Your lessons in Jewish history, Gaius, have been far better than what I'd learned from supposed experts in Rome."

"You never learn anything until you get on the scene, Pilate. Oh, I became a real Egyptologist in preparing for this post, but most of what I'd mastered in Rome was just a caricature of the truth, so bad are the geographies and histories. You'll have plenty of surprises yourself when you get to Judea."

"I know. For one thing, I still have to find out why the Jews there aren't happy with Rome—unlike here. But it's comforting to know that you and two Roman legions will be next door in case Judea breaks into revolt. I understand I'm allowed all of four or five cohorts." The satire was obvious.

"Pilate, it all hinges on the grain supply. Let an insurrection flare up in Palestine, and Romans continue eating. But if Alexandria revolts, a quarter of the populace back home has no bread. . . . Now, if something big develops and you get stoned out of Jerusalem, send word and I'll back you up. Probably with my Third or Twenty-second Legion."

"I'll write if I face any large problems," Pilate smiled, "so you should be hearing from me soon."

The next day, with copious thanks to Gaius Galerius and his wife, Pilate, his household and staff embarked on the final leg of their journey.

Chapter 5

A CRAFT only half the size of the *Trident* carried them on the short run to Caesarea, but its triangular lateen sail cut well against the exuberant gusts of the south wind, providing a rough but quick voyage across the Mediterranean corner. On the second day out, the sandy shores of Palestine showed clearly on the eastern horizon.

Pilate spent most of the trip trying out his Greek on the captain, since this was *the* predominating language of the eastern Mediterranean. Like most educated Romans, he had mastered Greek before donning the toga of manhood, but there was the usual gap between book and practice. Except for conversations with Procula, orders to his staff, and correspondence with Rome, Pilate would not use Latin again during his tenure as governor. Since he did not know Hebrew or Aramaic, all communication with his subjects would have to be in common, commercial Greek.

Caesarea, the Roman administrative capital of Judea, reflected a dusky gold from the setting sun at the close of the second day of their voyage. Pilate and Procula had been concerned about Caesarea because, like it or not, this would be their home for as long as Tiberius continued him in office. Seeing it the first time was a little like a groom unveiling a bride he had never previously met: one could only accept the inevitable.

As the ship neared the harbor, they were pleasantly startled by the size of the city. This was certainly not the smallest of Rome's provincial capitals and would, they hoped, offer a certain cosmopolitan way of life that might remind them of Rome. Nature had molded the west coast of Palestine into a very rectilinear shoreline, and there was hardly an indentation in the vast, extended beach to use in building a harbor. Undaunted, Herod the Great had created one artificially at Caesarea. By driving huge stone pilings into the sea bottom in a semicircular arc in front of the city, he fashioned a great mole which was 200 feet wide and absolutely impervious to Mediterranean storms. Jutting up from this jetty were towers in which mariners lived while their ships were in port. The great harbor, the captain assured Pilate, compared favorably with the port of Athens itself.

A sharp starboard tack carried the ship through the harbor narrows and between six great stone colossi rising from the ends of the interrupted jetty. A forest of masts and hulls seemed to grow out of the placid turquoise waters of the harbor, which were crisscrossed by a labyrinth of quays. Pilate had heard earlier the comparison between the ports of Caesarea and Athens, but had always written it off as exaggeration. Now he was less inclined to do so.

Caesarea's skyline seemed extraordinarily impressive to Procula, too grand for what she had heard of Palestine, and she asked the captain about it. He explained that the city was built at one time—a dozen-year period; of predominantly one building material—white stone; in one architectural motif—Hellenistic columnar; and by one man —Herod the Great. With such unitary planning, the result was a civic work of art. Herod had lavished vast sums on Caesarea and named it in honor of his close friend and patron, Caesar Augustus. His temple, resembling a slightly scaled-down version of the immortal Parthenon, crowned a summit overlooking the harbor. Just off the waterfront, they saw a series of government buildings, all gracefully columned in Doric, and, farther off, the unmistakable shapes of an amphitheater as well as a dramatic theater.

When their ship docked, an honor guard blew a trumpet fanfare and then escorted Pilate's party from the central receiving wharf to the palace of Herod. Procula thought it a bad omen: unquestionably, the retiring governor, Valerius Gratus, should have been at dockside to welcome his successor officially, a matter of common state courtesy. Certainly there were enough curious Syrians and Jews lining the harbor to witness the arrival of their new governor, even though it was getting dark and flickering torches started to appear. Pilate agreed that it was a breach of courtesy, and wondered what excuses Gratus would manufacture.

"I have it, Procula," he murmured. "Gratus is probably angry that I took so long in arriving. He's been writing for release ever since the new year, I understand."

"Maybe that's it," she agreed, "yet it's still no reason for such a snub."

But at the entrance to the Herodian palace, the wife of Valerius Gratus apologized, "Forgive my husband for not meeting you at the harbor," said the stately Roman matron, who was much older than Procula, "but he's been ill with a recurring fever. Today was one of his worst days."

She showed them to the guest quarters, and her manner was so gracious that they thought the medical excuse might have some validity. The next morning they were sure of it. Gratus greeted them with cordiality and regrets for his indisposition, which verified itself by his pallor and trembling hand.

"This sickness runs in cycles. Give me a short time and I'll be strong again," he said. "I must say, Pilate, I'm relieved by your arrival. I've put in eleven years here, so I think we exiles are entitled to return whence we came."

Gratus was a stout, middle-aged figure, balding, gray at the temples, but aging with dignity. Flashing, steel-colored eyes sparked his conversation and seemed to compensate for his ashen skin.

"I wish we'd arrived sooner than this," Pilate apologized, "but Tiberius showed a good bit of indecision on whether you should be replaced. One parts with good governors only reluctantly."

"Show that kind of diplomacy, my man, and you should have no trouble with the Jews," laughed Gratus. "But before anything else, you must tell me all the news from Rome. Out here we get only wisps of gossip and official reports."

For the next hour or so, Pilate had to reconstruct Rome as he had left it a month earlier. Clearly, Gratus was eager to return.

After wringing the last shred of information out of Pilate, he said, "We have much to accomplish in the short time we'll be together here. You see, we're all packed and ready to sail before navigation closes. An Alexandrian ship will pick us up in a few days."

While his wife showed Procula the dining salons, the

kitchen complex, storerooms, bedrooms, and the servants' quarters, Gratus took his successor on a tour of the atrium, peristyle, and state rooms. Herod's palace much resembled an elaborate Greco-Roman mansion, Pilate thought, but with such additional items as tropical courtyards, a private bathing pool, and the *praetorium* or government headquarters at the center of the structure. Then too, a military barracks adjoined the palace to ensure its safety. This would be Pilate's official residence throughout his tenure as prefect of Judea, and his cultivated tastes found Herod's beautifully ornamented palace an aesthetic delight.

The tour of Caesarea was equally impressive. Like Alexandria, the city was laid out with streets crossing each other at right angles and major arteries converging on a busy Forum-like public square. Less than forty years old, Caesarea lay almost painfully white in the brilliant Levantine sun, securely ensconced in a semicircular city wall. A huge hippodrome stood just outside the east wall, a consoling sight for the new prefect, since he would not have to surrender his Roman's penchant for sports and chariot racing. Indeed, Gratus told him that an institution called "Caesar's Games," a kind of Palestinian Olympics, was held there every five years. While Jews would not take part in them, the many gentile residents of Caesarea and neighboring cities participated with gusto.

"*Herod* built all this?" Pilate puzzled. "His name doesn't enjoy this kind of reputation in Rome. We remember him only as the man who was continually writing Augustus for permission to kill his own sons on suspicion of treason. Wasn't it the princeps himself who finally said, 'I'd rather be Herod's pig than his son'? Pork, at least, isn't slaughtered for consumption among the Jews."

"Yes," replied Gratus, "but that was when Herod was old and a little deranged. The *young* Herod cut a very dashing figure, with all the exceptional qualities of his father Antipater. By the bloody club of Hercules, that house surely knew when to switch allegiances! They shifted from Pompey to Caesar. After the Ides, they switched from Caesar to Cassius, then from Cassius to Antony. And finally they exchanged Antony for Augustus. Each time the proper substitution; so correct, so well-timed it nearly brings tears to the eye!"

"Yes, but—"

"The *young* Herod, I say. There was a man! It was four

years after the assassination of Caesar when Herod first came to Rome. He had no army, no money, no real support in Judea. He offered only the loyalty of his house, and that was enough, apparently. Mark Antony took up his cause and presented him to the Senate, citing the services of his father Antipater. The Senate debated briefly, then declared him King of Judea. And, ten years later, Augustus generously reconfirmed that kingship."

Gratus paused and reflected. "This is all part of Herod's gratitude—Caesarea," he said, spreading his open hands out over the city. "And the man never stopped building. He had a regular mania for constructing palaces, fortresses, temples, aqueducts, cities. His greatest project, of course, was the new temple in Jerusalem."

"Built at the cost of some very heavy taxation, I hear," Pilate added. "But tell me, where did he go wrong?"

"It's a tragic history," Gratus admitted. "The man eventually killed . . . let's see . . . his wife, her grandfather . . . his mother-in-law . . . his brother-in-law . . . and three of his sons. Yes, that's it. But the real villain in the story was his dear sister Salome. She was so jealous of Herod's wife that she sowed the seeds of suspicion in that family for years, concocting monstrous lies about everyone in the palace. And her brother believed them all!"

"Your predecessor Rufus told me—"

"Annius Rufus!" Gratus exclaimed. "And how is that son of Bacchus? I hear he's done quite well for himself in Rome."

"Rufus is fine. But he told me something so ghastly about Herod it must be a myth. Supposedly, Herod was worried that no one would mourn his death—a justified concern! So he issued orders from his deathbed that leaders from all parts of Judea were to be locked into the hippodrome at Jericho. When he died, archers were to massacre these thousands in cold blood, so there would indeed be universal mourning associated with his death. True?"

"That was the plan, and it did get as far as crowding the Jews into the hippodrome. But when Herod finally died, sister Salome countermanded his orders and released the Jews, the only good thing she ever did." Gratus pondered a moment, then continued, "Herod did succeed in committing one public atrocity, though. It was in his final months: a slaughter of babies in Bethlehem, a small village near Jerusalem."

"You're joking, of course."

"No, no. All the male infants in town were murdered. A horrible affair! It seems a caravan of astrologers came to Jerusalem and asked Herod one of the most undiplomatic questions imaginable: 'Where is the newly born King of the Jews?' Mind you, not a tactful, 'Where is the new prince who will one day succeed you?' but, in effect: 'Where is the *real* king, you imposter?' Imagine what must have gone through Herod's mind!"

"It's a wonder Herod didn't clap them in irons," Pilate smiled.

"Oh no. Herod was much too smart for that. He had to *find* his king first. He asked the astrologers how they came by this quest, and they told him they had seen a great, traveling star which led them to Jerusalem."

"How long ago was that?"

"Shortly before Herod's death, say, about the twenty-fourth or twenty-fifth year of Augustus' reign."

"Precisely, then. Thrasyllus, Tiberius' pet astrologer, told me to ask about that star when I arrived here. Can you tell me anything more?"

"No. I wasn't here at the time, of course."

"Well, how do the babies fit in?"

"Herod consulted the chief priests, and their sacred writings indicated that a Messiah-king would be born in Bethlehem. So he sent them there under the condition that they return to tell him where the regal infant was. But they suspected that the king was up to no good, and they never returned to tell him. Actually, it's a shame they didn't, because then only *one* baby would have died; whereas Herod was so angry at being tricked that he ordered his men to slaughter every last infant in town."

"So the little 'Messiah-king' died too, then?"

"Yes, evidently. At least no 'King of the Jews' has shown up in Judea since then. Every so-called Messiah who has turned up so far has been a fake, a rabble rouser, or self-appointed revolutionary who succeeds only in getting himself and his followers executed. But let me warn you of one thing, Pilate. If any impressive leader develops who speaks with authority and commands deep loyalties from a broad base of Jews, another Judas Maccabaeus or better, then prepare for the worst. He may declare a holy war of independence against Rome. In the long run, of course, Rome would merely pick up a swatter and swat the Judean fly.

But you and your auxiliary troops would probably be crushed before assisting legions arrived, unless you were flexible and prepared."

"In such a situation, I'd first call in Pacuvius from Antioch, correct?"

"Yes, he's acting legate there in place of Aelius Lamia, who never quite made it to Syria," Gratus smiled. "Pacuvius would probably send down his *Legio XII Fulminata,* the 'Thundering Twelfth Legion,' and, if necessary, *Legio VI Ferrata,* the 'Iron-Clad Sixth.' "

"Anything like this ever happen during your term of office?"

"No. And it probably won't during yours."

Pilate cupped his chin in his hand and commented, "There's one thing I don't understand. Why this desire for independence *here?* The Jews I saw in Alexandria seemed content, even happy, under Roman rule. They aren't—"

"You miss the point, Pilate. The Jew in his homeland and the Jew in foreign countries are cousins, not brothers. There's quite a difference. Here in Judea, the people think it's heresy not to be ruled by their own priests. Their normal form of government, they insist, is a theocracy, a rule by God. Any foreign control is regarded as a purely temporary arrangement, a divine chastisement which will be suspended when the Messiah comes. This land belongs to the Chosen People, they argue, and they must rule it. A Jewish priest once showed me a passage from their law which clarifies this attitude. It runs something like this: 'You must not put a foreigner over you who is not your brother.' "

"Gratus, your policies have certainly been successful here in Judea—"

"I doubt that the Judeans would agree," Gratus chuckled, with the attitude of one who failed to regard that prospect as a criterion of failure.

"Rome's been satisfied, or you wouldn't have remained here eleven years. Now what quintessence of wisdom can you leave behind to assist a neophyte provincial governor?"

Gratus thought for a moment, then replied, "Let the Judeans know that you are firmly in charge—at all times; that you are here to act, not react; that you will brook no civil discord. Let the Zealot party detect even a hint of irresolution, a solitary act of vacillation, and they will build on it, plan around it, and hound you into concessions. Be firm, Pilate, be firm."

On Gratus' final night in Caesarea, a warm evening fanned by fragrant offshore breezes, a state reception was held in the gardens of the Herodian palace. It served the dual purpose of officially introducing the new prefect of Judea and providing Valerius Gratus an appropriate farewell. A banquet would better have suited the occasion, but, it was explained, the orthodox among attending Jewish leaders would not have been able to eat with gentiles. As it was, the reception could not be held inside the palace, because all gentile homes were ritually unclean to Jews. Nor was it proper for women to attend. Procula and Gratus' wife had to watch the festivities from a balcony.

Gratus had arranged it cleverly. As he and Pilate stood near the center of the reception line, his master of ceremonies, using Greek, would introduce a local dignitary, who was then escorted on while Gratus gave Pilate a whispered run-down on the man in Latin. The chamberlain detained the next person in line with amiable pleasantries until Gratus had finished his brief commentary in time for the new introduction. Magistrates from Caesarea, Sebaste, and other cities were presented, but the most significant contingent of guests were leading members of the Sanhedrin, the ruling senate of the Jews. They had come from Jerusalem to meet the man with whom—or, if necessary, against whom—they would govern Judea for the next years. The Jewish officials, easily identified by their lengthy beards and magnificently flowing robes, were presented with strict ceremonial regard to rank, the highest first.

"His Excellency, the High Priest of the Jewish nation, Joseph Caiaphas," the chamberlain intoned. After an almost cordial introduction, and when the high priest was just out of earshot, Gratus quietly commented to Pilate, "Caiaphas you can work with. He cooperates with Rome. It took me a long time to find him. His father-in-law is Ananus, or Annas, the real patriarch and power behind the priesthood in Jerusalem. Annas probably didn't show up because I removed him from the high priesthood shortly after I became prefect. Ha! After that I appointed and removed three other priests until I found Caiaphas. But choosing him proved to be a good compromise because it placated Annas. The high priesthood was returned to his family through his son-in-law."

"Rabbi Eleazar, of the Chamber of Priests!"

After Eleazar was introduced and moved out of range,

Gratus whispered, "He's an ex-high priest, one of those I sacked. Amazed he came."

"Rabbi Jonathan, of the Chamber of Priests."

"Now here's a son of Annas who shows good promise," Gratus confided. "If Caiaphas ever gives you trouble, you might dismiss him and appoint this Jonathan."

"Rabbi Ishmael ben-Phabi, of the Chamber of Priests."

A handsome personage, redolent in scented satins, presented himself for introduction, chatted a bit, and moved on. "Another of my former high priests," Gratus disclosed, "and a pious and good man, though he has a problem with his sons."

"Rabbi Alexander, of the Chamber of Priests."

"Rich, very rich."

"Rabbi Ananias ben-Nebedeus."

"Quite a gourmand, this one, and what a table he sets! I've enjoyed one of his feasts. We went through twenty casks of wine, as many roasted calves, thirty fowl . . . but here comes Helcias."

"Rabbi Helcias, Treasurer of the Temple."

"An honest priest he is. A good man to have in charge of the treasury. Now, Pilate, we've met all members of the highest chamber of the Sanhedrin who made the trip here. The next group—here they come—are the scribes, members of the second chamber, some of the wisest scholars in the East."

"Rabbi Gamaliel, of the Chamber of Scribes."

"Gamaliel's the finest of the lot. His grandfather was the famed savant Hillel, who emigrated here from Babylonia shortly after Caesar's assassination. In breadth of knowledge, the Jews feel Gamaliel's another Hillel."

"Rabbi Jochanan ben-Zakkai, of the Chamber of Scribes."

"He's been studying the law of the Hebrews for almost forty years. It's been said, 'If the sky were parchment and all the trees of the forests pens, they would not suffice to record what Jochanan ben-Zakkai has learned.' "

"A modest claim!" Pilate smiled.

Ben-Zakkai turned and frowned at Pilate and Gratus, who were so caught up with the story that they had raised their voices somewhat. The rabbi, it seems, knew Latin.

Finally, members of the Chamber of Elders were introduced, the lowest of the groupings in the Sanhedrin. Names like Nicodemus and Joseph of Arimathea were announced, but Pilate had by now given up any hope of trying to remember all the Sanhedrists during this inaugural meeting.

It was Joseph Caiaphas who sought out Pilate later in the reception. Rather adroitly extracting him from Gratus' shadow, the high priest sounded out the prefect on his intended policies for Judea. Pilate let several harmless platitudes camouflage his real plans, which he did not intend to lay before the only man in Judea who might block them. He promised a general continuation of the principles of the Gratus administration; it seemed the safe, the convenient, thing to say at the moment. At least Caiaphas appeared contented. Pilate was merely satisfied that his Greek seemed to be holding up.

"Naturally we've been very concerned about the emperor's attitude toward Jewry ever since his expulsion of the Jews at Rome," said Caiaphas, "and we feared that the appointment of a new prefect might signify a change in policy also for Judea. We hope this is not the case." Before Pilate could comment, the high priest continued, "With proper respect for our traditions, which date back to Moses, there is no reason why Roman and Jew cannot dwell in peace in this sacred land."

Pilate agreed, but wondered if the olive branch waved by Caiaphas was as much a diplomatic screen as his own efforts. Yet the two men had met, the pair who would virtually control Judea over the next years, and this had been the primary purpose of Gratus' reception.

Early the next morning, the local auxiliary cohorts assembled for review in the drill grounds near the Herodian palace. Valerius Gratus bade his troops farewell, commending them for their loyalty and service, and officially transferred his authority to Pontius Pilate. Then, quavering from a fresh chill due to his malarial condition, he wished Pilate and Procula good fortune, escorted his wife onto the waiting ship, and sailed off to the Rome which he had not seen for eleven years.

Chapter 6

THE FIRST weeks in Caesarea passed with surprising ease. Pilate had to deal with some problems of adjustment, to be sure, and the usual new magistrate's miseries, but nothing more than he had expected. Gratus had left behind a small advisory council, which gently schooled him in the considerable skills required of a *praefectus Iudaeae*. Composed of his officers' staff, several local Roman and Hellenist civilians, and his own aides, the council assisted Pilate in some of the routine matters of his administration.

Procula, meanwhile, was kept busy putting her palace in order and meeting the important women of the city. But both soon sensed that something in their new life was not right. They found they were suffering from a galloping nostalgia, not so much for Rome as for Romans. Caesarea was a surprisingly cosmopolitan city, half-Jewish and half other nationalities, but very few Romans lived there. And nowhere else in Judea were there even that many.

As a former praetorian, Pilate had hoped for some camaraderie with his military, and he never quite forgot his shock the first time he talked to his troops. At some distance they looked like typical Roman soldiers, well-armed with the usual helmet, cuirass, greaves, and shield. But when he addressed them in Latin, they simply looked confused and replied in Greek, a substandard Greek at that. But for a few senior tribunes, there was not a genuine Roman in any of the forces in Palestine. Pilate's troops were auxiliaries, non-Romans of mixed Syrian or Samaritan nationality recruited locally for imperial service. Jews were exempted from military service because of dietary and Sabbath restrictions.

He knew these troops would be loyal enough to Rome in case of any Jewish insurrection, since Syrian pagans and Samaritans had little love for Jews, and vice versa. Whether or not the auxiliaries would be *consistently* dependable was another matter, the problem whenever mercenaries were involved. Fail to meet the pay allotments on time, over- or under-discipline the troops, or let some major grievance undermine morale, and the outnumbered Roman officers' staff could have a mutiny on its hands.

However, the overriding problem, Pilate feared, was not so much a matter of loyalty as of numbers. The whole of his military consisted of one *ala*, a cavalry company, and five infantry cohorts of five to six hundred men each, or about 3000 troops in all. If a well-organized general revolt did erupt in Judea, a mere 3000 men could hardly put it down. At best, they could stage a holding action in their fortresses until help arrived from Syria, hence Pilate's nagging concern about which legions were available on his borders.

As prefect, he had supreme authority in the military, judicial, and financial administration of Judea throughout the eleven toparchies or districts into which it was divided. Many of the juridical and fiscal responsibilities were assumed by ten local Jewish Sanhedrins in the toparchies, which, in turn, were responsible to the Great Sanhedrin in Jerusalem, with Pilate exercising only general surveillance and hearing appeals. In matters military, however, he could not delegate authority to non-Romans, so such tasks as manning the garrisons, rotating the cohorts, and ensuring logistics regularly occupied his day.

It was now November, and time to restation the five auxiliary cohorts for the winter. One regularly occupied the Tower Antonia, the great fortress that controlled Jerusalem. Another cohort or two was regularly based in Caesarea, while the rest manned various citadels across the countryside. By reshuffling the troops in his garrisons and camps, Pilate hoped to defeat restlessness and boredom among his soldiers.

After the first rain, which signaled the onset of winter, he recalled the Jerusalem cohort to Caesarea. To take its place in the Jewish capital, he dispatched the Augustan Cohort of Sebastenians, a unit from Sebaste that had distinguished itself in putting down a Zealot insurrection some years earlier. The emperor had rewarded it with a special honor, which permitted the cohort to name itself "Augustan" and carry in its identifying colors a special medallion with the emperor's image.

Just before setting out for Jerusalem, the tribune commander of the Augustan Cohort mentioned to Pilate, "We haven't been stationed in Jerusalem for some time, so I don't know how the Jews will react to our ensigns."

"What do you mean?"

"The other cohorts don't have *iconic* standards. There are no images of the princeps or anyone else on them, so the Jews don't mind them. But anything that's pictorial offends them."

"Why?"

"A special command from their deity. I believe it's in their sacred writings."

Pilate summoned a member of his council who was the authority on Hebrew religion. He read the following from a book the Jews called *Exodus*: "*You shall not make yourselves a graven image or likeness of anything that is in heaven above, or the earth beneath, or the water under the earth; you shall not bow down to them or serve them. . . .*"

"That's no problem," Pilate broke in. "The Jews didn't make those images. *We* did. And they certainly don't have to worship them."

"My men earned those medallions," the tribune added, "and removing them would hardly be good for their morale."

"True," Pilate said, "but there's no need to offend the Jews needlessly. Have your cohort enter Jerusalem late at night, when the standards wouldn't attract attention, and then restrict them to the Antonia. Would the Jews still be offended?"

"Hardly!" the tribune smiled.

"Farewell, then."

The tribune replied with a smart military salute, clenched fist crossing over to strike his chest.

On the march down to Jerusalem, the men of the Augustan Cohort amused themselves by singing bawdy songs, cursing happily, and exchanging ribald jokes. There was also a good deal of wagering, the stakes set on whether or not they would be back to Caesarea before April, when the rains stopped. They did not look forward to a winter in Jerusalem.

Their nocturnal entry into the city was made without incident, and the tribune thought Pilate's suggestion particularly well-conceived. Until the next morning.

It all began when an elderly Jew left the north portico of the temple after morning sacrifice and pronounced his daily malediction on the Tower Antonia, the Roman fortress growing out of the northwestern wall of the temple precinct like some incongruous tumor. Then he noticed the new set of standards fluttering from its battlements and squinted for sharper vision. Widening his eyes in disbelief, he scurried back into the temple enclave and climbed a wall for a better vantage point from which to confirm his horrifying discovery. There the unhallowed sight was unmistakable: several spears, standing on a dais, had crossbars from which wreaths and golden disks were hanging. And embossed on the disks in bas-relief were the effigies of human heads!

Compounding the horror of the aged Jew was the fact that just in front of the special shrine in which the ensigns were housed, two Roman centurions were burning incense or doing some mode of sacrifice to these standards. The old Israelite quivered with rage. His eyes ran with tears. The sacrilege! The idolatry! And directly overlooking the holy temple! Turning about, he shouted at the top of his frail lungs: *"Thoaivoh ne-estho be-yisroel ubi-yerusholaim! An abomination has been commited in Israel and in Jerusalem!"* "Abomination! Abomination!"

A cluster of early worshipers, priests, and temple guardsmen quickly surrounded the scandalized elder, all eyes toward the Tower Antonia. "Idolatry! Sacrilege!" they joined in the outcry, and hurried throughout the enclave to summon further witnesses. The trickle of news became a spreading torrent. Within an hour it had swept over Jerusalem in a riptide of fury, and the Antonia was besieged by an immense throng which now broke into an angry chant: "ABOMINATION! REMOVE THE IDOLS! PROFANATION! REMOVE THE IDOLS!"

Up on the Tower, one auxiliary, who had been watching the crowd mass with growing contempt, suddenly sneered, "I'll give the swine something to really squeal about!" Grabbing the large central standard with the images of Augustus and Tiberius, he tauntingly swayed it to and fro before the multitude. An enraged, deep-throated roar erupted from the crowd.

The situation was worsening when the tribune of the Augustan Cohort appeared and arrested the self-appointed antagonizer. The standards were jerked from his grasp and he was led off in custody, a sight that temporarily calmed the crowd. The tribune took advantage of the moment and called down from the parapets, "Send your representatives into the courtyard. I will hear your grievances." He looked at the thousands of faces tilted up in his direction and for some moments there was merely a picture of mass hesitation. Then slowly the raised fists were lowered, and the low-key din of discussion replaced the shouting. Several minutes later, the Rabbis Helcias and Jonathan, accompanied by several of the Jewish temple guard, met the tribune inside the Antonia.

"Your military standards are idolatrous!" Jonathan led off.

"Only your opinion," the tribune countered. "And how can you dictate what colors my cohort should fly?"

"The disks carry graven images. They violate the law of Moses."

"The medallions are engraved with the busts of Caesar Augustus, who sent gifts of golden candlesticks to your temple and favored you in other ways; and of the Emperor Tiberius, for whom you just sacrificed two lambs and an ox in the temple this morning."

"*For* whom, but not *to* whom!" Helcias objected. "Your soldiers were offering sacrifice *to* the ensigns, and the emperor cult which they represent."

"Our cohort won the privilege of flying these medallions from the emperor himself," the tribune snarled. "How dare you question our insignia!"

"We object to your using them to desecrate the temple of our God in his Holy City!"

The Roman had run out of arguments; it was time for him to refer to higher authority. "Our standards will continue to fly. Only the Prefect Pontius Pilatus can order them lowered."

The priest and the treasurer left the Antonia to address the crowd. There would be a meeting of the Great Sanhedrin that afternoon, Jonathan shouted. Meanwhile, everyone was to avert his eyes immediately from the Tower Antonia, lest the hated ensigns reappear.

In controlled fury, the multitude dispersed from the despised precincts of the Roman citadel. An emergency convocation of the Sanhedrin that afternoon decided to send a delegation to Pilate in Caesarea. Any citizens of Jerusalem who wished might accompany the deputation. What finally set out the next morning resembled an ethnic migration, so aroused was the populace at what it thought a deliberate provocation.

A courier had briefed Pilate on the confrontation in Jerusalem and alerted him to the approaching delegation. The news surprised but hardly troubled him, since friction between governor and governed was the anticipated rule for Judea. Better to face the encounter and have done with it.

But Pilate miscalculated the size of the protest. He had expected an embassy of no more than twenty, the usual size for Mediterranean diplomacy, since the point at issue seemed only a laboring of religious minutiae, a Judean analogue to a Roman controversy over whether thunder on the right were a good or bad omen if a person were left-handed. However, the great throng which now surged into Caesarea caught him entirely off guard, and he nervously put his cohorts on alert.

Swelled by Judeans from the countryside, the mass delegation was well-regulated by a corps of priests as it made its way to the Herodian palace and presented a formal petition that the offending ensigns be withdrawn from Jerusalem. In essence, the following arguments were cited: 1) the standards specifically contradicted the Mosaic law against graven images and were therefore idolatrous; 2) actual sacrifice to these standards had been perpetrated by soldiers in full view of the people of Jerusalem; 3) the ensigns themselves, as well as the shrine in which they were housed, were regarded as numinous, spirit-filled, and thus contrary to Mosaic law; 4) for these insignia to be present anywhere in the holy city of Jerusalem was sacrilege, but to have them fluttering over the temple from the proximity of the Antonia was absolutely intolerable. The petition was signed by all seventy-one members of the Great Sanhedrin.

Pilate received a committee of spokesmen and made only one inquiry: "Did the high priest, Joseph Caiaphas, or his father Annas accompany you?"

"No, Excellency," one of them replied.

"Honored Rabbis," said Pilate, "I shall reply to your petition tomorrow after consulting with my council of state. I am sure you understand." When this drew no objection, Pilate dismissed the Jewish leaders with a tactful suggestion that they do something to disperse the mass of people outside.

Later, he was appalled to learn that the multitude of Jews was not breaking up for the day, but simply adjusting to spending the night where they were, in the great square adjoining the Herodian palace. They had resolved not to move until their Holy City was rid of its sacrilege. It became a study in human adaptation. Those who had planned ahead now unloaded tents from the backs of braying burros, but most of the people simply spread out blankets and used staffs to support sheets for protection against the chilly November winds. Meanwhile, the merchants of Caesarea eagerly descended on this ready-made market with food, wine, and other items for sale at inflated prices.

Pilate viewed the scene from a lofty palace balcony. "I'll *not* negotiate under pressure!" he cursed softly. Rome never permitted it from anyone, ever, under any circumstances, and here it was taking place before his eyes. His resolve focused on two words, "Be firm"—the most-repeated piece of advice he had received from everyone with whom he had discussed Judea. Now, then, was the time to be firm.

In debating the crisis with his council, Pilate demanded to know why he had not been better informed on Jewish sensitivity to images. The advisers might have replied that their opinions had not been solicited at the time, but more diplomatically, they explained that the Augustan Cohort had not been stationed in Jerusalem since its iconic ensigns had been awarded, therefore the present issue was unprecedented.

All agreed that for Pilate to accede to the Jewish demands at this time would set a bad precedent for his administration. It might be misinterpreted as weakness, the one sin Rome would not tolerate in her governors, for weakness bred rebellion.

Pilate and his council drew up a reply to the Jewish petition which rejected any removal of the medallions, on the following bases: 1) The ensigns were designed for and owned by Romans and the Roman military, not Jews; 2)

Jews were not to draw religious conclusions from military customs which did not concern them; 3) Jews were not required to reverence the standards, and since Rome left Jewish practices and customs unmolested, why should Jews not exercise a similar tolerance toward Romans? 4) To tamper with its choicest military medallions would unnecessarily penalize the worthy Augustan Cohort.

A final item was written in darker letters to indicate its importance as an argument that could stand even if the rest fell away: "Removing their imperial effigies from the cohort's standards *would be a direct and unforgivable insult to the majesties of Caesar Augustus and Tiberius Caesar.*"

The next morning, the committee of spokesmen for the mass delegation was invited to appear before Pilate and his council, and the reply was handed to them in written form. The priests and scribes read it, then struck their breasts in sorrow. Several younger rabbis challenged the statement that Rome left Jewish customs unmolested by pointing out the obvious interference of Valerius Gratus in changing the high-priesthood five different times. But it became increasingly apparent that Pilate and his council would not concede on any point.

Finally, an elderly priest with sun-bleached beard and leather-brown skin consulted briefly with the rest, uttered a prayer in Hebrew, and then told Pilate defiantly, "We cannot allow the abolition of our ancient laws. We shall remain here in Caesarea and pray that God will lead you to remove the accursed abomination from Jerusalem!"

"Amen!" "Amen!" the others agreed. Then they left to join their people.

"Maybe they aren't representative," ventured Pilate. "Centurion, read this reply aloud from the dais in front of the palace. Perhaps the people will see the obvious logic in our stand." Then he added, "But save the part about our rejecting their petition until the end."

The centurion did as directed, but a roar of disapproval swelled as the refusal became obvious. At the close, the massed thousands took up the cry, "REMOVE THE ABOMINATIONS! AWAY WITH THE IDOLS!" The priests, it seemed, were representative indeed.

Pilate and his advisers listened to the tumult for several minutes from the palace balcony, then descended to a rear garden for an outdoor lunch. Pilate was making a strong effort to appear unruffled in this, his first crisis. That, he knew, would be in character for a strong governor. "A little wine, a little music, colleagues, and we transcend the clamoring crowd," he quipped, trying to cite an author he could not quite remember. A pipe, horn, and lyre ensemble tried heroically to defeat the sound of the chanting multitude, as the prefect dined with his council.

"That mob will soon tire of shouting, then tire of standing, and finally tire of Caesarea," a tribune laughed. "I'll wager half of them will be gone before sundown, and the rest will leave when the chill comes on after supper."

It seemed an accurate prediction, for by the time they had finished lunch, the chanting had indeed stopped and Pilate received congratulations for the way he handled his first encounter with the Jews.

Early the next morning, Pilate confidently climbed up to his balcony to survey the square in front of his palace, certain it would be empty of people but for a few fanatic diehards. He had already dispatched a squad of troops to clean up the litter that would be left by the departed throng.

He looked out over the balustrade and cringed; if anything, the masses had grown during the night. Scattered shouts began to ricochet among the Jews—"Look! There's the prefect!"—and a thousand arms pointed toward the balcony. A colossal blanket of people, ruddy orange in the rising sun, came quivering to life. They stood up and started shouting, "Remove the idols!"

Pilate jerked himself away from the railing and retreated inside the palace. Now angry rather than startled, he summoned his staff and announced orders for the day: "One cohort to guard the palace—yours takes over today, Tribune—but it will be normal routine for the rest of you. The mob can shout till its voice is a gravelly whisper! We've tried to reason with them, but the emperor's honor must be preserved. Tribune, tell your men not to antagonize the crowd, but be prepared to defend yourselves if necessary."

It became an exasperating day, with tempers getting shorter each passing hour. Periodically the clamor grew intense, then it would vanish for several hours. From the women's quarters of the palace, Procula looked down at the multitude, ill with uncertainty but trying to manage a confident front for her husband. She wanted to plead with him to give in. After all, what were a few military emblems compared to the peace of a nation? But she knew better than to inject herself into affairs of state. From the first reports of turmoil in Jerusalem, she had had a premonition that the affair would expand into major trouble for her husband, but she had not expected to have thousands camping on her doorstep. What if it came to violence? She was sure that the noisy mob could overwhelm the palace guard. For the first time in her life, Procula knew fear—haunting, numbing fear.

The third day it rained. Pilate looked up at the clouds and was jubilant. *"Ave, Jupiter Pluvius!* More, you Rainbringer!" And as if in response, a heavy squall blew from the Mediterranean, unleashing a deluge upon the protesting throng. A relentless, soaking drizzle followed.

Soldiers reported that some of the Jews were starting to leave the square. "Fine. How many?" Pilate inquired. He dispatched couriers to take counts at the three points of exit. A half hour later they returned to report, "According to our tally, about twenty-seven people left during the squall, and—"

"What! Only twenty-seven out of all those thousands?"

"They were the very aged. I understand the priests instructed them to leave."

"Incredible!"

That evening, dozens of campfires illuminated the square as the Jews dried their clothes and warmed themselves against the bleak November night. They joined in singing some plaintive folk songs, which penetrated the palace as if it had walls of gauze instead of stone. One haunting psalm tune seemed to be repeated often, with everyone joining in the singing. Procula asked one of her attendants who knew Hebrew about it. "Oh, that's very familiar, very sacred to them," she said, and then supplied a translation.

God is our refuge and strength—a well-proven help in trouble.
So we will not fear though the earth should change
 —or mountains quake in the heart of the sea.
The other nations rage, their kingdoms totter
 —He utters his voice, the earth melts.
He makes wars cease throughout the earth
 —He breaks the bow, shatters the spear, burns the chariots.

"Be still, and know that I am God.
    —I am exalted among the nations, exalted in the
      earth!"
The Lord of hosts is with us—the God of Jacob is our
refuge.

"Why that's beautiful poetry," Procula commented.

"Their mythology leaves no doubt as to who is in charge
of the world," Pilate observed.

"Only this isn't mythology to the Jews, Excellency," Procula's attendant replied. "They believe their god truly possesses this majesty."

"If Romans had one-quarter of *their* faith," Procula noted, "Augustus wouldn't have had to legislate religion or take citizens by the scruff of the neck and make them sacrifice to the gods."

"But if it breeds this kind of fanaticism—adult, presumably intelligent people inviting illness—then Judaism commands my sympathy, not my admiration."

Pilate, of course, could not forget the mass at his door, and that night he even dreamed about the multitude. He was on the dais in front of the palace, holding a huge ensign from which dangled two enormous iconic disks with the imperial busts. On the balcony were Tiberius and Sejanus, glaring down at him as if anticipating weakness on his part. The mob howled in a ghastly frenzy, but Pilate refused to give in. Finally the Jews stormed the dais, clutched at the disks, and triumphantly tore them to tatters. With a hideous scowl, Tiberius ordered a review of Pilate's cohorts and sentenced them to decimation, that terrible military punishment for failure which selected every tenth man for execution by flogging before the eyes of the rest of the troops. The grisly tally ended with a ninth man at the end of the ranks. Pointing a quaking finger at Pilate with a malicious leer on his pock-marked face, Tiberius ordered that he be the final tenth—a terror which lurched him awake. But behind the grotesque caricature of the nocturnal fantasy had been a certain grim logic, Pilate thought.

And now it was the fourth day. The crowd had not budged. Pilate turned the palace over to his highest-ranking tribune, ordered a carriage and guard, and retreated with Procula into the countryside. Since the conveyance could be closed against public gaze, there was no difficulty escaping the people, and Pilate felt entitled to a brief rest. They turned north up the coast road toward the grandeur of Mount Carmel, trying to shed their common concern before the spectacular seascapes along that part of the Palestinian coast. The storm of the previous day had cleared the air, and it seemed that spring, not winter, was approaching.

There was no conversation about the Jewish demonstration. They had finally discussed it the previous night, but without resolution. He would not retreat where Rome's honor was concerned, while she urged him to concede such minutiae as the medallions in order to keep the peace. Only she regretted using the word "minutiae," since Pilate had nearly exploded at it, delivering a heated lecture on the consequences if Tiberius learned that his bust had been removed from regimental colors.

For the first time Pilate wondered what would happen if events actually came to bloodshed in Caesarea. Would it spark a general revolt in Judea? An angry mob in one city was not that dangerous, but a whole province in arms was something else, and certainly more than five cohorts could handle. When he had suggested to Sejanus that Judea might be undermanned, the only answer he received was: "Just 1200 men, strategically placed, control all Gaul. A mere score of lictors keep the peace in Asia Minor. You should have no trouble in little Judea, Pilate. We need our legions on the frontiers." At the time he had recoiled with embarrassment. Now he wished he had expressed a strong counterargument: unlike Gaul or Asia, Judea was practically the only rebel province in the Roman Empire, having been torn by twelve major rebellions since its conquest.

The outing did little good. It was not even an escape, since nature seemed to conspire with the Jews in reminding Pilate of their protest. The panorama of whitecaps rolling in from the Mediterranean looked like the Jewish thousands. The tiers of pine trees staring down at them from the somber green hills were the Jewish thousands. Even the approaching rows of white clouds high in the northern sky were the Jewish thousands. Pilate ordered his driver to turn back to Caesarea.

The fifth day of the protest saw a dangerous complication developing. The gentile population of Caesarea grew hostile to the demonstration, for it had now interrupted business. In reaction against inflated local prices, the Jews were managing to import their own provisions. The Caesareans busily organized counterdemonstrations, which lavished appropriate insults and catcalls from the surrounding perimeter. One group of town youths released some stolen pigs into the plaza, which the Jews angrily beat off into a squealing retreat. Other gentiles drew rude, insulting portraits of Jews on large sheets of papyrus and hung them from buildings bordering the square.

A few more provocations and Pilate knew it would come to bloodshed, a civil war in his capital less than two months after his arrival—a handsome entry on his record back in Rome! Clearly, the disturbance would have to be terminated.

Following a strategy meeting with his council, he mobilized two local cohorts and ordered a third to come over from Sebaste. Early the next morning, trumpeters silenced the crowd for an announcement. A herald called out that the prefect of Judea would personally reply to their petition from his tribunal in the great stadium at the southeastern edge of town. The people were to assemble there within the hour. The throng hesitated, waited for instructions from the priests, and then did as directed.

The governor's tribunal or judgment seat could be set up anywhere at will, since it was the portable raised platform used by the Roman magistrate whenever and wherever he acted in official capacity. Obviously, the tribunal might have been erected in front of the palace to accommodate the multitude, but Pilate wanted to raise the siege of his palace and evacuate the plaza.

All the lower tiers of carved stone seats in the great hippodrome at Caesarea were filled with the mass of Jews. Preceded by lictors as he ascended his tribunal, the prefect of Judea was arrayed in a gleaming official toga that flashed more than a modest amount of imperial purple. To inaugurate the ceremonial, a trumpet corps blasted out a fanfare as the golden eagle which symbolized Rome and the purple governor's standard—Sejanus' gift at Puteoli—were mounted at the center of the dais. The fluttering pennant with its image of Tiberius caused no crisis, since the priests passed the word that Caesarea was not the Holy City, but merely the pagan capital of a foreign power.

As a concession, Pilate did refrain from taking omens or offering public sacrifice. The Jewish leaders were stationed in front of the tribunal, and now they renewed their petition for the removal of the hated medallions from Jerusalem.

"You permit no images of any kind? No pictures or portraits? No sculpture?" Pilate inquired.

"No," they replied.

"Perhaps I can understand your aversion to foreign themes in your art, but have you no representations of even Jewish people or Jewish things?"

"No. Making graven images contradicts the laws of Moses and the word of God," replied Rabbi Eleazar, who was one of the spokesmen.

"Have you no art, then?"

"No pictorial or representative art . . . only ornamentation and architecture."

"On that point, gentlemen, you are either playing with the truth or are amazingly uninformed," countered Pilate, with the half-smiling assurance of one armed with a surprise argument. "I've heard that Jews in Mesopotamia paint pictorial frescoes on the walls of their *synagogues,* no less, while I know for a fact that Jews in Rome draw and sculpt figures of human beings on their burial vaults."

"Don't conclude from the sins of our cousins, far-removed from the Holy City, what our true doctrines are," exclaimed Ishmael ben-Phabi, the incarnation of Judean orthodoxy.

"What about the golden eagle which Herod placed over the very gate of your temple?"

"That was torn down by the people even before his death."

"What about your coinage, then? Don't you carry silver denarii with Tiberius Caesar's image and superscription on them?"

Momentarily the priests paused to ponder Pilate's argument. Then Rabbi Helcias, the temple treasurer, replied, "Because we must pay tribute to Rome, we must perforce use Rome's money. But such denarii are never used for tithe offerings at the temple. Also, we attach no religious significance to coinage as you do to your standards. This is the difference."

"We *don't* ask you to *worship* our standards!" said Pilate, raising his voice, astonished that his argument did not penetrate.

"Our law *forbids religious images,* especially in the Holy City," Eleazar replied, equally amazed that Pilate could not grasp the concept.

"Enough!" Pilate shouted down from his tribunal. "Here is my final judgment: the ensigns of the Augustan Cohort *will remain in Jerusalem!* I shall not insult our emperor by permitting their removal. You must give me your immediate agreement and leave Caesarea at once."

For several moments there was a shocked silence. Then head turned to head and a furious rumble of discussion began. Finally the spokesmen filed up to the tribunal and said, with one voice, "We shall remain until the idols are removed." And the rumbling mass voice came to life once again, "REMOVE THE IDOLS! AWAY WITH THE ABOMINATIONS!"

Pilate clapped his hands twice, and suddenly the upper passageways of the great stadium disgorged hundreds of trotting, armed troops who surrounded the multitude in a ring of iron, three men deep. A low, quavering moan welled up from the astounded Jews.

"I convict you all of treason and sedition against Emperor Tiberius Caesar . . . unless you cease this protest immediately and return to your homes!" Pilate paused, then added, "And the penalty for treason is death."

His threat caused a great commotion. There was much anguished groaning, and several of the women began to cry hysterically. Many in the crowd recited psalms and prayers, with arms raised heavenward in supplication. Others dropped to their knees or covered their heads. But there was no sign of capitulation.

Pilate glared down at the leaders of the protest and snapped, "Surely you don't want the blood of these thousands to stain your hands. Lead them back to Jerusalem in peace."

There was no reply. "Auxiliaries . . . advance!" Pilate ordered. The armed circle constricted about the host of humanity.

"For the final time," Pilate announced, "anyone who shows his loyalty to the emperor by leaving Caesarea peacefully may raise his hand and the troops will allow him to pass through their ranks unmolested. Raise your hands and go in peace—now! Those who remain will be cut down where they stand."

A young boy began to cry, raised his hand, and ran out between the ranks of soldiers. Several women and a few more youngsters followed him. Rabbi Eleazar consulted with his colleagues and then announced, in a voice charged with emotion, "All women and all children under sixteen years of age may raise their hands and depart in peace. Go! But men of Israel, stand firm in the Lord!"

Many of the women and children left, but what appalled Pilate was the number who chose to remain with the men. And not a man left the arena.

"One final nudge," Pilate thought to himself, and called out, "Auxiliaries . . . unsheath your swords!"

A shrill and prolonged rasp of metal against metal rent the air. The Jewish leaders cried, "We would sooner die than see our law transgressed!" and threw themselves onto the ground, baring their necks for macabre convenience. The rest of the assembly also fell prone and joined in singing again, "God is our refuge and strength," the psalm that had impressed Procula.

Pilate was utterly thwarted. Certainly he had never planned to massacre thousands in cold blood. He was merely playing the time-honored game of bluff. Caesar had used it repeatedly in his campaigns, and it had always worked for him. What *should* have happened—Pilate had banked on it—was mass hysteria among the Jews and a stampede out of the stadium, then a headlong flight back to Jerusalem. But here they were, like so many docile sheep, bleating for their own slaughter. Pilate was almost angry enough to give the execution order anyway. But he came to his senses with the grimly humorous thought of how his report to Rome would begin: "Pilate to Tiberius: I killed 6000 Jews in my first six weeks here. With that average, I should wipe out the entire nation in a short time. . . ."

Now the disgusting, distasteful task of backtracking without seeming to, the gentle art of surrendering Rome's honor while appearing to preserve it.

"In the name of the clemency of Tiberius Caesar and of the Senate and the Roman People, sheathe your swords!" Pilate ordered his troops. "People of Judea, I was sent not to shed your blood, but to govern you with equity and justice. You will pardon this test of the sword, but I had to determine your sincerity in this matter. I see now that the military standards in question are truly offensive to you and that you are not simply testing Roman policy."

The Jews were listening in apparent but unforecast rapture.

"Do not misunderstand. I shall *not* dishonor the emperor by ordering his medallions removed from the standards of the Augustan Cohort. But I *shall* transfer that cohort back to Caesarea and send another in its place without iconic in-

signia. Now go in peace and be good citizens so that Jew
and Roman may live in accord."

A mighty roar of approval and thunderous waves of applause greeted Pilate's statement. Jew fell weeping on the
neck of Jew as they left the stadium in triumphant singing
and took the road back to Jerusalem. Even Pilate was
moved by the sight, though he quickly sobered to the further task of salvaging his prestige in this exasperating affair.

His council applauded the ingenious solution by which
the emperor's standards were not compromised, while Procula adoringly styled her husband's conduct as statesman-
like. Even the auxiliaries, though hardly Judeophile, were
glad to have been spared the gory task that had seemed unavoidable. When the Augustan Cohort learned of its recall
to Caesarea, few tears were shed. In fact, the Tower Antonia fairly rocked with an impromptu celebration at the
prospect of wintering in the capital.

So the affair of the standards, as it would later be called,
ended happily. Only Pilate was honest enough with himself
to acknowledge the confrontation for the personal defeat it
really was. The Jews had won the first round. But there
need be no dangerous repercussion from the episode *if* the
Jewish authorities did not misconstrue his concession as a
sign of weakness. If they did, or if they tried to press him
again, then, Pilate promised himself, blood might flow indeed. Another such episode and his first countermove
would be to replace Joseph Caiaphas as high priest, since
he seemed unable to control his people.

And where, Pilate reflected, *was* Caiaphas during the
whole affair? Annas was probably too old to make the trip
to Caesarea, but Caiaphas? The high priest was doubtless
caught in an embarrassing dilemma. On the one hand, he
had to—and probably wanted to—sign the Jewish protest
along with the rest of the Sanhedrin. But he would not go
to Caesarea and appear in an anti-Roman demonstration
antagonizing the new prefect, for he knew Pilate could replace him as Gratus had his predecessors. Well and good:
if Judeans could use such pressures to alter Pilate's decisions, Pilate could perhaps use Caiaphas to alter Jewish intentions.

Chapter 7

IT HAD been a blundering beginning for his administration in Judea, and it soured some of the idealism Pilate had originally brought to his office. Romanization of the Jews would be a formidable, perhaps impossible, task. That was now clear.

Fortunately, the standards affair did not, in fact, set up the pattern of trouble Pilate had feared, and once he adjusted to the routine of Judean administration, the government seemed to move with a momentum of its own. There was considerable correspondence with the various toparchial Sanhedrins, since these bodies were responsible for collecting the taxes and channeling them to Caesarea. There were judicial sentences to confirm, appeals to hear, disputes to adjudicate, especially the regular, small-scale unpleasantries perpetrated between gentiles and Jews, or Samaritans and Jews. But aides handled much of the dull routine and paper work. Governing Judea was a superable assignment after all.

Pilate spent his first winter in Palestine more as mayor of Caesarea than as prefect of Judea. The more he came to know the city, the more astonished he was at the engineering skill of Herod's architects and builders. There were touches of genius here which could have graced even the Capitoline Hill at Rome. The temple of the Divine Augustus, which crowned an eminence fronting on the harbor, was the civic symbol for which the city was known, Caesarea's Pharos. Two great statues commanded the interior

sanctuary, one of Augustus sculptured to resemble Olympian Zeus; the other of Roma, done after the likeness of
Hera, queen of the gods.

Herod's building materials were phenomenal: immense,
obelisk-like stone pillars up to fifty feet long, cut out of living rock in one gigantic bulk, not wafered into sections and
stacked on a core like columns in Greece and Rome. Only
Egypt could rival Herod's monumental architecture.

Maintaining it all in good repair was one of the subordinate tasks of the Judean governor. Pilate was more concerned about ensuring an adequate water and sewer system,
the dual problem afflicting most cities in the Empire.
Rome, he recalled, had done better with her water supply
than her drainage. Graceful aqueducts, converging on the
capital from all directions, cascaded an almost prodigal
supply of fresh water, but Rome's sewers were not always
equal to the task of removing the waste.

Caesarea was better off. Not only was her northern aqueduct sufficient, but Pilate soon found that it was unkind
to refer to "sewers" in that city. The capital boasted instead
a vast subterranean plumbing system, some of whose
arches were works of art that evidently only the waste
could enjoy. And Mediterranean tides made the system au-
tomatic: major conduits sloped gently to the sea, draining
the city's waste at ebb tide; later, with high tide, the Mediterranean herself returned to rinse out remaining impu-
rities.

On more visible levels at Caesarea, Pilate conceived a
project which would both enhance Herod's architecture
and solve the problem of how to accommodate the roistering ship crews wintering in port. Irked by idleness and
boredom, the sailors were creating serious waterfront dis-
turbances. Pilate planned to hire the men out for a construction project which he had envisioned ever since his
first promenade with Procula one evening on the great harbor jetty. In all the impressive skyline of Caesarea, one
type of building, dear to Romans, was conspicuously missing: a basilica. One of the most handsome yet versatile
structures of the Mediterranean world, the basilica was a
rectangular building with rows of columns framing a colonnaded interior hall, which could be used as a law court,
merchants' exchange, public auditorium, or even as a shelter for citizens caught in the rain.

Pilate wanted a basilica for his capital. Not a large one,

like those lining the Roman Forum, but a much smaller
version, adapted to the needs of Caesarea. The son of
Herod's architect for the city was commissioned to design a
plan, and he easily caught Pilate's ideas. Construction
began. At first, the winterbound sailors balked at being
hired out of their element, but once they had wined
through their savings, they proved much more cooperative.
Since Gratus had left Pilate a healthy provincial treasury,
he could pay a decent wage.

The basilica was built at a convenient location facing the
marketplace on one side and the sea on another. The sailors and construction crews did the heavy work, while
skilled craftsmen fashioned the beauty for months after the
crews had put out to sea in the spring.

Long before the basilica was completed, Pilate decided
to name the building in honor of Tiberius and had the following chiseled into its cornerstone in three inch lettering:

CAESARIENS. TIBERIÉVM
PONTIVS PILATVS
PRAEFECTVS IVDAEAE
DÉDIT

"Pontius Pilatus, Prefect of Judea, has presented the Tiberiéum to the Caesareans," a simple but proud sentence.*

The Tiberiéum project proved popular with the Caesareans. To be sure, the more sensitive Jewish citizens at
first disdained the construction, since they thought it would
be just another temple to a pagan deity—or worse, a
Roman emperor. But when they learned what Pilate intended with his Tiberiéum, they grew curious enough to join
the gentile population of the city in watching the basilica
take shape.

Strangely, the prefect of Judea had as yet had little contact with his neighboring rulers in Palestine, the sons of
Herod the Great. But Pilate's council had given him a full
briefing on the idiosyncrasies of these unusual brothers.

---

* This inscription is authentic. In the summer of 1961, an Italian
archaeological expedition found a two-by-three-foot stone with
this enormously important inscription while excavating at Caesarea—the first epigraphic evidence of the existence of Pilate to
be discovered. For further discussion, see the Notes.

One was Herod Antipas, the tetrarch of Galilee and Perea, lands bordering to the north and east of Judea. His half-brother Philip was tetrarch of an area northeast of the Sea of Galilee called by such near-medical names as Trachonitis, Auranitis, and Batanea. A third brother, Archelaus, had been named by Augustus as ethnarch over the rest of Palestine—Judea, Samaria, and Idumaea—areas which contained the majority of the Jewish population. If Archelaus had ruled wisely, he was to have been named king in accordance with Herod's will. But he proved a failure and was exiled, and to govern his critical areas of Palestine, Rome had sent her succession of prefects and now Pilate.

"Herod Antipas is the one to watch," Pilate's council warned him. "He's very ambitious, very clever and sly, very much the son of Herod the Great." Even back in Rome, Pilate had known that Antipas had diplomatically insinuated himself into the warm friendship of both the emperor and Sejanus. The naming of the handsome Greek-style capital he was building on the Sea of Galilee was no accident—Tiberias—nor was the renaming of the lake itself, the Sea of Tiberias. Sejanus, to be sure, had counseled Pilate to beware of any attempt by Antipas to transform his role from tetrarch into king, but he wondered if Antipas had not been given similar orders to watch the new prefect of Judea. Not that monarchy was an option for Pilate, but Rome always worried about her governors assuming too much personal power in the provinces.

As expected, neither Herod Antipas nor Philip had attended Gratus' state reception for Pilate in Caesarea, though both had dispatched diplomatically proper messages of welcome. At the time, Antipas had been harassed by Arab border raids on his Transjordanian territories. But he had deftly solved that problem by marrying the darkly beautiful daughter of the Arab king, Aretas. Hostilities quickly ceased.

Pilate now wondered if he should take the initiative in any correspondence or diplomatic exchange with the neighboring tetrarchs. "Nothing more than the present, normal channels," his advisers counseled. "Why stir up Herod's whelps? They might bite."

In the spring of 27 A.D., Pilate spent a week in Jerusalem at the time of the Jewish Passover. Each year, this festival developed a danger potential, since pilgrims from throughout Palestine and even overseas Mediterranean lands swelled Jerusalem to several times its size. The prefect of Judea was regularly on hand with troop reinforcements to quell any rioting which was prone to occur at this time, particularly by anti-Roman Zealots. But, mercifully for the new governor, this Passover was orderly.

Upon returning to Caesarea, Pilate found this message awaiting him:

L. Aelius Sejanus, *praefectus praetorio,* to Pontius Pilatus, *praefectus Iudaeae,* greeting.

The report of your first months in Judea was interesting to us. To reply to your questions: First, your erecting a "Tiberiéum" is praiseworthy. The princeps is pleased. But, no, he has no plans for travel to the East, so he cannot be present for the dedication. Second, your suggestion that at least one cohort in Judea be composed of Roman citizen troops has something to commend it, but this will require further review. Third, yes, apply to Pacuvius in Antioch if you need emergency reinforcements. Lamia, the "eminent legate of Syria" (our local lackey) has agreed to this. Fourth, yes, you do have authority to change the high-priesthood in Jerusalem whenever you see fit. If Caiaphas doesn't cooperate, replace him. But Valerius Gratus, who reported to us recently, thinks Caiaphas will suit your purposes.

Cornelius, the courier who brings this letter, can give you the latest news from Rome.

A final matter, Pilate. Writing me simply, "We recently dispersed a demonstration of Jews in Caesarea without bloodshed" is hardly an adequate account of what really happened. I was dismayed to learn that you had yielded to the Jews in recalling the Augustan Cohort from Jerusalem. You were right in not removing the emperor's medallions—that would have been treasonable—but I thought we had agreed about being firm in the face of Jewish provocations. Farewell.

"How did Sejanus learn about the ensigns?" Pilate growled.

"Caiaphas?" Procula suggested.

"Hardly. Jews dislike Sejanus as much as he despises them. They never approach him.—What about Gratus? No. He left before the trouble."

"Be sensible, Pilate. News of anything so spectacular as six days of shouting by thousands of people and a threatened mass execution in the hippodrome is bound to get to Rome. Anyone in Caesarea writing friends—"

"You're probably right. Yet normal mail to Rome takes some time in the winter months. Sejanus seems to have learned the details sooner than that. You don't suppose someone's been spying for him here in Palestine? Yes . . . What about Herod Antipas? Yes, Antipas! To further ingratiate himself with Sejanus as confidential informer while embarrassing a rival governor. Shrewd of him! But two can play that game."

"But you have no proof it was actually Antipas."

"Of course not. But he bears watching. Meanwhile, I'll write Sejanus a convincing defense of the way I handled the affair."

Pilate sent for the courier who had delivered the message from Rome. "Your name's Cornelius, I understand."

"Yes."

"One of the finest family names in Rome."

"But we're not from the patrician branch, sir."

"Now, lad, tell us all the news from Rome—and don't omit a detail."

Cornelius' briefing impressed Pilate. A week later, he entrusted the courier with a bundle of correspondence for friends in Rome, as well as his letter of justification to Sejanus.

"You're a good man, Cornelius," said Pilate. "When will you make centurion?"

"Not for three or four years yet, Prefect."

"When you do and it comes time for your overseas service, why not put in for Judea? Caesarea's a pleasant town."

"I'll give it serious thought, sir," Cornelius smiled. "Farewell."

The fellow was probably happy to get out of the province and back to Rome, Pilate surmised. But at least he had manners enough to manage a diplomatic fib.

Pilate heard nothing more from Sejanus on the standards affair. Evidently his carefully worded explanation of the incident had been satisfactory. But the source of Sejanus' information still troubled him. No one likes to be watched.

Pursuing his suspicion, Pilate began to take the measure of his co-rulers in Palestine. Intelligence proved easy to acquire. "A secret whispered in Jerusalem one day is shouted in Galilee the next," a local adage had it. In fact, there were few secrets in the land.

From all reports, Philip, tetrarch in northeast Palestine, was a rather pleasant fellow, honorable, just, and peaceable. A moderate who had no enemies, Philip was easily the paragon of Herod's progeny. He quite literally brought justice to the people. As he traveled with friends about the countryside, servants would set up his portable tribunal wherever and whenever adjudication was required.

"How does he feel toward Rome?" Pilate inquired, his consistent, crucial query.

"Romanophile," was the assuring reply.

That Philip's sympathies were strongly pro-Roman was evident from the names of two of his cities, Caesarea Philippi and Bethsaida Julias, and from two of his copper coins, which bore images of Augustus and Tiberius. Pilate wished that he had had that information earlier at the time of the standards affair. What were several military medallions compared to whole issues of iconic coinage, minted by a half-Jew? But since most of Philip's subjects were gentile, they took little offense at the coppers.

With this background, Pilate expected no trouble from Philip. The two had met in Jerusalem and found each other almost congenial. They parted with mutual invitations for state visits to Caesarea and Caesarea Philippi.

Genetics, Pilate decided, were partially responsible for the enormous difference between Philip and Antipas. The two were only half brothers. And unlike Philip, Antipas had had a near taste of royalty in being named heir to the throne in Herod's third will. The fourth had handed the crown to Archelaus, but now that he was in exile, only Roman Judea interposed between Antipas and most of his father's former realm.

Antipas' strategy, Pilate surmised, would be to impress Rome with his administration of Galilee, to discredit the Roman prefects wherever possible, and to conciliate the Judeans as potential subjects. His policies of ingratiating himself with Tiberius and Sejanus, his feverish "Tiberianizing" of capitals, seas, and coinage in his realm, and what must have been his recent report to Sejanus, embarrassing Pilate on the standards episode, all suited this pattern handsomely. He was playing a shrewd waiting game. For thirty-one years now, Antipas had successfully ruled Galilee and the Transjordan, while the government of Judea had changed hands five times. Might Rome not prefer continuity also for Judea? Might Tiberius not finally revert to using a buffer king in the tradition of Herod the Great to cushion the shocks between Roman and Jew? Doubtless, Antipas was grooming himself for such a role. . . . Or was he imputing false motives to the tetrarch, Pilate wondered. He had better test the situation soon.

He discovered that a younger half brother of Antipas named Herod-Philip (not to be confused with the tetrarch Philip) was living in Caesarea as a private citizen. From him, Pilate learned that Antipas was planning to sail to Rome on business. Deciding that it was high time he invited the tetrarch to Caesarea for a friendly visit, Pilate dispatched a letter to the Galilean capital, well-laced with cordiality, inviting Antipas and his wife to dinner at the palace on the eve of his departure, since he would be sailing from Caesarea. The guests would include brother Herod-Philip and his family.

Antipas was pleased to accept, though his wife, the Arabian princess, sent her regrets. "Since I wouldn't be returning with her," Antipas explained after his arrival, "she preferred to come another time."

Herod Antipas seemed older than Pilate had anticipated—he was now in his early fifties—but he looked very much the son of Herod the Great. The Herodian features —rectangular visage, square chin, deep-set eyes—were obviously dominant genes, since his half brother Herod-Philip, born of a different mother, shared them also.

Both were dressed as sophisticates of the Hellenistic East, though purple hems and signet ring betrayed the tetrarch, while Herod-Philip appeared merely the prosperous Levantine businessman which he was. Herod-Philip seemed a trifle uxorious, however, and took elaborate pains to see that his wife, Herodias, as well as their daughter, Salome, were carefully introduced to everyone.

These were the first women of the Herodian clan Pilate and Procula had ever seen, and during the dinner they watched them with curious fascination. Herself a granddaughter of Herod the Great, Herodias showed the family lineaments to good advantage. She was a rather handsome woman, Pilate thought, although Procula later insisted that her lavish make-up and almost male aggressiveness detracted from the impression she tried to make.

About halfway through dinner, Procula came to the shocking realization that the Herod-Philip—Herodias marriage was between uncle and niece, since Herod-Philip was half brother to Herodias' father. Salome, the product of this demi-incest, was a lissome, precocious sixteen-year-old. Maybe the nub of her firm, Herodian chin projected a shade too far to call the girl beautiful, but there was a sensuality about her that made Pilate almost uncomfortable.

Diplomatic niceties, lubricated by generous supplies of wine, commanded the first half of Pilate's feast. "How long do you plan to stay in Rome?" he asked Antipas.

"Several months. I need technical advice on several new projects I've in mind for Tiberias. . . . And how do you find Judea, Prefect?"

Antipas was edging up to it, so why not plunge in directly? "Except for a little problem about where we can carry Tiberius' picture and where not—fine!" Pilate smiled.

A round of laughter relieved the tension. The guests seemed grateful that the host himself had brought up the matter of his celebrated blunder.

"Amazing how different Jerusalem and Caesarea are," Pilate continued. "Here even the images of Sejanus among our standards cause no difficulty."

"It's rather easy to run afoul of Jews," commented Antipas good-naturedly. "My error was worse than yours, Pilate. When I started building Tiberias, everything went fine —stadium, forum, walls—everything, that is, except an oversight by my surveyors which extended the marketplace directly over an ancient cemetery. We had to exhume and transfer the dead."

"No great error. Why the difficulty?" Pilate inquired.

"For pious Jews, any contact with a cemetery or the dead causes ritual impurity. What I intended was a Jewish capital for Galilee. What I'm building is a forbidden city."

"How did you ever populate it?" asked Procula.

"I'm still in the process. We're importing people from the countryside who aren't so squeamish about evacuated cemeteries. Poorer Jews also seem less concerned."

"My brother Antipas is also a great emancipator," Herod-Philip volunteered, with a smirk. "He's freed droves of bondservants and slaves in order to manufacture townspeople. He even built homes for them in Tiberias . . . under the condition that they wouldn't move out of town."

It was a borderline reference, born of wine running in his veins, which did not please Antipas. Angrily, Herodias went to his defense. "At least," she bit her words, "Antipas built a city, as tetrarch of Galilee, while *you* live off the inheritance from your father as a *nobody!*"

Pilate exchanged a shocked glance with Procula. Herod-Philip, glaring at his wife, took a long draft from his goblet. Then he lowered it slowly and replied, "My inheritance? Oh, yes. But I could have lived much better off my *original* inheritance."

"What Father means, Prefect, is that Herod's first will had named *him* as successor to the throne," Salome intruded.

"Only in case your Uncle Antipater died," Herodias corrected the record.

"You may think it impudent of me to speak of 'Herod' rather than 'Grandfather,'" Salome explained to Pilate, "but, you see, Herod is also my *great*-grandfather on my mother's side, so I don't know which name to—"

"All right, child, all right!" Herodias interrupted.

A long pause descended on the conversation, which had nearly degenerated into a family squabble.

"Uncle Antipas," Salome suddenly chirped, "do you suppose you'll ever become king instead of tetrarch?"

Silence virtually thundered at the ingenuous query. Antipas reddened.

"My, how you prattle, child!" Herodias covered.

"I'll tell you when Antipas will become king!" Herod-Philip called out, a little unsteadily from drink.

"When?" Herodias snapped.

"The first."

"The first of what?" she snarled.

"The first chance he gets!" tittered Herod-Philip, until he discovered that he was laughing alone. Then another deadly silence descended.

"Salome, why don't you play the lyre for us like a good daughter," Herodias urged.

"Oh yes, please do, Salome," Procula added.

"Must I, Mother?"

In a pleasant sing-song voice which only barely disguised the urgency, Herodias said, "You must."

Pouting, Salome moved to her task. While the performance would have won no trophies at the Panathenaea festival, it did serve Herodias' purpose in changing the mood and direction of the dinner party. At one point, Pilate almost thought he saw Antipas giving his brother a brief jab in the shin as they reclined to listen to the recital.

Later that night, after the guests had gone, host and hostess were reviewing the evening, their usual after-party hobby. "I begin to understand Herod-Philip," said Procula. "With a wife like that, one who delights in humiliating him publicly, small wonder he cuddled his wine goblet as his dearest friend."

"True, though he certainly did his own bit to exhibit the soiled family laundry. And wasn't it surprising how Antipas revealed his blunder at Tiberias?"

"And what about Salome's innocent question?"

"And Antipas' reaction? Wonderful!" They laughed.

"Pilate," Procula asked in a more serious tone, "how did you manage to stay in such good control of yourself all evening while they were all getting drunk and loose-lipped?"

"Not too difficult," he replied grandly, as if he had been waiting all evening for that question. Walking over to a cabinet, he pulled out a large, silver wine flagon which his steward had used earlier that evening to keep all goblets brimming. "Look closely into the neck of the flagon. See its double throat? The larger passage leads to a main reservoir, which was filled with the strongest vintage I could find in the palace wine cellar. The other leads to a smaller chamber, which contained a color-matched grape juice. See this valve? One flick and it opens one throat while closing the other, and vice versa, with no one the wiser."

"Pilate, you didn't . . ."

"Precisely. Now, you know I love my wine, but this evening we had a little work to do. So, with the steward's deft hand, it was wine for everyone, grape juice for me. They had the loose tongues; I had the information."

"Why did you let me have wine, then?"

"My pet, you drink like a sparrow."

"Well, we do know a good deal more about our friends, the Herods. . . . Something else struck me about Antipas. Did you notice it, too?"

"Yes, if we're thinking about the same thing."

"The way his eyes fastened on Herodias?"

"And hers on his."

"It was almost indecent."

"It *was* indecent."

They prepared for bed; but, before falling asleep, Procula offered a final comment. "Pilate, you don't have portraits of Sejanus on any of your regimental standards, do you?"

"No."

"Well, why did you tell Antipas you did?"

"You'll find out shortly."

That interim proved to be two months, when another letter arrived from Sejanus. Pilate seized on the following and read it jubilantly to his wife:

> . . . The Jews, as you know, do not wish me well, so it is doubly appropriate that you are flying my medallion as an object lesson. . . .

"I never wrote Sejanus about posting *his* standards. It seems we've authenticated our suspected channel of information."

"But what if Sejanus checks on whether his medallion really is hanging from your ensigns?"

"He won't. Why should he? But if it comes to that, we can fall back on the governor's pennant he gave me. Antipas will just have gotten his facts garbled about the image."

One day, soon after Antipas' return from Rome, the scandal broke across Palestine in fury, horrifying the orthodox and scandalizing even liberals. Antipas had fallen hopelessly in love with Herodias, and she, fired by ambition, reciprocated. In flagrant violation of Jewish law, she divorced her husband, and Antipas his Arabian wife; they then married each other. Hebrew scripture also forbade marrying a brother's wife, and, to compound the scandal, Herodias was also Antipas' niece. While marriage of uncle and niece was actually permissible under Jewish law— Herodias had taken the same route with her first husband —such a union was thought incestuous by Antipas' gentile subjects.

In the settlement, Salome would live with her mother at Tiberias, though she could visit her father periodically at Caesarea. Herod-Philip was too disgusted to contest the affair. Apparently, he despised Antipas with all the enthusiasm that only Herodian siblings could generate. Other rumors had it that he was in fact relieved to be rid of Herodias.

The only person to emerge from the sordid affair with personal honor intact was the innocent wife of Antipas, princess-daughter of the Arabian King Aretas. She had learned of her husband's plans with Herodias almost as soon as they were contrived. Instead of making a scene, she adroitly asked if she might not spend a brief vacation at Machaerus, a palace-fortress overlooking the Dead Sea. Unaware that she knew his intentions, Antipas readily agreed. But since Machaerus lay on the border between his domains and those of her father, it was simple work for one of Aretas' officers to spirit the princess away from the castle and back to the safety of her childhood home at Petra.

The old hostility between King Aretas and the House of Herod now blazed anew. With a righteously angry father determined to avenge his daughter's honor, bloodshed seemed inevitable.

In the duel for respectability and leadership in Palestine, the prefect of Judea was now clearly ahead of the tetrarch of Galilee and Perea. And Pilate had several plans for remaining in front. By blending firmness with conciliation, he would try again to win the people of Judea for his cherished program of Romanizing Palestine.

Chapter 8

LATE IN the summer of A.D. 28, Pilate took Procula on the sixty-mile trip to Jerusalem. For her first visit, he intentionally avoided a Jewish festival, so that she would have a chance to see the city rather than milling masses of people.

Their route led south along the fertile Plain of Sharon to Lydda, then diagonally southeast up through winding hills toward Jerusalem. Only a small cavalry escort accompanied them, since this visit was to be unofficial, and, hopefully, unobtrusive. Pilate's fiscal officer and a small committee of city engineers from Caesarea were part of the entourage.

Hardly a cloud was overhead, a vast blue purchased at the expense of a parched countryside. No rain fell in Palestine during the summer months, and Judea demonstrated the result. Its pinkish-beige soil had turned to powder, and the only remaining green in the landscape was furnished by the hearty pine, a drab and very thirsty green. Sheep, goats, and other livestock clustered at waterholes which had shrunk to muddy saucer-shaped depressions.

When Jerusalem finally appeared beyond a high ridge, the city seemed more like a mirage shimmering upward in the heat, a glistening sight quite painful to the eye. Its lime-white walls and buildings formed too stark a contrast in reflecting the afternoon sun against a background of brown hills and azure sky.

Procula confessed that it was one of the most fascinatingly odd-shaped cities she had ever seen. Whereas most metropolises had their focus of importance in a central citadel, marketplace, or forum, Jerusalem had apparently shoved hers off to one side. Nothing in the center of the city compared to the broad rectangular area wedged into its northeastern corner. This was the sprawling temple enclave, bordered by a maze of colonnaded porticoes and gates, which occupied nearly a quarter of Jerusalem. To the Jews, this was the center of the world. In the middle of the uncluttered terrace and gleaming in Hellenistic style, yet Semitic opulence, stood the great temple itself.

But just northwest of it was an architectural error, the Tower Antonia, so-named by Herod for his patron, Mark Antony. "That ugly fortress doesn't belong there," Procula objected. And it was true. The Antonia, while not ugly, was clearly out of place in its setting. It was a square citadel, a turret rising from each of its corners, with the colors of Pilate's second cohort fluttering from the battlements. The fact that the stronghold was taller than the temple and dominated the sacred precinct had magnified Jewish irritation at the time of the standards affair. Nature was partially responsible, the base of the Antonia being a sharp butte of living rock which had always loomed over the temple area; and to protect the city, that rocky rise had been fortified long before Rome arrived in Judea.

Pilate and Procula were still at the summit of a suburban ridge, a splendid vantage point for viewing the whole of Jerusalem. "It's clear that Herod's been here," Procula observed. "Look at the theater over there."

"Yes, and there's a hippodrome just south of the city. And see the little Greek forum just off the west wall of the temple? Back of that colonnade there's even a gymnasium."

"A Hellenization of Jerusalem?"

"Oh, Herod didn't really Hellenize the city—it was his supporters, the Herodians, and some of the local gentiles who used these facilities."

"Down there, Pilate, just below us—what are those poles stuck in the ground on that rise?"

"That's Skull Place, as the Jews call it. Golgotha in their language. A good name, because capital cases are crucified there."

Pilate signaled his cavalry escort to move on, and the retinue clattered into Jerusalem through the western or Water Gate. Immediately, Procula felt engulfed by another

world, at least a millennium more ancient. Jerusalem's lab-
yrinthine lanes and passages were a confusion of Oriental
sights, sounds, and smells. An aroma of aged mutton hovered over the city, exuding from countless little butcheries
along the streets, no two of which seemed on the same
level. There were choruses of sheep bleating, donkeys braying in ridiculous staccato, and above it all, citizens calling
to each other in a tongue Procula could not decipher. It
was Aramaic, the everyday language of Palestine, though
some of the sages in Jerusalem communicated in pure
Mishnaic Hebrew.

Slowed by the crowded streets, their retinue attracted
some attention. The pointing hands and craning necks
spoke a language of their own but the message was clear:
"Look—there's the governor and his wife." Neither happy
nor hostile, the people merely seemed curious. But because
there were so many of them, Procula felt a pang of self-
consciousness and kept rearranging her shawl to hide more
of her face until a sharp turn brought them into the relative
privacy of Herod's palace courtyard, just south of the west
gate.

Styled in the finest Hellenistic tradition, with lavish use
of porticoes interrupted by pools and fountains, the palace
was sybaritic in its luxury. Plainly, it was even larger than
the temple itself, although its surrounding terrace was not
comparable. The royal residence was divided into two
wings, which Herod had named the Caesareum and the
Agrippeum, in honor of his two most important friends.

Inside, Procula admitted that she had seen no mansion in
Rome which could match the sweeping height of the interi-
or chambers, all trimmed with alabaster, and only the imperial palace on the Palatine harbored the exquisite gold
and marbled furniture that Herod had accumulated here
from distant lands. The palace at Caesarea was opulent;
this one was prodigal. The difference, easily explained, was
that Herod had spent most of his time in Jerusalem.

Pilate stationed his cavalrymen at one end of the Agrippeum, in handsome barracks Herod had constructed for his
bodyguard. Their revelry that night could not even be
heard in the main atrium of the Caesareum, testimony
enough to the size of the place.

Procula spent the next days digesting the Jewish capital.
While her husband was occupied with official business, she

explored the city with several women of the Herodian palace staff. The great temple she found particularly intriguing, but her first visit to the sacred enclave nearly caused a riot.

While her attendants were chatting with a friend in the outer courtyard of the temple, Procula moved beyond a low balustrade on the terrace and was climbing the steps to peer into the sacred interior of the sanctuary. Suddenly a cry shattered the air, and in a trice she was surrounded by a band of angry temple guards, each brandishing a short stave. Their captain unleashed a furious torrent of Aramaic.

Procula's women rushed up to where she stood and almost hysterically shouted back in the same language. Several of them were in tears and nearly beside themselves.

Glowering at Procula, the captain demanded, "Why have you, a gentile, violated our Holy Temple?"

Both afraid and yet angry, Procula merely stared fiercely at the man, since she could not understand him.

"Don't touch this woman!" one of her attendants cried, "she's the governor's wife!"

Momentarily stunned, the captain of the guards asked, "But why did she try to subvert our law?"

"She didn't know about the restriction! It was our fault for not warning her. But don't worry, she didn't defile the temple itself."

The captain pondered momentarily, then said, "No matter. She must pay the penalty."

"You utter *fool!* You'd execute the wife of your governor? Have you lost your mind?"

The captain hesitated. "Well, we'd better take this matter before the high priest and the Sanhedrin."

"You'll do nothing of the sort, you blunderer!" Procula's attendant hissed. "Unless you want the armies of Rome to destroy Jerusalem for your folly in arresting the wife of a Roman prefect!" Then, switching to Greek, she said, "Come, Lady Procula."

The guards, completely befuddled about what to do in such an unprecedented circumstance, stood aside and let Procula return to the women. Only then did she follow their pointing fingers to a stone tablet embedded in one of thirteen similar columns surrounding the temple. They all bore this inscription, in Greek:

Let no gentile enter within the balustrade and en-
closure surrounding the sanctuary. Whoever is caught
will be personally responsible for his consequent death.

First then did Procula realize the mortal danger into which
she had innocently strayed.

Legally, Pilate could not have saved his own wife had
the Jewish authorities—as seems unlikely—condemned her
for this infraction. But the brave bluff of the women had
prevented any extension of the incident, and they all hurried back to Herod's palace.

Pilate was angry at the confrontation. Several times he
asked the women if any of the guards had laid a finger on
Procula. Then, recalling his role as governor, not just husband, he inquired if any imbroglio had developed among
bystanders at what they might justifiably consider an out-
rage. A negative to both queries closed the book on the incident.

Understandably, Pilate accompanied his wife on future
excursions about Jerusalem. As a typical woman, she preferred parks to civic buildings and monuments, but Jerusalem had few public gardens as such. The topography had
provided two likely areas for vegetation in the upper arms
of the y-shaped valley which flanked the mesa on which
Jerusalem was set. But the western arm, the Valley of Hinnom or Gehenna, had been ruined by its use as city dump,
and the fires constantly burning refuse there so resembled
the Jewish picture of hell that the word Gehenna became,
in fact, synonymous with hell.

In contrast, the eastern branch of the y, the Kidron Valley, remained a place of natural beauty, with some greenery splashing up the slopes of the Mount of Olives, which
hovered over Jerusalem on the east. The grayish verdure of
olive trees was particularly concentrated near the base of
the hill at a grove called Oil-Press Garden, named for a
gethsemane or oil press located there.

But the brook which was supposed to flow through the
Kidron ravine was only a dry ditch at the time. An aide explained to Pilate that the stream had water only during
winter months, when Judea caught its first rains. It was another piece of the parched picture of a dry and thirsty city.

Coming from a land where aqueducts gushed water at
many gallons per second, Pilate could not comprehend how
Jerusalem could exist without a better supply. Jews, of

course, used far less water than Romans, who had an insatiable appetite for baths, fountains, and pools. In countless cisterns throughout the city, the people of Jerusalem hoarded the meager winter rainfall which drained from their roofs, and used water only sparingly throughout the year. Even Herod's palace was supplied from a reservoir of rainwater, built into the top of one of its fortress towers.

Pilate called a meeting of the city engineers and architects who had come with him from Caesarea, and their Jewish counterparts for Jerusalem. By now it was no secret that the prefect wanted to improve the local water supply, and the men agreed that Jerusalem had a water problem, especially during the great festivals, when the area population at least quadrupled. The specialists debated the question. "Improve the Gihon," one suggested. Pilate requested an explanation.

Nature had endowed Jerusalem with but one, solitary spring named Gihon, he was told, and even that gurgling rock lay just outside the city walls in the Kidron Valley. But seven centuries ago, the Hebrew King Hezekiah feared that invading Assyrians would seize the exposed spring just when Jerusalem needed its waters most. So he had his builders carve out a reservoir, the Pool of Siloam, just inside the city; and then, starting from both ends—the new reservoir and the existing spring—they hacked a tunnel under the city walls through 1752 feet of solid rock, which diverted Gihon's water into the new and protected cistern. The grotto surrounding the exposed spring was then walled up and camouflaged. The Assyrians missed it. A feat of superb engineering had saved Jerusalem.

Since the Gihon was still flowing, Pilate and the engineers went down to the Pool of Siloam, where they found the water level disappointingly low. Wading into the shallow waters of the tunnel at the point where it emptied into the pool, they lit torches and began their underground journey inside the conduit. Soon they came to Hezekiah's proud inscription, cut into the rock of the tunnel wall. It was translated for Pilate's benefit:

> The Tunnel. And this is the history of the tunnel. While the bronze picks [of the two teams of workmen] were still opposite each other, and while three cubits still remained [to be excavated], the voice of one calling to the other was heard, for there were hollows in the rock

toward the south and the north. And on the day of
the boring through, the stonecutters struck pick against
pick, one opposite the other. And the waters flowed
from the spring to the pool, 1200 cubits in length. And
100 cubits was the thickness of rock above the heads
of the stonecutters.

After some minutes of sloshing along, Pilate and his
party came to an abrupt deviation of five feet, after which
the tunnel continued again. One of the men held his torch
close to the wall and said, "Notice the pick markings are
now aiming down *toward* us, rather than *away* from us.
This shows we're at the juncture of the two teams of workmen mentioned in the inscription."

Pilate was impressed. "Do you mean that Hezekiah's
tunnelers could calculate this accurately that long ago—
why, about the time Rome was founded—so that the two
teams were only five feet off?"

"Yes, indeed."

The men splashed their way further through the conduit
and up a slight grade. Their ruddy torches painted a grotesque panorama of shadows on the walls of the tunnel.
Just before reaching the spring, one of the Jewish engineers
pointed to a narrow shaft that rose directly upward from
the roof of the tunnel. "Here's the passageway dug by the
Jebusites, the original inhabitants of Jerusalem, so they'd
have access to the spring in case of siege. But King David
learned about the shaft just when he was scheming how to
penetrate Jerusalem's defenses. This made it simple: his
commandos stole into the Gihon grotto by night, climbed
this shaft, and took the city."

"The Trojan Horse of Jerusalem," Pilate commented.

A few more steps brought them to the Gihon spring, a
circular pool bordered by rocks from which cool and deli-
cious water was gurgling.

"Is there any way to increase the flow?" Pilate inquired.

One of the men swung a pick into the water source,
causing a fountain to squirt up to the ceiling of the grotto.

"Careful!" one of Pilate's aides cautioned. "Too much
water and we'll be trapped and drown down here."

"Watch that fountain."

For several minutes it spurted well enough, but gradually
the column of water dwindled in height until it was only a
gentle swell on the surface of the pool.

"Hit it again," someone suggested.

After several swipes of the pick, the answering water jet was smaller than the first spurt. In a short time, the spring looked the same as when they first arrived. The engineers inspected the grotto for supplementary water sources but found none. So ended any thought of increasing the flow of the Gihon.

In the next days, Pilate continued debating the problem with the engineers. Could waters of the Jordan be tapped for Jerusalem? Impossible, because the river flowed 3500 feet *below* the level of the city. The Asphalt Lake [Dead Sea] was even lower, and its waters useless. Were any lakes or streams in the area higher than Jerusalem? No. Any large brooks? No.

"Gentlemen," said Pilate impatiently, "I ask you to think: are there water sources of *any* kind within, say, a twenty-mile radius of Jerusalem?"

"Well, there are pools and cisterns, of course."

"*Living* water: springs, rivers."

"Yes," one of the older Judeans recalled, "there are several springs near Bethlehem. They converge on an age-old pool out there—Solomon may have built it—but Herod added two more reservoirs to supply his nearby castle, the Herodium. That's also where he's buried."

"Well, since Herod obviously has no further need of the water, why don't we tap it for Jerusalem?"

"Wait," an architect from Caesarea interjected, "are these pools higher or lower than Jerusalem?"

"I really don't know."

The next day they visited the site, which lay some seven miles southwest of Jerusalem. Pilate and his party found five springs in the area, while a sixth, further in the hill country, had been tapped by Herod and connected to the pool system by an aqueduct. Though badly in need of repair, Herod's watercourse would constitute an important segment of the aqueduct Pilate began envisioning.

The whole scheme hinged, of course, on whether the pools were higher or lower than Jerusalem. Locating a point near Bethlehem from which both the reservoirs and Jerusalem were visible, they sighted on the temple through a hollow viewing cylinder and noted the angle described with a plumb line to the ground. Then, maintaining the same angle, they turned the tube towards the pools and tried to sight them. If blue sky or even the reservoirs themselves were sighted, then the area would be level with or lower than Jerusalem, making an aqueduct impossible.

The sighting showed a section of beige-colored terrain, broken by outcroppings of white limestone. Pilate looked through the tube, then sighted over it. "Yes!" he exclaimed, "I think it can be done." The section observed was on a hillside well below the lowest of the three pools.

They hurried over to the limestone scars and calculated the vertical distance between them and the lowest pool. "About fifty-three or fifty-four cubits," an engineer called. This was eighty feet higher than the temple.

"Is that enough fall for water flow?" asked Pilate.

"Oh, yes. If our aqueduct meanders, we might have no better than a 500-to-1 drop, but that will move water."

"A fall of one cubit for every 500 in length?"

"Yes."

The next days were spent in verifying the preliminary survey and planning a route for the aqueduct. This proved difficult, since the terrain between the pools and Jerusalem was a natural obstacle course of hills and valleys, not to mention the town of Bethlehem, which lay directly across the proposed route.

"We'll have to tunnel under Bethlehem," Pilate decided.

The planned aqueduct would resemble a stone-lined ditch over much of the route, hugging the contours of the hills ranging toward Jerusalem and, therefore, winding and twisting until its length became twenty miles—to cover a direct distance of only seven. And then there was the final engineering problem of crossing the Valley of Hinnom into the city. The architects planned a traditional Roman arched aqueduct for this segment in order to "bridge hell," as Pilate fondly put it, once he learned the significance of Gehenna.

After reconditioning Herod's equally long upper aqueduct, which fed the pools, the entire water system with all its windings would extend more than forty miles. This length, plus the construction necessary within Jerusalem to prepare it for the happy onslaught of water would make Pilate's proposed aqueduct very expensive. Preliminary estimates showed that the costs would run several times that of the Tiberiéum in Caesarea. His problem, apparently, was less mechanical than fiscal.

The financing for construction projects in the provinces regularly came from local taxation, but there was no provision in the budget for Judea to cover an expense of this magnitude. Extra taxes would therefore be necessary. Pilate consulted with his fiscal officer and asked him to jot down the various taxes which Jews paid to Rome.

He was handed this list, with brief explanations:

tributum soli—land tax
tributum capitis—head tax
the *annona*—levy of grain and cattle to support the military
the *publicum*—customs duties, salt tax, sales tax, etc.

"Do you know which tax the Jews hate most?" the fiscal agent asked Pilate.

"The tribute, most likely."

"No. The *publicum*, because it's farmed out to the private tax-collecting companies."

"Oh, yes, our friends the publicans, always collecting more than their quota and pocketing the surplus. Rome should never have resorted to that disgusting system. . . . This is the whole tax picture, then?"

"Yes, our side of it. But the Jew must also pay his synagogue tithes and temple dues."

"It seems fairly oppressive, this total tax load."

The officer told Pilate that in Gratus' administration, Judean resentment had spilled over into an appeal to Tiberius to lower the tribute, but he had not granted the request.

Against this background, Pilate thought it futile to increase taxes just when the Jews wanted them lowered. There was also a question of ethics. Was it justifiable to add to the tax load of someone in Caesarea for a local improvement in Jerusalem? The money, Pilate decided, would have to come from another source.

Toward the close of his stay in the Jewish capital, he invited Joseph Caiaphas and Rabbi Helcias to the Herodian palace in order to discuss the proposed aqueduct. As Pilate laid before them the architects' routing and structural plans for the water system, the Jewish leaders seemed pleased. The high priest admitted that the shortage of water was particularly noticeable at the temple, the focus of activity in Jerusalem.

Then Helcias, the temple treasurer, added, "But I hope,

Prefect, that the aqueduct can be built without increasing taxes. In fact, we look for a reduction."

"That, gentlemen, is a final item we must discuss," Pilate interposed. "According to our estimates, the aqueduct will cost 750 talents up to the point where it pierces the south wall of the city. Building an appropriate reservoir system for it in Jerusalem would be extra, of course."

The sum gave his two guests pause.

"And this is assuming we use bargain labor," Pilate added.

"But how will you raise the money?" inquired Helcias.

"I could do it by doubling the tribute for several years. . . ."

"No! Not that," blurted Helcias. "Or . . . pardon me, Excellency, it's not for me to instruct the prefect of Judea, but—"

"That's all right, Rabbi," Pilate smiled. "The fact is, I agree with you. It *would* be wrong to increase taxes. I think you Judeans are taxed enough."

Caiaphas and Helcias exchanged glances of relieved surprise, though the high priest sagaciously sensed that Pilate might be leading up to something.

"Therefore, I propose that the temple treasury defray the cost of the aqueduct."

The rabbis were thunderstruck. For some moments not a sound was heard.

"Our treasury?" Helcias finally exclaimed. "You would touch the Sacred Treasury of the temple?"

"Not I. You would . . . as temple treasurer."

"But why this source, Prefect?" Caiaphas challenged.

"A matter of ethics, which you, as high priest, should particularly appreciate. Now tell me, for what purpose is the temple treasury used?"

"For the support of the temple, of course; to pay for the sacrifices, priests' and guards' salaries, upkeep, repairs, and the like. Therefore it's called the *Corban*, which means sacrifice."

"All right. But don't you have a large surplus of unexpended funds each year in the Corban, Rabbi Helcias?"

"Well, there is *some* surplus, but—"

"Come, come, Rabbi. I'm informed that adult male Jews all over the world provide a compulsory half-shekel tribute to the temple treasury, not just the citizens of Jerusalem. Add to that the votive offerings and gifts of gold which are lavished on the temple, and you have—I'm reliably advised —an annual income that approaches 800 talents."

"It isn't that much," Helcias protested.

"Whatever it is, by now you've many times that amount accumulated in a vast store of wealth lying in your temple coffers and doing no one any good, least of all the Jerusalem which badly needs water."

"Sacred money shouldn't be used for such a purpose," Caiaphas objected.

"Can you think of a better purpose, after the primary obligations of this treasury have been met? In this way, no one need pay higher taxes."

"Couldn't Rome underwrite such an expense?" Caiaphas suggested. "After all, she has our tribute money, and can *you* think of a better purpose for which the tribute might be used?"

"The tribute is spent for the protection given you by our military and for the normal costs of government."

"Ah, but don't *you* have a surplus after you've met the primary obligations of the tribute?" Caiaphas countered, argument for argument.

"No. All surplus in the provinces goes to the emperor, who uses it for government. Running the Empire is enormously expensive."

"Well, the sacred money can't be used in this manner," Helcias insisted.

"But if the offerings are given for the maintenance of the temple, this must certainly include provision for an adequate water supply."

"Providing water is a secular, not a religious matter," Caiaphas argued. "It is the concern of the civil and political authorities, not the priests. Therefore the Corban may not be used for this purpose."

"But the temple is the largest user of this 'secular water,' if you will, in the city of Jerusalem. Stones and mortar may be secular construction materials, but they built your very religious temple. Your sharp distinction between temple and state suggests a refuge from fiscal responsibility."

Caiaphas glared at Pilate. "If you don't respect my opinions in this matter, respect the people's, then. The people would not permit the Corban to be used for this purpose."

"The people will be grateful for a copious water supply. Probably only the ultra-orthodox would object to such an application of the treasury, and then only if they learned about it. You see, you need not publicly announce that the temple treasury will underwrite the aqueduct."

"I doubt if the Sanhedrin would allow it."

"That's your affair, Pontiff Caiaphas. But do point out to the Sanhedrin an interesting group of traditional laws taught by your sages concerning the use of *shekalim*. They may have some bearing on this question."

Pilate was smiling. He had played his trump, and he knew it ended the discussion. Astonished that a Roman prefect even knew of the existence of the *halakoth* or Jewish traditional laws, Caiaphas and Helcias excused themselves, promising to bring the matter before the governing council of the Sanhedrin.

His adviser on Hebrew affairs had alerted Pilate to the traditions concerning the use of *shekalim,* the half-shekel temple dues, and these approved using any surplus from the temple offerings for the upkeep of "the city wall and the towers thereof, and all the city's needs." And foremost among the needs of any metropolis was adequate water supply. In fact, maintaining the temple water channel was one of the items specifically sanctioned as proper expenditures of the temple treasury.

Two days later, Caiaphas and Helcias informed Pilate that the Corban would help defray the cost of the aqueduct, but only under the following conditions:

1. The temple authorities agreed to the arrangement only under protest.

2. Since this was a private agreement between the prefect and the temple authorities, the financing of the aqueduct was to be kept in confidence by both parties.

3. If the public learned that the sacred treasury was subsidizing the aqueduct, the temple authorities would state that their hands had been forced in the matter.

4. Instead of supplying some new reservoir in Jerusalem, the aqueduct was to lead directly into the system of underground cisterns already in existence under the temple. These basins, enlarged to receive the new flow, would, in turn, supply the rest of the city.

The last item surprised Pilate, since he had imagined that there was nothing but rock under the temple. His engineers surveyed the ancient cisterns cut into the temple mount and reported that some were of great capacity, fifty to sixty feet deep. One of the larger basins, called The Great Sea by the priests, had an estimated 2,000,000-gallon capacity, though it was nearly bone-dry at the time. The cisterns could easily be expanded without weakening the temple foundations, and the enlarged capacity would receive anything the proposed aqueduct could provide. And since the temple mount was higher than much of Jerusalem, the cisterns could supply continuous water pressure to the city conduits.

Now it was merely a matter of haggling between Pilate and Caiaphas on final terms of their agreement. Caiaphas understandably insisted on an absolute upper limit to the amount of the Corban's contribution, whereas Pilate would have preferred submitting a final statement reflecting actual expenditure. They finally compromised on a formula whereby the temple treasury would underwrite the full cost of extending the underground cisterns, but only three-quarters of the estimated expense for the rest of the aqueduct. Pilate reasoned that his Jerusalem cohort could provide the extra labor which would enable him to make up the difference. Now he could slake Jerusalem's thirst without upsetting his ledgers in Caesarea.

Pilate and Procula left Jerusalem with the satisfaction of seeing preliminary construction crews already at work. The populace was delighted with the prospect of a better water supply—it was rumored that new public fountains would be installed—and, as happens so often in civic ventures, no one bothered to ask who was footing the bill.

Chapter 9

THE PRESTIGE of the prefect of Judea was now more than salvaged. His subjects were starting to forget the quarrel over the military standards, since Pilate had kept his part of the agreement: no more offending medallions were brought into Jerusalem. On the contrary, and unlike previous governors of Judea, this Roman was apparently interested in public welfare; the new water system under construction in Jerusalem attested to that. The Jews were prepared to forgive.

Inevitably, Pilate was more popular with his gentile subjects. During the winter of 27-28, Caesarea's Tiberiéum was completed, although artistic embellishments would be added to the structure for the next decade. But it was now open to the citizenry, and at the formal dedication a letter from the emperor himself was read, dispatched directly from Capri. There was no question that Tiberius had authored it. Who else would thank the Caesareans for not having honored him with a temple, and then suggest that even the Tiberiéum might be excessive? Who, but the same person who would regard it as an insult if the structure had *not* been named in his honor! The letter concluded with an accolade for Pilate, which, of course, had been one of the desirable side effects of the entire project.

The following spring, Pilate took Procula north to Antioch, the Syrian capital, on a business-and-pleasure visit. He had administrative matters to discuss with Pacuvius, the legate and acting governor in place of the absentee Aelius Lamia.

Pacuvius, Pilate discovered, was an epicure who had one of the strangest habits imaginable in an era of bizarre conduct: he regularly held mock funerals for himself. In the midst of the feasting and drinking at his own wake, he would have himself carried to the bedroom while his eunuchs sang, "He has lived his life! He has lived his life!" He explained it to Pilate thus: "This way I get to enjoy my own funeral, and each new day is a bonus for one fully prepared to die." Pilate did not try to plumb Pacuvius' logic.

Procula, meanwhile, went sight-seeing in Antioch. She found the city corrupt, confusing, crowded, but a richly cultured and altogether fascinating place. To the unskilled observer it seemed another Alexandria, but this was no center of learning, as the Egyptian capital. Antioch was rather given over to trade and pleasure, with emphasis on the latter. Daphne, one of its suburbs, was known throughout the Mediterranean as a hedonist's paradise, a Levantine center for sacred prostitution.

One afternoon while her husband was busy with Pacuvius, Procula paid a cautious visit to Daphne and was enthralled with the natural beauty of the sprawling park. Lushly wooded with thick groves of laurel and cypress, the delightful pleasure resort was gushing with brooks, rapids, and waterfalls. At the center of it all stood the great shrine to Apollo, which conferred the right of asylum on the entire preserve and, incidentally, attracted to the park a variety of society's outcasts.

"Please, pretty maiden, in the name of Apollo and Aphrodite I implore your favors." Procula whipped about and saw a handsome young Syrian barely beyond his teens. "Let me show you a beautiful grove yonder," the youth continued.

"No!" Procula hurried away in alarm. Several other men also accosted her, only more brazenly. Quickly wrapping a shawl over her lower face, Procula ran away from the park in terror. The men laughed, but did not try to run after her because there were so many other girls about. Only later did Procula learn that unescorted women went to Daphne for only one purpose. . . . No, she would not tell Pilate about Daphne.

The next day, she shopped zealously to replace her dwindling supply of necessities, which Pilate thought better called luxuries. For their palace at Caesarea she purchased rich tapestries, bas reliefs, urns, statuettes, ivories, an inlaid table, Damascene silver, and other magnificent wrought furnishings. Pilate had to hire an extra wagon just to cart it all back to Judea.

His larger interests that spring were in Jerusalem. When he returned to the city at the Passover, Pilate spent most of his time on the hills with the construction crews. The aqueduct was taking shape. Herod's segment had been repaired and was now channeling water into the pools near Bethlehem. The lengthy conduit from the pools to Jerusalem was nearly completed, and the Hinnom water bridge was rising from the valley. However, the tunnel under Bethlehem had been plagued by cave-ins, and disagreements between priests and workmen were delaying modification of the temple cisterns.

However, most of the engineering problems had been surmounted, and Pilate noted, with the consummate satisfaction only administrators can generate, that project costs were not exceeding estimates by too vast a margin. His architects promised him that water would be flowing into Jerusalem the following spring.

And the schedule held true. For the inauguration of his water system, Pilate paid an official visit to Jerusalem late in May of 29. A slender aqueduct of Romanesque arches now bridged the Hinnom Valley, the largest visible change wrought by the project. At the point where the flume penetrated the south wall of Jerusalem, sluice gates had been constructed, and it was here that Pilate and his aides assembled with the temple authorities for the ceremonial opening of the water system.

At high noon, a polished, sun-reflecting shield had signaled a relay station halfway to the pools, which, in turn, flashed that reservoir to open its valves into the aqueduct. It had taken more than an hour for the water to reach the Hinnom bridge and finally the sluice gates, where it was now overflowing and spilling down the sides of the city wall.

Pilate knew better than to give a long public address on that muggy afternoon. The people wanted to hear the gurgle of water, not the grandiloquence of a governor. After a few remarks on the rather obvious theme, "Judeo-Roman

Friendship," Pilate signaled the men of the Antonia cohort, who snapped to attention in ranks along the south wall. Trumpeters blasted out a brassy fanfare, which was answered by the flapping of terrified doves taking to the air. Solemnly relishing his grand moment, the prefect of Judea lifted open the valve and the waters gushed into Jerusalem.

Pilate was highly pleased with the success of his project, though disappointed that more townspeople had not turned out for the opening ceremonies. But a tour of the city's new fountains the next day showed that the water was being used and appreciated. Children merrily splashed each other in the surrounding pools while their mothers filled waterpots. And it even seemed as if the sheep population of Jerusalem was bleating less plaintively.

Toward nightfall, a servant of the high priest named Malchus appeared at the Herodian palace with an urgent message for Pilate.

"Pardon my disturbing you, Excellency," he said with Oriental obsequiousness, "but my Lord Joseph Caiaphas regrets to inform you that despite his best efforts, word is out about the temple treasury's being used to finance the aqueduct. The populace is very angry."

"Who told them?" asked Pilate, struggling to keep his temper under control.

"If I may venture an opinion, sir, many in the Sanhedrin knew of the arrangement, and Rabbi Helcias will certainly have had to account for the expended funds, so it would have been difficult to suppress the information in any case."

"I didn't ask for your opinion," Pilate snapped. "It's clear that the confidence was well kept until today. Who told the people?"

Malchus hesitated a moment, then replied, "It was late this afternoon . . . in the outer court of the temple. A zealous young orator of the Herodian party—they're pro-Romans, as you know—well, this man was praising you, the aqueduct, and Rome itself. He got carried away and started taunting those who oppose Roman administration of Judea. 'Rome built an aqueduct, but what have *they* done for the city?' he cried. Just then, someone from the crowd shouted, 'Rome didn't pay for the aqueduct! *The Corban did!*' "

"Who called out?"

"We don't know, Excellency. We really don't know."

"Then what happened?"

"Chaos broke out. They started yelling for Helcias, the temple treasurer. In tears he told the crowd that the Jewish authorities had been forced in this matter. But finally he regained control of himself and told the people that, after all, the aqueduct *was* necessary, and that they should go home and not make trouble."

"What will happen now?"

"My Lord Caiaphas hopes the matter will pass, but he fears the worst. This is why he sent me to forewarn you, so that you could take the necessary precautions."

"Decent of him." It was said in a marginal tone, indicating either mockery or sincerity. "That will be all, Malchus."

Pilate summoned several aides and dispatched them into the city to check on Malchus' story and sound out the mood of the citizenry. They returned to report a gathering storm. Ironically, each fountain at the various crossroads of Jerusalem was serving as a rallying point for excited clusters of people. Young extremist orators, members of the violently anti-Roman Zealot party, were moving in to capitalize on the situation, and Jerusalemites were being summoned to a mass rally at the temple early the next morning.

Another high priest's messenger brought word that a raiding party had smashed the sluice gates of the aqueduct, but that Caiaphas had dispatched some of his temple guard to protect the Jerusalem segment of the water system. He suggested that Pilate send auxiliaries to defend the Hinnom bridge.

Pilate alerted the tribune at the Antonia, who dispatched the necessary troops. Later that night they held a strategy session. That there would be a mass demonstration the next morning was beyond all doubt. The only point at issue was how to control it. Pilate gave much thought to this problem, well aware that he could not afford another defeat such as he had been forced to accept on the matter of the standards. The tribune at the Antonia urged him to saturate the city with well-armed troops, arguing that the mere visibility of such power would stop any trouble well before it began.

Pilate, however, remembering how the throng had behaved at sword-point in Caesarea, was reluctant to display his troops unless it were absolutely necessary. He was convinced that the people, seeing themselves surrounded by troops, might react with peculiar frenzy, forcing a slaughter that might otherwise be avoided. But Pilate had no intention of losing control of the populace. After much deliberation, he devised an unorthodox plan. Somewhat skeptical of its success, the tribune accepted his orders and left the palace to prepare his troops for the following day.

Pilate slept fitfully that night. Calls, cries, angry shouts, and chanting broke the silence of the city. At 2 A.M., he walked over to a palace window and looked out across Jerusalem. The Jewish capital seemed ablaze with moving torches. He was glad Procula had not accompanied him on this trip.

Returning to bed, he searched for sleep. His last thoughts seemed to be a conversation between two unknowns. "Why the rioting?" someone asked. "Be firm!" someone replied. Then he dropped off.

"PI—LIT! PI—LIT! PON—SHUS—PI—LIT!" The thundering chant awakened him.

He looked out. A huge crowd filled the gray-white expanse of the esplanade in front of the palace. "PON—SHUS PI—LIT!" The cry continued.

Pilate summoned a herald, who went out and announced: "The prefect will ascend his tribunal shortly and hear you. But your shouting must stop immediately, or the square will be cleared by force."

The din of the crowd gave way to a reduced, but still colossal, murmur.

When he had breakfasted and dressed in official garb, Pilate appeared before the crowd and mounted his tribunal, an elevated dais just in front of the palace. A small bodyguard of auxiliaries flanked him on either side. Beyond that, there were only a few Roman soldiers in sight, stationed at the edges of the crowd.

"What do you wish?" Pilate asked the mass assembly.

A spokesman for the throng edged his way closer to the tribunal, a middle-aged Judean whom Pilate did not recognize. "The sacred treasury dare not be used for building a Roman aqueduct," he said. "Sacrificial gifts cannot be desecrated! You must return the money to the temple treasury. This abomination must not continue!"

The statement was seconded by a swelling cry of affirmatives.

"Is this your appointed spokesman?" Pilate asked.

"Yes . . . Yes," the people replied.

"And why not the high priest Caiaphas?"

There was a general grumbling.

"And why not the temple treasurer?" Pilate probed further. "Surely he above all should be concerned about the Corban."

Further murmuring greeted the statement, but no reply.

"Perhaps, then, one of the chief priests of the Sanhedrin should speak for you, rather than this man."

The people were growing impatient, but Pilate persisted, "Is any chief priest present?"

He quickly scanned the plaza, and seeing no hand raised —though of course he did not wish to see any—continued, "Your leaders aren't present because they concurred in this equitable arrangement, whereby, according to your own traditions regarding *shekalim*, the Corban *may* be used for such important purposes as ensuring a good water supply for the city of Jerusalem."

"But you forced the high priest, the treasurer, and the other leaders into this arrangement!" The spokesman was pointing his hand directly at Pilate.

"I didn't *force* them. The only threat I used was cancellation of plans for the aqueduct."

"Would that you *had* cancelled them, Prefect!" someone called from the crowd. The people laughed and applauded.

"And *you* probably enjoyed a drink of water from that very aqueduct before coming here this morning," Pilate countered.

"I *spat* in the water!" he shot back. The crowd roared its approval.

In the absence of troops, the people were in a very spirited mood, feeling free to speak their mind. This was as Pilate had hoped. So far, all the energies of the crowd were verbal, with no hint of physical violence. Again he tried to combat emotion with logic.

"Men and women of Israel: listen closely to my final statement," he called out. "I planned this project for the welfare of Jerusalem. Not one of you can deny that the city was badly in need of a better water supply. Now, if our government had paid the entire cost of the aqueduct, your tribute would necessarily have been doubled for several years, which would have been hard on all of you. But since there's an annual surplus in the temple treasury, and since your own traditions permit excess funds to be spent for such needs as this, the water system was financed in the best manner for all concerned. Besides, where does the water flow? Into the temple! You and your children can enjoy the water with no additional taxes to pay. You should be grateful to your prefect instead of staging these hostilities."

"*Grateful* we should be?" someone yelled. "We'd be grateful if you'd remove yourself!" Pilate's soldiers clapped their hands to their swords.

"And take your cursed standards with you!" cried another.

Pilate ground his teeth, fighting to control himself. "How can a governor deal with you people in rational terms? You know I removed the ensigns!"

One of the young Zealots hoisted himself onto the shoulders of another and cried, "Stand fast, my compatriots! We won at the stadium in Caesarea, and we'll win here too!" Then, pointing to Pilate, he said, "We shall stay here until you return the money to the temple!" A great affirmative chorus reinforced the threat.

"Hear me, my young friend," Pilate shouted, "and all of you: the funds will *not* be returned. They were spent for a justified purpose, approved by your own leaders. The money certainly didn't go into *my* pocket—I had nothing to gain by this aqueduct—it was built for the public good. Don't now make the mistake of interpreting my reasonable explanations to you as weakness. I tried to be fair. You've been unreasonable. This plaza will be cleared at once! With the first trumpet blast, you will leave in orderly fashion. At the second, my auxiliaries will advance and clear the square by force. Do not wait for the second trumpet!"

He turned and signaled his trumpeters. A rising commotion smothered the dying echoes of their brief flourish. The people seemed divided. Some felt that Pilate was bluffing. Others sensed he was not, and started to move toward streets leading away from the esplanade.

Pilate watched the crowd in an agony of suspense. According to his plans of the night before, he was far more prepared than they realized. He had ordered two hundred of his soldiers to dress as civilians, concealing swords and cudgels beneath their robes. These troops were now well distributed in the crowd with orders to subdue the most vocal of the agitators at Pilate's signal.

Ten minutes passed, but at least two-thirds of the multitude remained defiantly. Pilate seemed reluctant to give the second trumpet signal. The most vociferous in the crowd began taunting him.

"We call your bluff, noble Prefect. You wouldn't slaughter us all."

"Remember Caesarea!"

"Brave Pilate! Why don't you clear Judea of Romans instead? Then we'd both be happy."

"Go back and make love to your pretty wife, Prefect. You've no stomach for this kind of thing!"

Livid with rage, Pilate gave signal for the second trumpet. The notes spat out in the strains of the Roman battle charge and ricocheted across the vast plaza. Troops poured in from adjoining streets, but most of the riot control fell to the auxiliaries dressed in Jewish clothing, who now began cudgeling those who had taunted Pilate. Then they savagely went after others with their flailing staves.

A full-dress Near Eastern riot broke out, a gory melee in which it was difficult for the auxiliaries to spare the innocent. They waded into the people, their clubs impartially knocking whatever heads and bodies lay in their path. Although Pilate had cautioned his men not to use swords, the stinging insults to their chief, and to Rome itself, were too much for some of his men. Blades began to glint with furious enthusiasm, slashing and carving their way into human arms, legs, trunks. Many of the Jews managed to escape. Others bravely resisted, grabbing weapons from fallen troops and fighting back. But the people had not really expected the sickening spectacle of anguished screams from the wounded, the sweaty stench of people fighting for their lives, the dull and ugly thud of wood against flesh, the flashing of forbidden swords, and the bloodshed.

Finally the square was cleared. The dust settled. Bodies, bruised and brutally torn into shreds of red flesh, lay strewn in clusters near the two major exits, trampled to death by the panicking crowd. Hysteria had claimed as many lives as had Roman clubs and swords.

The plaza quivered with wounded demanding immediate attention. One bewildered casualty tried to stand up, but collapsed because his left foot was missing. Pilate ordered his troops to give aid to the injured, but few Jewish mothers wanted his men to so much as touch their wounded sons and husbands.

Jerusalem's new water supply was used for a quite unexpected purpose: washing the wounded, cleansing the dead. Slowly, the square was cleared. There were no further protests. And everyone began using Jerusalem's improved water system—a victory hollowed, Pilate knew, by his resort to force.

Frustration, resentment, and especially apprehension swirled in the cauldron of his emotions. Would the violence go down in Jewish memory as "The Jerusalem Massacre," or rank simply as "Riot Number 13" in the perennial quarrel between Jew and Roman? On the answer to that question hung the chances of his success or failure as prefect of Judea.

When he returned to Caesarea, Procula wanted to know everything, and this time he had to recount events that she had missed with something less than enthusiasm. As if to compound his mood, he found her asking some searching questions about the aqueduct riot.

"I know you were in a terrible spot," she admitted, "but put yourself in place of the Jews. They had imagined all along that Rome was paying for the aqueduct, only to discover that it was their own temple treasury instead."

"What we should've done, I see now, was to announce from the start that it was legal to use temple funds for that purpose, so people would've gotten used to the idea. Because our action *was* legitimate. No one seems to remember that."

"All right, but once the protest was made, did you really have to resort to force?"

"I tried to avoid it. They left me no choice. You should've heard the insults, some even involving you."

"The people wouldn't move away from the palace. Is that right?"

"Yes."

"Why didn't you simply leave them standing there and go on about your business?"

"For days on end, like the first time here in Caesarea?"

"Why not? Wouldn't that have been better than bloodshed? Eventually the crowd would have dispersed itself in boredom."

"Maybe. Maybe not. Some fanatics would probably have camped there permanently. But you fail to see that this demonstration was a direct challenge to Rome. To have let it go unopposed would have flaunted weakness and encouraged a Jewish revolt. That point is simply beyond debate."

"But why *kill* anyone?"

"I told you," Pilate snapped, "I ordered my men *not* to use swords. They exceeded my orders. Some had to. We were greatly outnumbered, of course."

"I wonder. Your men were armed and prepared. The crowd was not."

Now at the end of his patience, Pilate fairly exploded: "What do you take me for, Volesus Messala, the proconsul of Asia who beheaded three hundred provincials one morning, then strutted among the corpses, boasting, 'What a kingly deed!'? I hate this kind of thing."

"But . . ."

"But why go to Asia? Let's look at the record here in Judea. At the time Herod died, our legate Varus had to put down an insurrection in Jerusalem. He ended by *crucifying two thousand* Jews. And if you think that's bad for a Roman—and it is—remember what the *Jewish* King Alexander Jannaeus did to fellow Jews who opposed him. While that wretch was lounging with his concubines at a public feast, he had eight hundred of them crucified for his entertainment; and, while they were still alive, he ordered the throats of their wives and children cut before their very eyes."

"Stop, Pilate!"

"Well, against this kind of cruelty, don't quarrel with a necessary police action which unfortunately resulted in some casualties."

"Tell me, Pilate, can one justify a wrong by resorting to favorable comparison with a greater wrong?"

Pilate clenched his hands until the knuckles whitened. "I had to do it, Procula."

Chapter 10

JERUSALEM WAS quiet now. No further anti-Roman demonstrations followed the clash over the aqueduct, but deep resentment against Pilate lingered. That this did not ignite sympathy riots elsewhere in Judea was due less to any chastened mood of the Jews than to their greater concern over the Antipas-Herodias scandal in Galilee.

The smoldering indignation of the people at this notorious misalliance was being fanned into flame by a newly popular desert prophet named John the Baptizer, who was holding forth in the rugged badlands east of Jerusalem toward the Jordan River. John would have escaped Pilate's notice but for two factors which could prove dangerous when combined: first, the man was apparently announcing some oncoming world crisis—"Repent, for the kingdom of heaven is at hand!" was his most typical pronouncement in reports Pilate gleaned concerning the wilderness preacher; second, great numbers of Judeans of all classes were marching out into the desert to hear him. Many were being converted and washed at the Jordan in a purification rite called baptism.

Prophets of judgment and doom were familiar enough in Pilate's world; they cluttered public squares from the Athenian agora to the Roman Forum. But they had few listeners, fewer converts. The Baptizer, by contrast, was commanding multitudes with his oratory, and the locale was not sophisticated Rome or Greece, but volatile, ever-turbulent Judea. Here, possibly, was another pseudo-Messiah in the making, another religio-political troublemaker who could add to the administrative woes of the prefect of Judea.

Pilate dispatched an Aramaic-speaking aide down to the Judean wilds to hear John and report back to him on the movement. The intelligence that he provided, after his return, answered a few questions, but raised so many more that it left Pilate thoroughly perplexed.

"This John makes no Messianic claims for himself, so you can bury your anxiety on that score," the aide told Pilate. "One look at the man, of course, would convince anyone that he's not the Jewish Messiah. Hardly," he laughed. "He wears a straggly beard and a rough camelskin tunic with a leather belt. I inquired about his background, and it seems he was associated for a while with the Essene monastery just above the Asphalt Lake. Then he launched out into the wilderness on his own, keeping himself alive on a diet of honeycombs and—would you believe it—insects, locusts!"

"Friend, fried grasshoppers are a delicacy on Roman tables," Pilate advised. "It seems your Baptizer is something of a primitive gourmet. . . . But how do you know he doesn't have Messianic ambitions?"

"While I was there, some priests from Jerusalem asked him about it, and he said, 'I am not the Messiah.' Then they inquired, 'Are you the prophet Elijah?' He said, 'No.' Finally, they demanded point-blank, 'Who are you then? What do you have to say about yourself?' "

"How did he answer that?"

" 'I am the voice of one crying in the wilderness: Make straight the way of the Lord.' "

"What's that supposed to mean?"

"That he's the forerunner of the Messiah, who's just about ready to appear in Judea."

Pilate frowned. "How did this news strike the people?"

"Hard to say. Some seemed disappointed that John himself was not the Messiah, since he preaches a powerful message and is regarded as a kind of oracle for advice. For instance, some of the pious folk asked him how they ought to live, and he gave them a simple message about sharing. But then some tax collectors also wanted counsel, and he suggested, 'Collect no more than your due.' "

"Would that they did just that!" Pilate grunted.

"Part of our cohort from the Antonia was out there to

police the crowds, and several of the troops asked John, 'And we, what shall we do?' "

Pilate moved forward in his chair to catch every syllable of the reply.

"The Baptizer told them, 'Rob no one, either by violence or by fraud,' I believe he said, and . . . oh yes: 'Be content with your wages.' "

"By Hercules, that's good advice!" Pilate chuckled. "I'm beginning to like the Baptizer. How did the Jewish authorities react to this fellow?"

"With extreme suspicion. And you can't blame them. When some of the Pharisees and Sadducees came to hear him, this John blasted them with such a verbal assault as I've never heard before. 'You brood of vipers!' he snarled. 'Who warned you to flee from the approaching wrath? Repent!' "

"Brood of vipers?" Pilate laughed. "A real Demosthenes!"

"That's about it. Oh, later in Jerusalem I heard a rumor that the Baptizer had actually singled out some Galilean in his crowds as the coming Messiah."

"What? Any demonstration by the people in support of this Galilean?"

"Nothing I heard about."

Pilate paused to think. "And John the Baptizer . . . what, if anything, should we do about him?"

"I think he's moving beyond the Jordan, so we can't touch him. That's Herod Antipas' territory."

"And even if he stays in Judea," Pilate said, "I think we should let him alone. Unless, of course, he raises a sedition. He may be a good counterpoise to the Jerusalem authorities. The greater the number of divisions among the Jews, the harder it'll be for them to unite against us. Pharisees, Sadducees, Herodians, Essenes, followers of the Baptizer— several more parties wouldn't hurt at all." Pilate reflected, then smiled, "And John's attacks on the tetrarch of Galilee and his beloved Herodias make me look positively virtuous by comparison."

As it happened, John the Baptizer was no long-distance critic. Instead of castigating Antipas from the safety of Pilate's Judea, the desert prophet boldly crossed over into the territory of the tetrarch to continue his preaching.

During the remainder of the year 29, Roman travelers visiting Caesarea told Pilate of dramatic changes taking place back in Rome. An era had passed, they said, with the death of the aged empress-mother Livia, wife of Augustus. Surprisingly, Tiberius had not left Capri to attend his own mother's funeral. Public business detained him, he claimed. But all Rome knew that mother and son had been estranged ever since her attempt to interfere in affairs of state. Indeed, many gossiped that Livia herself was the real reason for Tiberius' prolonged sojourn at Capri.

Shortly after Livia's death, Pilate was told, the long struggle between Sejanus and Agrippina came to a head. Ever since the praetorian commander saved his life at The Grotto, Tiberius had placed progressively greater confidence in Sejanus, and the after-effects of the Sabinus affair now gave him an enormous advantage.

Titius Sabinus, a leader of Agrippina's party, had been indicted for plotting to murder Tiberius and raise Agrippina's son to the throne. The Senate ordered the execution of Sabinus, and his corpse was pitched down the Stairs of Mourning, that steep flight of steps over which bodies of traitors were hurled into the Tiber.

Although there was no proof that Agrippina and her son Nero* were implicated in the plot, Tiberius added to the climate of suspicion by sending the Senate a letter which faulted Agrippina for pride and arrogance, and accused Nero of homosexuality and profligacy. Since the letter contained no direct charge of treason, the Senate found itself in a terrible dilemma. Any motion of censure would be a mortal offense to Nero, the heir apparent, while failure to act would antagonize the reigning emperor.

During the debate, the Senate house was surrounded by a mob which brandished images of Agrippina and her son, pleaded for their safety, and shouted that the princeps' letter was a forgery. The demonstration turned into a riot, which cowed the Senate into dispersing without acting on Tiberius' communication. At that report, Pilate derived a bit of comfort from the fact that he was not the only Roman magistrate to face angry crowds.

Sejanus, of course, quickly mastered the situation with his praetorians, but warned Tiberius that sedition was in the air and that a coup in favor of his adoptive daughter-in-law and grandson was possible. The emperor dispatched an angry missive to the Senate, rebuking the Roman rabble for

---

* Not the future emperor.

disloyalty and calling the Senate's temporizing an insult to the imperial majesty.

Senators, in fright, hastened to fall in line. They vied with one another in a scramble to introduce motions declaring Agrippina and Nero public enemies. The decrees passed unanimously, leaving their punishment up to the emperor.

Tiberius soon banished Agrippina to Pandateria and Nero to Pontia. Both were islands, some thirty-five miles off the Italian coast near The Grotto. Sejanus had triumphed.

News of these events relieved Pontius Pilate, since his very career was staked to Sejanus' success. Had Agrippina been victorious and Sejanus been exiled, all Tiberius' appointments which had been made with the advice of the fallen prefect would likely have lapsed. Pilate would have been recalled. At best, his political career would have been at an end; at worst, if Agrippina wished to institute a vindictive purge, he might well have shared in Sejanus' disgrace and exile.

Early the next year, news of Sejanus' further success reached Caesarea. The Senate had continued its campaign against the house of Agrippina by pronouncing another of her sons a public enemy; and the youth, Drusus, was imprisoned in an underground chamber at the Palatine palace. Romans now ventured to speak openly of Sejanus as virtual successor to the imperial throne, since only one son of Agrippina remained—Gaius (Caligula)—but he was barely eighteen, and if he proved disloyal and went the way of his brothers, it would be Emperor Sejanus, pure and simple.

Throughout 30 A.D., successive reports reaching Pilate added brush strokes to the portrait of Sejanus' prospects. The Senate voted that his birthday should be a public celebration, and gilded statues of him were appearing throughout Rome. Whenever public officials consulted Tiberius, they now always consulted Sejanus as well. His mansion was besieged with delegations. Public prayers and sacrifices were offered "in behalf of Tiberius and Sejanus."

Pilate peered into his own future, quaffing the news from Rome like heady wine. He reckoned himself in the inner circle of Sejanus' closest political adherents, and had not the prefect personally promised greater honors if he proved himself in Judea? Sejanus had climbed the praetorian stairs to success, a route similar to his own, and what would be more natural for Sejanus as emperor than to extend a helping hand to one who was standing where he once stood?

What appointment would Sejanus give him after Judea? Another province, perhaps Egypt? More likely, one of the major administrative posts in Roman government. Sejanus would want to be surrounded by his own men. Nearly any office would be open to Pilate, including the privilege of sitting in the Senate, or even that proven springboard to limitless power, praetorian prefect, vice-emperor of Rome.

Or was he fooling himself? How high did he really rank in Sejanus' favor? Would Sejanus' accession actually spell his own advancement? With a twinge of regret, Pilate recalled how Sejanus had criticized his handling of the standards episode. But surely his firmness during the aqueduct riot more than counterbalanced any image of a "weak Pilate" Sejanus might have conjured up for himself.

Indeed, Sejanus had reacted to Pilate's report of the aqueduct imbroglio with enthusiastic approval of his use of force. His only regret, in fact, was that many more rioters had not been killed as a standing object lesson to any would-be Jewish revolutionaries. Pilate noticed that the anti-Semitic streak in Sejanus was now blossoming into a full-blown hatred of the Jews, magnified also by the burning glass of political hostility, for many Jews had supported Agrippina's Julian party in tribute to Caesar's memory. According to reports, the Roman Jews, in turn, were becoming thoroughly alarmed at Sejanus' continuing triumphs.

Pilate had a different cause for concern: Sejanus had not written him in months. All this information was coming from unofficial sources. But one day, finally, a praetorian courier delivered a communication which was virtually imprisoned under heavy seals. Pilate whittled away at them with his dagger and read:

L. Aelius Sejanus to Pontius Pilatus, greeting. The task of securing Rome against our enemies must excuse my interrupted correspondence. By now you must have heard that victory is ours.

Does this mean we can relax our guard? The gods forbid! The princeps hints that he may pardon the sons of Agrippina. And who is the enemy which silently plots my destruction and secretly assists the cause of Agrippina? The Jews of Rome. Here, I think, is their line of communication: the Jews contact members of

Herod's house living here in Rome, particularly Berenice. (She is the mother of that Herodias whom you wrote about, the one who recently married Herod Antipas.) And Berenice has the ear of the Lady Antonia (Mark Antony's daughter and sister-in-law of Tiberius), who has access to the princeps. And what message runs from the Jews to Berenice to Antonia to Tiberius? "Sejanus is a danger to the state."

I have warned the Jewish leaders in the Trans-Tiber that I will no longer tolerate *their* schemes against the state. In reprisal, you must now move to restrict the Judean authorities in some way. Write me what specific measures you will undertake. My reasoning should be obvious: pressure on Judaism is applied much more effectively at the heart than at the extremities.

How far has your project of Romanizing the Jews proceeded? Not far, I fear, but you had set yourself a virtually impossible task to begin with. Continue firm in Judea, Pilate, and you will have an auspicious future. Farewell.

Pilate was perplexed by the letter, if not alarmed. Small wonder it had been sealed so tightly. Never before had Sejanus betrayed such emotional anti-Semitism. Although he was anything but a pro-Jewish partisan, Pilate wondered if Sejanus was justified in ascribing all of his woes to the Jews of Rome. He found several glaring chinks in Sejanus' logic. If, indeed, the Jews had used a Berenice-Antonia-Tiberius route for attacking him, it might only have been in defense against Sejanus' prior attacks on them. Even more likely would be Antonia's own aversion to Sejanus: Agrippina, after all, was her daughter-in-law. It would hardly take a Berenice to suggest to her that the praetorian prefect was ruining her family.

Fulfilling the directives in Sejanus' letter would be difficult, but there was no alternative to compliance. The idea of some restriction on the local Jewish leadership might be feasible; it might also prove disastrous to the peace of the land. It would have to be some token which looked big to Rome, but was not that fundamentally important to the Sanhedrin, Pilate decided.

He took his clue from a curious custom regarding the robes of the high priest. In order to control the Jewish priesthood, Herod had gained custody of the sacred vestments and Rome succeeded Herod in that prerogative. Worn by the pontiff only four times a year, at major festivals, the robes were locked in the Antonia until the feasts approached, when they were given back to the priests, who had to return them immediately afterward. It was a token of Roman supremacy which had never sparked a riot. Pilate looked for a similar symbolic restriction of the Sanhedrin.

He found it in the *jus gladii*, the "law of the sword," the right to execute in cases of capital punishment. Until now, the Great Sanhedrin had full authority to conduct trials and execute sentences for capital crimes perpetrated by Jews in Judea. To implement Sejanus' directives, Pilate now planned to withdraw from the Sanhedrin the right of execution and add it to the *jus gladii* already possessed by the Roman prefect. From now on, the Sanhedrin could continue to try Jews in capital cases, even find them worthy of death, but the actual sentencing and execution would have to be carried out by the prefect of Judea.

Pilate was pleased with the idea. In Roman eyes, nothing showed sovereignty so much as the right to control sentences of death. He could easily play this up in his report and so satisfy Sejanus. As to Jewish feelings in the matter, he could assure the Sanhedrin that their right to try capital crimes was not grossly affected, since the prefect would usually confirm the sentence determined by them. It might actually be a convenience to the Jewish authorities, since the nasty business of execution would be taken out of their hands.

During his visit to Jerusalem at the Passover of 30. Pilate discussed his planned revision with Caiaphas. Confiding to him the pressures from Sejanus which had prompted the change—and as diplomatically as he could—he gave the high priest no choice but to accept.

Caiaphas brought the news to the Sanhedrin, and fully a week passed before he reported their reaction. They had grudgingly accepted, but with the stipulation that Pilate and his successors never alter their verdict in a capital case. Pilate said that he would discuss the proviso with his superiors. At any rate, in symbolic response to the new limitation, the Sanhedrin ceased meeting in the Hall of Hewn Stone near the inner temple, their senate chamber as unrestricted leaders of the Jewish nation, and moved to the market of Annas, farther over on the temple mount.

Pilate tried to sweeten the pill by granting a Jewish request that he release one prisoner, chosen by the people, at each Passover, a festival amnesty which was unparalleled in the Roman Empire, but a concession with no great implications.

Chapter 11

PILATE'S INVITATION to visit Herod Antipas finally arrived. It had taken the tetrarch of Galilee almost three years to return Pilate's hospitality in Caesarea. Although the sensitive Procula resented the apparent slight, her realist husband pointed out that social amenities necessarily had to wait until the popular scandal at Antipas' marriage to Herodias had exhausted itself.

Antipas would be celebrating his birthday shortly after the approaching Feast of the Tabernacles, the invitation read, and in case Pilate and Procula should be in Jerusalem for the festival, he would gladly escort them to his nearby Perean palace, a delightful place overlooking the Asphalt Lake, for a week's stay. Procula had not intended accompanying her husband to the Jewish harvest festival, but now she changed her mind. They accepted, and made the now-familiar trip to Jerusalem.

Following closely in autumn on *Rosh Hashana,* the Jewish New Year, and *Yom Kippur,* the Day of Atonement, *Sukkoth,* or the Feast of Tabernacles, was one of the most joyous and certainly the greatest of the Hebrew festivals. It was a time when both Pilate and Antipas, neither of whom would win any popularity contests in Jerusalem, could appear in the city without inspiring hostile demonstrations. People were too happy for that kind of thing.

Sukkoth passed without incident. With the eight-day festivity ended, Antipas, his bride-of-a-year, Herodias, and a sizable group of Galilean leaders and court retainers conducted Pilate and Procula on a carriage caravan which wound its way eastward down the rugged Judean hills. Between curves, the grand expanse of the lush-green Jordan valley came into view, a welcome contrast from the adobe-colored wilderness surrounding them. The Jordan itself meandered back and forth ridiculously, as if unsure in which direction to flow. But finally, near the palms of Jericho, it seemed to orient itself and aim reluctantly for an oblong, finger-shaped basin of slate-blue water called the Asphalt Lake or Dead Sea, a body of water nine miles wide and nearly fifty long, rimmed by mountainous cliffs along its shores.

"Spent much time in this area, Pilate?" inquired Antipas, as they jogged down the roadway in the same carriage.

"Just a short visit to Jericho two years ago."

"We're entering one of the most fascinating regions in all your Roman Empire, no, perhaps in all the world."

"A rather comprehensive statement."

"But true nevertheless. Look just north of Jericho. See those outcroppings of earth beyond the spring and the palm groves? They mark the site of the oldest city in the world, a civilization going back literally thousands of years."

"Any proof of that?"

"My father, Herod, was interested in antiquities and once had his men dig into those mounds. Near the bottom they found stone tools of such crudeness and age as have been found nowhere else."

Pilate pointed to the south and asked, "What's that establishment up on the hill overlooking the sea?"

"Where? Oh, there. That's the monastery of the Essenes, a truly unbelievable collection of scholars. They follow the law so closely they refuse to urinate or defecate on the Sabbath. No women are allowed in their community. All wealth is held in common."

"Oh yes, I understand that—what was his name—John, yes, John the Baptizer was associated with them for a while."

"You've heard of the Baptizer?" Antipas' eyes had widened in surprise.

"Hasn't everyone?" Pilate laughed. "Where's the man holding forth lately?"

Hesitantly, Antipas replied, "In one of my prisons. His movement was getting dangerous. . . . But look, Pilate, we're almost at the shore of the Asphalt Lake." Cupping his hands around his mouth, he shouted, "Everyone dismount!" Then he proceeded to tell his guests about the geographic miracle which was the Dead Sea.

"You're looking at the very lowest surface in the Empire, nearly a quarter-mile *below* sea level. If some mad engineer cut a canal from the Mediterranean to this lake, waters would rush in to drown the whole Jordan valley to a depth of 1300 feet." He paused to see if his guests were impressed. "And don't let the cool blue of the lake fool you. Its waters are a hot, oily fluid, about one-quarter salt and asphalt. Here, Pilate, put your hand in the water."

It felt like warm, sticky soup.

"Now watch this, Pilate," said Antipas, taking an egg from the commissary carriage. "Do eggs float in water or sink?"

"They sink, of course," Procula answered for him.

Antipas dropped the egg into the sea, where it bobbed like a cork. "Now, Chuza"—he turned to his chief steward —"why don't you take a swim for us?"

"Must I, Excellency?"

"On second thought, no. You're normal size. You wouldn't float until chest level. Send in your roly-poly friend there instead."

One of the chefs in Antipas' commissary, a man of huge girth, stripped to his undertunic and waded out into the Dead Sea. He got no further than seven or eight paces, for when the water reached just above his paunch, he actually began floating, pitching about and rolling out of control, to the cheers and guffaws of the whole entourage.

In a final demonstration, Antipas had an ox dragged into the water, bellowing and groaning, and that frenzied animal also floated. "The water's so dense a man could break his legs if he jumped into it from any height," the tetrarch commented. "And it's so brackish no living thing can exist in it. No fish, nothing."

The chef had neglected to rinse himself off after his briny dip and soon resembled a walking pillar of salt, so quickly had the fiercely hot and dry air evaporated the watery residue on his skin, leaving an ugly, itchy deposit of chalk white.

"You can wash off at Callirrhoë," Antipas called, as the party wound its way around the northeastern corner of the Dead Sea and continued south toward their destination, the fortress-palace of Machaerus.

Procula was riding with Herodias in the carriage just behind Pilate and Antipas. Periodically, Pilate turned around to see how his wife was faring in the company of the woman who was the talk of Palestine. She flashed him a knowing smile to convey the message, "Everything all right . . . so far."

Pilate was holding up his end of the conversation with Antipas. "Doesn't Strabo's new *Geographica* speak of subterranean gases and fires around this lake?" he asked.

"Nature has a simmering furnace under this area. Usually its vapors filter upward in pleasant form, as in the hot springs just ahead. But sometimes the furnace explodes into volcano-like eruptions of gas, fire, and brimstone, like those which destroyed Sodom and Gomorrah a little south of here. But that was many centuries ago."

The retinue stopped briefly at Callirrhoë, where Antipas showed his guests the thermal springs resort while the chef washed off his sultry, stinging stickiness. This celebrated spa was known throughout Palestine for its sweet, bubbly mineral waters. Herod had spent some of his last days here, trying desperately to shake off the horrible malady that would shortly claim his life. But the feverish convulsions, tumors, and gangrene proved terminal.

"As a Roman used to his daily baths, this place should have special fascination for you, Pilate," Antipas bantered, "but we can return here later. Machaerus is just beyond the next hill."

Herod Antipas had inherited Machaerus from his father, who built the fortress-palace to safeguard his southeastern frontiers against the Moabites and Arabs. The huge, trapezoidal mound on which it was situated further isolated the castle from surrounding hills, and it was easy for Pilate to appreciate its legendary invincibility as a military stronghold. Supposedly, Machaerus ranked second only to Jerusalem's Antonia as a citadel. The arduous ascent along hairpin curves was so taxing to the horses that the entourage got off their carriages to spare the animals.

It was nearly sundown when they reached the portico around the base of the citadel. The view westward was spectacular, commanding at least half the Dead Sea, which lay lifeless several thousand feet below in its water-hewn tomb. Later that evening, the gathering night only improved the vista. A rising moon shed a frosty incandescence over the rugged wilderness of Judea, as though new

snow had fallen in an area fifty degrees too warm for it.
Beneath the center of it all lurked the sepulchral, now-mis-
ty torpor of the Dead Sea, trapped by surrounding mountains and scarred by a glittering swatch of moonlight. Only
some pinpoints of light to the northwest, marking Jerusalem, gave any evidence of habitation.

After retiring, Pilate and Procula finally had the chance
to compare notes on the day's events. "And how does it
feel to be safely imprisoned in your enemy's fortress?" she
led off.

"Please, *Carissima*, we're on a diplomatic visit, so let's
call our host friendly rival instead," he chuckled. "Wait,
are you serious?"

"Why, yes," she said in a half-tone, betraying neither
truth nor jest.

"Well, you can sleep securely. Our auxiliary bodyguard
is certainly—"

"Of course, of course," she laughed. "I'm just wondering why he invited us to Machaerus instead of Tiberias. Remember what happened here about three years ago?"

"No. What?"

"This is where Antipas' first wife, King Aretas' daughter,
'vacationed' on her escape from Antipas. From here she
fled to her father."

Procula's comment gave Pilate cause for some political
considerations. His informants had told him that Antipas
feared Aretas would make war on him for the way he had
treated his daughter. And if it came to blows, Antipas
would probably want the prefect of Judea to assist him
with his cohorts.

"Tomorrow, Procula, when we start discussing politics,
be prepared for a blackening of King Aretas to prepare me
for a possible war against him. But I wouldn't send a single
auxiliary to fight Antipas' battles for him. Do you know
why?"

"Why?"

"Because if the tetrarch of Galilee disgraced himself further by losing a frontier war with the Arabs, Rome could
use that as an excuse to add Galilee to the province of
Judea. Sejanus told me of eventual plans to move the Herodians out of their control of Palestine in favor of direct
Roman administration."

"And if this happened under the governorship of Pontius

Pilate, it would look awfully well on his record, wouldn't it?"

Just before drifting off to sleep, they were startled to hear some plaintive chanting from the depths of the palace, which echoed throughout Machaerus.

"Probably Antipas offering his bedtime prayers," Pilate suggested. "That fox can afford to pray."

The week at Machaerus turned out pleasantly. The hosts, it seemed, were on their best behavior. As predicted, Antipas did indeed vilify Aretas, but it was done by means of some histrionics which only amused Pilate. A presumed Arab spy, "caught" near Machaerus during their visit, was made to confess that King Aretas was planning an invasion not only of Galilee but of Judea as well. Pilate had one of his guards who knew Arabic go down to the dungeon, talk to the spy, and report back to him privately.

"From his knowledge of the language," the guard confided, "I'd say that as an Arab that clown was a good Galilean. But I left the impression that I believed his story."

Yet, the daily hunting expeditions into the wild countryside, the nightly feasting, and the delightful baths at Callirrhoë easily compensated for Antipas' tricks. It was not until later in the week that the tetrarch got a bit tiresome in trying to pick the brains of the prefect.

"Just what *is* happening in Rome, Pilate?" asked Antipas, in the course of a night's revelry.

"How do you mean?"

"Is it to be Tiberius or Sejanus?"

"An impossible alternative. After Tiberius dies, then perhaps Sejanus."

"You're heard what they're saying in Rome, 'Sejanus is emperor; Tiberius, only an island potentate.' "

"Are you trying to impugn the loyalty of the emperor's praetorian prefect?"

"Of course not," Antipas corrected himself. "What I meant to ask," he nervously snickered, "was, 'Will it be the young *Gaius Caligula* or Sejanus?' "

"I really don't know. Possibly Sejanus as regent for the young Gaius."

It was a safe statement. Probably, he thought, Antipas' original alternative of Tiberius or Sejanus better expressed his true thought, and had Pilate answered such a treasona-

ble choice incorrectly, it might have doomed his career
should Antipas try to compromise him.

"Well, then, put the case that Sejanus *is* regent for the
young Gaius," Antipas persisted. "Who, ultimately, would
control Rome?"

"That, my friend, is in the hands of the gods." The
nonreligious Pilate resorted to religion at such times. Antipas only smirked, realizing that Pilate had affixed a period
to their conversation on Roman politics.

That night, Pilate's sleep was again disturbed by the
haunting voice from the bowels of the castle, apparently
chanting its prayers and singing melancholy hymns. Equally
mystifying was the conduct of Antipas' chief steward the
next morning. Answering a knock on his door, Pilate found
Chuza. "Excellency," he said, "I must discuss an urgent
matter with you. A request . . . " Just then, one of Antipas'
servants came by and Chuza broke off. "Breakfast will be
served shortly, Excellency." Then he whispered, "Later."

But the "later" never materialized, since all Machaerus
was in an uproar of preparation for the tetrarch's birthday
feast that night. His half brother, the tetrarch Philip, arrived just in time to help celebrate, as did Antipas' half
niece-stepdaughter, Salome, who had been visiting her half
uncle, Philip. The daughter of Herodias, Pilate and Procula
noted immediately, had completed the metamorphosis from
the spoiled girl they remembered in Caesarea to a sensually
attractive young woman.

The banquet was attended by all of Antipas' many guests
at Machaerus, including tribal leaders from Galilee, as well
as his officers and courtiers. It was a formal affair, carried
off in the best Hellenistic tradition. Some of the viands Pilate had not tasted since his own wedding banquet. As to
beverages, he commented, "For a non-Roman, Antipas,
you're a worthy connoisseur of the vine."

"My fellow son of Bacchus," he responded with a wine-
reinforced amiability, "you forget that the family of the
Herods *have* Roman citizenship. We're enrolled in the Julian gens."

"A toast, then, to the cousin of the Caesars," Pilate
laughed, a little too loudly. Procula poked him with her
sandals.

"Why so dour a face, my Chuza?" Antipas called across
the table to his chief steward. "You can worry about my
estates when we return to Galilee."

Chuza brightened up, though later in the evening he cast worried glances in Pilate's direction. Procula saw it and alerted her husband. Both shared a twinge of concern, wondering what message Chuza had failed to communicate. Surely he wasn't trying to warn them of physical danger?

When the fourth course had been cleared away, Antipas snapped his fingers and the flute and harp melodies which had serenaded the feast now gave way to a program of entertainment. Some of it, Pilate noticed, was a bit ostentatious, but that was forgivable, since all floor talent had to be imported to that solitary location. The jugglers from Jericho were a bore, easily upstaged by the acrobatic apes of a local bedouin. Someone proposed that the monkeys be given a little wine to liven their act. It had the desired effect.

Then Herodias rose from the table, inviting Procula and the other ladies to follow her out of the banquet hall to the women's quarters of the palace, since Antipas' celebration was now over so far as they were concerned. In Greek style dinner parties, the women would not even have appeared at the table, but the more civilized Roman custom allowed them to participate, until it was time for the *comissatio,* which was exclusively for the men. Since the culminating *comissatio* or post-banquet social drinking bout often involved risqué entertainment, some of the more conservative Galilean elders paid their respects to Antipas and Pilate and also retired.

Antipas now pulled a cord, which released a cloud of rose petals and flower garlands from the ceiling. Servants picked up the floral wreaths and arranged them about the heads and necks of the men. Then they carefully sprayed perfume on each. Flowers and perfumes were used, not for adornment, but because their fragrance was thought to prevent, or at least delay, drunkenness.

"Let's choose a king!" Antipas called, for the next stage in the ritual was to pick someone to preside over the festivities. A servant brought dice to Antipas. He shook them, calling out, "Herodias, help me" and threw an eight. Then he handed the dice on to Pilate, who cried, "Procula, help me" and threw a six.

Next, the dice went to Philip, who shook and cried, "Salome, help me" and shot eleven. This raised a few eyebrows, since each was to call on the spirit of his wife or sweetheart to assist his throw, and Salome was neither to Philip—so far as anyone knew.

Since no one exceeded Philip's eleven, he was formally declared "King of Drinking." From now on Philip would have to direct the *comissatio,* determining the order for proposing the toasts, and in what proportion water was to be mixed with the wine.

"We drink to the health of our honored host on his birthday—at a good, stout one-half!" Philip led off. Slaves quickly measured out equal portions of wine and water into a large mixing bowl, and stirred the blend. Then they ladled out exactly seven-twelfths of a pint into the goblets of each of the guests, who had to drain them in a single quaff. The precise quantity was no accident: one-twelfth pint was meted out for each letter in the name of the man whose health had been proposed. "Antipas" made seven twelfths.

The entertainment continued. A small corps of pantomimes performed several indecent playlets, which did not go over as well as Antipas had hoped. Philip then rose to his feet and said, "We drink to the health of our honored guest, the prefect of Judea. May his tenure be long! A hearty two-thirds!"

Amid cheers of the guests, slaves measured out two portions wine to one of water and again hastily ladled out seven-twelfths pint of the mixture to each guest, for the seven letters in "Pilatus."

The final floor routine was a troupe of very badly coordinated dancing girls, clearly local talent hastily conscripted for the evening. There was a bit of grumbling disapproval from the guests. Then Philip accidentally knocked over a flagon of wine onto the tunic of a Galilean chief sitting next to him. A slave, hurrying to assist the man, collided with another servant, who dropped a tray of dishes. The resounding clatter shattered the mood of the banquet, and the furious tongue-lashing given the hapless slave by the rotund chef helped matters not at all. Antipas' birthday party was coming apart at the seams. He called Chuza to him, whispered something, then sent him scurrying off.

Four toasts, and several degrees of intoxication, later, Antipas arose to announce that Salome had consented to honor their *comissatio* by performing a dance. Everyone put down his chalice and stared at the host for this precedent-shattering idea. Entertaining at a *comissatio* was only for lewd servant women or actresses and prostitutes, not members of one's own family. Philip glared at his half brother with all the fury of a wounded animal. Pilate wondered if Antipas were really that drunk.

Two lyrists, concealed behind curtains, started playing at each other in graceful counterpoint, and then the precocious Salome appeared. Clad in the festival costume of a Galilean peasant girl, the nineteen-year-old performed a sprightly folk dance which was popular during the Feast of Tabernacles. Salome whirled close to the banquet tables so that she could be seen to proper advantage, since only torches and candles illuminated the hall. Pilate was amazed at what three years had done to the girl. She looked arrestingly lovely, no longer the passionate teen-ager, but now a richly voluptuous woman. Enhanced by the ruddy warmth of the fireglow, her exquisite performance of the dance captivated Pilate as much as Antipas and his friends. She was careful to lavish elfin gestures on each important guest and especially Philip, the "King of Drinking," who sat enthralled with infatuation for Salome.

Slaves suddenly appeared by each candle and torch, and, at a given signal, all lights were extinguished. Startled, Pilate sat up and grabbed for his dagger until he saw a brazier flaring up in the middle of the darkness. Then the lyres started plucking out a very different rhythm, a slow and languid staccato which gradually picked up tempo. A small drum now added its hollow thump to the music.

Then Salome reappeared, dressed only in the gauzy tunic she had been wearing under her peasant costume. It was a girl-size garment hugging the lush contours of a grown woman, and Pilate noticed at once the brief distance the hem extended down her upper thighs. Salome's whole body seemed to gyrate and throb a perfect response to the music as she darted up to and back from the fire, caressing the warmth, then swiveling away from it. Several times Pilate and the other men gasped as she vaulted right over the flames unsinged. With the brazier as the only light in the hall, gigantic shadows played on the ceiling, enlarging her nubile form to heroic dimension. The source of it all was a symphony of sensuality, her fair skin painted a golden russet by the flames, the diaphanous white tunic clinging precariously to the rest of her.

Pilate was distracted by some labored breathing next to him and he pried his eyes away for a moment to find the cause. It was Herod Antipas, gaping at Salome in a near-

hypnotic trance, a man so helplessly captivated by the sight
that his lower jaw sagged limply and he was almost snort-
ing with emotion. A slave approached with a napkin to absorb a string of drool which was starting to dangle from
Antipas' mouth. Ignoring the wiping, Antipas mumbled,
"Salome, my daughter. Salome . . . my *own* daughter? No,
thank the Fates, my *step*daughter." Then he smiled.

Salome concluded her dance with a deep bow in front of
Antipas. Then the brazier was extinguished and the torches
relit.

Pilate, Antipas, and the other guests rose as one man to
cheer and applaud. Salome's performance was the breath
of excitement which had resuscitated the corpse of Antipas'
party. And, somewhat tipsy now, but overflowing with
gratitude to his stepdaughter, the tetrarch fawned, "Splendid . . . magnificent, my darling Salome! And now you
must have a reward for your performance. Ask me for
anything: I'll give it to you!"

"Thank you, Father. But . . . how do you mean?"

"I said, Lovely One, ask me for anything and it's yours,
by Heaven, even if it's half my kingdom."

Antipas' comment was seconded by approving cheers.
"Ask for Perea," Philip laughingly suggested. "Or all of
Galilee—that would be *exactly* half his kingdom."

Further advice was silenced by her reply. "Thank you,
noble Father, but your appreciation is enough reward."

"*Ask* for something, Salome! I *want* to give you a gift!"

"Well . . . do you mind if I ask Mother first?"

"Not at all," Antipas chuckled.

While Salome retreated to the women's quarters for
Herodias' advice, the host was the target of a good bit of
banter. "Beware, Tetrarch," said the commander of his
guard at Tiberias, "and remember, you *swore* to fulfill her
request!"

"Did I?" wondered Antipas, showing a trifle of mock
concern.

"You said 'By Heaven,' which is one of the stronger
oaths."

"Ahahaha!" exulted Philip. "Excuse me, gentlemen. I'm
going to tell Salome to ask for Galilee. Then I'll marry her,
and add Galilee to my own tetrarchy. And *then*," he
paused, "I'll be the size of your Judea and Samaria, Pilate!"

Antipas frowned fiercely for a moment, then released a
colossal guffaw.

"Laugh, will you?" Philip said, as he got up from the table. No one knew if he were staging a practical joke or not.

But Salome returned. Stillness descended on the hall as everyone wondered what she would choose. Only a soft tread of her sandals was heard as she carefully walked up to Antipas and looked at him with a puckish smile.

"Yes, dearest," he said, "What have you chosen?"

"As reward, Father, I want you to give me—immediately —the . . . the head of John the Baptizer on a platter."

But for a few indrawn breaths, there was total silence. Salome repeated her request, more firmly.

"Aha," Antipas emitted a force chuckle, "you're joking, of course, Salome."

"No, Father."

"Your mother . . . did she suggest . . . insist?"

"She told me to remind you of your oath."

There was no sound, and this compounded the unreality of the situation. In the course of a raucous evening, nothing is louder than silence.

In his mind, Antipas at first tried to discount it all as a drunken nightmare, but that would not work. He had imprisoned the Baptizer as a punitive act to stop his haranguing him: "It's not legal for you to have your brother's wife." Herodias hated him for that and had nagged Antipas to have him executed. But John was a holy man, and Antipas had not intended to bother a hair on his unkempt head. Fact was, when Herodias was not around, he even enjoyed talking with the desert prophet, nimbly dodging the verbal arrows John fearlessly shot at him.

But it was no longer a question of himself and the Baptizer. It was now a public matter of state, confirmed by oath, due to his own carelessness and Herodias' fiendish stratagem. He would settle scores with her later. But what to do now?

Chuza was at his side, whispering, "Excellency, I would *not* consider myself legally or morally bound by that oath, for your intention was to provide the young Salome a gift of great monetary value. Now surely the head of—"

"I gave her my word."

"Fear the people, then, Excellency. They consider John a prophet."

Salome now tilted her head upward and stared directly into the eyes of Antipas with an unmistakably challenging expression. Her mien spoke eloquently what remained unspoken: "I dare you to break your word, Tetrarch Herod Antipas, in front of all your guests."

Pilate, at the outer edge of that stare, caught the smirk of success spelled out by Salome's limpid blue eyes and firmly pressing, perfect lips. But he did not intervene. He had overheard Chuza's advice to Antipas, and it was obviously correct. Only a fool would fail to heed it, and the Tetrarch of Galilee and Perea was no fool.

But Pilate was a Roman, a practical man who could temper absolutes to suit circumstances, as Rome herself had been doing for the last seven hundred years. Here in the East, however, absolutes were not so easily adjusted, and the spoken word was thought to have a reality all its own. For this reason the Jews never expressed the truest name of their deity, Yahweh, believing it would intrude on the divine itself. Similarly, the "Law of the Medes and Persians," once enunciated, could not be retracted.

"I gave my word," Antipas muttered, looking up and down the tables at what was left of his *comissatio*. It was the steel look in the eyes of his chief officers from Galilee that decided the issue for him. To back down on his oath would expose weakness in front of the very men he could least afford to have see it. Summoning a guard, he gave him the command.

"No!" Chuza cried, but a look from Antipas silenced him. Pilate was aghast, a feeling of disgusted helplessness numbing him.

Suddenly the silent halls of the cavernous castle resounded with a cry from below: *"Repent, Antipas! The kingdom of God is at hand! The Messiah has—"* The words were cut off.

The gory trophy was brought in on a platter, as requested, and handed to Salome. The head, propped in an upright position, still fastened its open eyes on Antipas with prophetic fury. Pilate was nauseated. Chuza wept. Salome turned about and carried the reddening platter to her mother. Antipas' birthday party was over.

Pilate and Procula prepared to leave early the next morning, two days sooner than planned. Just before their departure, Chuza finally managed to see them privately.

"What were you trying to tell me yesterday morning?" Pilate asked the steward.

"Oh . . . nothing," he said mournfully, "too late now."

"But what was it?"

"I wanted to ask you to use your influence with the tetrarch to secure the release of John the Baptizer. He was a prophet of God."

"It was a disgusting, nasty business. Reminds me of the time when Cicero's head was impaled on a spear in the Forum, and Antony's wife stuck pins into the tongue which had attacked her husband. Women can be the most vengeful of creatures . . . But why was the young Salome so hostile to the Baptizer?"

"Like mother, like daughter. John insisted that Herodias was living in sin with Antipas, which would make Salome the daughter of a harlot."

"Why didn't you alert me sooner? I didn't even know the prophet was at Machaerus."

"You didn't? Couldn't you hear him singing hymns each night?"

"So *he* was the one. . . ."

"Yes," Chuza said mournfully. Then he brightened. "But John did not live in vain. He was the forerunner of the Messiah. He has come, Excellency, he has come!"

"Who has come?"

"The Messiah. Already he's preaching in Galilee and working great wonders."

Pilate took leave of Chuza, mystified by the fanaticism of the land. Here was the presumably sensible chief steward of a neighboring government, who witnessed the execution of one prophet one evening, then declared for a new one the very next morning.

Antipas and Herodias saw them off, somewhat apologetic for the events of the previous night. Pilate's thanks were just barely tactful.

With no effort on his part, he was leaving Machaerus in a much stronger political position than Antipas. Their rivalry, in fact, was now over, with Pilate the victor. Drawing subsidies from the temple might look bad in Jewish eyes, and killing rioters even worse; but these were mere foibles compared with executing a prophet of God. News of the dramatic demise of the Baptizer was all over Palestine in a week.

Chapter 12

THE YEAR 31 A.D. dawned auspiciously for the prefect of Judea, now in his fifth year of office. The land was prosperous and quiet. For months no demonstrations had disrupted the calm. To be sure, several Zealot leaders in Galilee continued agitating their followers, but they were Antipas' problem.

The tetrarch had other difficulties, Pilate learned. His Galileans so hated Herodias and Salome for their roles in John's execution that they never ventured far from Tiberias without a large bodyguard. Salome soon left Galilee entirely. The tetrarch Philip, evidently, was thoroughly smitten with the girl and finally married her. It was a normally abnormal romance for the House of Herod, half niece marrying half uncle. But with the blood of a prophet quite literally on her hands, anything else Salome did would look quite acceptable by comparison.

Early that year, Pilate and Procula explored Egypt as guests of their friends, the prefect Gaius Galerius and his wife. The foursome took an extended trip up the Nile on Cleopatra's refurbished royal barge to view the monuments at Luxor and Thebes, imposing in their incredible proportions. During much of the excursion, Galerius chatted excitedly about his nephew, a brilliant young equestrian who was now cutting a widening swath of success through Rome as a Stoic philosopher. His name was Seneca.

As it happened, however, this would be the final happiness for Galerius. After sixteen years of distinguished service to Rome as prefect of Egypt, he took sick shortly after Pilate's visit and resigned his office, hoping to return to Rome before death. But on the voyage home he died.

Saddened, Pilate wondered if Galerius' successor in Egypt might alter the military power structure of the Empire so far as Sejanus was concerned. The new prefect was Vitrasius Pollio, who was unknown to Pilate. But such speculation was now unnecessary. Sejanus had achieved a long-cherished goal. He was elected consul for the year 31, the highest office of the old Republic, and with the emperor himself as colleague. It was an almost tacit declaration that the praetorian commander was indeed heir apparent.

There were other clues that the purple mantle of empire was all but draped around the shoulders of Sejanus. Agrippina's son, Nero, a former heir to the throne, had committed suicide on the isle of Pontia. Gone was any possibility of Tiberius relenting in his favor, as Sejanus had feared in his letter to Pilate. Now also, at last, the princeps sanctioned Sejanus' betrothal to his niece and daughter-in-law, Livilla, that long-standing romance on which Tiberius had at first frowned. The marriage would tie Sejanus into the imperial blood line.

One day it was all but official. Tiberius recommended that the Senate confer the proconsular *imperium* on Sejanus, and it was done. This promoted him to virtual half emperor, since it was by means of the proconsular authority that Tiberius could legally govern the empire beyond Rome. Constitutionally, Pilate could now take his orders from either Tiberius or Sejanus. In fact, only the tribunician power was lacking for Sejanus to be joint emperor with Tiberius. For the prerogatives of tribune would make the prefect, like the princeps, personally inviolate, and with full executive veto powers to boot.

Procula's father wrote that Sejanus' mansion was now so jammed with followers that one of his large couches had broken down under the crowds seated in his waiting room. With the same dispatch came a letter from the great one himself, in which Sejanus raised Pilate's salary from 100,000 to 200,000 sesterces per year, awarding him the grade of a *ducenarius.* This promotion, Sejanus hoped, would inspire Pilate to even greater efforts in Judea. The last, Pilate presumed, would mean more anti-Semitic directives from Rome. But a doubling of one's salary was always welcome.

It was her father's letter which gave Procula the idea of returning to Rome for a vacation at home. Gaius Proculeius was not well, and his lines betrayed a wistful desire to see his daughter again. Pilate encouraged her to make the trip.

As Roman marriages went, theirs was proving a success. With a fifth anniversary nearing, a time when it was quite fashionable for each partner to be halfway through a second marriage, Pilate and Procula were remarkably happy. His trials as governor had tested their love, bringing stresses which Procula, in her sheltered life, had never known before. But facing them together had deepened their relationship, and they cheerfully admitted that they needed each other, especially in a far-off province like Judea.

At times Pilate wondered if they would have been as faithful to one another had they remained in voluptuous Rome. Perhaps their virtue was sheltered by the insular position in which they found themselves in a foreign land. There simply was little opportunity to sin in Caesarea, at least with members of one's own social stratum. Yet Procula was returning to Rome—alone. Pilate felt a ripple of concern, even a tinge of jealousy at that prospect. But, knowing his wife, he banished it immediately.

Curiously, their quarrels were usually over matters of state, not personality. Procula was not the typical Roman wife, preoccupied with running the household or flitting from one social engagement to the next. Gifted with superior intelligence, she showed a lively interest in what her husband was doing, or leaving undone. In moments of crisis, she wanted most to offer her advice, but she was sensible enough to realize that precisely then Pilate would least tolerate any intrusion. So she supplied her ideas only when the government was running smoothly. While Pilate never formally acknowledged her help—that, she knew, would have been unmagisterial and un-Roman—Procula's delight was to find some of her best suggestions incorporated from time to time.

Their personalities were attuned by curious harmonies. Pilate was the realist; the calculating, ambitious, even opportunistic public official; the sub-emotional man; the religious neutral. She was the sensitive, imaginative idealist, with a creative focus toward the worlds of art, literature, and religion. What had held this polarity in balance was not simply romantic love—the romantic part of it was waning—but a flexible, mutual understanding, the undergirding necessary whenever a man and a woman must live together for life.

There was one considerable flaw in their marriage: they had no children. The first year or two they had tried to avoid them, but now that they wanted a family, it was apparently denied them. Procula promised that she would consult the Proculeius family physician after her return to Rome.

In late May, when the Mediterranean would be at its calmest, Procula set sail from Caesarea. Several tribunes' wives and attendants accompanied her on the voyage to Rome. It would be some months before Pilate saw his wife again. Depending on her father's illness, Procula might not return until the new year.

Later that summer, three large, unidentified ships approached Caesarea. A lookout on a tower near the harbor mouth reported that the craft seemed to be teeming with armed men. In the ensuing alert, Pilate led an auxiliary cohort and a company of archers down to the waterfront. *Ballistae* were readied atop the towers rising from the jetty, catapulting machines which could shoot 150-pound stone balls over a range of 300 yards.

The harbor alert was a standard procedure against piracy. Although Pompey had driven the buccaneers off the Mediterranean a century earlier, random companies of maritime cutthroats might still descend on an unsuspecting town, plunder it, and make off with the spoils before help arrived.

Pilate was about to order a warning shot across the bow of the lead ship when he saw it posting its colors—somewhat tardily. To his chagrin, these turned out to be Roman military standards. As the ships approached the narrows, a herald called across the water, *"I-den-ti-fy your-selves!"* Pirates had the nasty habit of using any disguise, even that of Roman legionaries, to put their victims off guard.

"Cohors Secunda Italica Civium Romanorum Voluntariorum!" was the shouted reply.

Pilate's face was transformed by a huge grin. The Latin for "Second Italian Cohort of Roman Citizen Volunteers' was perfect—he knew of such a unit—and as the ships slipped into the harbor of Caesarea, the Italian faces crowding the railings were unmistakable. Pilate's cohort let out a cheer and scrambled to convert its image into that of an honor guard, while the artillery men sheepishly crawled out from behind their *ballistae* and waved greetings from the turrets.

As the lead ship docked, a voice called down, "What were you trying to do, Prefect, sink your fellow Romans?"

The comment came from the smiling face of a centurion leaning over the starboard gunwale.

"Why you . . . you're the courier . . . Cornelius, aren't you?" said Pilate.

"Honored that you remember me. Four years ago you invited me to return to Judea. So here I am."

"*Salve*, Cornelius! But why didn't Rome tell me the Second Italian Cohort was being dispatched here? Or are you only visiting?"

"No. We're assigned to Caesarea. The Prefect Sejanus wrote you about it some weeks ago, I understand."

"Strange! I never got word!"

But he did when the arriving cohort delivered a bundle of communications from Rome, a sad commentary on the imperial mail service. The letter stated that Sejanus was finally adopting Pilate's suggestion that a nucleus of Roman citizen troops be sent to such outposts as Judea, rather than having the governor rely entirely on local non-Roman auxiliaries. The new cohort, recruited from Italian volunteers, would add five hundred genuine Romans to Pilate's military arm and so improve the security of the prefecture.

Although as a centurion Cornelius was only a junior officer, Pilate soon found him more congenial than the newly arrived tribune who commanded the Italian Cohort. While he showed him no partiality in official or military matters —that would have created dangerous jealousies within his officers' staff—Pilate soon came to depend on Cornelius for discreet, off-duty camaraderie. The centurion had a blazing wit and the kind of stability and common sense that Pilate had not really enjoyed in a fellow Roman since Gaius Galerius.

In midsummer he had a special assignment for Cornelius. "This will be something of an intelligence operation," he told him. "We've heard rumors of some kind of unrest developing up in Galilee—that's the breeding ground for the insurgents in Palestine, the home of the Zealot party. And it's been some time since we've learned what Herod Antipas and his subjects are up to."

"You mean Antipas might be behind this unrest?" Cornelius inquired.

"Hardly! It's just that his administration—or maladministration—helps create the climate both there and here. And when clouds form in Galilee, it rains in Judea. The Zealots do a little demonstrating up there, but they reserve their full fury for riots in Judea."

"Because Rome is in charge here."

"Exactly. For instance, just last month it came to bloodshed. Several Zealots were inciting the people to riot, from the very steps of the temple in Jerusalem. The gathering crowd insulted the guards at the Antonia, and it came to a clash. Several Galilean pilgrims were cut down. And who gets credit for all this?"

"The prefect of Judea, of course."

"Precisely, even though I wasn't there at the time. The Galileans are now martyrs, identified as 'those whose blood Pilate mingled with their sacrifices.' "

"Naturally. But what's my role in your plan?"

"Take the east highway for about twenty miles. You'll come to our frontier post, a place called Legio. It controls the pass through the Carmel mountain range into the plains of Galilee. Since Legio is so close to the border of Galilee, it's our listening post for what goes on there. Now, after you interview our frontier officers, use one of our Aramaic guides to inquire casually among the merchants using the Megiddo Pass."

"What sort of information are we after?"

"Find out what Antipas is doing . . . how the people feel now about his beheading John, the desert prophet . . . and, particularly, what the new commotion is in Galilee. See if the Zealots are involved in it and what their plans are. Can Rome expect more trouble from them? If so, where? This kind of thing, plus whatever else you can learn."

Since Pilate was eager for answers, Cornelius' absence seemed much longer than the three weeks he was actually gone. In the interim, Pilate received the first letters from Procula. The voyage was delightful, she wrote—no seasickness—and her father's health was slowly improving. Rome was torrid but tolerable, since her girlhood friends were hosting a string of parties in her honor. She missed Pilate, and wouldn't it be possible for him to join her in Rome later in the year, even for a short month?

It was only after picking through the gossip and succulent morsels of news in her second letter that Pilate found the marrow he had sought. Tiberius was still on Capri. Rumor had it that he was finally going to confer the tribunician power on Sejanus. Procula chanced to meet the exalted prefect himself one afternoon in the Forum. Her letter continued:

> . . . Sejanus actually remembered me! He gallantly introduced me to the senators and clients surrounding him as "the beautiful wife of our efficient prefect of Judea." Imagine! Then he asked about you and the Jews, and he even invited me to have dinner with him sometime. And guess what he said as they moved on: "Mark my words, countrymen. Rome will hear more of Pontius Pilatus." So, dear husband, it looks as if you're carrying winning colors in your political chariot race. . . .

Pilate digested these lines with double satisfaction. Not only was his own star rising in the cluttered skies of Roman politics, but there was this second success: even Procula, that partisan of Agrippina, now had kind words for Sejanus!

"Herod Antipas is definitely on the defensive," Cornelius reported to Pilate on his return. "He's not panicking, but he'll do anything to conciliate his subjects. The people haven't forgiven him for beheading the Baptizer though it hasn't come to open rebellion."

"What about King Aretas?"

"Still seething. The commandant at Legio has it from the tribune at Jericho that Aretas is building up his army for an attack on the Transjordan."

"What about the Zealots?"

"Nothing much going on. It may be the calm before the storm, or it may not. They just aren't out agitating."

"Doesn't make sense, Cornelius," Pilate replied, apparently piqued at not getting the information he had expected. "We've received definite reports of some kind of turmoil going on up there—crowds, hill meetings . . ."

"I was just coming to that. You're right. Something *is* afoot. A prophet up there seems to be attracting quite a following. He teaches the people by various means, usually unorthodox, I understand. The merchants reported that he's preached in many of the synagogues of Galilee, and when these are denied him he takes to the open air . . . in the fields, on the hills. Once he even launched out onto the Sea of Tiberias and preached to the crowds from a boat. But there's always a multitude around him, wherever he goes."

"What's his message?"

"Repentance. Prepare for—what was it?—the approaching 'kingdom of God.' "

"That was the Baptizer's message."

"This prophet's, too, though he also teaches a whole program for the new era which he claims has dawned on earth. The Pharisees, the Sadducees, and the priestly clan in Jerusalem are doing a poor job of leading the people in this new time, he contends."

"Does he preach revolution?"

Cornelius thought for a moment, then replied, "No, not that I've heard so far. A spiritual revolution, perhaps, but no call to arms. The changes are to take place *inside* people, and then society will improve. People are to love, not hate . . . help, not hurt. A rather different message, what?"

"What do the Jewish authorities think of this prophet?"

"They're divided. A few support him enthusiastically, but most are wary. The Pharisees hate him for his stinging attacks, and the Sadducees think he's upsetting the *status quo*. But they haven't bothered him yet."

"I wonder why. . . ."

"Because of the people. The man seems to wield enormous authority over the *people*. And small wonder! After each of his discourses, he supposedly starts healing them, curing their diseases. . . ."

"That's not very unusual, Cornelius," remarked Pilate, a little condescendingly. "The eastern Mediterranean is full of faith healers. Some of them even get as far as Rome. I remember once when I was young—"

"I can too, Prefect. But here's the difference: all reports agreed that the people actually *were* cured."

"Of *course* they're cured!" Pilate grinned, "else how could the faith healer stay in business? The 'cures,' of course, are done in people who never had anything wrong with them in the first place, aside from their minds or overwrought imaginations. Sometimes they're part of the charlatan's entourage. The thing is staged. The 'cripples' have been hired to hobble by on crutches, which are then thrown away. Or, in cases of real disease, the fever was about to break anyway . . . coincidence."

"Yes," laughed Cornelius. "Wouldn't you love to expose the fakers by bringing them someone genuinely ill, no, handicapped—say, a person blind from birth—and *then* see if they could be cured?"

"Yes, that *would* be a good test."

Cornelius was silent a moment. Then, slowly, he replied, "Well, this is exactly the kind of thing being done by this prophet: people blind, paralyzed, deaf, dumb—*from birth* —being given sight, hearing, speech, the use of their limbs."

Pilate frowned at Cornelius. "I don't believe it," he said coolly.

"Well, those are the reports, anyway," the centurion shrugged. "And there are others."

"What do you mean?"

"This prophet does more than heal, the people say. He also performs other 'signs,' as they call them. One report has it that wine was running low at a wedding, and he transformed one hundred gallons of water into wine. And not just everyday, run-of-the-press vintage, but *aged* choice Judean Red!"

"Aha! A prophet with taste."

"There're other stories. For instance, during a storm on—"

"Enough, Cornelius! All this is simply the old thaumaturge phenomenon. Every religious culture I've come across has its wonder workers, its magicians, and the Jewish tradition is more religious than most."

"I suppose you're right. But you can see why he has such a hold on the people."

"Of course." Pilate closed the conversation and was about to dismiss the centurion when he had an afterthought. "Wait, Cornelius. Just who *is* this prophet? Did you learn anything about the man himself?"

"Some people think he's the Baptizer, returned from the dead. Herod Antipas is supposedly terrified at the thought."

"He must be losing his mind to believe that."

"Others claim he's none other than Elijah, the most famous of past Hebrew prophets."

"Equally ridiculous! Come, come, man, couldn't you get a better identification than that?"

"Yes. I did. The prophet's name is Joshua. He comes from Nazareth in Galilee."

"Hmmmm. Joshua, eh?"

"Yes, Joshua or Yeshua. In our language it would be Jesus."

Chapter 13

WHEN THE blow fell, Pilate felt his career cracking under it. The shattering happened at Rome, but the fissures radiated across the Mediterranean world. This was more than a passing crisis, for it threatened the very life of the prefect of Judea, and hundreds like him. Pilate would never be able to shake off the searing memory of what happened when Procula returned, unexpectedly, after an overland trip from Rome in the winter of A.D. 31-32.

Overtired, distraught from the cruel journey—Romans never traveled in winter except for emergencies—Procula could only report the horror in Rome and collapse from exhaustion. Pilate spent a night of agonized despair, trying to sort the fragments of fact into some mosaic of reason until Procula could explain it all the next day.

She was composed enough the following morning to furnish the details about October 18, A.U.C. 784,* a date which changed their lives, and which marked probably the most dramatic event in the long cavalcade of Rome's past. Procula told the story slowly, fully, deliberately, consulting a long scroll of notations she had made of the entire episode, knowing that Pilate would have to have precise information. Much of the detail was supplied by a cousin of Procula who was a senator and an eyewitness.

Tiberius had not written the Senate for some time, she

---

* The Roman date for 31 A.D. "A.U.C." signifies *Ab Urbe Condita,* "from the founding of the city," i.e., Rome.

said, but now the praetorian commander at Capri, Sertorius Macro, was delivering to the Senate a lengthy and important document from the emperor. Sejanus, of course, wanted to know the contents of that communiqué, for rumors swept the city that here, at last, was the conferral of tribunician power which would make him joint emperor.

Early on the brisk and beautiful morning of the eighteenth, Procula continued, Sejanus led his crack first cohort of the Praetorian Guard to the Temple of Apollo on the Palatine, where the Senate would sit that day. The site was thronged with cheering Romans. Anyone who hoped to rank in Sejanus' favor wanted to be on hand when the great man was rendered even greater. At the door of the temple, Macro, who had Tiberius' letter in hand, encountered Sejanus.

"Why the fretting, Sejanus?" he wondered good-naturedly.

"The princeps hasn't written in some time. Naturally I'm concerned."

"Shall I break the seals on this and let you have a look ahead of time?"

Sejanus merely smiled at the pleasantry, for it would have been treason to open the letter before it was presented to the Senate.

"Come here, friend," Macro smiled, "I've something confidential to tell you."

Bystanders and arriving senators saw Macro whisper something to Sejanus. They could not know what, but when Sejanus' frown melted into a smile of satisfaction, they could guess what Macro had in fact confided: the tribunician power was his! The news immediately flashed through the crowd and a volley of cheers arose.

Elated, Sejanus hurried inside the Senate chamber, receiving felicitations from every side. His partisans were jubilant, applauding him openly, and even his enemies now had to wear a counterfeit mask of joy, Sejanus noted with double satisfaction.

The conscript fathers took their places as a lictor signaled with his fasces and all excited talk in the chamber died instantly. The presiding consul, Memmius Regulus, led a file of magistrates to curule chairs in front of the chamber, and then solemnly threw several pinches of incense over coals glowing on Apollo's altar. Next he offered hallowed grain to a coop of sacred chickens, while a venerable senator, clutching a spiral-headed crosier, watched them closely. The excited cackle of the hens signaled the senators that the omens were favorable even before the augur could announce, *"There is no evil sight nor sound."* A relieved murmur filled the chamber. Business could now begin.

After disposing of preliminary matters, Regulus, one of the *consules suffecti,* or substitute consuls for the year, rose to read Tiberius' letter.

There were no surprises in the opening paragraphs, though it did seem to many that they had never heard the emperor quite so verbose. His words seemed to compete with each other, rather than serving to support a uniform train of thought.

Sejanus waited anxiously for the prolix ramblings to reach their theme, but Tiberius, at his discursive best, was first taking the senators on a tour of the Empire's problems. He shambled on over a gamut of topics ranging from wheat production in Sardinia to the offensive garlic breath of the masses at public games.

"He's obviously getting senile," one senator in the front row whispered to another.

The princeps' first reference to Sejanus finally came, a bit of criticism over his fiscal policies. This raised a few brows, but the letter next digressed to the need for public rest rooms in the Forum. Then, just as abruptly, Tiberius returned to Sejanus for a slighting reference to the prefect's ambitions, but quickly the lines skimmed over to another topic.

"What do you make of it?" the consul Trio asked Sejanus, after he had sidled over to him.

"Typically Tiberius. He wants to keep me humble, and he also loves to shock. Watch. First he shoots his barbs. Then, just when the Senate is ready to write me off, comes the emperor's surprise: the tribunician power. Sejanus is closer than a son after all, even if he does need a little discipline."

"It's an old man's game."

"Quite." Sejanus noted the concerned glances from some of his partisans and smiled to reassure them. After all, he knew how the letter would end.

But many in the Senate were beginning to doubt that the message would ever end. Regulus droned on and on and on.

Sejanus grew impatient. This was to be his moment of glory, but the princeps was injecting a massive dose of tedium into the occasion. He looked around for Macro, but could not find him.

Then he heard something which brought him up short. Regulus raised his voice at this passage:

> . . , Finally, Conscript Fathers, I regret to inform you that our trusted minister and prefect, Lucius Aelius Sejanus, is a traitor. He has endangered the state, indeed, the princeps himself, by his fanatic persecution of Agrippina and the House of Germanicus, his lawsuits against members of the Julian party, his overwhelming personal ambition, and the conspiracy he has undertaken against Rome. Sejanus is another Catiline. I ask you now to show your loyalty by immediately arresting the prefect Sejanus and keeping him under close guard until I come to Rome. And since I am an old man, in the very peril of his life, I ask that you send a guard to Capri under the command of the consul Regulus to escort me to Rome. Farewell.

Silence blanketed the chamber. A few senators quietly got up from their benches to move away from Sejanus. The first sound was a crescendo of muttering, then a full discordant chorus of condemnation from the very mouths which had cheered the prefect an hour earlier.

Thunderstruck, Sejanus flashed about to summon his praetorians. But they had vanished. The entire cohort had been replaced by guards of the night watch, who were now filing into the Senate chamber. Their commander, Graecinius Laco, stood between Sejanus and the nearest exit. A knot of tribunes and lictors was encircling him.

"Sejanus, come here."

Paralyzed by icy disbelief, he did not respond.

"Sejanus, come here!" the consul Regulus called a second time, now pointing his finger at the accused. 'Here! Now!"

"Me? You are calling *me?*" Dazed, unaccustomed to receiving orders, Sejanus slowly stood up and faced the Senate, while Regulus repeated the final paragraph of Tiberius' letter, now as a formal bill of indictment. The face of the prefect looked white as a waxen death mask.

When he finished reading, the consul called on a single, reliable senator for an opinion, asking, "Should Sejanus not be imprisoned?" He dared not submit the matter to general debate, since the Sejanian faction in the Senate might recover to defend their man.

"He should be imprisoned," came the reply.

Regulus then adjourned the Senate, while Laco and the night watch surrounded Sejanus, bound his hands, and then led him out of the Temple of Apollo. The news blazed through downtown Rome so quickly that swarms of people were already converging along the Via Sacra to witness the incredible sight: the second man in the Empire, a halter about his neck, being led like a donkey westward across the length of the Forum to the Tullianum dungeon.

Pilate begged Procula to stop temporarily, while he rose to adjust his nerves. Perspiring profusely, a sickly knot of anxiety churning his stomach, he ordered a flagon of strong wine and then paced back and forth with rippled brow, his hands wrestling with each other. When the wine was brought he gulped a goblet in one draft and refilled it. Finally he sat down in a slump and asked his wife to continue.

The Roman populace hailed the fall of Sejanus with a wild rampage of joy, Procula resumed, toppling his statues and desecrating his memorials. Partisans of Agrippina led the demonstrations, of course, but followers of Sejanus were desperately eager to change sides and now outdid themselves in trying to show that they had always hated the man.

But where were the praetorians? Sejanus, languishing in prison, had one powerful hope: that 9000 praetorian guardsmen, marching across Rome, would tear open the Tullianum, rescue him, cut down his enemies. But there was no stirring from the *Castra Praetoria.*

The reaction of the citizenry combined with the inaction of the praetorians now firmed the Senate in its resolve. Reconvening later the same day, it listened to angry fusillades of oratory denouncing Sejanus. Then, just before supper, Consul Regulus called for a vote. There was little need to count the waving thicket of human arms. Regulus announced, "The Senate and the Roman People sentence Lucius Aelius Sejanus to death for high treason!"

Roman law required that nine days elapse between sentence and execution, but Rome was in no mood to wait so long. That very night, a committee of consuls and praetors visited the Tullianum, and gave orders to the executioners. Under the flickering glow of torches, Sejanus was pulled out of his cell and led to the black-walled death chamber.

"No!" he cried. *"This is a violation of Roman law! The praetorians!"* he roared. *"Get the praetorians!"* But a rag was stuffed in his mouth and poked down his throat. Then a long strap of leather was wound around his neck, and the free ends were pulled by guards on each side of him. Sejanus tried to struggle free, but his hands were tied behind his back. The pressure around his neck only increased. Now the lack of air was torturing, excruciating, but the strap kept tightening. The man who had begun the day as virtual co-emperor of Rome was strangled to death at its close.

His body was pitched down the Stairs of Mourning, yet it failed to reach the Tiber. The rabble had to play with it first. For three days and nights the corpse was made to preside over mock ceremonials, then abused and dragged by hooks through waterfront streets until mercifully dumped into the Tiber. Or was it? According to another rumor Procula heard, the mob tore Sejanus' body into pieces so small the executioner could not find one big enough to expose on the Stairs of Mourning.

In the week following the death of Sejanus, Rome rocked in a chaos of disorder and rioting. The rabid, unforgiving riffraff went after the well-known associates of Sejanus and lynched them in what became a general massacre. Meanwhile, the praetorians, furious at being thought less loyal to Tiberius than the night watch, vented their ire in burning and plunder instead of policing the mobs.

The record of the Senate in that crisis was not much better. Obsequious to the point of nausea, senators scrambled to introduce these measures, all of which passed with acclamation:

1. A statue of liberty was to be erected in the Forum.
2. October 18 would henceforth be an annual holiday, to be celebrated by games and spectacles.
3. In the future, no excessive honors would be granted anyone, except the princeps.
4. Henceforth, Tiberius would be known as "Father of his Country," and his birthday was to be observed by ten horse races and a banquet.

5. Macro and Laco would receive splendid honors for their roles in felling Sejanus.

The Roman people had sampled blood; they now seemed to develop something of a taste for the scarlet beverage. In another stormy session of the Senate, one old patrician observed darkly, "The blood of Sejanus still pulses in his offspring, the kind of blood which conspires against the state!" Concurring in this masterpiece of logic, the conscript fathers, conscience of the state that they were, condemned Sejanus' children to death. The eldest was executed six days after his father, another later, and finally the turn came for the youngest brother and sister.

Too young to understand what was happening, the little girl was carried off to the dungeon sobbing that she was sorry, crying that she would never again do whatever she had done that was wrong, that she would forever be a good girl if they would just spank her and let her go.

In the murky depths of the Tullianum, the executioners first thought this was rather amusing, but then, just as they were about to put the garrote on her slender neck, someone remembered that never in Rome's past had capital punishment been inflicted on a virgin. This caused them to hesitate, but, according to the stories Procula had heard, the delay was short-lived. A brute of an executioner jumped the girl, threw her on the moist floor of the dungeon, and raped her then and there to solve the legal problem. Only then were she and her brother strangled to death in the same halter.

At that point in Procula's report, Pilate shuddered with horror and loathing at that species of the human animal known as Roman man. Despising his own city and countrymen—it was a new experience for Pontius Pilate.

"But it doesn't make sense," he protested. "There are too many unanswered questions. *Why didn't the praetorians defend Sejanus?* And why did Macro, his own subordinate, lie to him about the tribunician power? Who baited the trap for October 18, and why?"

"Well," Procula explained, "only young Caligula remained as an obstacle between Sejanus and the throne. Finally it was Antonia who—"

"Caligula's grandmother?"

"Yes. She learned that Sejanus had an agent ready to denounce Caligula before the Senate on trumped-up charges, which she could prove false. She also had other evidence pointing to years of intrigue and conspiracy by Sejanus—"

"What? Sejanus *actually guilty?*"

"More on *that* in a moment. Antonia's problem was how to get the information to Tiberius on Capri, with Sejanus controlling all communications between the island and the mainland. She managed to send word via Pallas, her most trusted slave, who luckily wasn't searched. So, at long last, Tiberius' eyes were finally opened. Immediately he summoned the young Caligula to Capri for protection, and then plotted the fall of Sejanus."

"The princeps certainly proved himself a master deceiver. . . ."

"He *had* to be, Pilate! Imagine, even Capri was crawling with Sejanus' agents. The Praetorian Guard was his. The nearest legions were his. So Tiberius had to take him off guard, which explains those rumors about the tribunician power all but conferred on Sejanus. Fortunately for the emperor, Macro, as guard commander on Capri, was privately critical of his prefect, and Tiberius took him into his confidence. He told him to deliver the letter indicting Sejanus to the consul Regulus, *not* Trio, who was Sejanus' friend."

"If only he'd known! Sejanus would simply have surrounded the Senate with his praetorians. *Why* did they leave?"

"When Sejanus swallowed Macro's bait about the tribunician power and hurried inside the Senate, Macro went back outside and confronted the praetorians. He produced a special commission from Tiberius, which appointed himself as new praetorian prefect to succeed Sejanus. Naturally the guardsmen were dumfounded, but when Macro added that the princeps promised them a large bonus for quiet obedience, they obeyed his order to return to camp."

"Incredible! Evidently Sejanus spent so much time in politics that he neglected to maintain close contact with the guards, his power base."

"No sooner had the praetorians left than Laco, who was party to the plot, moved in to surround the Senate with his night watch. Tiberius' letter was intentionally as long and rambling as possible to give Macro time enough to hurry over to the *Castra Praetoria* and establish command over the other praetorian cohorts before Sejanus could take countermeasures. By the way, Tiberius was so worried that the guards might stay loyal to Sejanus that he had escape ships waiting in the harbor of Capri which would take him to loyal armies in the provinces. And just to make sure he'd have a head start on Sejanus, he watched constantly from the high cliffs of Capri for a fire signal from the mainland which would alert him in case his counterplot failed."

Pilate sat quietly for some moments, searching for moorings of logic in this flood of information. Then he turned angrily to his wife. "Wait a minute. Sejanus chasing down his own emperor? Are you suggesting he plotted against the very life of Tiberius?"

"It's not clear yet. When I left Rome, the trials against Sejanus' partisans, those who escaped the mobs, were just getting underway."

"But would it have been reasonable for him to attack the only man who could name him heir apparent? And even if Sejanus were as black as you picture him, wouldn't he have let Tiberius live out his life on Capri before making his move?"

"Perhaps. Though after Tiberius' letter was read to the Senate, the Roman Empire wasn't big enough for the two of them."

Immersed in his own train of thought, Pilate now lashed out angrily. "The more I hear of this, the more convinced I am that probably the most monstrous injustice in history has taken place against a man who gave his emperor a lifetime of service, protecting him against a dozen plots. And what was his reward? Death—and the slaughter of his innocent family. What was this alleged 'conspiracy' and 'intrigue' of Sejanus? Likely a fable spun out by Antonia! After all, she *is* the mother-in-law of Agrippina and therefore prejudiced against—"

"*Stop, Pilate!*" Procula cried. "I've tried hard to avoid the I-told-you-so attitude in view of our political differences. You know how we've gone round and around on Sejanus and Agrippina. But Sejanus' plot, his horrendous guilt, is now a sober *and proven* fact!"

"How proven?"

"Besides what I've already told you, one of the conspirators, Satrius Secundus, turned state's evidence and supplied absolute proof. Some of Sejanus' correspondence with provincial governors was intercepted, and it's equally incriminating."

Pilate looked as if his soul had been lacerated. For some

time he deliberated, then admitted, "Sejanus' letters did hint that some kind of showdown was approaching. What if they go through his files and find drafts of those letters to me which mentioned the approaching crisis? They may think *I* was party to the plot!"

Slowly, solemnly, Procula replied, "It could well mean the end of your prefecture, Pilate." Both were silent. Tears ran down her cheeks. "You have to face the truth," she finally cried. "Just having been a friend of Sejanus may incriminate you enough not only to lose your office, but"— she burst into tears—"your life itself."

"Now, now," Pilate consoled, "isn't that a little extreme?"

"No! Before I left, Father warned me that you could be recalled at any moment. The prisons of Rome are bulging with supporters of Sejanus, and the trials may turn into a legal terror."

"But Tiberius *won* his power play. Why is he now so vengeful?"

"Are you finally ready to hear the *whole* truth? You wouldn't have believed it earlier."

"Of course. . . ."

"Do you remember Drusus?"

"Agrippina's son?"

"No. The other Drusus—the only son Tiberius ever fathered—the one who died three years before we sailed for Judea."

"Yes. Obviously. What about him?"

"What did he die of?"

"Some kind of fever, wasn't it?"

"That's what everyone believed at the time, including the princeps, who was heartbroken at not having his own flesh and blood succeed him on the throne. But the horrible truth was finally revealed by Apicata, the divorced wife of Sejanus. After she'd seen her children strangled and thrown down the stairs, she committed suicide, but not before she wrote Tiberius that Drusus had *not* died a natural death."

"What?"

"Sejanus had seduced Drusus' wife Livilla . . . and the two of them *poisoned* Drusus, hoping to marry after his death."

Pilate was too stricken to speak.

"When Tiberius learned the tragic truth, he nearly went

mad. He now refuses to leave Capri, and lives only to avenge himself on everyone connected with Sejanus."

"Sejanus . . . *poisoned* . . . Drusus?"

"Tiberius wouldn't believe it from Apicata's letter alone. After all, she might have invented the story in revenge for the execution of her children. But the slaves and attendants of Livilla corroborated the poisoning."

"What did Tiberius do to Livilla?"

"She died of compulsory starvation. . . . And by the way, do you recall now Nero died?"

"He committed suicide on Pontia."

"Yes, but now it comes out how *that* happened. Sejanus' agents lied to poor Nero that the Senate had condemned him to death. They even had an executioner stalk about the island, testing out a strangling rope, until it was too much for Nero and he took his own life."

Pilate slumped in his chair. "Sejanus plotted that too?"

"Yes. And what, do you suppose, caused all the quarreling between Tiberius and Agrippina which led to her exile? Sejanus telling Agrippina the princeps was plotting against her, then telling the princeps Agrippina was plotting against him. And who imprisoned the younger Drusus on the Palatine? And who planned the judicial murder of the young Caligula? It was all part of Sejanus' huge conspiracy to win the throne for himself, a plot which duped Tiberius for almost ten years!"

Slowly Pilate reacted. "And now, of course, he'll make his move against *all* supporters of Sejanus."

"You can't blame him for that."

"I. . . . I must have time to think, Procula. It was good of you to get me. . . . the facts."

Chapter 14

PILATE KNEW that the next months would determine his future career, even his life itself. That he could share in the fall of Sejanus was easily possible, since he heard that friends, supporters, and appointees of the fallen prefect were being imprisoned to await trial by the Senate on charges of *maiestas,* treason in "diminishing the majesty of the Roman People." The end might come in the form of a letter of recall, delivered by a praetorian courier fresh from Rome. More likely, a newly commissioned prefect of Judea would land in Caesarea with orders for him to return to Rome for trial. Each large ship arriving at the harbor struck a twinge of uncertainty in him.

Or might the fates be kind and allow Tiberius to forget his close association with Sejanus? It was nearly six years since his last visit with the princeps under Sejanus' patronage, and the only thing Tiberius might likely recall from that occasion would be the collapse of the grotto. No, that was wishful thinking. The rockfall would only anchor the entire visit, and what had preceded it, more securely in the emperor's mind.

But the Tiberiéum. Pilate's last direct word from the princeps before the fall of Sejanus had been favorable, a message of appreciation for the now-completed basilica and an accolade for Jerusalem's new water system. The fact that the aqueduct cost Rome hardly a sesterce had been especially appealing to Tiberius, who made an act of worship out of balancing the imperial budget. Yet if he did remain in the emperor's good graces, Pilate's *acta* for 31, an end-of-the-year report, should have received some acknowledgment, some indication that it would be "business as usual" in Judea despite the unheavals in Rome. But no word from Tiberius had arrived.

In making policy, the princeps would probably lean heavily now on Sertorius Macro, the new praetorian prefect. Pilate reviewed his relationship with Macro, whom he had known casually as a fellow tribune at the *Castra Praetoria,* but there was little from this earlier acquaintance to indicate how he would advise Tiberius concerning Judea. A good hater, Macro was already happily at work, bringing Sejanians to trial.

New policies and changes of officials in the Near East now seemed the order of the day. Aelius Lamia, the absentee governor of Syria, was graduated from that phantom post to become urban prefect of Rome, while Pomponius Flaccus succeeded him in Syria. And Flaccus actually sailed east to assume his governorship. For the first time, then, Pilate would have a higher-ranking colleague overlooking his shoulders from the north, a possible hamper on his freedom.

Down in Egypt, Vitrasius Pollio had been in office only a matter of months when he died, and, after an interim appointment, Tiberius sent another man named Flaccus, A. Avillius Flaccus, to succeed him. So change was in the air, and Pilate could only wonder when it would be his turn, especially after the execution of his patron. But still no letter from Capri or Rome.

He made his usual trip to Jerusalem for the Passover festival in 32, but this time his retinue carried along some well-wrapped and crated pieces of freight. During the journey he kept an anxious eye on the joggling bundles, for they represented his latest proof of loyalty to Tiberius, something of which he had maximum need at the time.

Ideally, there should have been something like the Tiberiéum for the other capital of his province, Jerusalem, a public edifice in honor of the emperor. Pilate now cursed himself for not having thought to name the new water system there the "Tiberian Aqueduct." Herod Antipas, with his perennial courting of the princeps, his "Tiberianizing" of every place name in Galilee, might now rank higher in the emperor's favor than in the days of Sejanus. Pilate had to find some way of honoring the princeps in the heart of

the Holy City itself, but without offending the Jews in the
process. The solution lay in the packages.

This time he had to be especially careful not to antagonize the Jews, for rumors poured out of Rome that since
Sejanus had been anti-Semitic, Tiberius was now veering
toward a pro-Jewish policy. As a first step, exiled Jews
were being encouraged to return to Rome. Jerusalem, of
course, had hailed the fall of Sejanus with rejoicing, and
in view of the restored status of Jews in the Empire, Pilate
had cautiously ordered his provincial mint to stop producing coins with a *lituus* symbol, the Roman augur's spiral-
headed staff which Pilate, under pressure from Sejanus,
had intended as a Romanizing gesture in Judea. But now
was no time to offend his subjects with the pagan crosier
motif, and the pressure behind such coinage was dead anyway.

After arriving at Herod's palace in Jerusalem, Pilate
carefully unwrapped his bundles and had servants polish
the contents. They were large heraldic shields, heavily coat-
ed with gold, which bore the simple inscription:

In Honor of
TIBERIVS CAESAR
Dedicated by
PONTIVS
PILATVS

His goldsmiths in Caesarea had worked the shields handsomely, and Pilate carefully hung them in the great reception hall of the Herodian palace.

He thought the gesture well-suited to his purposes. The
gleaming escutcheons were a public demonstration of his
loyalty to the emperor, in the very city which had once demanded the removal of medallions with his image. A sample of the shields was already en route to Capri, along with
a notice of their forthcoming dedication in the Jerusalem
palace. Tiberius was known to like that kind of thing: trophies, citations, plaques, and other tokens of recognition
fairly cluttered his personal offices both on the Palatine and
at Capri.

And the shields could hardly offend the Jews. They contained no tracings or engravings to represent anything ani-
mate or inanimate. No images. Only lettering. Nothing on

the shields, then, was contrary to Hebrew law, for the law did not condemn written inscriptions.

The next morning, Pilate was doubly glad that he had been careful regarding Jewish sensitivities. A courier arrived from Caesarea, bringing a long-awaited—and long-dreaded—message from Tiberius. Pilate had just missed receiving it when he set out for Jerusalem. With throbbing pulse he nervously slit the seals with his dagger and read the following, written before the sample shield had arrived:

Tiberius Caesar Augustus, *pontifex maximus,* consul five times, acclaimed *imperator,* holding the tribunician power for the thirty-third year, to Pontius Pilatus, *praefectus Iudaeae,* greeting. If you are in health, it is well. I also and the army are well.

Following the death of the traitor, murderer, and enemy of Rome, Sejanus, I have learned that the accusations he made against the Jews of Rome are false slanders, invented by him to do away with the Jewish nation. From henceforth, penal measures will extend only to Jews guilty of actual crimes, and not to their entire people as such.

I have written my prefects elsewhere in the Empire to conciliate the Jews living under their jurisdiction, and not to disturb their established customs. On the contrary, they are to protect them. The same must certainly apply to the Judean homeland. I herewith charge you to maintain the peace of Judea by disturbing none of the Jewish institutions. Farewell.

Given the Ides of February, A.V.C. 785, in the consulship of I. Gnaeus Domitius and M. F. Camillus Scribonianus

So his first word from Tiberius was a directive in behalf of the Jews—and Pilate could not have been happier or more relieved. The imperial message had not ordered his return to Rome to stand trial for complicity with Sejanus. In fact, the last sentence of the letter nearly implied a reconfirmation of his office.

Possibly, then, Tiberius had forgotten his close association with the fallen prefect. Or had he? There was no commendation for him in these lines, nothing in response to his glowing report for the year 31, so Tiberius might still be in the process of constructing a case against him prior to official recall. In that event, dispatching the golden shield to

Capri had been a good bit of timing, even though that gesture alone would hardly avert disaster.

Jerusalem celebrated the Passover of 32 with more joyous fervor than Pilate had ever noted before. The reason was hardly a mystery. The anti-Semite who ranked second in Rome was no more, and pilgrims streaming into Jerusalem from all parts of the Empire were spreading the news about Tiberius' now conciliatory policy toward Judaism. A special service of thanksgiving saw the vast terraces of the temple submerged under a sea of humanity. Four sons of Herod the Great had come to Jerusalem for the occasion—probably to capitalize on the popular good will of the moment, Pilate reasoned.

But he was not above doing the same thing. Calling a conference with Joseph Caiaphas and leaders of the Sanhedrin, he announced the new imperial policy toward Judea, reading them excerpts from Tiberius' letter. The Jewish authorities were heartened at the dramatic change, and there were tears in the eyes of saintly Rabbi Zadok, who, two years earlier, had begun what became an intermittent forty-year fast for the safety of Jerusalem. At long last, it seemed to them, healing might yet close the inflamed wounds of Judeo-Roman relations. And when, during the Passover, Pilate appeared publicly before the crowds to announce from his tribunal the annual release of a popular prisoner, he was actually cheered by the people. He could scarcely trust his ears.

Just when Pilate's relations with his subjects were finally improving, a new storm suddenly chilled the atmosphere. The first rumblings had been the report of a crowd advancing on the palace, led, incredibly, by Herod's four sons.

But it was an orderly demonstration—there were no hoots or shouting—and the leaders of the procession were admitted into the palace when they requested an audience with the prefect.

Pilate came out to the vestibule and saw the tetrarch of Galilee. "Greetings, Antipas," he began affably. "Have you come to repossess your father's palace?"

"No, friend," he smiled. "The Hasmonean palace is quite enough for us. You know my brother Philip the tetrarch."

"Of course. Congratulations on your marriage to the beautiful Salome, Philip."

". . . and my brother Herod-Philip."

"Pleased to see you again." Pilate could hardly refrain from saying instead, "Oh yes, Herodias' one-time husband, cuckolded by the man introducing you!"

". . . and my third brother here you've not met. His name is also Herod, my father's son by Cleopatra of Jerusalem. . . . And several of the chief priests and members of the Sanhedrin have joined us, as you see."

"You are welcome, gentlemen," said Pilate, still wondering what had prompted such a visit, reinforced, as it was, by several hundred citizens at the palace gates.

"I wonder if we might be permitted to view the interior of the great reception hall of the palace," Antipas inquired.

"Of course. This way, gentlemen."

Pilate conducted the delegation into the hall, now handsomely ornamented with the golden shields. Immediately an animated conversation in Hebrew broke out among the Sanhedrists, while the Herodian brothers said nothing. Pilate could not understand the priests, but they were obviously discussing the shields, since they approached each and examined it carefully. There were sighs, headshaking, and louder Hebrew. Then the priests called the sons of Herod into a huddled consultation, from which Pilate was again excluded. Minutes passed.

Finally Antipas broke out of the group and asked, "How long have these gilded shields been hanging here in the palace, Prefect?"

"About a week. Why?"

Antipas drew in a long breath and said, "It's simply that the Jews finds the shields offensive, and they—"

"Do you mean that your delegation and all the people outside came to complain about these simple shields?" Pilate snapped, his ire building.

"Yes. . . ."

"How did you all even learn about the shields in the first place?"

"Several of the Jewish palace servants were troubled about them," replied Rabbi Ananias, "and they inquired if the shields were contrary to our laws. Later, the public learned about the new abominations and—"

"*Abominations!*" Pilate fumed. "I took extreme care that the shields be fashioned so as *not* to offend your laws. They represent no living thing in heaven or earth. Or hell, for that matter! Look at them. They have no *images*, gentlemen. *Why* the objection?"

Ananias replied with a cool serenity which contrasted with Pilate's agitation and further infuriated him. "The shields are pagan trophies erected by a foreign power within the walls of our Holy City. Doubtless they also have a sacred significance for you."

"They have *no* religious implications whatever!"

"Naturally we have no objection to your honoring the emperor in any way you see fit *outside* the Holy City. But these engraved shields cannot be tolerated within Jerusalem. In the name of the Sanhedrin and of the Jewish nation, we respectfully request that they be removed as soon as possible."

"But you misinterpret these ornaments. They bear only the emperor's name and mine, as the donor. What sacral implications could possibly be involved?"

"Do you deny that the medallions which you tried to introduce into Jerusalem some years ago had religious significance?" Rabbi Alexander interjected.

"How long do you people carry a grudge? How long, I ask you," Pilate exploded. "Or did you forget that I *removed* the standards?"

"It's just this, Prefect," Philip interposed, trying to play a mediating role. "The people knew that the ensigns had a strong religious significance for the troops, and what is a shield but as much a part of military equipment as standards. How then can the people believe the shields are free of cultic significance?"

"And not only that, Tetrarch Philip," the illustrious scribe Jochanan ben-Zakkai interjected. "Prefect, are you being entirely honest with us when you say these shields are religiously neutral?"

"Are you daring to impugn my veracity?"

"Certainly not. But does the term *ancile* mean anything to you?"

Suddenly Pilate caught the significance, though he could not imagine ben-Zakkai learned enough to know of that minute detail from Roman history. At the same time, he could not afford to bluff in case the rabbi knew his ground, so he asked, lamely, "What are you driving at?"

"It was in the era of the early Roman monarchy, during the reign of your King Numa Pompilius. A sacred oval *shield*, the *ancile*, supposedly fell from heaven. Your priests declared that the shield guaranteed divine protection for the city of Rome, so it was zealously guarded. Numa was so worried that someone might steal the holy shield that he had eleven others fashioned exactly like it, so that the genuine one could not be distinguished and stolen. The twelve shields were then entrusted to the pagan god Mars and his priests. And Prefect, I find it significant that you also had a plurality of shields prepared. . . . But the meaning of your inscription must now be clear: May Mars guard the emperor and the city of Rome through the sacred shield of Numa! And this paganism in our Holy City!"

Pilate was impressed by ben-Zakkai's knowledge, even if he himself had not recalled the myth of Numa's shield when preparing the trophies for his palace. "I applaud your knowledge of our past, learned Rabbi," he said, "and you are right about Numa and the shields. In fact, the priests of Mars troop through Rome every March, clutching their shields as they sing and dance. But I swear to you by your own god that I was *not* motivated by the story of Numa. For that matter, I don't even believe in the myth, or in Mars either—I'm not a very religious person, in fact. And you are wrong in supposing that this style of shield harks back to Numa. His were small oval shields, whereas these are round military shields which we call the *clipeus,* not the *ancile.*"

The delegation briefly exchanged thoughts in Hebrew. Then Rabbi Ananias said, "In the context of your previous indiscretions concerning our customs, and in view of the pagan significance of Roman shields in general, however unintended on your part, we must insist that they be removed from Jerusalem."

Now angry again, Pilate countered, "But one of your own rabbis in Caesarea stated that nothing offensive was engraved on the shields. I took pains—"

"And we would agree. The written message does not offend us; but the shields themselves do."

Pilate knew it was time to unleash his master stroke. He did not think he would have to use it, but apparently nothing less than such a logical bolt would convince the priests. "Have any of you visited the synagogues in Alexandria?" he inquired. "Do you know how your brothers in the faith honor the emperor in Egypt? They dedicate *votive shields* to him. And they hang the shields on the very *walls of their synagogues!* Not in the public basilicas, mind you. Not in their homes. But in their houses of worship. Their synagogues also boast pillars, golden crowns, plaques—all inscribed *in Tiberius' honor!* I saw them when I was in Egypt. And now you object when a Roman governor honors his emperor within his *own praetorium* in a similar fashion! Have you no sense of fair play, no decency? Must your people complain and object, agitate and demonstrate continually, and for no justified cause—just when we had hoped our relations would improve?"

Several of the priests looked somewhat nonplused. But Rabbi Ananias replied in his now-familiar, lofty tone, "So far as our brethren in Alexandria are concerned, we shall pray for them. They erred in ignorance and we shall so inform them."

Antipas, who had remained aloof from the discussion thus far, gently urged Pilate, "You'd better remove the shields. They *have* become a pagan symbol, an unnecessary show of Roman dominance in the very heart of the Holy City. You're doing the same thing my father tried to do: please Rome at the expense of Jewish sensitivities. And the Jews hated him for it.—You won't be able to convince the people."

"Well, why don't *you* convince them, then, Antipas?" Pilate glared. "As a fellow governor of this troubled territory, you'd do better supporting a colleague than helping to lead a demonstration against him. Does your own record in Galilee show you off as a paragon of Jewish orthodoxy?"

The debate had now reached the level of personalities, and Antipas was quick to reply in kind. "I find it amusing, Prefect, that you should hurry to hang up these shields just at *this* time. Could it be because of a certain crisis, involving the fall of a certain individual in Rome?"

What nettled Pilate was not so much the verbal thrust, which was true to the mark, but the sneer with which Antipas spilled the words from his mouth. And this new pose as champion of the Sanhedrin was nauseating—brother's wife-stealing adulterer and prophet-killer now playing hero of the faith.

"My past association with Aelius Sejanus is certainly common knowledge," Pilate stated with all the dignity he could muster. "And so is yours, Tetrarch."

The two glowered at each other briefly before Pilate turned to the rest of the delegation and said, "A matter of principle is involved here, gentlemen. If I were to remove the shields, not only would it be a tacit admission that they were in fact religious after all—and they are *not*—but this would be *the* supreme insult to Tiberius Caesar. Imagine his learning that six gilded shields were dedicated in his honor at the Jerusalem *praetorium,* and then discovering that they had to be removed because of popular pressure."

"Nevertheless," objected Ananias, "unless you can produce a document from the emperor indicating that our customs are to be subverted, we must categorically insist, as a matter of conscience, that the shields be removed from Jerusalem. Don't be responsible for destroying the peace, Prefect. You don't honor the emperor by dishonoring our laws. If you fail to grant our request, we shall have to choose envoys to present our case before Tiberius Caesar."

The suggestion of going over his head would have been unwelcome to Pilate under any circumstances, but in his present tenuous position it was particularly distasteful. On the other hand, Tiberius' learning that the sample shield sent to Capri was just a mockery since the originals had been taken down would be even worse. Besides, the priests were probably bluffing. Pilate would meet the test.

"Choose your wisest representatives then, Rabbi Ananias," he replied, "for their mission will not be a happy one. In essence, they'll have to ask, 'O, Emperor, may we please dishonor you by removing trophies inscribed in your honor?'" Pilate paused, then continued, "I repeat: these are harmless, secular mementos, which have nothing to do with religion, and they're hanging in Roman territory, in a Roman *praetorium,* and away from any possible glimpse by the public. Therefore the shields will not be disturbed. And so far as that crowd is concerned, I'll hold all of you personally responsible for dispersing it peacefully. Good day, gentlemen."

The Herodian brothers and the Sanhedrists left the palace to address the people. Pilate could not hear what was said, but it must have been something placating, since the crowd turned away without incident and dissolved into the city.

There were no subsequent riots in Jerusalem. When Pilate left the city for Caesarea at the close of the Passover celebration, he felt for the first time that he was governor of Judea in fact.

Chapter 15

ONE DAY, the centurion Cornelius proposed "a fresh solution to the problem of Jew versus Roman." Pilate, of course, was more than curious, but all Cornelius suggested was "Intermarriage." Pilate was sure he had not heard correctly. Then the centurion broke his glad news. He, an imperious Roman, had surrendered to the charms of a Jewish girl from Caesarea, and they planned to be married—with Pilate's permission, of course. It was quite the only solution to Judeo-Roman antagonisms, Cornelius twitted.

Pilate assumed he was jesting, until the centurion presented his bride-to-be. She was a striking girl of seventeen, whom Pilate already knew well as one of Procula's palace attendants. Cornelius claimed she would have no trouble lowering the raised eyebrows of Caesareans. The city's Jewish community frowned on marriages between The Chosen and pagans, while gentiles in the capital were just as convinced that Cornelius would demean himself by "such a misalliance." Though startled and somewhat skeptical, Pilate would deny nothing to his favorite, and so approved the marriage. He could hardly blame his officer, for he himself had been noticing the girl's charms.

The wedding was a discreet compromise between a Roman civil marriage and the Jewish ceremony, which apparently satisfied those attending the nuptials, the first such social mixing between Jewish and gentile elements at Caesarea in anyone's memory. The couple had settled their religious differences by simple inertia. Since Cornelius was as

177

skeptical as Pilate about the deities of Roman mythology, he believed in nothing supernatural. But his bride, as a good Jewess, had a strong faith. And since something is usually better than nothing, Cornelius promised to let his wife practice her religion unhindered, with the stipulation that she not try to make a Jew out of him. They had not yet agreed on how their children would be reared.

The secret matchmaker in this unlikely romance was Procula. She did not want her role a matter of public knowledge for fear it might embarrass her husband, but since the bride had been one of Procula's favorite attendants, it was she who first introduced her to Cornelius and then watched their romance ripen into marriage. Procula had always been liberal in such matters.

She also had a higher respect for Judaism than did her husband. The hysteria and political bloodshed at Rome had shaken her once-unquestioning confidence in Roman state religion. What kind of deities could have been in charge of the Empire to let such atrocities happen? In contrast, the Jewish belief in one god, and only one, seemed to her less confusing than juggling loyalties to several dozen gods, goddesses, demigods, spirits, and dead emperors. More than that, the Jews had a dynamic code of conduct—their law—which guided their lives far more meaningfully than watching the gustatory habits of sacred chickens or poking around a sheep's liver. Romans, she felt, had been getting their omens from animals for so long that they were starting to live like them also.

Pilate was happy to learn of his wife's disenchantment with Roman paganism, but her new admiration for Judaism worried him. He feared she was becoming a Jewish proselyte, and right under his governor's nose.

"Tolerance is not conversion," Procula replied.

"But tell me, then," he probed, "why did you choose the young Cornelius for your experiment in interethnic romance?"

"Experiment? This will be a *very* happy marriage. You'll see. But why Cornelius? Because he's as much a favorite of mine as yours. In fact," she said, "I saw quite a bit of him while you were away in Jerusalem. We've had long conversations. . . ."

"Oh?" Pilate raised his left eyebrow. "Should I be jealous?"

"I hardly think so," she said coyly. "We had a wedding

to plan. But there was also something which you never even told me about."

"What's that?"

"The fascinating reports about that new prophet up in Galilee."

"Who *now?*" he grumbled. What Pilate needed least at the moment was a new prophet in the land.

"He's called Yeshua."

"Oh, him. Yes, I know about that Jesus. He seems to be some kind of faith healer."

"More than that, apparently. While you were in Jerusalem watching the Jews prepare their Passover Seder, this Jesus provided his own kind of Passover feast for more than 5000 people who were hearing him teach near the Sea of Tiberias."

"Well, that was kind of him . . . but hardly spectacular. Caesar's friend Crassus once threw a banquet for the entire citizenry of Rome, and several times 50,000 crowded to the tables he set up in the streets—"

"Let me finish, Pilate. This was entirely different. Jesus hoped to get away from the crowds by taking his twelve student followers on an excursion across the Sea of Tiberias. But the people moved along the shore and intercepted him just after he landed. So he spent most of the day teaching and healing the people anyway, but when evening came they were all hungry and the nearest market was miles away. A little shepherd boy sold them five barley loaves and two carp, but that was hardly enough—"

"Procula, this is a moving little tale of dedication, but does the story have a point?"

"I'm coming to it. Jesus had the people sit down on the grass. Then he prayed and started handing out the loaves and fish. He *multiplied them,* and everyone had so much to eat that twelve baskets full of crumbs were collected afterward."

"All from five loaves and two fish, I suppose?"

"Yes."

"What they did was to unload food supplied from their ship."

"No."

"The people brought lunch baskets along for the day's outing and shared."

"No."

Pilate reflected a moment, then commented, "Well, I don't know what you heard or what the people actually saw, but what you report is impossible, that's all."

"I knew that would be your attitude, but Cornelius says there are people here in Caesarea who ate bread and fish up there that evening."

This time Pilate was intrigued enough to trace down the fantastic story and find a reasonable explanation for it. He asked Cornelius to locate and bring to the palace any Caesareans who had actually participated in the now-famous outdoor meal. Two days later, the centurion presented six people who had made the pilgrimage to Galilee. They were rather nervous at being summoned before the governor of Judea, but when they understood that he only wanted to hear their versions of the event which was now being discussed throughout Palestine, they readily told their stories.

But the accounts agreed substantially with Procula's version, though there were differing opinions on the size of the multitude. And one old woman insisted it was two loaves and five fish, rather than vice versa. Pilate dismissed the people with thanks.

Later he related the interviews to Procula, but insisted, "Regardless of what they saw, there *has* to be some explanation. If I'd been there, I'd have found it, I'm sure." Then he wrinkled his brow. "But *one* bit of information from these people rings true."

"What's that?"

"The reaction of the crowd. Once they were fed, some shouted, 'Let this man be our *king.*' Now that part of it I believe. A man who can heal the sick and produce food for the masses, he *could* become king. But fortunately for this Jesus, he made the right decision when the people offered him a crown."

"By withdrawing into the hills? Why do you say 'fortunately'?" Procula asked.

"Because if he had in any way accepted the title of king, Herod Antipas would have had to indict him for high treason against the emperor."

Something else about this phenomenon bothered Pilate. The people referred to Jesus as "the Christos." He knew that this meant "the Anointed One," but he was startled to learn that it was merely the Greek translation of the Hebrew term "Messiah." Messiahs were dangerous to Rome.

Throughout 32 A.D., Pilate scanned every straw in the winds from Rome, and the news was very discouraging. Tiberius remained in his self-imposed exile on Capri, except for one sailing excursion up the shores of Italy to the mouth of the Tiber. Here he landed, and Rome prepared a glittering welcome for the returning emperor only to learn that Tiberius had changed his mind and returned to the rocky solitude of Capri. Tongues wagged that the lusty princeps could not stand being away from the lewd games he concocted in the villas and groves of Capri. But Pilate was skeptical about the gossip. Would an embittered seventy-two-year-old actually engage in such gymnastics, especially when his only real appetite now was for revenge on the partisans of Sejanus?

Since the prefect had fallen late in 31 A.D., most of the treason trials took place in 32. Pilate learned that the actual reign of terror had ended in the weeks following the execution of Sejanus, when senators finally wore themselves out attacking each other. But now the more orderly trials were taking place. Typically, a letter would arrive from Capri, charging some high official with complicity in the Sejanian conspiracy and supplying what evidence there was. If the Senate found the man guilty, he was executed or allowed to commit suicide. The innocent, fewer in number, were acquitted. In the judiciary storm sweeping Rome, Pilate found one fact abundantly clear: friendship with Sejanus, once an asset, was now a mortal liability. Many prominent Romans were living, like him, in daily dread of being cited for *maiestas,* treason against state and emperor.

Pilate and Procula were deeply concerned also for their parents. So far, they had escaped any accusations, although Proculeius did appear as a defense witness in the trial of one of his friends. But their point of contact with Sejanus had been Pilate, so the first indictment to blight their families would likely be the case of Rome *vs.* the prefect of Judea.

By now, Pilate had accustomed himself to living under this political sword of Damocles, although reports that the princeps was reaching down into the equestrian class to ferret out Sejanians was hardly comforting. More disturbing was Tiberius' failure to acknowledge the golden shield. Certainly he was busy with his incriminations, but might not his secretary on Capri have had the decency to write that the trophy had been received?

The princeps was always unpredictable, of course, but now he was touchy too. A letter from Proculeius gave the latest example of the imperial spleen. A senator named Gallio moved that retired praetorians be given the honor of sitting with equestrians in the lowest fourteen rows of seats at the theater. But a letter from Tiberius blasted the proposal, suggesting that Gallio was trying to turn the guards' heads in a treasonable manner. As reward for his innocent motion, Gallio was banished from Italy. Then, when it was learned that he planned to live on the beautiful island of Lesbos, he was dragged back to detention in Rome, since Tiberius thought such an exile too pleasant for him.

It was late summer when Pilate received another letter bearing the large, purple imperial seals, his second from Tiberius since the fall of Sejanus. The mere act of opening messages from the princeps made him taste anxiety, but this time Pilate had more confidence. Here, finally, would be the emperor's acknowledgement for the golden shield. The letter read:

> Tiberius Caesar Augustus, *pontifex maximus,* consul five times, acclaimed *imperator,* holding the tribunician power for the thirty-fourth year, to Pontius Pilatus, *praefectus Iudaeae,* greeting.
>
> Have you forgotten that a prefect represents the will of the princeps in his province, rather than his own? Or did you fail to read my last letter which expressed that will? Or are you, perhaps, still taking orders from the shade of Sejanus rather than the living Tiberius? In that case, you ought to join him!

A shuddering horror clutched at Pilate and beads of perspiration broke over his face, blotching with dread. His hand shook so much that he had trouble reading the quivering scroll. Finally he set it down on a table.

> In my last letter—I shall not say "if memory serves me correctly," for it does—I told you distinctly that you were *not* to disturb Jewish customs, but, on the contrary, to uphold, even defend them. What, then, is this new indiscretion of yours regarding the golden shields? I shall not play the ingrate and withhold my appreciation for your motive in this gesture. But it was a gesture in the wrong place, since the Jews are nearly fanatic about what does or does not happen in their Holy City. You ought to know that by now.

Herod Antipas, his brothers, and the chief priests of the Sanhedrin have written me, pleading that the shields be removed from the palace in Jerusalem. I have written them that their request will be honored. You will remove the shields immediately. But they are handsome and should be exhibited: I suggest that you transfer them to the Temple of Augustus at Caesarea.

You are to conciliate the Jews, Pilatus. Do not try our patience again, or we shall have to review the full extent of your past relationship with the murderous traitor Sejanus—after recalling you to Rome. Farewell.

Given the Calends of July, A.V.C. 785.

Pilate spent the next minutes collecting himself. Could one man fear, hate, despair, and be shocked, frustrated, angry, and vengeful all at the same time? He could. Most of all he was swept with a sickening anxiety for himself and a deadly hatred for the Herods.

His first strictly logical thought was to send a courier to the tribune of Jerusalem with an order to remove the shields from the palace. Only then could he indulge his fury at the audacity of Antipas and the Sanhedrists in making good their threat to contact Tiberius, which he had thought only bluff.

Obviously he should never have gotten himself into this predicament in the first place. Hanging the trophies in Caesarea would have been quite enough for his purposes. Why, then, had he chosen Jerusalem? The reason he had given his council was: to neutralize any lingering memory Tiberius might have had of the old standards affair, which, technically, had been a symbolic disgrace for the emperor. The shields would honor Tiberius in the very city which had rejected his images—without offending the Jews. But was this the *only* reason, Pilate finally asked himself. Or had removal of the medallions really vexed the princeps? Crises have this merit, that they often shake a person into candor with himself. Pilate probed his motives and finally uncovered another explanation for his shields scheme. The standards had been a personal setback for him, in Jerusalem; the shields were to be his personal vindication, in Jerusalem. No one likes to be thwarted.

Yet even in his mood of personal honesty, Pilate branded Herod Antipas as the chief cause for his plight, not himself. He had sincerely thought the shields would not offend the Jews—there was the glittering precedent of the synagogues in Alexandria—and the objections of the chief priests were not supported by any Hebrew law. Nor had they proved their case logically. If Tiberius could only have heard the dialogue, he would surely have exonerated, no, applauded him for unholding Rome's interests, Pilate felt. In this light, Antipas knew he was justified in putting up the kind of ornaments he wished in his *own praetorium* and yet he switched out of character, wrapped himself in the mantle of Jewish piety, and went over Pilate's head to complain, instead of providing his good offices to soothe the ruffled feelings between the prefect and the priests. The hypocrite! He objected to *imageless* shields, the man who offended Judaism by adorning his own palace in Tiberias with images of animals. It was another item Pilate wished he had recalled earlier.

Why did Antipas deal him this low a blow? Clear. If, at Rome, friends were informing on friends in their anxiety to appear anti-Sejanus, why not a rival accusing a rival in Judea? Though Sejanus had openly patronized Antipas, the tetrarch had always managed to keep a solid reserve of favor with Tiberius. By casting Pilate in the role of a disobedient prefect who was spurning the emperor's directives, possibly with hints at Pilate's previous dependence on Sejanus, Antipas would contrast favorably in the princeps' estimation. And if it came to Pilate's recall, who might better succeed him than the only man who had proved he could get on well with both Roman and Jew? "The tetrarch of Galilee . . . *and Judea*," a virtual restoration of the kingdom of Herod the Great. Before this, it would not have been possible, since Antipas was disliked by the Sanhedrin. But now that he had successfully championed their cause before Rome, his stock would soar in Judea. After his marital misadventures, his antagonizing of King Aretas, and his beheading of the Baptizer, Herod Antipas had finally staged a diplomatic coup. The fact that it had also been at Pilate's expense must have been doubly sweet to him, as it was twice as bitter for Pilate.

His future now seemed drastically uncertain. Without telling Procula, he drew up a last will and testament. Tiberius' letter implied that one more provocation would cause his recall, and the awful language about "reviewing the full extent of your past relationship with Sejanus" only brought into the open what he had long suspected anyway: Tiberius had not, in fact, forgotten.

After living a week under the precarious new circumstances, Pilate composed a long reply to the emperor. He wrote and rewrote it several times, then tried it out on Procula and finally edited it again. The language had to be perfect, the argumentation flawless. Above all, there could be no double meanings for the suspicious and resentful Tiberius to interpret the wrong way. It was an incredible situation: his very life might depend on the arrangement of ink scratchings on a slip of papyrus!

The letter began by assuring the emperor that the shields had been removed immediately, but it went on to explain why Pilate had originally hung them. Prominent reference was made to Jewish law and the Alexandrian synagogues. The letter closed with the statement that he had not seen Sejanus for five years prior to his fall, and that he had certainly had no idea of his treacherous conspiracy.

Such a reply was a calculated risk. It was not servile, for that would only have further demeaned him in Tiberius' estimation while saving his skin. But in defending his conduct, he might hazard immediate recall if Tiberius were in a black mood when he opened the letter. Yet there are times when personal integrity allows no other option. For Pilate, this was one of them.

The next weeks would tell. A quick response from Capri would augur doom even before the seals were broken. No word, on the other hand, would be good word indeed.

The autumn months of 32 brought no further communication from Tiberius. Pilate's attention now shifted back to Jerusalem. Ever since the shields episode, he had warned the Antonia cohort, under threat of severest military discipline, not to offend the Jews in any way. Many of the Judean riots over the years had been triggered by incidents of friction between soldiers and people. A thumbed nose, a yelled curse, an obscene gesture easily escalated into bloodshed. Pilate simply could not afford another uproar of any kind at this time.

He also asked the tribune of Jerusalem to report on the activities of the puzzling personage who was high priest of the Jews. Joseph Caiaphas had not been part of the delegation which sought the removal of the shields. And so it had been with the other crises between Pilate and the Jews, including the water system and the standards. Caiaphas never openly opposed him. Why?

Reportedly, Caiaphas was a worldly-wise Sadducee, a reasonable pontiff who disliked rioting and disorder as much as Pilate did. In fact, the Zealots and most of the Pharisees thought him too Rome-serving for their blood. Yet if his sympathies *were* pro-Roman, Pilate wished he would better exercise them in moments of crisis to save him repeated embarrassment. But was Caiaphas truly Romanophile? Pilate doubted. The most obvious reason for the high priest's failure to move against him publicly was a simple matter of self-preservation. Since Pilate could replace him at the drop of his governor's staff, he would necessarily remain in the background during any anti-Roman demonstrations, even if his sympathies would naturally be with his fellow Jews—up to a point. If a protest broke into civil disorder or open rebellion, Caiaphas would wash his hands of it. Indeed, he would probably conspire with Pilate to put it down, for such turmoil could invite massive Roman intervention, and then his own position would be lost. Nor would he be apt to agitate for Pilate's replacement, since a new governor might well mean a new high priest.

The pontiff, then, was another man-in-the-middle between Jerusalem and Rome, Pilate reasoned. What he now feared was that Caiaphas might be tempted by Tiberius' new Jewish policy to upset the arrangement by which the two had controlled Judea for the past six years and venture into occasional open defiance of himself. This is why Pilate had directed the tribune in Jerusalem to keep the high priest's activities under surveillance.

But the tribune reported that lately Caiaphas and his ruling coterie had no time for any hostility to Rome, since their attention was claimed by growing domestic turmoil. The people were restless, excited, he wrote, and the Sanhedrin was trying to keep them calm. Probably it would not come to insurrection, but something was in the air. There were anti-Roman elements in the movement, but just as much anti-Sanhedral feeling.

"Cornelius," Pilate called, "read this note from the Jerusalem commandant and see if you can make any sense out of it."

The centurion studied the communiqué, then admitted, "Seems like gibberish to me."

"A good tribune should have ferreted out better information than that. I'm concerned. Maybe something dangerous *is* developing; maybe it's only everyone's nerves. But I can't afford to be caught off guard. Why not go down to Jerusalem, Cornelius, and sniff out what's happening?"

"I'll do my best."

"Take your time. Don't come back till you have all the facts."

Cornelius left for Jerusalem in mid-December, returning to Caesarea in late January of 33. He began his extended report with a curious statement: "The leaven of Messianism is at work throughout Judea."

"What's that supposed to mean?" Pilate scowled.

"This is how my wife's relatives in Jerusalem explained the present mood. The common people are longing for a patriotic and religious deliverer, who will inaugurate some great era of independence and peace and plenty here in Palestine."

"The old hope for the Messiah-king. Well, has he shown up yet?"

"There seem to be several candidates. In Samaria, one of the favorites is a charlatan named Simon Magus, a practitioner of black magic who astounds the Samaritans with his tricks and modestly calls himself 'the Great Power of God.' But the Jews pay him little heed. Now, the Galilean Zealots have an aspirant called Jesus Bar-Abbas, which means, 'Savior, Son of a Priest,' but there's a rabbi's son who went wrong! He lost his head and raised an insurrection near Jerusalem. He succeeded only in robbing and killing some defenseless Jews. Our Antonia cohort crushed that uprising in short order, and now Bar-Abbas and his gang are in prison awaiting your judgment."

"Did he have any support from the people?"

"No. The Jews knew he was the falsest of false Messiahs. He only wanted to turn a fast shekel by capitalizing on the popular mood."

"By the way, whatever became of that other Jesus who supposedly fed that crowd in Galilee but refused a crown?"

"He's a logical candidate for Messiah."

"What?"

"Don't misunderstand—Jesus doesn't seem to be after political power. You see, there are two schools of thought on the Messiah concept, my relatives told me. One believes that the Messiah will be a political monarch, a conquering king. The other insists he'll be a spiritual reformer who will rule as 'king' only over men's hearts and minds. Jesus seems more this type."

"Learn anything more about him in Jerusalem?"

"Quite a bit. Herod Antipas seemed to protect him for a while, but then he wanted to arrest him, so Jesus came down into your territory."

"Into Judea?"

"Yes, Prefect. And it's not the first time. He's been to several Passovers in Jerusalem. And last week I finally caught a glimpse of him myself on the terrace of the temple at the Feast of Dedication."

"What sort of man is he?"

"Flowing hair and beard. Kindly face. Clean clothes. But otherwise indistinguishable from anyone else in the city, except for one fact."

"What's that?"

"A crowd is always around him. Usually it's friendly, but sometimes not. When I saw him, some of his enemies were asking, 'How long will you keep us in suspense? If you are the Christ, tell us plainly.' Jesus replied, 'I told you, but you do not believe. The works which I do in my Father's name, they bear me witness'—I think that was it."

"So the man *does* give himself out as the Messiah!" Pilate's brow wrinkled with concern. "What did his interrogators say to that?"

"They picked up rocks and were going to stone him for blasphemy. But he escaped."

"What blasphemy?"

"His statement: 'works I do in *my Father's* name.' He made claim to a special kinship with the Jewish god."

The theological implications of such a claim were far beyond Pilate. He merely thought it interesting that the Jews apparently knew how to keep their visionary Messiahs in check. "Then this Jesus doesn't really have much of a following?"

"I didn't say that. After the attempted stoning, his crowds, if anything, were even larger . . . especially after that extraordinary event in Bethany. If I hadn't been in Jerusalem gathering information on the Sanhedrin, I might have seen it."

"What happened?"

"Jesus either raised a man from the dead, or performed

the most magnificent trick in the history of magic. The man's name was Lazarus, a friend of Jesus. He lived in Bethany with two unmarried sisters till he took sick and died. Jesus got there four days later and ordered the stone rolled away from the entrance to the tomb. One of the sisters protested that the smell of decay would be too strong, but Jesus shouted, 'Lazarus, come forth!' At the door of the sepulcher, a mummy-like figure appeared and then staggered out, tripping over the grave cloths which were binding his hands and feet. They unwrapped him. It was Lazarus, live and healthy."

"Nonsense."

"The news was all over Jerusalem that night—Bethany is only two miles away. I went there the next day and found the tomb open, but there was such a mass of people milling around the home of Lazarus that I didn't try to talk to him."

Pilate fretted, tapping his open palm with his other fist. "Fantastic," he said. "How do you suppose he brought it off?"

"How do you mean?"

"I mean, making it look as if he raised a man from the dead. You see, the story comes apart on the point that Lazarus was a friend of Jesus. Well, the two friends decided to stage something truly spectacular in order to convince the people once and for all."

"I don't know, Prefect. I just don't know. The doctors said the man was dead."

Pilate smiled.

What Cornelius could not have reported was a crucial meeting of the Sanhedrin, which convened on the day he returned to Caesarea. The Lazarus phenomenon had precipitated this extraordinary session, whose agenda had but one item: what action was to be taken regarding Jesus of Nazareth? If he were allowed to go on performing his signs, he would win over the entire population, they reasoned. "And then the Romans will come," warned an aged scribe, "and destroy our temple and our nation." A rising commotion followed this opinion.

Then the high priest Caiaphas raised his hands for silence. "Use your sanctified intellect, brethren," he said. "Is it not more expedient that *one man* die for the people, rather than the *entire nation* perishing? Our only problem is . . . how shall that man die?"

On or about February 22, A.D. 33, the Great Sanhedrin published the following notice for arrest and punishment. A court crier had to announce publicly or post such an official handbill in the major towns of Judea some forty days prior to a trial.

——— WANTED FOR ARREST: ———
Yeshu Hannosri or Jesus the Nazarene

He shall be stoned because he has practiced sorcery and enticed Israel to apostasy. Anyone who can say anything in his favor, let him come forward and plead on his behalf. Anyone who knows where he is, let him declare it to the Great Sanhedrin in Jerusalem.

Chapter 16

THIS WAS the year which would shift the course of human history and dislodge many strata in the world's culture, from its dating system at the surface to its religious and philosophical values at the depths. But no one could have guessed this during the early months of 33. No one could have known that for once Rome would not determine world events, or that Jerusalem would.

For Rome it was a year as dangerous as the last. Tiberius, suspicious as ever, requested a special bodyguard to attend him whenever he should finally visit the Senate. Sheeplike as ever, senators not only bleated their approval, but passed a law requiring that they be searched for concealed daggers at the door of the Senate whenever the emperor visited. Implicit was their promise that there would be no repetition of the Ides of March.

But Tiberius never returned to the capital. Once again he ventured to within four miles of it, spending some time in the suburbs, but suddenly he found an excuse to return to Capri. "Like an insect circling a candle," his critics said, "attracted to the light, but afraid of getting burned."

And the trials and executions continued, though the emperor now wanted an end to them. He took two drastic measures to stanch the blood. He issued orders that all persons in prison condemned for complicity with Sejanus should be killed. And so the hapless partisans were dispatched and their bodies pitched down the Stairs of Mourning into the Tiber. Then, with a certain grim but po-

191

etic justice, Tiberius had the bodies of some of the most notorious accusers who had disrupted the state thrown after them into the river.

The public applauded him for that final gesture, and his popularity slowly edged upward in other ways. He refused further honors from the toady Senate. And when an economic crisis that year threatened to plunge Rome into financial ruin, Tiberius shrewdly pumped money back into circulation by setting up a fund of 100,000,000 sesterces, from which debtors could borrow interest-free.

For a time, A.U.C. 786 would be known as the year of Rome's economic depression, but later ages would call it A.D. 33 because of what was happening that spring in Palestine. The prefect of Judea, of course, could hear nothing of any drum roll of destiny as he prepared to leave Caesarea for his appointment with history in Jerusalem. Plagued with the petty problems of government and living under imperial probation, Pilate paid scant attention to Jesus of Nazareth. If he worked his wonders like a good, orderly thaumaturge and did not preach rebellion, there would be no need to deal with him.

Pilate was a little nettled when the notice for the arrest of "Yeshu Hannosri" was posted in Caesarea, for it suggested that the Sanhedrin might be trying to reassert its ancient right to execute capital sentence by stoning. Cornelius pointed out that "stoning" did not necessarily mean "stoning to death," in Jewish custom, though this was the extreme to which it usually went. To clear the air, Pilate dispatched a note to Caiaphas which, without mentioning Jesus, warned him, in effect, "Try whom you wish, but remember that the *jus gladii* remains in the hands of the prefect of Judea."

The Passover that year would fall at the beginning of April, and Pilate planned, as usual, to spend several weeks in Jerusalem around the time of the festival. Because of the Messianic longings in the land, he gave serious thought to having a large contingent from the Italian Cohort accompany him, but then he dismissed the idea. Genuine Roman troops would have been introduced into the Holy City for the first time in thirty-seven years, and Jerusalemites would surely manage to find something dreadfully symbolic in that gesture. Better to take only the usual company of local auxiliaries, and rely on the Antonia cohort for security.

Procula wanted to make the trip also, but Pilate refused

to consider it. "Too risky," he warned. "The city is seething with unrest."

It took her several days of indirect persuasion, gentle coaxing, and even a tear or two to achieve what most wives accomplish in a far shorter time, changing a husband's "unalterable decision." But she dared not disclose her real motive in wishing to go along, for that would have ended the matter: Cornelius had told her that Jesus might attend the Passover in Jerusalem. The various reports about the Galilean prophet had at first only tickled her curiosity, but now she was intrigued by what the extraordinary man said and did. She had even thought of asking her husband for permission to go and hear the prophet, but his veto would have been so certain that she had not bothered. Yet her native religiosity kept feeding a blazing interest in the Galilean. Even if he did not show up in Jerusalem—he was, after all, a hunted man—she might at least interview those who had seen him.

Their journey to Jerusalem lagged behind schedule, because the roads were choked with crowds on their annual pilgrimage to the Holy City. But traffic was lighter on Saturday, when no pious Jew would break the Sabbath by traveling more than a half mile, so Pilate's entourage arrived almost as planned on the last Sunday in March.

Even now, as they approached the final rise of the northern road into Jerusalem, the highway was increasingly congested with pilgrims chanting psalms and singing the traditional Passover songs. Freight donkeys squealed, sacrificial sheep bleated an accompaniment of their own. Old people were being helped along by the young, children were getting lost, mothers were calling them, and men were swearing at recalcitrant burros or scampering to keep the sheep in line. A smell of dust and reeking animal dung hovered over the highway, broken only intermittently by gusts of wind from the west.

When they reached the summit of the last ridge and all Jerusalem lay before them, much of the caravan fell on its knees in tearful joy and prayer. Pilate and his retinue moved on through the worshipers toward the Water Gate. Great clusters of canvas suburbs ringed Jerusalem, a larger tent city than Pilate had seen at previous Passovers. Since the Jewish capital could not hope to house the hordes of pilgrims arriving for the festival, such hillside shelter was a necessity. Before the week was over, Jerusalem's population would temporarily increase by 250,000.

"A regular religious army," Pilate commented. "Imagine what would happen if each of them were armed. We wouldn't stand a chance." He had a magistrate's wariness of crowds, and certainly the experience to rue them.

Suddenly Procula tugged at his arm. "Look to the east, up the slopes of the Mount of Olives there. . . ."

Pilate squinted. Parallel bands of wriggling green were hovering over the heads of an enormous, oblong throng of people, split in two by a roadway. The crowd seemed to be waving branches of some kind, perhaps palm fronds. A tumultuous roar, muffled by the distance, welled up as a small knot of people came down the roadway.

"I can't make it out, Procula," he said. "Now if this were Greece, that would be a demonstration in honor of a returning Olympic victor. We'll find out when we get to Jerusalem; they seem to be heading toward the city."

It was not until evening that Pilate received a full briefing on the palm-waving phenomenon from the tribune at the Antonia. But the explanation hardly satisfied him, since it was so full of contradictions. Yes, the demonstration was in honor of a man, the prophet Jesus, who had evidently come out of hiding. Yes, the event might have serious political overtones. Many Jews thought their Messiah would be declared as king on that very Mount of Olives. The crowds had also shouted praises to "the son of David," a loaded name if Jesus should claim to be heir of King David in a restored Judean monarchy. Even the waving of palm branches could be symbolic, for the palm was the national emblem of Palestine. These were Jewish flags. . . . And of the extra quarter million people jamming Jerusalem, how many were members of the Zealot party from Galilee?

Yet others told him that Jesus was a nonpolitical person, the commandant continued, and that he was misunderstood by the swarms of pilgrims. Still others insisted that the people knew this and were only cheering on their favorite prophet. His vehicle was not a golden chariot but a jogging ass, certainly a poor prop for any kingmakers. And when he reached Jerusalem, Jesus made no incendiary speeches to the masses or flaunted pretensions of any kind. He simply walked over to the temple, enjoyed the view across the Kidron Valley, and then returned with his disciples to Bethany, for it was getting on toward suppertime.

Pilate was baffled by the significance of it all. The episode was either harmless or it was meaningful in the extreme. But the fate of the puzzling prophet would clearly depend on what he did or did not do from now on in the face of such enthusiastic support. If Jesus veered into politics, Rome would intrude, much as Pilate hated the thought of getting involved.

But then it occurred to him that even if the prophet remained strictly within a religious sphere, he would still be in trouble with Caiaphas and the Sanhedrin, who had posted the notices for his arrest throughout Judea. In that case, why hadn't the Jewish temple guard seized him during his afternoon visit to the temple?

In the Herodian palace that night, Pilate retired more bewildered than ever. But Procula barely concealed her satisfaction that Jesus had come to Jerusalem after all. At last she might have the chance to hear him, perhaps even meet him. Would he accept an invitation to have dinner with them in the Herodian palace, she wondered? After all, Roman governors were always giving dinners for famous people in their provinces. Maybe she could see with her own eyes whether or not he actually performed wonders. At least she could try to learn something about the secret power he had over people, whether it was in his personality or in his message. But the bubble of her idea burst on the thought that her husband was not about to entertain Messiahs of any kind.

On Monday, while reviewing the Jerusalem cohort at the Tower Antonia, Pilate warned his auxiliaries to be on especially good behavior during the coming week. He then went to the south wall of the city to inspect his beloved aqueduct. Due to heavy rainfall that spring, the water was gushing along better than ever.

Later in the day, he presided over a meeting of the chief regional tax collectors for Judea. He was in the process of assigning toparchial quotas for the annual tribute when little Zacchaeus, the diminutive superintendent of taxes for Jericho, announced, "Noble Prefect, in going over my accounts, I find that I made an error of 50,000 sesterces in last year's tribute."

"Zacchaeus," Pilate sniffed, "securing a tax rebate from the imperial treasury is impossible."

"No, no, Excellency. I *owe* the treasury 50,000 sesterces. And here they are." Zacchaeus' eyes were blazing happily.

Pilate's jaw sagged. "What's come over you, Zacchaeus? You usually battle me down to the last quadrans."

"Last Thursday, while I was up a tree in Jericho, the prophet—" He stopped abruptly, then laughed, "Oh . . . nothing, gentlemen. Now, Excellency, how much did you say poor Jericho will have to 'contribute' this year?"

That drew a general chuckle, since Jerichoans had the highest per-capita income of any purely Jewish city in Palestine.

When the fiscal conference adjourned, the tribune of Jerusalem arrived to report something he felt would be of interest to Pilate. "Just an hour ago it happened, Prefect. At the Antonia we heard a commotion in the temple area. I took a squad of men up to the outer courts, but by then it was too late."

"For what?"

"The prophet Jesus. He had a whip in his hands and was flailing away with it against the cattle and sheep merchants in the temple courtyard, who sell their animals for sacrifice. He drove them out—cattle, sheep, and all. You should have heard the bellowing and bleating. And cursing!"

While recounting the incident, the tribune's face broke into a low smile, which Pilate found a bit contagious. He asked, "Did Jesus give any explanation for this . . . unusual conduct?"

"He said, 'My Father's house is for *prayer*. You have made it a den of robbers!' Oh, but he was scowling furiously! Then he went after the dove dealers, and while they stood by gaping, he opened their cages and let all the pigeons fly away. And finally the money-changers. That was a scene! Jesus stormed into their stalls and pushed over the change tables, sending the coins clattering across the courtyard. Hah! You should have seen the bankers scramble!"

"Tell me more!" Pilate begged.

"He simply purged the place of commercialism. If you'll pardon my opinion, sir, I think he had the right idea. The temple was getting to look like a Persian market."

"I dare say, or a zoo. But Tribune, didn't you or your men try to interfere?"

The tribune winced a bit. "Well, no, sir. I didn't want to infringe on the authority of the temple guard."

"Why didn't they act?"

"They wouldn't have dared arrest Jesus at that time and place. He's too popular with the pilgrims."

"Suppose there were no crowds and no temple guard. Then would you have tried to stop the prophet?"

"I'd have been awfully slow about it."

"You're a good man, Tribune," Pilate clapped him on the shoulder. Then he grinned. "I just recalled that most of the concessions in the temple courts are owned by the family of Annas and Caiaphas. What I wouldn't give to have seen the looks on their faces when they learned the news!"

At supper that evening, Pilate rehearsed the incident for Procula's benefit, and they enjoyed a round of laughter. She intended to go to the temple the next morning in hope of seeing Jesus, but Pilate knew nothing of the plan. Nor would he have approved.

She succeeded in her mission the next day, for during that famous week, Jesus appeared at the temple on a daily basis to address the people. Insulated by a bevy of women attendants and several auxiliary guardsmen, Procula came within fifty feet of the young prophet, but was afraid to press forward to meet him. There were too many people, and she did not want to make a scene.

Pilate took the news of her reconnaissance at the temple with less displeasure than she had feared, because he was curious about what Jesus had to say.

"You should have heard the man, Pilate," she recounted. "He held the people spellbound. When he was finished speaking, some Pharisees shouldered their way to the front of the crowd and brought up something which you'll find rather interesting, I think. They asked him, 'Master, what is your opinion: is it lawful to pay the tribute money to Caesar or not?'"

Pilate's eyes widened with concern. "What did he say, Procula? Recall it excactly. I don't have to tell you that the fate of this Jesus may depend on how he answered that question."

"My girls gave me a running translation. He said, 'You hypocrites. Trying to trap me in my words, are you? Show me a piece of tribute money.' So they handed him a silver coin. He held it up and asked, 'Whose image is this, and whose inscription?' 'Caesar's,' they replied, and Jesus said, 'Then pay Caesar whatever is due Caesar, and pay God whatever is due God.'"

"Ingenious," Pilate admitted, "ingenious. Even Cicero would have been proud of that line."

"Then the Pharisees—"

"I mean, look how sharp were the horns of that dilemma. If he'd said it was wrong to pay the tribute, he'd have been a hero to the people, but I'd have had to arrest him for treason. If he'd simply answered that it was right to pay the tax, the crowds would have called him a Roman lackey."

"Anyway," continued Procula, "the Pharisees disappeared. Then one of the lawyers asked him, 'Rabbi, what is the greatest commandment in the Torah?' and one of my Jewish girls said it was an awful question. Their Law is supposed to be equally great in all its parts. But Jesus replied, 'Love God with all your heart, soul, and mind; and your neighbor as yourself.' There was dead silence until someone cried, 'Wise Rabbi, in *one sentence* you have summarized the whole Law!' Then the people actually cheered. Imagine, at the temple."

"How did this sit with the authorities?"

"How do you think? Then Jesus launched a bitter attack on them. 'Woe to you, scribes and Pharisees, hypocrites!' he said, several times. Once he called them 'blind fools.' Then, I think, 'a brood of vipers.' Even 'white-washed tombs,' nice outside, decaying inside."

"How could they take that kind of language?"

"The people . . . remember?"

"Yes. I see it now. That's why Caiaphas couldn't arrest this Jesus despite his notices—the people. But now what will he do?" He paused and then smiled, "Caiaphas had better not come to me for help. For once *he's* on the hook, while I can relax and watch him wriggle. . . . Yes," he murmured contentedly, "this is one Passover I think I'm going to enjoy."

On Wednesday, Pilate set up his court. The first two days in Jerusalem he had been imperial fiscal agent. For the rest of the week and part of the next he would be provincial judge. Appeals, capital cases, all local disputes between Jew and gentile, and any political offenses involving a threat to the Roman administration would come before his tribunal. Because Pilate's visits to Jerusalem were so infrequent, his docket was bulging.

Court was held in the main reception hall of the Herodian palace, now stripped of its golden shields, with Pilate sitting on a raised dais. Sennsion lasted from early in the morning until noon, and then, because there were so many cases, from two to four o'clock in the afternoon. In Rome, courts usually had large juries, but in provinces like Judea, the prefect constituted judge and jury. However, he had to conduct trials carefully, since law was a Roman specialty.

It was an exhausting day for Pilate, including two acquittals, one condemnation to imprisonment, and one capital sentence. In the last, the condemned was crucified before nightfall. Perhaps humanely, punishment, in Roman justice, was inflicted at once.

But these were merely routine cases. The more important trials would come in the following week, culminating in the case of Rome *vs.* Bar-Abbas. This was the major one, for which Pilate began preparing even now. Not that he had any doubt of Bar-Abbas' guilt, but this trial would far and away attract more of Jerusalem than any of the other cases. The man on the street had already tried the political brigand, and was speculating only on whether the governor might devise some unusual means of executing him. Pilate's problem would be to avoid that temptation, while showing Rome's wrath at murderous insurgents like Bar-Abbas. On that occasion too, Pilate sensed, he would be judged by a fellow judge. Herod Antipas had just arrived in Jerusalem for the Pesach, as the Jews called their Passover, and he would hardly miss the opportunity of evaluating Pilate's performance at the Bar-Abbas trial.

Late that night, Caiaphas' servant Malchus appeared at the palace to deliver this note:

Joseph Caiaphas, High Priest, to Pontius Pilatus, *praefectus Iudaeae,* Peace!

Were it not a matter of utmost urgency, involving the security of the state, I would not disturb you at this hour. Yeshu Hannosri, a deceiver and false prophet who has broken our Law on repeated occasions and whose heresy has been condemned by the Great Sanhedrin, is in Jerusalem for the Pesach. You must have noticed his great following, which could break out into seditious rioting at any moment. So dangerous is the situation that, although the Sanhedrin has issued warrants for his arrest, we have not dared apprehend him because of the people. Our decision now is to arrest

Yeshu at night, when he will not be surrounded by
supporters. A close adherent of his has defected and
will inform us of his nocturnal whereabouts so that
our temple guard may arrest him.

We respectfully request that a large contingent from
your Antonia garrison assist our guard. Of the vast
numbers of pilgrims camped on the hills surrounding
Jerusalem, how many are followers of Yeshu, who
would attack our police if they knew we had the deceiver in custody? If you are amenable, we can arrive
at a mutual strategy concerning time and place for the
arrest. The blessings of peace be yours.

Pilate hated to make decisions when he was sleepy and
preparing for bed. He resented the intrusion, but he had little choice in the matter. Gritting his jaw so that the muscles
bulged a bit below the ear lobes, he dictated a reply to an
aide, who handed it to Malchus:

Pontius Pilatus to Joseph Caiaphas, greeting.

I sympathize with your concern. We also have been
kept informed of Jesus the Nazarene over the past
months, and have been ready to arrest him if he
preached rebellion. Thus far, it appears, he has not.
He may well have offended you on religious grounds,
but I am hardly qualified to judge on that score.

Accordingly, I do not feel justified in committing
Roman auxiliaries to apprehend Jesus, even if the
temple guard would make the actual arrest. I feel certain that if your police proceed with any strength, they
will have no trouble arresting Jesus by night. Were
our troops to join yours, would this not advertise your
purpose to all the pilgrims? If your men are attacked,
our garrison will, of course, march to their immediate
assistance. Farewell.

There was an unexpressed reason for Pilate's refusing his
auxiliaries. Why should he, rather than Caiaphas, bear the
popular opprobrium for arresting a prophet? Certainly
the people would be inclined to blame Rome, rather than
their own countrymen in the temple guard. He would not
make Antipas' mistake and cut down a Jewish prophet,
especially not in his present, probationary status. In fact, it
looked as if Caiaphas also disdained the role of prophet-
killer, and was trying to wrap himself in a Roman mantle
for the distasteful task.

At that moment, the high priest was meeting with his father-in-law Annas and the inner council of the Sanhedrin at his mansion, not far from the Herodian palace in that part of Jerusalem called the Upper City. The Sanhedrists were unanimously in favor of arresting Jesus, but divided on whether the arrest should take place before or after the Passover. Those who favored delay argued that there would hardly be enough time for trial and punishment before the Pesach, and no prosecution was possible once the feast got underway. Better to wait until the close of Passover week and the departure of the pilgrims—then apprehend the man.

"But what if Yeshu leaves then also, surrounded by his followers?" Caiaphas asked.

"What may sooner happen is this," Annas interposed. "The deceiver will use the Pesach as the time to raise his followers against us. You know what he said and did at the temple! Therefore we must strike at once."

This opinion carried. They would now alert all members of the Sanhedrin to be available at a moment's notice. The temple police were to arrest Jesus when this could be done *conveniently*. It would have to be at night, when he was away from the crowds. It would have to be in or near Jerusalem, for if the guard were sent as far as his lodging place at Bethany, the thousands of tenters on the eastern hillsides might get word of his arrest and raise a riot.

To fulfill all these conditions required the services of an insider who could alert them when Jesus was in such a vulnerable position. They found such a man, or rather, he had found them.

"His name," said Caiaphas, "is Judas Ish-Kerioth, a mercenary sort, willing to sell out his teacher for thirty denarii. But there may be more to it. You see, he's the only *non*-Galilean among Yeshu's disciples. Probably he realized his heretical allegiance and wanted to relieve his guilt by coming to us. He said he'd try to get their plans for tomorrow night."

"How difficult do you suppose it will be to deal with Pilate?" Annas asked.

They had the answer when Malchus arrived with Pilate's reply. Caiaphas read it aloud, then commented, "He won't commit his auxiliaries, but he suggested that our temple guard should have no trouble making the arrest. Reading between his lines, I think we get the following message: 'This is your affair. Rome won't interfere.' "

Thursday was equally crowded for Pilate. Again his tribunal was besieged with cases, but fewer people than usual attended court as observers, since the day of preparation for the Passover began that sundown. Others, including many Galileans, would eat the Pesach meal that evening, for there was a divergent calculation among the Jews as to whether the week of Passover celebration began then or the following day. The majority, with the priestly establishment of Jerusalem, would begin celebrating at sundown Friday.

Pilate's docket fell behind schedule, so again he resorted to an afternoon session of his court. The two most serious cases of the day were now introduced, a pair of highwaymen who had assaulted and robbed a small group of Passover pilgrims trudging up the desolate Jericho-Jerusalem road on their way to the Holy City. The brigands encountered resistance and killed several of the party before despoiling them, but their luck failed them almost immediately. A patrol of Roman troops from the Jericho garrison, guided by surviving pilgrims, flushed them out of the hills and sent them, shackled, to Jerusalem.

In Roman law, prosecutors were private, not governmental, individuals, so Pilate opened the trial by calling on three women of the assaulted party to act as plaintiffs. Tears and hatred in their eyes, they pointed accusing fingers at the two highwaymen and charged them with robbery and murder. Witnesses, including other pilgrims in the party, as well as several auxiliaries from the Roman patrol, then gave evidence for the prosecution.

The defense in the case was very weak. The bandits had no attorney and tried to defend themselves. They supplied a witness who claimed they were in Jerusalem at the time of the felony, but the alibi fell apart when written evidence was introduced into the trial. The Jericho patrol had extracted signed confessions from the two just after capture.

Both sides now presented summations, the Roman patrol captain prompting the women on what to say, while the brigands threw themselves on the mercy of the court. Finally, it was time for sentencing or acquittal.

But the proof of guilt was conclusive. The only complication in what would otherwise have been a simple case was the problem of sentence and execution. It was too late in the day for crucifixion, and yet punishment had to follow immediately upon sentencing. Pilate solved the matter by announcing, "Judgment and sentence will be suspended until tomorrow morning. This court is adjourned."

At the temple, a priest who had been carefully scanning the darkening heavens shouted that he could see three stars overhead. Answering trumpets shattered the hush of evening. For the Jews, a new day, Friday, Nisan 14, had begun, since they reckoned from sundown to sundown. Pilate heard the trumpet flourish while dining with Procula. For them it was still Thursday, April 2, since Romans counted from midnight to midnight.

In a borrowed upper room a few blocks directly south of the Herodian palace, a group of thirteen men were eating an early Passover Seder of unleavened bread, greens, bitter herbs, meat, and wine. It represented the diet of the Israelites on the night before their hurried exodus from Egypt some 1300 years earlier. Yet this meal had a different ending. The controversial teacher from Galilee distributed bread and wine around the table and then, strangely, called it his body and blood.

But the thirteen diners now dwindled to twelve. It seems that one of them, Judas Ish-Kerioth, had pressing business elsewhere.

Chapter 17

THERE WAS an urgent rapping at the door of the high priest's palace. Malchus opened it and brought Judas in to join Caiaphas and the leading Sanhedrists he was hosting at dinner. Judas was a swarthy, somewhat obsequious Judean of slender build.

"Most Noble Excellency," Judas bowed to the high priest, "they are planning to go to Oil-Press Garden across the Kidron after their Seder this evening. Soon now, I think. I just left their table."

"Yeshu, and the eleven others? Anyone else?" Caiaphas inquired, a touch of excitement in his manner.

"No."

"You're quite certain none of his other followers will be there?"

"Yes. Yeshu said he wanted solitude for meditation. And they're fond of the grove anyway, always going there by themselves."

"Are they armed?"

"Only two of them have swords, Peter and James."

"How far along was their Seder when you left them?"

"Nearly finished."

Caiaphas thought for a moment, then said, "The Lord has shown us that tonight must be the night, my colleagues, for it's also our last chance to arrest Yeshu before the Pesach."

"Wait . . . a word, Caiaphas," said Rabbi Ananias. "It will be very dark out there. How can we be sure to arrest the right man? It would be chaos if a mistake were made and Yeshu slipped away."

"If you will permit, Excellency," said Judas, "I will identify Yeshu by giving him a kiss of salutation."

"Agreed. Malchus, tell the captain of the temple police to await us with his entire corps fully armed. And see that the members of the Sanhedrin are alerted."

"He'll be brought to my place first?" Annas inquired.

"Yes, Father."

Several hundred men, clutching swords, cudgels, and torches, filed out of the temple precincts, crossed the Kidron Valley, and quickly cordoned off the grove beyond. Judas led the officers and chief priests up to a small knot of people in the shadows of the garden. Singling out one figure whose perspiration gleamed in the moonlight, he kissed him.

"Whom do you seek?" said Jesus.

"Yeshu Hannosri," an officer answered.

"I am he. But do you take me for a bandit, that you have to use swords and staves to arrest me? Day after day I taught in the temple, yet you did not seize me there. But let the Scriptures be fulfilled."

Few arrests were made so easily. With a servant's eagerness to please his master, Malchus was the first to reach out and grab Jesus. That was too much for one of his followers, a burly fisherman who pulled out his sword and slashed through Malchus' right ear.

Jesus intervened with a quick command. "Sheathe your weapon, Peter! All who take the sword die by the sword." Sheepishly, Peter wiped the blade clean and shoved it back into his scabbard.

The other disciples looked terrified, cringing in a huddle of horror at the edge of the grove. Jesus saw it and said, "If I am the man you want, let these others go." They ran away and lost themselves in the darkness among the olive trees. Jesus was bound and led back to Jerusalem.

When the posse returned, Caiaphas learned the details of the arrest from Malchus, who was still clutching the right side of his head in bewilderment.

"Splendid work, Malchus!" the high priest commended. "Oh . . . I'm sorry about the ear, but we'll need you at the trial as evidence that they were armed and gave resistance. Now go and see the doctor."

Still dazed and in semishock, Malchus slowly removed his hand and showed Caiaphas a normal right ear, attached where it should be. "Yeshu," he said, "picked it up . . . put it back . . . healed—"

"Fool!" Caiaphas slapped him. "We have no time for your idle lies. Get hold of yourself! Now take this over to the Herodian palace." He thrust a note into the servant's hand and sent him out, muttering, "A little excitement and the knave hallucinates."

Pilate and Procula were preparing for bed when Malchus arrived with this message:

> Joseph Caiaphas to Pontius Pilatus, Peace. Our guard have arrested Yeshu Hannosri near the Kidron Valley. There was little resistance. But we urge you to keep the Antonia cohort on full alert from now until this case is concluded. Rioting may break out when the news reaches the people tomorrow. Yeshu will, of course, receive a fair trial by the Great Sanhedrin. Peace.

"What does it say, Pilate?" asked Procula.

He handed her the note, then watched her face for the reaction which came almost with the first line, a flash of concern, nearly a sad frown.

"A fair trial," she said. "Do you think there's any chance he'll get a fair trial?"

"Perhaps. After all, they're only trying to head off a possible rebellion and preserve the peace. They *could* be after the death penalty, though Caiaphas would probably have told me if that were the case. What they may do is imprison Jesus as an object lesson, or humiliate him in some way which will compromise him with his following. Anyway, his support will melt away from Jerusalem after the Passover."

With that, Pilate dispatched orders to the Antonia commandant: "Put your men on full alert, in shifts, until further notice."

Meanwhile, Jesus was taken to the house of Annas for a hearing prior to formal arraignment before his son-in-law Caiaphas. For several moments the white-haired priestly patriarch stared at the prisoner. "Are you Yeshu Hannosri?" he finally asked.

Jesus nodded.

"So you're the man tongues are wagging about from here to Galilee. What is it, then, Yeshu? Why are you so bitter at our leadership here in Jerusalem? You've said and done some fearful things in the temple . . . and elsewhere."

Jesus made no comment.

Annas continued, "How big is your movement? Who are your chief supporters? What is your doctrine, your message? What are you telling the people?"

But Jesus, knowing that his appearance before Annas was simply a lower-court hearing before the inevitable confrontation with Caiaphas, blunted the interrogation: "My teachings are a matter of public record. I taught openly in the synagogue and in the temple. Ask the people what I said."

One of the temple police thought his attitude impertinent and struck him on the cheek, snarling, "Is that the way you answer a former high priest?"

Jesus turned to him and said, "If I spoke wrongly, produce the evidence. But if correctly, why do you strike me?"

Annas glowered and said, "If the accused will not cooperate, this hearing is ended. Guards, bind the prisoner and take him to the high priest."

Members of the Great Sanhedrin were gathering at the palace of Caiaphas for an extraordinary night session. With the gates of the temple mount locked at night, they could not meet in their regular chamber. All seventy Jewish senators now took their places in a semicircle which fanned out around Caiaphas, the president of the Sanhedrin, and two clerks of the court. The great hall of Caiaphas' palace was bathed in the rosy amber glow of flickering torches. The place smelled resinous and smoky.

Excited crosscurrents of conversation hushed when Jesus was led into the hall and directed to stand in front of Caiaphas. The prisoner glanced up at the rising tiers of benches arced about him and felt the stare of 140 eyes. Witnesses and some of the public which had been attracted to the trial crowded into the hall behind him.

Caiaphas, clad in his official garments, called the Sanhedrin to order and opened the case by soliciting witnesses who had any evidence to bring against Jesus. In Jewish law, a minimum of two witnesses was necessary to support a given charge or it would have to be quashed.

A dozen or more elbowed their way to the front and were formally interrogated by Ananias, who was known for his skill in crossexamination. Most of the witnesses reported isolated acts in which Jesus had apparently violated the Sabbath, but each told of a different occasion, no two the same, so their otherwise damaging evidence had to be disallowed.

Caiaphas called for more witnesses, and more struggled through the press to the front of the court. Some of these were riffraff from the streets who wanted to have a part in this great hour, but they were expelled after their false testimony proved ridiculous. Other witnesses agreed on technically incriminating evidence, but Ananias hesitated to admit it when it dealt with a kindly or serviceable action of Jesus such as healing on the Sabbath day, for example. Even the learned rabbis disagreed on that, though it was firm tradition that medical help was allowed only if life itself were in danger. A mere broken leg, for example, could not be set on the Sabbath.

Further evidence was offered, but even statements about the same incident did not tally. Finally Ananias thought he could derive a solid charge from the allegations of two men who agreed that Jesus had said, "I will destroy this temple, and rebuild it in three days." Since any threat against the temple was capital blasphemy, this charge alone, if proved, could result in the death sentence, and Ananias pursued it like a hawk.

Then someone from the crowd shouted, "Yeshu meant the 'temple' of his body, not the great temple." A loud murmuring developed, and Caiaphas called for order. Then, fixing a piercing glare at the defendant, he asked, "Have *you* no answer to the charges these witnesses bring against you?"

Jesus did not reply. Legally, he did not have to, since no proven evidence had been introduced into the proceedings. Caiaphas knew it. For the last minutes he had been deploring the situation which had brought him to this legal impasse. Because of the inordinate haste in this trial, they had neglected to weed out the false witnesses and secure those with truly incriminating evidence. It was a wretched oversight on his part. In an agony of frustration, he realized that the goal to which he had been pressing over the past months might now elude him. For unless a proven charge were introduced, the prosecution would collapse and the Sanhedrin would be legally bound to declare Jesus innocent and free him. That would render him more popular than ever with the people, while disastrously embarrassing the religious establishment in Jerusalem.

All eyes in the hall were fastened on Caiaphas. As a "Caiaphas" (meaning inquisitor), he was belying his name. Perspiring profusely, he groped for fundamentals. What evidence did *he* have. . . . Why did *he* despise Yeshu Hannosri? Four reasons: 1) he was a lawbreaking false prophet, who deceived the people with dangerous doctrines; 2) he attacked the Jewish authorities abusively; 3) he was probably planning sedition, which would lead to Roman intervention; and 4) he did not repudiate Messianic claims. Alas, without proper witnesses, no case could be constructed on the first three charges. . . . But the fourth! No witnesses? Why not create seventy of them!

Caiaphas stood up from his judiciary seat and walked over to the prisoner. The other members of the Sanhedrin also rose to their feet, for custom demanded this honor for the president. "You will not answer these charges?" the high priest asked. "Then perhaps you will respond to this: I adjure you by the Living God to tell us. . . . *Are you the Messiah? Are you the Son of God?*"

Caiaphas had prefaced the question with the dreaded Oath of the Covenant. Once it had been spoken, even a reply of silence would be criminal, while a false answer would be damnable. But the question need not have been charged with this explosive, for the mysterious time to which Jesus had repeatedly referred in his public ministry when he said, "My hour has not yet come," had now come in fact.

"*Are* you the Son of God?" Caiaphas repeated.

His gaze penetrating to the very soul of the high priest, Jesus replied, "*I am* . . . as you have said. And you will see the Son of Man sitting at the right hand of the power of God."

There it was, an answer complete and categorical. Caiaphas tore his priestly garment in fury. Straining to be heard above the great commotion, he cried, "*Blasphemy!* Do we need any further witnesses? You've heard his blasphemy. *You* are now the witnesses! What is your judgment?"

Each member of the Sanhedrin would now have to decide whether Jesus' statement was sober truth, or the worst blasphemy a Jew could frame with his mouth. Caiaphas had just said it was the latter, virtually a directed verdict of capital blasphemy, but the Sanhedrists might think differently.

All attention now focused on the youngest of the seventy members of the Sanhedrin, who were sitting at the edge of the semicircle, for, in standard procedure, the voting would begin with him and end with the eldest member, the president casting the final vote. The youthful Sanhedrist stood up in the hushed chamber and said, "He is worthy of death."

A chorus of whispering erupted. The next member got up and said the same. Commotion in the hall rose steadily as the tally continued, "Guilty." "Death."

A look of satisfaction softened the features of Joseph Caiaphas, and when thirty-seven condemnations were recorded, he had triumphed. Only a simple majority of two votes was necessary for a sentence of condemnation. Nevertheless, all seventy would be polled.

When the clerk read the name Joseph of Arimathea, a richly clad man of medium build stood up and said, "I abstain." There was a brief hubbub in the chamber and Caiaphas glared at Joseph, but then the voting continued.

One more abstention from a man called Nicodemus caused a flurry, but finally Caiaphas cast his concluding vote and announced, "Bretheren, there are 69 votes for condemnation and 2 abstentions. Yeshu Hannosri is herewith sentenced to death."

The hall broke into a great commotion of shouts and applause as the Sanhedrin adjourned. Temple police now grabbed Jesus and hauled him into the courtyard, where they beat and abused him, standard procedure for one condemned. Several spit in his face, while others blindfolded him and taunted, "Now prophesy for us, you Messiah, who just slapped you?"

One glaring difficulty remained. The trial was illegal, according to Jewish law, since only cases involving monetary matters were heard after sunset. Capital trials could take place only in the daytime. That technicality was removed shortly after dawn the next day, when Jesus was brought before an official session of the Great Sanhedrin, which convened on the temple mount. After bare formalities, Caiaphas again requested a verdict from members of the Sanhedrin. Once more the court clerk read off each name, beginning with the youngest. Each, in turn, arose and replied, "Death," until, except for the same two abstentions, another unanimous decision was reached.

A final complication was simply disregarded. To avoid hasty convictions, Jewish law stated that a capital sentence could not be pronounced until the day following a trial. Therefore a Friday trial which ended in condemnation was illegal, since it would be followed by the Sabbath, when sentencing or execution were impossible. The only verdict permitted a court on Friday, if it took formal action, was acquittal. But in this emergency, the Sanhedrin did not feel bound by such a restriction.

If Judea were not a Roman province, Jesus would now have been executed by stoning, probably below the east wall of Jerusalem. On the way there, a herald would have preceded the execution detail, calling:

> Yeshu Hannosri, son of Mary of Nazareth, is going forth to be stoned because he has uttered blasphemy and is a false prophet and deceiver. Members of the Sanhedrin are witnesses against him. If anyone knows anything in favor of his acquittal, let him come and plead it.

About ten cubits from the place of execution they would say, "Make your confession."

"May my death be an atonement for all my sins," would have been a standard response, though Jesus would not have made it.

At the place of stoning, his clothes would have been stripped off. Then one of the Sanhedrists, as witness to his "blasphemy," would have shoved him off a precipice onto the rocks below. If he were still alive, a second member of the Sanhedrin would have dropped a boulder onto his heart. If he still survived, the entire Sanhedrin and any others present would have been obliged to hurl stones down on him until he died.

However, with the *jus gladii* now reserved for the Roman prefect, Pilate would have to review the Sanhedrin's verdict, pronounce sentence, and issue orders for execution—or dismiss the case. Had he been in Caesarea and the Antonia commandant otherwise occupied, the Sanhedral authorities might have risked taking matters into their own hands and stoning Jesus anyway, claiming mob action. But Pilate was very much present in the Holy City of Jerusalem.

Chapter 18

IT WAS six o'clock in the morning of Friday, April 3, A.D. 33—to Jews, Nisan 14, of the year 3793. In the sumptuous royal bedroom of the Herodian palace, Procula was sleeping later than usual. Her husband glanced at the tousle of hair spilling over the pretty face on the pillow next to him and did not disturb her as he pulled himself out of bed. He needed an early start for the docket of cases awaiting him at the tribunal.

Pilate looked out over Jerusalem on that crisp spring morning. The sun was starting to daub a hazy luminescence on the mists hovering over the summit of the Mount of Olives. Soon it would be unseasonably warm. He gave orders to have his official dais set up in the inner shaded courtyard of the palace, as on the previous morning. It would be transferred to the front of the palace in the afternoon when he no longer had to face the sun.

After a quick breakfast, Pilate mounted his tribunal and glanced at the small knots of people before him who would play some role in the day's litigation. He now called for unfinished business from yesterday. The two highwaymen whose sentencing had been postponed were brought before him.

"I judge you guilty," Pilate told them. "The sentence, in both cases, is death." The men did not flinch. The extreme penalty was standard punishment in that era for offenses less than theirs, and they fully expected it. *"Staurotheto kai staurotheto,"* Pilate called to his guards while nodding at

212

the two culprits, "Let him be crucified, and let him be crucified." And the pair were prepared for that dreaded punishment, the regular Roman method of execution for slaves and criminals who did not possess Roman citizenship.

While this case was concluding, a rather remarkable procession of priests, temple guardsmen, scribes, and a great crowd of people were filing into the esplanade before the palace. In the interior courtyard, a man came running up to the tribunal. Angrily, Pilate asked him, "What do you mean by this interruption, Malchus?"

"Forgive this intrusion, Excellency. My Lord Caiaphas and the entire Sanhedrin are outside to ask your confirmation of their verdict against Yeshu Hannosri."

"Do you mean they've already tried him?" snapped Pilate.

"Yes," replied Malchus, with a slight frown.

"But there hasn't been enough time. . . ."

"Hardly enough, though two sessions of the Sanhedrin have been held since the arrest."

"What was their verdict?"

"Guilty."

"The punishment?"

"They seek the death penalty."

"Death?"

"Yes. Otherwise they would not have brought the prisoner here."

A centurion broke into their conversation. "Pardon, my Prefect, but you should know that a huge crowd is gathering in front of the palace. Shall I send to the Antonia for reinforcements?"

"Yes, but keep them out of sight." Then, turning back to Malchus, he said, "This is extraordinary. The high priest should not have dared to interrupt my tribunal in this manner." Pilate thought seriously of making the Sanhedrin wait its turn for a hearing, perhaps until after the Bar-Abbas trial the following week. But, sobered by past confrontations with the Jews and with another eye to the throng which was gathering for obviously this case, he thought better of the plan.

"My Lord Caiaphas told me to express his profound regret for this interruption," Malchus continued, "but he said you would understand the danger of serious rioting if this matter were not adjudicated promptly. He also stated that the Sanhedrin does not expect you to interrupt your schedule with a trial at this time—the trial has already taken place—they merely request a simple confirmation of their sentence, which should not take long."

Pilate was angry. "Let them come in, then," he said quietly.

"Unfortunately, Sire, they must remain outside the *praetorium* to avoid defilement, so that they can eat the Passover Seder tonight."

Struggling to control his fury, Pilate waved Malchus away. Then he ordered his ivory *sella curulis,* the magistrate's chair, moved outdoors to the regular afternoon location facing the esplanade. The transfer made, he emerged from the palace to face the multitude, ascending his elevated tribunal.

Pilate sat down in his curule chair, grasping the arms of it with a grip which whitened his knuckles. For some moments he pondered the issue. . . . How the Sanhedrin could have given the complex case of Jesus a fair hearing in the brief interval since Pilate received the note which promised it, he could not fathom. . . . And the death penalty? While not surprising, in view of the hatred between the Jewish authorities and Jesus, it was at least inexpedient, considering Caiaphas' concern about a riot erupting. Kill the prophet and disorder *would* break out. . . . Then, without advance word, to confront him like this. . . . And finally the implication: "Don't bother judging him, Pilate. You wouldn't be qualified. This is a religious case. Just countersign our order for execution, like a good prefect."

"But I *will,*" he decided. "I will judge this case. And thoroughly."

He looked down from his dais. Jesus was stationed directly in front of the tribunal, with members of the Sanhedrin flanking him on both sides. Ranging off to Pilate's right were the familiar faces of Annas, Caiaphas, Ananias, Zadok, Helcias, Eleazar, and Jonathan. He guessed that they would constitute the chief accusers if, as they thought unlikely, it came to a formal trial; for without accusers, there could be no trial in Roman law. Behind Jesus stood the leading Pharisees, Sadducees, scribes, elders, and the temple guard. Beyond the semicircle of these principals, some 200 in number, ranged the vast and growing mass of spectators.

But only one face in this rising lake of humanity intrigued Pilate. He scrutinized the figure immediately in front of him and was a trifle disappointed. In the past months he had heard so many reports about the mysterious powers of Jesus that the man was becoming larger than life in his imagination, and yet here he was, bound, unkempt, evidently powerless. His dark hair, parted roughly in the middle, fell to shoulder length. This, along with his mustache and beard marked him as a typical Palestinian Jew of the time. Still, the erect and tallish figure seemed to speak eloquently through his eyes. They were tired, but they were not the eyes of a prisoner—not imploring, fearful, or ashamed; nor were they vindictive or threatening. Pilate had seen all these eyes in prisoners whom he had condemned. Those of Jesus registered only serenity, with a trace of disappointment and resignation.

By this time the crowd had hushed to hear the governor's first statement. Turning to the chief priests on his right, he asked, in common Hellenistic Greek, "What charge do you bring against this man?"

The Jewish leaders were thunderstruck, for this was the opening formula of a Roman trial, the *interrogatio*. Pilate was not going to endorse the action of the Sanhedrin; instead, he was reopening the case and beginning his own hearing!

"If he were not a criminal, we would not have brought him before you," replied Ananias defiantly, caught off guard by this turn of events.

Stung by this insolent reply, Pilate retorted, "Very well, then, take him out of this court and judge him according to your own law."

"That is not possible according to your law," said Caiaphas, speaking for the first time. "We are not allowed to put anyone to death."

A trace of a smile warped Pilate's lips. Were it not for the mass of observers and his own problems in Rome, he would have ended the hearing then and there.

Again he asked, "What charge do you bring against this man?"

This time several of the chief priests prepared to act as the principal *accusatores* or prosecutors. They presented a formal bill of indictment, which opened the case against Jesus: "We found this man subverting our nation, forbidding the payment of tribute money to Tiberius Caesar, and claiming that he is Messiah, a king."

It was a triple accusation, magnificently tailored to alarm

a Roman prefect, since the charges were thoroughly political. Of the religious grounds on which Jesus had been condemned by the Sanhedrin there was not a word, since the Judean authorities knew that Pilate would not likely put a man to death for the purely theological offense of blasphemy.

Touching the tips of his fingers together, Pilate paused to review the charges. The first, that Jesus was an instigator of sedition, a resistance leader, was very serious. According to a Roman legal compendium, those who caused sedition or incited the populace were liable to crucifixion or were "thrown to the beasts, or deported to an island." But the subversion charge would have to be proven, since, from all reports, Jesus seemed to shy away from political involvement.

The second accusation, that he opposed payment of the tribute, Pilate knew to be a lie, but he checked himself from flinging it back at the prosecutors. They might have used the charge in good faith from garbled reports, although their attitude seemed hypocritical. Many of these plaintiffs, especially the Pharisees, spent their days protesting payment of the Roman tribute, yet here they were patriotically defending it.

But the third indictment, that Jesus was giving himself out as "Messiah, a king," was the gravest. Depending on the nature of that kingship, the claim could be construed as *maiestas,* high treason, the most heinous crime known in Roman law. The weary succession of trials in Rome after the Sejanian conspiracy had all been prosecuted under the rubric of *maiestas.* With Tiberius as emperor, here was a provincial allegedly daring to call himself king. It could be harmless, perhaps a delusion of grandeur. But it could also be deadly treason.

Since no one seemed ready to defend Jesus, Pilate thought it fair to give him a brief, confidential hearing before proceeding with the trial in order to learn something more about the defendant away from the glare of his accusers. He stepped back into the palace, summoning Jesus inside the reception hall.

"*Are* you the king of the Jews?" asked Pilate. "How do you plead?"

Jesus looked up at him. "Do you ask this of your own accord, or did others tell it to you concerning me?"

"What! Am I a Jew? Your own nation and the chief priests have brought you before me. What have you done?"

"My kingship is not of this world. If it were, my followers would fight to defend me. But my authority as king comes from elsewhere."

"So? You *are* a king, then?"

"It is as you say, that I am a king. For this I was born, and for this I have come into the world: to bear witness to the truth. Everyone who is of the truth hears my voice."

"A kingship of *truth,* you say?" Pilate asked quizzically. "What *is* truth?"

What was truth indeed, Pilate reflected. As a child he had believed in the mythological gods and goddesses, only to repudiate them as a thinking adult. Truth used to be the word of Sejanus, yet Sejanus was a liar. Once he could swear by the nobility of Rome, but that city murdered innocent children and flung them into the Tiber. Truth was the Roman state, yet now the Senate itself could not trust the princeps, nor he the Senate.

The private hearing, however, convinced Pilate that Jesus' claims for kingship, his visionary "kingship of truth," had no political implications, so it would hardly be possible to construct a case of *maiestas* against him. But he might do well to avoid using the dangerous term king in the future.

Pilate led Jesus back to his outdoor tribunal and announced, "I find no guilt in him." Ordinarily, this would have signified a quashing of the major indictments, if not of the entire case itself. In Pilate's now-tenuous status in Judea, however, it was more a way to test the prosecution, which was already greeting Pilate's statement with loud murmuring.

"I find no case against Jesus thus far," Pilate repeated. "What evidence do you have to substantiate your charges?"

Annas bent over to whisper something to Caiaphas, who then relayed the information to Ananias. After a quick review of strategy by the principal *accusatores*, they now summoned witnesses by name, some of them Sanhedrists, to lend stature to their testimony. In ranks of two or three at a time, they supplied their evidence to Pilate, for Roman law also required plural witnesses. A scribe in a conical hat told of hearing Jesus attack the Jerusalem authorities on three different occasions and inciting the masses thereby. A gray-bearded priest spoke eloquently of his violence at the temple. An elder member of the Sanhedrin, his story well-corroborated by colleagues, reported Jesus' claim to be Messiah-king in front of the entire Sanhedrin.

Clearly, the prosecution was better organized than at the Sanhedral hearing. Caiaphas had chosen his witnesses well. But a certain, seemingly contrived sameness in the evidence Pilate found less than convincing, while such other items as Jesus' supposed opposition to the tribute he knew to be false.

After providing testimony on the principal charges, the plaintiffs now introduced additional subsidiary accusations against the defendant, indicting him also for magic and sorcery. In planning his confrontation with Pilate, what had worried Caiaphas most, if it came to a trial, was how to neutralize the testimony of witnesses for the defense, if any dared show themselves, since their evidence would largely concern good deeds, healings, and other apparent miracles wrought by the accused. He now shrewdly forestalled such testimony by producing his own witnesses to these spectacular deeds, who explained them as products of the black arts. Sorcery was also punishable under Roman law.

When the prosecution rested its case, Pilate turned to Jesus, who had remained silent the whole time, and asked, "Have you *nothing* to say in your defense? Don't you hear all this evidence against you?"

But Jesus remained silent. He supplied no defense, not even to a single charge. Pilate was astonished at this conduct. In his seven years on the provincial bench, this had never happened. Innocent defendants at his bar usually could hardly wait to launch their counterattacks on the prosecution, and even the obviously guilty at least pleaded some mitigating circumstance and sought leniency. But Jesus was making no defense. And no advocate was pleading in his behalf.

Pilate addressed the crowd, "Can anyone offer evidence favoring the defendant, Jesus?" A buzzing developed throughout the palace esplanade, which by now had filled with people.

"Louder, Prefect!' someone yelled.

"I said, can anyone offer testimony in defense of Jesus of Nazareth?"

Some hands, it seems, were waved at the edge of the crowd, while others were trying to make their way toward the tribunal in response to Pilate's invitation. But so many in the multitude supported the prosecution that the few who seemed to venture forward were being jostled or blocked. Whenever a lone voice protested, "He is innocent!" a great chorus responded with the antiphon, "He is guilty!"

This was enough to steer Pilate's sympathy toward the defenseless accused, though he was growing impatient with Jesus for refusing to say a word. Once more he called out, "Will anyone testify in behalf of Jesus?" The only reply was more growling from the mass assembly and several violent fist fights at the periphery. The mood was getting ugly.

"You see, Prefect, Yeshu Hannosri means trouble wherever he goes, even here at your tribunal," Rabbi Jonathan argued. "The man is a born troublemaker. You know of the riot he caused in the temple just this past Monday: illegally, without any authority whatever, interrupting people at their worship by driving away their sacrifices! And in overturning the exchange tables with great financial loss to the temple, Yeshu is, in effect, a temple robber. . . . Now, you may not feel concerned over what takes place inside our sanctuary, but this firebrand may one day upset your provincial finances in the same way. We've already cited his attitude toward the Roman tribute. But did you know that he lured a tax collector away from his profession? He's now one of his disciples, a man named Matthew. Yet financial harm is as nothing compared to Yeshu's role as political agitator. His teachings are inflaming the people through-throughout all Judea, starting from Galilee and spreading even as far as this city."

Something in Jonathan's summation caught Pilate's attention. "Wait, Rabbi, did you say that Jesus began teaching in Galilee?"

"Yes. . . ."

"What's his home town?"

"He came from Nazareth, of course, but lately, I understand, he was lodging at Kephar Nahum."

"Where?"

"A town on the Sea of Tiberias. You probably know it as Capernaum."

"Both places are in Galilee. Are they not?"

"Yes. . . ."

Pilate thought for several moments, then said, "The defendant, thus, is clearly a Galilean, and, as such, under the authority of the tetrarch Herod Antipas." Pilate's eyes brightened as he spoke. "And since Herod is in Jerusalem at this very moment, I think it eminently proper to remand this case to his jurisdiction."

"But Prefect, surely this isn't necessary," Caiaphas objected. "The crimes committed by Yeshu Hannosri took place also in Judea. You would certainly have the legal right—"

"Thank you, noble Pontiff, but I need not be schooled on points of Roman law. Yes, I would have the legal prerogative to try this man in Judea as the *forum delicti* of his alleged crimes, the place of the offense. But yes, I also have the option of remanding this case to the jurisdiction of the sovereign of the accused, since Galilee is his *forum domicilii*, the place of residence. And I believe it most appropriate to bind the defendant over to his own tetrarch, particularly because your charges have religious implications within Jewish law which Herod Antipas could adjudicate far better than I."

Caiaphas and Annas went into brief consultation with Helcias and other chief Sanhedrists, after which Ananias said, "Very well, Prefect, we shall accept adjudication by Herod the Tetrarch, if he is willing."

Pilate then announced officially, "This court takes no action in the case of Jesus of Nazareth. This tribunal is adjourned."

While temple heralds instructed the crowd to proceed immediately to the Hasmonean palace, where Antipas was lodging, Pilate stood up from his curule chair, walked off the dais, and entered his palace with a sense of victory. He was enormously pleased with himself. The change of venue rid him of a sticky case involving a probably innocent man whom it would have been wrong to convict, and yet dangerous to acquit, in view of the Sanhedrin's attitude. It was also a bit of diplomacy toward Herod Antipas, who could not fail to recognize this as an olive branch in their perennial feud. It was like saying, "You stabbed me in the back in the shields affair, Antipas, but that's history now. In transferring this case, you can see my consideration for the Jews. So quit stirring up the lion on Capri." Pilate quaffed some wine; then returned to judge the cases awaiting him.

The Hasmonean palace lay due east of the Herodian, about two-thirds of the distance to the temple, and the leaders of the Sanhedrin argued strategy while marching in

front of their manacled prisoner en route to seeing Antipas.
Several suggested that it might be more difficult to get a
conviction from the tetrarch, since his hands were already
stained with the Baptizer's blood and he might not wish to
redden them again with that of another so-called prophet.
Antipas had not wanted John killed, and might now choose
to defend the Nazarene as a fellow Galilean. After all, he
had not arrested Yeshu during his three years of teaching
in Galilee, though he had threatened to.

But Caiaphas countered confidently, "Antipas has shown
much more sensitivity to our laws than Pilate. Undoubtedly
he'll convict Yeshu with the same fine cooperation he
showed us in the case of the golden shields."

Since the tetrarch had few official duties to perform in
Jerusalem and was largely on vacation, he and Herodias
were entertaining their relatives Philip and Salome at a lei-
surely breakfast when a courier brought news of the immi-
nent arraignment. While Antipas had learned of Jesus' arrest, this development caught him off guard and he hastily
prepared for the hearing. But he was pleased with the turn
of events, since he had wanted to meet Jesus for some
months. Even before he had finished grooming himself, a
mass of people was pressing against the gates of the Hasmonean palace. Officialdom, the Sanhedrin and its prisoner, and a few representatives of the people were allowed
into the atrium of the palace, but much of the throng had
to wait outside because of limited space.

While Herodias, Philip, and Salome watched from the
wings, Antipas mounted his tetrarch's throne and ordered
the hearing to begin. The priestly plaintiffs produced political charges similar to those raised before Pilate, but this
time they did not demur at introducing also the religious issues which had led to Jesus' conviction before the Sanhedrin.

Antipas listened intently to the accusation, then startled
everyone by his unorthodox procedure. Turning to the
chief priests, he said, "Thank you, honored Rabbis, for
your presentation of the case. Actually I'm quite familiar
with the charges against Yeshu Hannosri, but I've never yet
had the occasion to meet him." Then, in an almost kindly
tone, he addressed the prisoner, "Yeshu, will you step forward?"

For several moments Antipas studied the manacled figure in front of him. Then he said, "I've wanted to see you
for some time. You've been given credit for certain . . .

rather magnificent exploits, especially in our Galilee. I wish I could have witnessed some of them."

Antipas noticed that the plaintiffs were looking uneasy, even alarmed at his gentle treatment of the prisoner. Jesus himself showed no reaction, but continued gazing into Antipas' eyes.

"Several times I looked for you in Galilee," the tetrarch continued. "You probably thought I meant you harm, but I didn't. I only wanted to see a prophet for myself. If, indeed, that's what you are. John the Baptizer was supposed to be a prophet, but he didn't perform any miracles. And yet *you* can, I understand. Well, I've never seen a miracle. Why not show us one now?"

All eyes shifted from Antipas to Jesus. The chief priests were apprehensive, for Herod's tone was serious, not taunting. What would he do if their prisoner actually performed a bit of magic—declare him a true prophet and free him? But they need not have been concerned. Jesus made no move whatever, other than shutting his eyes in inner concentration and then opening them.

"Come now, Yeshu," said Herod, "I know you once called me a 'fox,' and for the shrewdness implied, why, I thank you for the compliment." This raised a bit of laughter from Antipas' guards. "But my request has no further slyness than this: you're either a true prophet or a false one. The latter achieves wonders by tricks; the former by the power of God. Now I believe that I can see through tricks. So if you perform an actual sign for us, wouldn't that demonstrate that you are a true prophet?"

Jesus said nothing, did nothing.

"Look, don't just stand there, man!" Herod was losing his temper. "You haven't much of a bargaining position, and no one's speaking in your defense. I'm showing you a way out. Do a *miracle!* Even a simple one . . . say . . . have those fetters break off your wrists."

Jesus was silent.

"Well, if you can't *do* anything, can you *say* something?" Herod glared, starting to lose all sympathy for the prisoner. The tetrarch of Galilee was simply not disobeyed, especially not by one on trial, and yet here was a defendant mocking him by his silence.

But Jesus held his peace. Antipas might have known he would stage no spectacle for a man who had executed his close friend, forerunner, and cousin, John. He would not entertain the fox.

At this point, the chief priests and scribal lawyers quite logically broke into the silence, vigorously pressing their case against Jesus. "Do you know why he won't perform any wonders, noble Tetrarch?" asked Jonathan. "Because he can't! The signs ascribed to him are merely tricks—hoaxes."

"And according to your own flawless logic," Ananias added, "Yeshu must therefore be a false prophet."

Much affirmative head-nodding supported that observation. Antipas let the *accusatores* speak on to a summation. Then he addressed Jesus a final time. "No defense, Nazarene?" After the now-expected silence, Antipas broke into derisive laughter. "Of course there's no defense for a charlatan—a fraud! I must marvel at the people of Judea and Galilee—to consider this one a prophet. Ridiculous! At least the Baptizer had the courage to speak out, even in prison. But the Nazarene can't even find his tongue. Guards, I think it's time for you to show due reverence to our Messiah-king here."

Antipas' troops converged on the prisoner for a round of mockery and ridicule. Playfully they dropped to their knees or bowed deeply. Several fell flat on their faces before him and pounded the floor. Trumpeters blew a fanfare directly into his ears. Then they dressed him in a brilliant white robe, one of Antipas' discards, for the Messiah was expected to wear such.

"All right. That's enough," Herod directed. "Now take this magnificent prophet-Messiah-monarch back to Pontius Pilate."

The Sanhedrists thought they had not heard correctly, and Helcias asked, "Did the tetrarch say 'back to Pilate'?"

"He did. I herewith waive my jurisdiction over this subject. Since most of your accusations focus on events in Judea, let the prefect of Judea judge him."

"But Excellency," protested Rabbi Zadok, "the prefect remanded this case to *your* tribunal, and—"

"And I'm referring it back to his. Do you suggest I don't have the prerogative? My Galileans are judiciable in Judea if they break the law here. Besides, those charges of yours which involve Yeshu calling himself king are something for Rome to adjudicate, not I."

Finally Caiaphas himself, who had remained silent

throughout Antipas' hearing, approached his throne and said, "Worthy Tetrarch, you have protected our most holy faith in the past. You have defended our cause admirably, as in the appeal to Tiberius regarding the golden shields, and on other occasions. Why do you now fail to condemn this arch-heretic who blasphemes the name of our Holy God by calling himself His Son?"

"Most Honorable Pontiff Caiaphas, I think this tongue-tied wretch deserves our sympathy, not our stoning. Today we've proven him a hoax. How could he possibly have a following after this? But if you think he deserves punishment, just remember this: *I didn't set him free.* I might have acquitted him entirely, rather than returning the case to Pilate. As it is, you can simply resume his trial before the prefect at the point where you left off."

Caiaphas was about to reply, but Antipas ended the hearing by standing to announce, "This court is adjourned."

Slowly, the chief priests filed out, followed by members of the Sanhedrin, the temple guard surrounding Jesus, and then all the rest who had crowded into the atrium of the Hasmonean palace. The parade of accusers headed back to the Roman *praetorium*. But now it was almost nine A.M.

Surrounded again by his wife and relatives, Antipas watched them leave. He knew he had been less than candid with Caiaphas in posing as something of the forgiving humanitarian. This was only to mask the real motive behind his failure to judge the case. Many of his Galilean subjects believed in Jesus, and some of them were in Jerusalem at the time, camped on the surrounding hills. Even if riots did not break out, were he to condemn the Nazarene, he could still look forward to reaping a fine harvest of hatred upon his return to Galilee, for then he would have killed his second prophet. Besides, two of those who believed in the man were standing very close to his own tribunal during the hearing: Chuza, his chief steward; and Manaen, his close friend and adviser. Antipas was man enough to taunt Jesus before people who believed in him, but not to have him stoned.

And why should he relieve Pilate of this thorny case? Let Rome and Rome's prefect bear the odium for prophet-killing, if it came to that. But it was decent of Pilate to make such a conciliatory gesture as deferring to his tribunal; very decent, in fact, especially after the shields altercation. Perhaps Pilate was basically a good man after all, and he had been misjudging him all these years.

Antipas took a stylus, prepared a note for Pilate, and sent it to the Herodian palace by a courier who was told to reach the prefect before the multitude returned. The message commended Pilate for having referred the case of Jesus of Nazareth to him, but he thought in view of the *forum delicti*, the mood of the Sanhedrin in having approached the Roman tribunal in the first instance, and the political implications of some of the charges, that Pilate's would be the more appropriate court. He herewith waived his jurisdiction over Jesus. Nevertheless, he appreciated Pilate's kind gesture, and could he and Procula come over to the Hasmonean palace the following Tuesday evening for a dinner party?

The communication reached Pilate at his inner tribunal. He read it with only moderate surprise. A political sixth sense had told him Antipas might react as he did. With a renewed frown, he rose from his ivory *sella*, postponing the remaining cases, and went out to face the crowds, which by now had largely reconvened in the palace square. There, again, were the chief priests, the Sanhedrin, Jesus, the masses—the same unpleasant cast which had confronted him earlier in what evidently had been merely Act I of a Greek tragedy played by Jewish actors before a Roman judge.

This time, without waiting for the prosecution to enter a formal request for a reopening and continuation of the trial, Pilate seized the initiative and announced, "You brought the defendant before this tribunal on a charge of subversion. But, after personally and publicly examining him, I did not find this man guilty of any of your prime charges against him. Neither did the tetrarch Herod Antipas, for he has referred the case back to me. Even if he committed infractions of your religious law, Jesus of Nazareth has done nothing to deserve death."

This provoked a general outcry from the crowd for the first time, a rising, sullen rumble of disapproval, punctuated by isolated shouts of "Away with him! Convict him! He's guilty!" The sickeningly familiar atmosphere of tension was building.

Pilate looked down at the plaintiffs, speaking in a conversational tone so that only they would hear him. "I see you've managed the masses rather well. But this also means that if the people get out of hand, you'll have to answer for the consequences. Now, in order to preserve the peace, I ask that you withdraw the charges against this man, since they've not stood up in court. Such a gesture will effectively end this hearing, without my being compelled to declare the defendant innocent. Perhaps you can build your case against him another time when you have more conclusive evidence. For my part, I'll flog him as an object lesson for disturbing the peace and release him."

He searched the faces of the Sanhedrists for some sign of concession, but found only unbending resolution. Therefore he had no choice but to reopen the sorry business. But to what good? All the evidence for the prosecution, such as it was, had been presented in the earlier hearing. The defense, such as it was, had also been enunciated in the one sentence, "My kingship is not of this world." Perspiring in the mid-morning sun, Pilate groped for a solution.

Inside the palace, meanwhile, Procula had awakened to find Pilate gone to his morning's business. She felt somewhat ill—the change of diet from Caesarea to Jerusalem often brought her dysentery—so she decided to stay in bed for the rest of the morning and soon dropped off to sleep again.

But the trial being conducted in front of the palace disturbed her, and she was shocked to see that Jesus was being judged by her husband. Yet, as she watched, she grew proud of Pilate. He was the only one who seemed to be defending the innocent prophet; no one else had a word to say in his behalf. Now, as the case was reaching its climax, Pilate formally declared Jesus innocent.

"Away with him!" the people cried. "Condemn him! Crucify him!"

Pilate looked nonplused. But finally, with a nobility Procula was sure had always been a part of his character, he announced to the crowd: "Hear me! As prefect of Judea and representative of his imperial majesty, Tiberius Caesar, and as judge of the provincial tribunal of Jerusalem, I herewith declare Jesus of Nazareth *not guilty* of the charges you have brought against him. I am releasing the defendant. This court is adjourned."

With that, Pilate rose from his curule chair and ordered a contingent from the Jerusalem cohort to untie Jesus and escort him under imperial safe-conduct as far as Galilee.

Then, while the dumfounded multitude watched the last auxiliaries leave the esplanade with Jesus securely in their protection, a young scribe pointed to Pilate and cried, "Crucify *him!*" A bloodcurdling yell arose as the people, now a lynch mob, stormed up to the tribunal from all sides and tore into Pilate before any of the palace guards could assist him, pommeling his head and body and lacerating his flesh. Pontius Pilate was dead even before he could be hoisted onto a crude cross fashioned by the mob from scrap timbers.

With a muted scream, Procula awoke from her grisly nightmare, that amalgam of truth and grotesque fantasy of which morning dreams are made. Shouts from the crowd had in fact penetrated the palace, and her fears had supplied the framework in which to arrange those shouts.

Overcome with relief, she summoned an attendant to ask where her husband was. Learning of the trial in progress, she was alarmed once again. Ever since the notice of Jesus' arrest was delivered to the palace, Procula had intuited that Pilate would eventually have to hear the case, since capital charges were involved. But she had not imagined the trial would take place that soon. Now her dream took on prophetic dimension, the usual posture for Roman dreams. Every school child in the Mediterranean knew about Calpurnia's dream of Caesar's torn and bloodied toga on the night before his assassination in the Senate house. In anxiety, Procula called for a wax tablet and quickly scribbled this warning:

Procula to Pilate: keep your guard closely about you. And have nothing to do with that innocent man, for I have suffered much today in a dream because of him.

Sitting on his dais in front of the palace, Pilate had finally found a solution to his judicial quandary, one prompted by the Jewish calendar itself. Since it was his custom each Passover to release one prisoner chosen by the people, he now reminded the multitude of this annual festival amnesty. But instead of allowing unlimited free choice of candidates for pardon, he narrowed the selection to just two. "Whom do you want me to release?" he asked, "Jesus Bar —Abbas . . . or Jesus of Nazareth?"

Momentarily, the throng seemed to hold its breath. Then it broke into a bubbling cauldron of contention, for Pilate's

alternatives had been cleverly chosen. Against the controversial Jesus he had pitted one who was guilty beyond all
controversy, a notorious public enemy. Pilate had calculated that the present hatred of Jesus would be far outbal-
anced by public dread at having a murdering insurrec-
tionist turned loose in Jerusalem. Also, the people would
never want to forego the Bar-Abbas show trial.

The prosecution huddled for strategy, then sent messen-
gers throughout the crowd. At this point, Procula's message
was delivered to Pilate. Recognizing his wife's handwriting,
he almost cast it aside as nothing more than a housewifely
note which should not have bothered him at such a time.
But since it was brief, he read it—a strange message, he
thought, though Pilate placed little credence in dreams.
Perhaps Procula was ill. At any rate, the warning could
hardly apply, since he was well guarded, and he quite un-
avoidably did indeed have something "to do with that innocent man," even if he agreed with his wife's own, albeit un-
solicited, verdict on Jesus.

"Well, which of the two Jesuses shall I release for you?"
he called out, now quite sure of victory, "The Nazarene . . .
or Bar-Abbas?"

A great, almost unified cry arose, "BAR-ABBAS! . . . BAR-
ABBAS!" A few lone voices called "the Nazarene," but they
were hopelessly drowned out by the majority of the crowd,
which took up the name of the public enemy as a near war
chant.

Now it was Pilate's turn to be dumfounded. The prosecutors had done their work well. In the interval, which Pilate had interpreted as confusion, they had marshaled the
crowd through couriers who persuaded the people, in the
name of the Great Sanhedrin, to demand the release of
Bar-Abbas instead of Jesus. Theologically, they said, the
crime of the Messiah-so-called was far more serious than
anything Bar-Abbas had committed.

Bewildered, Pilate finally found his tongue. "Then what
am I to do with Jesus of Nazareth?"

Again the great voice cried out, "LET HIM BE CRUCIFIED!"

"Why? What evil has he done?"

They shouted all the louder, "AWAY WITH HIM!" "GIVE
US BAR-ABBAS!" "CRUCIFY HIM!"

Stung by the intransigence, Pilate challenged again,
"Why? For what crime? I have not found him guilty of *any*

capital offense. I will therefore flog him and then free him."

Amid further shouts for a death sentence, Pilate had Jesus brought inside the palace courtyard for scourging. The captain of the troops who had been keeping an eye on the crowd from inside the *praetorium* now barked a command to his auxiliaries. They gathered round the prisoner, stripped him, and administered the *fustigatio*, that Roman flogging which punished someone as a warning against further wrongdoing. It was lighter than the severe scourging which preceded capital punishment.

Pilate witnessed the scene, half hoping that the stripes would bring Jesus sufficiently to his senses to make a better defense of himself. Playing on human behavior, he also intended the scourging to win the people's sympathy for the accused.

Then it came time for a Roman magistrate to turn his back on a prisoner's punishment while the soldiers played their games of mockery with him, a barbaric custom which Rome had not shaken off from her ancient past. The only charge against Jesus which had registered with the troops was the claim that this unlikely figure should be a king in any sense, and of the Jews in particular. As anti-Semites, they found the idea doubly humorous. So their mockery focused on this theme. A sneering centurion who had located a purple lictor's mantle draped it around Jesus' shoulders and his men broke into lusty laughter. One hulking veteran with fat calluses covering his hands tore out several branches from thorn bushes growing in the courtyard and braided these into a prickly crown which he solemnly planted on Jesus' head in a sham coronation. A reed shoved into his right hand as scepter completed the royal ensemble. The whole rowdy company of troops now fell on their knees and jeeringly saluted him, "Hail, King of the Jews!" Then, one by one, they filed by to do him honor, slapping his cheeks and spitting in his face. When Jesus refused to hold the reed and dropped it, the centurion picked it up and used it to beat the crown of thorns into his scalp. Bleeding from scourge and thorn, Jesus said nothing.

Pilate reappeared in the courtyard and halted the mock homage. Then he led Jesus out to the tribunal and exhibited him to the multitude. "Here he is," said Pilate. "I bring him out to let you know that I find no crime in him, but this scourging has punished him for offending you. Look at him! You charged him with claiming to be king. Well, here's your king . . . wearing the purple, but crowned with thorns."

The soldiers started laughing, and Pilate encouraged it, hoping that mockery might slake the crowd's thirst for blood. It was one thing to demand execution of a healthy and unharmed prisoner, quite another to insist on it for a defenseless, beaten, and ridiculed wretch.

"Behold the man," said Pilate, in a tone of condescending compassion.

"Crucify! Crucify!" the chief priests and the elders exclaimed. At first the shouting came only from the comparatively small knot of prosecutors below the tribunal, since some sympathy for the beaten Jesus had been generated in the mass assembly. But soon more and more took up the chant, and the general mood was once again galvanized for condemning Jesus.

Pilate was losing his patience. *"You* crucify him," he snarled. "Take him and crucify him yourselves, for I've found no case against him."

This invitation went begging, of course, for it was merely angry sarcasm. At this point, Pilate was preparing to announce final acquittal and the closing of court.

The chief priests took quick counsel. Then Caiaphas walked up to the tribunal and spoke with Pilate face to face. "We have a law, Honorable Prefect, and according to our law this man ought to die, because he has claimed to be the *Son of God."*

"The Son of God?" asked Pilate, plainly disturbed, but also irritated.

"Yes. This is the greatest offense in Hebrew law, the worst blasphemy."

While a ripple of superstition was aroused in Pilate by the new information, his juridical sense was infuriated. The prosecution was introducing an entirely new charge, a religious one, which was apparently unrelated to the previous political indictments. In fairness to the judge, the court, and the defendant, it should have been cited much earlier. However, Pilate understood why it had not been: the Sanhedrin feared that he would not adjudicate in matters religious. Now, however, backed against the wall by his refusal to condemn, the prosecution was honest enough to supply what had undoubtedly been their main charge against Jesus at the Sanhedral hearing.

Scowling at the plaintiffs, Pilate finally grumbled, "This

is an entirely new charge. You should have raised it when I called for accusations at the start of the trial. Now I'll have to hold a private hearing on this alleged claim to be . . . 'Son of God.' " With that, Pilate had Jesus brought back again into the palace.

A claim to divinity was always a bit unnerving for Romans. Fundamentally, they were a rather religious—or at least superstitious—breed, even if, like Pilate, they thought themselves enlightened skeptics.

He began his careful probe into Jesus' alleged claim to divinity with a frankly metaphysical question. "Where do you come from?"

Jesus did not reply.

"You won't speak to me? Don't you know that I have the authority to release you or to crucify you?"

"You would have no authority at all over me if it had not been given you from above," Jesus responded. "Therefore the prosecution has the greater sin."

The inscrutable language, the reference to higher, possibly fatalistic powers, for which he was evidently a tool, convinced Pilate that further conversation with Jesus would lead nowhere. The man seemed resolved not to enter any defense for himself.

Pilate left Jesus inside the *praetorium* while he returned to his tribunal. He then realized that for the second time Jesus had in fact mentioned something in his defense. It was only a sentence, like the first occasion ("My kingship is not of this world"). He had said, "The prosecution has the greater sin." The last word also meant "failure" or "error." Pilate knew, and clearly Jesus also knew, that the legal process now taking place was "sin . . . error . . . failure."

Pilate's conscience would not allow him to condemn an innocent man, so he now renewed his efforts to release Jesus, despite the uncompromising attitude of the people. He wondered to what extent they were a hired claque rounded up by the prosecution.

The prefect of Judea cajoled, debated, argued, and finally threatened. The prosecution countered that because this was a case involving religious offense, Pilate need not have reopened the trial. He should simply have countersigned the execution order of the Sanhedrin, for it had supreme jurisdiction over all religious questions affecting Jews. If Rome had not removed the *jus gladii* from that body, the

prefect would not even have had the unpleasant task of trying to fathom Jewish law to understand why such supreme
blasphemy could be punished only by death.

Pilate found it difficult to answer that argument. He had
private reservations about the motives which led Caiaphas
and the priests to seek Jesus' death. To what extent were
they based on the alleged blasphemy? Or did they stem also
from envy at Jesus' success? Or was this merely a case of
retaliation for his attacks on them? But it was impossible to
debate such motives publicly, for that would have im-
pugned the veracity of the Jewish authorities before their
own people, an offense which would have terminated Pilate's usefulness in Judea.

It was while he was hesitating that the leaders of the
prosecution pressed their final attack. Rabbi Ananias was
chosen to voice the decisive appeal. "Noble Prefect," he
said, "our very beliefs, our way of life, our religious future,
are at stake in this trial. If this deceiver is released, he will
subvert our nation and also our most holy faith. If such
cardinal blasphemy which we have all heard with our own
ears is not punished, then Israel is lost. However, Tiberius
Caesar has charged you to uphold *all* our religious customs." He paused to lend emphasis to what would follow,
raising his voice at the same time. "Therefore, if you let
this man go free, you are *not Caesar's friend.* Furthermore,
anyone who would make himself a king *treasonably* defies
Caesar!"

There it was, a linking of the religious and political
charges against Jesus raised to the highest level of appeal,
that of the emperor himself. Pilate was beaten. He had lost.
The priests were victorious, though it took him some moments to recognize that fact in all its fullness.

Pilate glanced down at the gold ring of a "Caesar's
friend" which Tiberius had sent him upon embarkation at
Puteoli. With his thumb he twirled it round his finger, the
symbol of an *amicus Caesaris,* with all rights and privileges
pertaining thereunto. The significance of the ring was not
lost on the brilliant Ananias, who had focused on it while
making his statement. Release Jesus and the ring would
surely be plucked from Pilate's finger, with all the attendant indignities and loss of status. Yes, that was it. Call it
political blackmail or just strategic threat, but Ananias'
statement could be translated in only one way: "If you free
this man, the Sanhedrin will send a delegation to Tiberius

to bring the following two charges against you: 1) disobedience to the emperor in failing to uphold Jewish law; and 2) criminal neglect of duty for failing to punish someone who committed *maiestas* in setting himself up as subversive counter-king to the Roman emperor." Considering Pilate's probationary status ever since the fall of Sejanus and his various troubles with the Jews, such a dual arraignment before Tiberius could lead to loss of office, political career, or even life itself if the charge of treason were sustained. Fantasy? Hardly. If the Judean authorities had complained to Tiberius about something so minimal as a few gilded shields, they would most certainly appeal to him in a matter they obviously considered of much greater import. The trial was over.

It was getting late in the morning. The sun was hot. Pilate wanted to have done with the sorry affair. He ordered the prisoner brought out of the palace for sentencing.

His practical Roman mind did remind him that there was one alternative to sentencing an apparently innocent man to save oneself: acquitting Jesus . . . and sacrificing himself. Pilate canvassed history to see if any man, were he in this situation, would so immolate himself on the altar of principle. Possibly the blind Appius Claudius, or crusty old Cato from Rome's heroic past? Perhaps Socrates? No. Even these idealists would have surrendered their lives for some cause higher than one visionary and unfathomable prisoner, a man seemingly so resigned to death that he made no defense for himself.

Whenever one acts in opposition to conscience, several justifying crumbs are usually thrown in its direction to ensure peace of mind. While preparing as graceful an exit as possible for himself, Pilate gathered his crumbs. The first would be that he would continue to defend Jesus until the end. So when the prisoner, still dressed in purple and thorns, was brought out for the last time, Pilate announced, "Here is your king!" It was more of the same, defensive mockery which might yet wring some kind of sympathy from the people.

A smallish scribe, hatred twisting his features, clenched his fist at Jesus and cried, "Away with him!"

"AWAY WITH HIM! AWAY WITH HIM!" the mass responded. "CRUCIFY HIM!"

"Shall I crucify . . . your king?"

"We have no king but Caesar," the chief priests objected, thus appearing to be even more loyal to the emperor than Pilate, his representative. It was a shrewd underscoring of their latest threat.

Another self-justifying gesture Pilate found in Roman law. Those who did not defend themselves in Roman trials were usually given three opportunities to change their minds before sentence was pronounced. And so Pilate asked, "Jesus of Nazareth, have you anything to say in your defense?"

Jesus did not reply. He was bleeding, perspiring, and apparently weakening physically.

"Jesus of Nazareth, do you have anything to say in your defense?"

There was no response.

And a third time Pilate asked the prescribed question, but heard no reply. Legally and juridically, he could now hope to salve his conscience. Since there was no defense, he had no alternative but to convict.

Pilate's temporizing was cut short by the multitude. Simmering under the sun, they were restive and impatient by now, each contributing to an aroma of sweat which hovered over the palace plaza. For almost three hours they had stood, watching one man defy their will and that of the Great Sanhedrin. Some young firebrands had started mixing catcalls with the shouts for crucifixion, and several were screaming obscenities at Pilate. Isolated scuffles had broken out between auxiliaries and people at the edge of the esplanade. Demands for crucifixion were droning on to a sickening crescendo, as if the crowd were trying to change Pilate's mind by the sheer force of sound itself. The palace square was a writhing mass of shaking fists. Some of the people were holding their arms straight out in cruciform fashion while yelling "Crucify!" so Pilate would not miss the message. All the storm flags, indicating the approach of a full-dress uproar, were being hoisted. Pilate eyed his troops. At that moment he did not feel he could take another riot, so he waved his arms overhead to silence the tumult, an indication that he was finally ready to pass sentence.

He had a golden basin of water brought out to the tribunal. Then he announced, "Hear me, Men of Israel! This court cannot pronounce Jesus of Nazareth guilty, but because your Great Sanhedrin has condemned him to death, and since the Roman prefect must respect and protect Jewish religious law, the prisoner will be crucified."

A great roar of approval filled the air. When it finally subsided, Pilate, in full view of the multitude, washed his hands in the basin. "My hands are clean of this man's blood," he said.

"HIS BLOOD BE ON US AND ON OUR CHILDREN!" the people cried, using the words of the Old Testament formula to assume accountability for themselves.

Pilate dried his hands. With inner revulsion he ordered the release of the murderous insurrectionary, Bar-Abbas. Then he looked at Jesus. *"Staurotheto,"* he told a centurion of the guard, "Let him be crucified."

The soldiers took the condemned into the courtyard, stripped off the purple cloak, and, after additional mockery, dressed him in his own clothes again. Then they made him shoulder the *patibulum,* a wooden transverse beam which, to form the cross, would be fastened to one of the upright stakes already standing at Skull Place.

A contingent of Pilate's auxiliaries led Jesus out of the palace esplanade and directly north to Golgotha. The two convicted bandits, whose sentencing had been postponed to that morning, were also marched in that procession of death, since Pilate's execution detail preferred handling all distasteful crucifixion cases at the same time.

The route out to the lethal hillock, just beyond the northwestern walls of Jerusalem, was clogged with people lining the streets. Many were part of the crowd which had called for Jesus' condemnation, and they lavished ridicule and derision on him. But some were admirers or followers of the condemned, who commiserated his fate. Most of them had learned of the trial only after it was over. Clearly, Jesus' enemies had been organized; his friends had not. Fear of a Galilean-style political rebellion under his aegis had proved a fantasy. In fact, the only finger in all Jerusalem raised in Jesus' behalf was unintentional. Half way to Golgotha, he stumbled under the weight of his crossbeam. The execution squad cursed him for clumsiness, then compelled a broad-shouldered bystander named Simon, from Cyrene in North Africa, to carry the beam for him.

A courier from Pilate ran to catch up with the procession before it reached Golgotha. He bore the *titulus* or inscription which had to be carried before a condemned man to identify him and the cause for his execution. The sign would then be affixed to the cross. Written with gypsum on a wooden board, the *titulus* was spelled out in Latin, Hebrew, and Greek so that nearly everyone would be able to read: "Jesus of Nazareth, the King of the Jews."

Pilate had barely returned inside his palace when several of the chief priests asked to see him.

"What now?" he demanded.

"The *titulus*, sir. It should not read, 'the King of the Jews,' but 'He claimed to be king of the Jews.'"

"What I have written, I have written." Pilate stalked off, leaving the priests standing at the door. There would be no further capitulation to the Sanhedrin.

Actually, Pilate had chosen the wording of the *titulus* for a purpose. There was subtle sarcasm, to be sure, directed less at the crucified and more at the crucifiers: "Jews rate such a king as this" was one clear implication. But there was also a legal consideration. For the record, Pilate wanted a solid reason for conviction. Crucifixion would not be an appropriate Roman punishment for the purely Jewish crime of blasphemy, but it was perfectly proper for high treason perpetrated by a self-styled king.

In his office at the Herodian palace, Pilate dictated a memorandum to one of his aides which would explain the legality of Jesus' case for his records:

Form of trial: cognitio [investigation] of the prefect.
Advisers or jury: none
Sentence: crucifixion
Stated basis of sentence: constructive treason—implied *maiestas*
Secondary basis of sentence: endorsement of Sanhedrin's conviction of Jesus on a capital religious offense.
Appeal: none. The convicted was not a Roman citizen.

Chapter 19

DRAINED BY the events of that morning, Pilate reclined alone for lunch. Procula sent word that she would not join him until dinner because of her indisposition. He drank more wine than usual, since he would not be holding court that afternoon. He drank also to dull the immediate memory of the morning's ordeal.

Governing Judea was a corrosive experience, Pilate decided. One day soon he might follow Gratus' example and ask to be relieved of the prefecture and transferred elsewhere, hopefully back to Rome. Almost seven years had passed since he'd been there. Too long; too terribly long. Seven years of confrontation with the Jews—could anyone really govern them successfully? Except Jews themselves? Perhaps that was the real reason for their agitation. They felt that only they could rule themselves. Though even that was debatable, considering their intense inner rivalries. "Two Jews, three opinions," went the aphorism, and Pilate thought it sober truth.

After lunch and a fitful nap, he called for his afternoon bath earlier than usual. He took it outside in the garden pool just off the inner courtyard.

While splashing about in the crystal blue waters of Herod's lavish natatorium, Pilate continued his musing. . . . How would Herod the Great have judged the case this morning? He certainly wouldn't have shied away from it like his son Antipas. Pilate grinned. No, Jesus would never even have come to trial. Very quietly, very efficiently,

237

Herod would have had him assassinated, since he dreaded anyone using the term king . . . like the time those sages came to Jerusalem asking about a newborn king of the Jews.

Now there's a coincidence, Pilate startled . . . a baby and a man I just condemned to death both called "king of the Jews." Herod killed the baby, I the man. Does that make me as bad as Herod? No, I was forced into it. . . . I wonder how he's doing out there—Jesus of Nazareth, king of the Jews. Probably silent, determined, resigned as ever.

Why didn't he make a defense? Why was he so uncooperative? Or too cooperative for his own conviction? I had to act not only as judge, but his defense attorney too. . . . I wonder if Procula knows. "Have nothing to do with that innocent man," she wrote. She'll think I spurned her note, of course. . . . "That *innocent man*." Where have I heard that before? Yes, I was reading it in Plato.

Pilate pulled himself out of the water and walked over to a chair where he had left a scroll of the *Republic*. Turning back a few sections he found the passage:

> The innocent man will be scourged, tortured, bound, blinded with fire, and finally, after enduring every extremity of suffering, he will be impaled *on the cross*. . . .

A strange coincidence, he thought to himself. And how curious of Plato, writing against the background of Socrates' martyrdom, to use the figure of the cross when Socrates had quietly sipped his hemlock. . . .

He dove back into the pool and swam its length, then turned over to float. By this time, he noticed, something distinctly uncanny was happening. Shortly after lunch, the sun had started to dim from some kind of overcast, and the sky was now a dreadfully glowering purple. Pilate thought a severe thunderstorm was brewing, but there was no wind, no lightning, no approaching rumbles.

He slipped out of the pool, dressed, and then climbed to an upper turret of the palace. The sky was blackening more deeply, yet no rain fell. He was startled to see that the entire countryside was darkened—no patch of brighter blue showed anywhere on the horizon. He could barely see across Jerusalem to the cluster of people gathered at Golgotha around the silhouette of the three crosses. Was it a solar eclipse? In the city below, oil lamps were flickering—at three o'clock in the afternoon.

Suddenly, Pilate seemed to hear and feel it at the same time. A tremor shook Jerusalem, then a moderately severe earthquake filled the air with grinding and buckling, tearing and clatter. Down on the esplanade he watched a fissure yawn open, which seemed to run eastward across the city to the temple mount. Foundations near the crevasse were ripped apart, and there were screams from the city. Pilate heard a creaking from the south and looked in horror as one of the arches of his aqueduct parted and crumbled into the Hinnom valley. Water cascaded from the ruptured trough.

Summoning his palace guard, he dispatched them through Jerusalem to report on the damage. Then he ordered the Antonia cohort out of their barracks to patrol the city and maintain order. His engineers were to take a construction detail out to the aqueduct and make emergency repairs.

It was all very weird. First the mysterious darkness, then the earthquake. But the crisis seemed to pass as quickly as it had come. The sun and a normally bright sky nearly burst upon Jerusalem, and in minutes the heavens resumed their regular blue, the strangest celestial phenomenon Pilate had ever witnessed.

He was just rearranging his nerves when an aide reported that the high priest's servant requested a moment of his time. "Will they never leave me in peace?" Pilate fretted. "Let him in. . . . Yes, Malchus?"

"Excellency," he bowed, "since the most solemn Sabbath in the Jewish year begins at sundown, my Lord Caiaphas and the priests request that toward the end of the day you permit the legs of the crucified prisoners to be broken so that they will die and can be buried. Then their bodies will not be left hanging on the crosses to desecrate the Sabbath."

Pilate dashed off a note, authorizing the centurion at Golgotha to do as the priests requested, and gave it to Malchus. Breaking the legs of those who were crucified hastened death by suffocation, since the diaphragm and rib cage were severely pressured by being hung from the arms above, rather than resting on the normal support provided by the legs.

Late in the afternoon, a member of the Sanhedrin requested an audience with the governor. His patience ebbing, Pilate was about to roast the caller when he saw that this one had never bothered him before. "Didn't I meet you some years ago in Caesarea, Councilor?" he inquired.

"Yes, Excellency. I am Joseph of Arimathea. I'll take only a moment of your time. My colleague Nicodemus and I seek your permission to bury the body of Jesus of Nazareth. I have a sepulcher rather close to Golgotha."

"Jesus is already dead?"

"Yes," said Joseph, lowering his eyes, for he did not want to betray emotion in front of the prefect.

"When did he die?"

"Shortly after the ninth hour. At the time of the earthquake."

"But men don't die on the cross that quickly."

"If you will pardon, Excellency, very little about this crucifixion was normal."

"True. But after the great rebellion under Spartacus, it took days, not hours, for his men to die on their crosses along the Appian Way . . . Are the other two still alive?"

"They were when I left."

"Did Jesus say anything before he died?"

"Yes, something quite loudly, which surprised us since we thought he was unconscious. 'It is *accomplished,*' he said. 'Father, into thy hands I commit my spirit.' With that he died." Joseph looked down for a moment, then resumed, "The bystanders were already frightened by the intense darkness, but when the earth shook they ran back into the city terrified. Even your centurion was struck by it. He looked up at the body of Jesus and said, 'Truly this man was a son of God.' "

Brushing his hand slowly across his brow, Pilate asked, "Was he, Councilor? Was he a 'son of God'?" and before Joseph could reply he continued, "Then why would he choose to die? And on a cross. What kind of divinity is that?"

He saw his execution squad returning and asked the men, "Did you break their legs?"

"Yes," the centurion replied. "They're all dead now. But we didn't have to smash the prophet's legs. He had already died. Just to make sure, though, one of the men shoved a lance into his side. He was quite dead."

"Tell me what happened, Centurion."

Still shaken from his afternoon at Golgotha, the officer

gave Pilate a full briefing. He reported confiscating the prisoners' clothing, as was their legal right, then shaking dice for the prophet's seamless tunic, which the centurion won . . . Jesus asking his "Father" to forgive them, whoever "them" was . . . offering the crucified the usual drugged, narcotic wine, but the prophet's refusal to take any . . . Caiaphas and the Sanhedrin waiting in vain for the man to recant so that they could absolve him and let him die a blessed death . . . the strange conduct of the bandits, one mocking him; the other asking his blessing . . . bystanders challenging him to use his touted supernatural powers to climb down from the cross . . . the eerie darkness . . . Jesus' farewell messages to his mother and several followers who were there . . . the troops giving Jesus a little *posca* via saturated sponge on a reed . . . and then his death and the frightening earthquake. "It almost seemed as if the gods were angry, Prefect," the centurion declared. "Whom *did* we crucify?"

During the narration, Joseph of Arimathea was trying to attract Pilate's attention. Finally he succeeded. "Oh yes, Councilor," Pilate turned to him. "Sorry to have kept you waiting. You may bury the body of Jesus."

At the temple, meanwhile, the busiest afternoon of the year was concluding. Townspeople and pilgrims alike had converged on the sanctuary in order to have their Passover lambs slaughtered according to sacred ritual, and this had greatly reduced the crowd which might otherwise have thronged Golgotha to witness Jesus' crucifixion. Indeed, Caiaphas and members of the Sanhedrin had left Skull Place by 1:00 P.M. in order to conduct the Passover preparatory liturgy at the temple and supervise the sacrifice of lambs.

The ceremonial had not gone well that afternoon. The sudden darkness frightened the worshipers, and the earthquake, while not causing any loss of life, had still terrified the people. The worst news was shielded from them: the large fissure from the quake had torn in two the sacred curtains which screened off the Holy of Holies from the rest of the temple. The portent was so terrible that the priests did not try to interpret its significance, except for Rabbi Zadok, who resumed his intermittent forty-year fast for the safety of Jerusalem. However, since most worshipers were in the outer courts and did not see the damage, no panic resulted.

The ritual now ended with a final sacrifice of three official lambs. Caiaphas, resplendent in his robes of office with gleaming breastplate and sacred ephod, presided over the ceremony, assisted by three Levites. The animals were unblemished specimens, and their throats were cut in a single stroke. There was no anguished bleating, just the sound of blood dripping into golden vessels. When enough was collected, the incarnadine was splashed onto a sacred stone. The victims were then flayed and the viscera carefully examined. In Rome, augurs would have determined the future from such probing; here it was only to authenticate that the lambs had been in perfect health, for nothing less than flawless sacrifices were offered to God. The lambs proved physically impeccable, the ceremony successful. The people returned to their homes, where the Seder was in final preparation.

Procula felt well enough to join Pilate for dinner that evening, but her taciturnity cued him that she was informed of the day's events. Pilate was equally silent, not looking forward to the criticism from his wife he fully expected.

"Procula," he finally ventured, "why did you send that note out to the tribunal today? What sort of dream did you have?"

After she described her nightmare, Pilate laughed. "But there is some truth to it. I *was* trying to free Jesus. And I was almost tempted to have Caiaphas crucified instead. Then the people really *would* have lynched me!"

Slowly she raised her eyes to his and transfixed him with a chilly stare. "How does it feel, Pilate, to send an innocent man to his death?"

Immediately abandoning his whimsy, he replied, "It's not that simple, Procula."

"Was he guilty or innocent?"

"Guilty, as far as the Jews are concerned."

"And the Romans?"

"Technically guilty of the charge of treason for calling himself king, *rex*. Remember, 'king' is one of the most despised terms in our language. We had seven kings after Rome was founded, but that was enough. And what was the Senate going to debate on the Ides of March? Whether to confer the title of *rex* on Caesar. It didn't happen! Even the emperors, with powers greater than any king, never allow themselves to be called by that hateful title."

"Stop, Pilate. Was Jesus' kingship intended in any political sense?"

"No. . . ."

"How could you condemn him then?"

"Were you given a full report of the trial? The whole thing, my *defense* of Jesus throughout—"

"Yes, the centurion told me everything. You were doing so well, Pilate, acting nobly, in fact. I might even have forgiven you for ordering him scourged if I could be sure it was only to win sympathy from the people."

"It was."

"Then why did you fail?"

"How fail?" A touch of ire was seeping into his voice.

"Fail the cause of justice. You condemned a man you knew was innocent, the worst thing any judge can do. Freeing a guilty man is far more forgivable than what you've done."

"But—"

"You knew what was just and right. You knew what you should have done." She now had tears welling in her eyes. "Yet you didn't have the moral fiber to do it. I . . . I didn't know I married a man without a spine—"

"Stop it, Procula!" he thundered. "I *had* to do it. Don't you understand? If I would have released Jesus—no, the crowd wouldn't have attacked me as your dream had it—but Jesus would likely have been lynched anyway once we left Jerusalem and our guard was removed. And if I hadn't given in, another riot would have broken out, shedding far more Jewish blood than that of one visionary prophet. Which would have been worse? Sometimes a little evil is necessary to bring about a greater good."

"You've opposed Jewish crowds on other occasions."

"And you know the result. If the long shadow of Sejanus weren't touching us, I might have countered the crowd. But with Tiberius committed to his new pro-Jewish policy, it would have been insanity."

Procula was silent for some moments. Then she said, "What if it were true, Pilate? What if he were the Son of God?"

"Are you serious?"

"Yes."

"You always were the superstitious one, weren't you?

Well, you may find it hard to believe, but even I gave a moment's thought to that possibility when I was searching for a way to release him. Yet I reasoned that if, in some fantastic unlikelihood, I actually *were* judging divinity, the whole affair wouldn't get very far. Jesus would have waited for my judgment, then laughed at me and the screaming mob and either struck us all down or simply walked away from the tribunal. And none of us could have done a thing about it. But the fact that he couldn't prevent his punishment proves that he was not, in fact, what he claimed to be. A true 'son of God,' if such exists, wouldn't allow himself to be beaten, mocked, insulted. Therefore, when the scourging took place successfully, when the first drop of blood reddened his back I knew we had a mere mortal on our hands, and that, if crucified, the man would actually die. You see, Procula, no divinity could die."

"You make the logical error of assuming that what *did* happen, *had* to happen. Because Jesus *did* not defend himself doesn't prove he *could* not defend himself. Perhaps he meant to suffer. Anyway, none of this excuses you from judicial murder."

"Watch your language, Wife!" He glared at her. "Now, we've established that this was no son of God in fact—"

"We established nothing of the sort."

"All right. The one body qualified to judge such arcane matters, the Sanhedrin, decided that this was no son of God. Therefore, they condemned him as a false prophet and blasphemer. Now, even though I think it's barbaric to execute someone who uses his tongue the wrong way while involving their deity, this is their law. And Tiberius ordered me to uphold their law. What else could I do?"

When Procula did not respond, he pressed his case. "Four years ago, Jesus wouldn't even have come before my tribunal. The Sanhedrin still had the *jus gladii* over Jewish nationals at that time. But under pressure from Sejanus I withdrew their right to execute; yet it was understood that I'd usually *endorse* their verdict in capital cases. It was extraordinary on my part even to conduct a second hearing."

"Why did you do it, then?"

"Because I wanted to determine if the man were really guilty, also according to their law. This was a very rare situation, since they hardly ever seek capital punishment. One rabbi told me: 'The Sanhedrin which issues a verdict of death more than once in seven years is a slaughterhouse.'

So you can see how important this case was to them. But the point is this: if Jesus' trial had been held four years ago, they could simply have stoned him to death without asking our permission."

"Doesn't it seem a rather strange argument, Pilate? 'I can crucify an innocent man, because four years ago they would have stoned an innocent man.' "

Pilate fumed, "You keep calling him innocent. Remember, he was *guilty* in the eyes of the Jewish authorities. Should I blithely have disregarded Tiberius' orders to respect their ancient and holy laws?"

Procula hesitated, then asked, "Was there no chance of sending him to a higher court, or appealing to Caesar?"

"No, for two reasons. He made no appeal. And he couldn't have appealed, since he wasn't a Roman citizen. But put the case that he had been. Tiberius still wouldn't have heard the appeal, since he's not bothered with such affairs on Capri. Probably Macro, as praetorian prefect, would have handled this appeal, and you know Macro."

Procula said nothing for the next minutes. Finally she asked, "If you had to judge the case over again, would you give the same sentence?"

With only a moment's hesitation, Pilate replied, "Yes, of course. I would have had to. My hands were tied."

"I thought they were washed, Pilate."

"Enough!" he bellowed. "There simply was no other way. Would you have preferred a riot, then an angry delegation to Tiberius? In his present testy mood, he'd have listened only to their side of it, and I'd be recalled in disgrace, imprisoned, exiled, or 'invited' to commit suicide, while you'd be stigmatized for the rest of your life. It was simply a choice—a choice between us and this man Jesus. Can't you see that? Be honest now, Procula!"

"Yes . . . that's probably true."

"Well?"

Slowly and deliberately, she said, "To have acquitted him anyway would have been a glorious demonstration of principle, an act of supreme altruism."

"Supreme folly!"

Saturday mornings were always quiet in Jerusalem, and this one especially so. Except for the faithful attending worship, there was no activity in the city during that high and holy day, for this Sabbath was also the Passover. Pilate was doubly surprised, then, when a number of priests and leading Pharisees paid him a visit about mid-morning.

"Your Excellency," said Rabbi Helcias, "we recall how that deceiver once said, while he was still alive, 'In three days I will rise again.' Not that he will, of course." The temple treasurer smiled. "But could you arrange to have his sepulcher guarded until after that third day? Otherwise his disciples may come and steal the body. Then they would announce that he had risen from the dead. And this last fraud would be worse than the first."

Pilate wanted no part of it. He had washed his hands of the case once and for all. "You have your own guard. Take your temple police and make the tomb as secure as you can," he retorted, amazed at a fanaticism which could hound a man not only to his grave, but beyond it.

The priests followed Pilate's advice, dispatching a detail from the temple guard to surround Joseph's tomb. They secured the precinct, sealed the stone which had been rolled in front of the sepulcher, and remained on guard.

The rest of Saturday lazily exhausted itself in a torpor which served as welcome contrast to the previous day. It was an unusually warm Sabbath for so early in spring, but the evening was beautiful, as were all nights that week, shimmering in a silvery sea of moonlight. The Passover fell at the time of the first full moon on or after the vernal equinox.

The fact of the full moon was bothering Pilate. He was still somewhat intrigued by the atmospheric phenomena which had blackened part of Friday afternoon. At first he had written off the unnatural darkness as a solar eclipse. Though hardly an astronomer, he now realized that when the moon was full, any eclipse of the sun was utterly impossible. The moon was in a diametrically wrong position.

Pilate shrugged his shoulders. Perhaps Joseph of Arimathea was right. . . . nothing was normal that Friday.

Chapter 20

SUNDAY DAWNED clear and bright, though the northwestern part of Jerusalem was shaken by another mild tremor just before sunrise. The quake evidently centered in a small park or garden just west of Golgotha, for reports reached Pilate that knots of people were starting to cluster there, perhaps to survey a deep fissure of some kind. Before the day was out, the clusters had grown to sizable groups.

On Monday, the groups developed into crowds, and all Jerusalem buzzed with rumors that the dead Jesus of Nazareth had risen from the dead, as he had predicted. Pilate learned that it was no fissure at all which was attracting the people west of Golgotha, but the sepulcher of Joseph of Arimathea in which Jesus had been buried. Supposedly it was empty.

Pilate scoffed at the report, but toward evening he and the tribune of the Antonia garrison visited the site. Escorted by troops who shouldered them through the ranks of curiosity seekers, they peered inside the tomb. A large, circular stone which served as door had been rolled aside to reveal an ample rock-hewn sepulcher, hollowed out of the side of a hill. Inside were linen grave wrappings lying on the slab of stone where a body would repose, and at the head end, rolled up separately, was a burial napkin intended to cover the face of the corpse. The cloths still exuded a spicy and resinous odor of myrrh and aloes. But there was no body.

"Are you sure this is the right tomb?" Pilate asked his tribune.

"This was the one sealed up by the temple guard."

"And just where *is* the guard?"

"They left after the earth tremor early Sunday morning. We couldn't learn much from them over at the Antonia, but it seems this stone broke its seal and rolled open in connection with the earthquake."

"How? And the body—how did it disappear?"

"The guards claim the disciples of this Jesus stole the body while they slept."

"Right from under their noses?"

"We couldn't get any more out of them—they're pretty sheepish about it."

"Small wonder, the incompetents," Pilate sneered. He examined the seal, which was fractured in two, part attached to the edge of the door stone, and part hanging from the lintel. He also searched the walls and floor of the tomb chamber for any hidden exits or passageways, but found none.

"Tribune, find Joseph of Arimathea, a member of the Sanhedrin, and bring him here. Check with him if this is the sepulcher in which he buried Jesus. If not, we'll put a Roman guard on the right one. Any police who can let a dead man 'escape' are stupid enough to seal and guard a wrong tomb!"

Late that evening, the tribune reported that he had taken Joseph of Arimathea to the sepulcher which they had examined. It was the right one.

Pilate reflected for several moments, then grinned. "Those rascally disciples of his, they certainly brought it off. Imagine, right under the noses of the guards!"

"Shall I have his followers rounded up and arrested, sir?"

"No, I don't think so, Tribune. Rome doesn't much care who has possession of a body after crucifixion. Besides, Caiaphas will be hard pressed to explain an empty tomb. Why should we help him out by locating the body?"

For all his jocularity, Pilate still had trouble falling asleep that night. His logical Roman mind first had to find a solution to the puzzle which had been thrust on him by the missing corpse. Of course it was the disciples' work. Who else would have a motive for stealing the body? Caiaphas' thinking was correct on that score. But how could that Galilean cadre have been clever enough to outwit a detail of some fifteen temple police? Granted even that they were *all* sleeping Saturday night, which was unlikely, rolling away that huge stone should have caused a commotion and a grinding which would have awakened them. No. It was impossible. The disciples would probably have had to step on their slumbering faces in order to move the stone and extricate the body. . . . How did it happen then? Pilate ground a fist into his other palm, weighing the riddle.

Of course! The solution was so delightfully obvious that anyone would have missed it at first blush. The chief priests had come asking for a guard on Saturday morning. Jesus had died late Friday afternoon. Therefore there was *no guard at the tomb during all of Friday night!* The disciples must have come that very night, while all Jerusalem was sleeping off the Passover meal, and removed the body of their dead teacher, replacing the stone at the doorway to hide the empty tomb. That was it! Rather pleased with himself, Pilate could now drop off to sleep.

The dinner Tuesday evening at the Hasmonean palace was a feast of friendship to honor repaired relations between Herod Antipas and Pilate. Not that either of them had any delusions about a genuine cordiality being established. It was more an unofficial peace treaty or at least a truce, an agreement to cooperate with each other in maintaining their separate positions in the uncertain world of a suspicious Tiberius. There would be no more tattling to Rome, they agreed, which was a small diplomatic victory for Pilate, since Antipas had been the chief offender on that score.

Not much was said about the trial and crucifixion of Jesus. Though Antipas was privately happy that he now had company in the select fraternity of Palestinian prophet-killers, he did not want to embarrass his guest. What talk there was centered rather on speculations about the empty tomb and the resurrection rumor which had now saturated Jerusalem. It was all that Antipas' aides Chuza and Manaen seemed able to talk about, Pilate noticed. They were exchanging the latest information, cheerfully careless of the fact that the man who had condemned Jesus was sitting at the head of the table and overhearing them.

Antipas would have silenced the pair, but for his own inordinate interest in the supernatural and the spectacular.

The man who once feared that John the Baptizer might have risen from the dead now cocked his ears to learn the latest gossip on the empty sepulcher. When his guests left that night, he would ask Chuza and Manaen for all the details. Pilate would also learn them from Procula.

As was fitting for Jerusalem, the ladies of the party were dining separately, and their whole evening was devoted to bartering news about the missing body. One of them could speak authoritatively, but earlier in the banquet she had hesitated to do so. It was only after much coaxing that Joanna told her story. She was the wife of Chuza, Antipas' chief steward and general manager of estates.

"Our Joanna was there when it happened," Herodias told Procula with a sarcastic leer. "Why she's been a follower of Jesus ever since he supposedly healed her in Galilee. She used to keep that confidential, but now she doesn't care who knows, do you, Joanna?"

"Please, Joanna, tell us your story," Procula interrupted, to stop Herodias' badgering.

A little hesitant, yet deliberate, Joanna began. "Well, several women followers of his and I were worried that he had not been buried properly. So we went out to Joseph's tomb early Sunday morning to anoint the body of Jesus with spices. You see, we didn't know this had already been done."

"You say you went out *Sunday* at dawn?" Procula inquired.

"Yes."

"Why not Saturday morning, just after he died?"

"The Sabbath, Lady Procula."

"Of course."

"Just as we got to the sepulcher, the earth trembled and the great stone rolled away from the entrance to the tomb. We were frightened, of course, but also a little relieved because we had no idea how we women would be able to budge that stone." She smiled shyly. "But then we were terrified: standing inside the sepulcher was some white and radiant personage, who said, 'Don't be afraid. You're looking for Jesus who was crucified. But he is not here. He has risen, as he promised. Come, see the place where he lay. And then go quickly and tell his disciples that he has risen from the dead.'"

"*Who* said all this?" Herodias snarled. "And where were the guards?"

"I think he was an *angelos*, Mistress, a messenger from God. The guards were there, but they were horrified. I believe they ran back into Jerusalem."

"My, but the story grows!" Herodias observed sardonically.

"Please continue, Joanna," urged Procula.

With a look of joyful serenity, she said, "Naturally, we were still shaken by it all. But thrilled at the incredible news. Then we hurried off to tell the disciples. But—but—"

"Out with it!" Herodias snapped.

"I fear you won't believe me, Mistress. . . ."

"Trust us and tell us, Joanna," begged Procula.

"As we were returning to Jerusalem, we suddenly saw Jesus in our path."

"What!"

"Of course we fell down in adoration before him. It was the Lord! It *was!* You *must* believe me! He smiled and reminded us of his mission. He also told us to alert his disciples, which we did."

After they returned from the Hasmonean palace that night, Procula excitedly reported Joanna's story to Pilate. What stupefied him was not just the fantastic information, but the almost sympathetic ebullience with which Procula related it. "Don't tell me *you* believe this bizarre business?" he sniffed.

"I didn't say I did. I didn't say I didn't," she trifled. "I'm just reporting what Joanna told us at dinner. Of course, Herodias tried to laugh it all off, but I thought she was cackling rather nervously. The wife of Manaen had tears in her eyes."

"Procula, I don't really care about their emotional reactions," said Pilate testily. "I just want to know if you, a sensible Roman matron, can give any credence to such myths, such hallucinations on the part of this Joanna. That woman was delirious with grief."

"She was *not* suffering from delusions," Procula retorted angrily. "She's one of the most sensible women I've met. And she wasn't flaunting this information. We had to worm it out of her, since she was afraid of Herodias."

"Oh—the whole thing was a wish or illusion. Do you notice how it was *women* who claimed to see a resurrected Jesus? Of course women! You creatures are *far* more imaginative than men. We could never dream up such a story!"

He laughed, then frowned. "Jesus is dead, Procula. Accept the fact and be done with it."

"I'm not finished, Pilate. Joanna and the women hurried to tell his disciples, but, like you, the men thought it was all nonsense. Evidently they have the same opinion of women which you seem to hold. But that night, Sunday night, it was different. While they were gathered at the house they're using here in Jerusalem, Jesus appeared to them. The disciples thought it was a ghost, but he ate some of their food and had them touch his scarred hands and feet to show that he was very much flesh and blood."

Pilate began perspiring. Gone was the carefree bravado. But it was not fear which clouded his features so much as anger. "You say there are *men* who would swear they saw Jesus alive?"

"Yes . . . and women too!"

Pilate jerked his head about and yelled for a servant, who came running. "Go to the Antonia and summon the centurion and the three auxiliaries who crucified Jesus of Nazareth."

"At *this* hour, Master?"

"*Yes,* at this hour—now—immediately!"

Procula let her husband vent his steam. Then she ventured quietly, "What do you hope to learn, Pilate?"

"A solution to this ridiculous mystery which has been addling my wits, an alternative I'd not thought of till this moment. Let's say I believe your story, Joanna's story. Suppose Jesus *is* alive. You know why he is? *Because he never died,* that's why. It would explain everything. Why he 'died' *too soon* on that cross, for one." Pilate paced the room. "Yes, it all falls into place now. Someone gave him a drink from a sponge, the centurion said, and shortly after that Jesus presumably died. What likely happened was that one of his disciples had put a deep narcotic into the *posca* soaked up by that sponge. . . . You'll remember that they did *not* break his legs so he never suffocated. After he was carefully 'buried' by Joseph, another of his henchmen in on the scheme, he revived in the cool of the tomb as the drug wore off. There were no guards on Friday night, so he climbed out without anyone's help; or his followers were there to assist with the stone. He rested through Saturday. He recuperated by Sunday. Then he went back to the tomb to make his appearance."

"Magnificent, Pilate," said Procula quietly. "But re-

member, one of the troops did something more lethal to
Jesus than breaking his legs: he thrust a spear into his
heart."

"That's why I called for the execution detail."

The quaternion of soldiers arrived and reported to Pilate. "Centurion," he demanded, "what was in that sponge
from which the crucified Galilean drank shortly before he
died this past Friday?"

The four troops peered drowsily at Pilate. Their getting
out of bed and hurrying across a sleeping Jerusalem only to
hear a question like this gave an air of unreality to Pilate's
query. The centurion asked that it be repeated. Then he replied, "What was in that sponge? Plain, ordinary *posca*—
vinegar and water. What else? It came from my canteen."

"No one tampered with that canteen?"

"Of course not. At the beginning, some of the women
tried to offer the Nazarene some drugged wine, but he
wouldn't take it. All he drank later was our own good old
sour *posca.*"

Procula looked at her husband, who avoided her eyes.

"Now, Centurion, this is a far more important question,"
he said. "Tell me again why you didn't break the prophet's
legs. Wasn't that my order?"

"With all due respect, sir, not quite. Your message read,
'You may break legs to induce death near sundown.' But
the one on the center cross was already dead, so we didn't
have to—"

"How did you know he was dead?"

"That was clear, Prefect. There was no breathing, not
the slightest twitch of a muscle, the pallor, the glassy stare
of death in his eyes—there was no question." The other
men nodded in agreement.

"Then why did you feel it necessary to spear him with a
lance?"

"Just an executioner's gesture, I suppose, to make assurance doubly sure."

"Which of you threw that spear?"

"I did, sir," a burly young auxiliary replied, "only I
didn't throw it. He was too close for that. I just drove it
into his side as far as I could."

"How far was that?"

"Well over a foot, sir."

"Then what happened? Did he gasp, or cry out?"

"No, not a thing. He'd been dead for at least an hour, I'd say. When I pulled the lance back out, blood and water followed it."

Procula looked as if she would faint. Pilate had an attendant assist her from the room.

"Show me where that spear went in."

The fellow opened his tunic and put his finger between the fifth and sixth ribs on his left side.

"It missed the ribs?"

"Well, it went between them."

"At what angle?"

The soldier took his dagger and pointed it, describing a thirty-five-degree angle from his chest.

"It could hardly have missed the heart, could it?"

"No, Prefect. Nor the lungs."

"No question, then, about him being quite dead?"

"I'd wager my life on it, sir."

"Do you know why I had to recheck all this with you?" Pilate asked the centurion.

"To be honest, Prefect, we have heard rumors about the Nazarene. . . . coming back to life."

"That will be all, Centurion. Take your men back to the Antonia."

The next morning, Pilate summoned Joseph of Arimathea to inquire exactly how he had buried Jesus. The councilor replied that he and the fellow Sanhedrist, Nicodemus, had been somewhat hurried, since the Sabbath was approaching, but all the usual customs had been observed, including the placing of a downy feather just below Jesus' nostrils for about ten minutes. The feather had not moved. Jesus was dead.

Pilate asked Joseph the final query he could logically muster: Did Jesus have a twin brother? But Joseph shook his head.

Wearily, Pilate returned to his original supposition of a dead Jesus, whose body was stolen by his disciples on Friday night. Subsequent "appearances" to his followers would have to be hallucinations or optical illusions of some kind—or lies.

This, at any rate, seemed to be the explanation over at the temple, for Malchus, Caiaphas' servant, delivered the following message shortly before noon:

Joseph Caiaphas to Pontius Pilatus, peace.

The followers of the Nazarene will stop at nothing, as you have doubtless heard. They came by night and stole his body while the guards were sleeping. Therefore if any claims are made to his so-called "resurrection," you will know how to interpret these. We are grateful for your cooperation. Do not think harshly of our guards for falling asleep. They have been exhausted over the last days in pursuing this case. Peace.

Pilate had contempt for such an excuse in behalf of sleeping guards. Didn't they set up shifts? They would not have come off so lightly were they Roman auxiliaries.

Suddenly the import of Caiaphas' note struck him with crushing force. Why had the high priest not resorted to the obvious loophole of an unguarded tomb on Friday night to account for the disappearance of Jesus' body, rather than blaming it on guards sleeping on Saturday night? Friday night was the one hiatus in the grave's surveillance to which Pilate had been clinging in his maddening quest for a logical explanation to the events of the weekend. Why had Caiaphas overlooked it? Unless his guards had proof that the theft occurred between Saturday night and Sunday dawn.

"Malchus! If you ever spoke the truth in your life, don't fail to do so now."

"Yes, Excellency?"

"Do you know any of the police who were sent to keep watch over the sepulcher in which Jesus of Nazareth was buried?"

"Yes, I know several of the men who were on duty."

"Did you talk to them about what happened?"

"Yes."

"Good. Now, when they set up their bivouac around the tomb on Saturday morning, they certainly wouldn't have bothered to roll back the stone to . . . to see if the body of Jesus were still inside, would they?"

"Yes, they would, Excellency. In fact, the chief priests instructed them to do that even before setting up their watch. The body was there, wrapped in linen bands. Certainly they wouldn't have sealed the stone without first determining that there was something inside to seal."

Pilate had worded his question so as to elicit a negative reply most easily. He wanted a negative answer. The puzzle would have been solved. Since stealing a body from a fully guarded tomb had to be impossible, the theft would have occurred Friday night, with the watch sealing a tomb they didn't know was empty on Saturday, and then imagining the robbery had transpired Saturday night when the earth tremor shoved the stone aside Sunday morning to reveal the empty tomb. But now the last exit had been blocked, the last straw of logic wrenched from the clutch of a man sinking into an intellectual quandary.

"Well," Pilate finally shrugged, "at least Caiaphas was honest enough not to use a Friday night theft as a convenient excuse."

"He wasn't being honest."

Pilate was certain he had misunderstood Malchus. "What did you say?" he asked.

"I said, my master wasn't being honest."

"What do you mean?" Pilate asked in astonishment. Now the servant grew frightened and hesitant.

"Go on, Malchus. I give you my word that I'll not report anything you say. Speak on."

"The prophet's body was not stolen by his disciples. I was there when the guards reported everything to the chief priests. They said it happened at dawn. Half of them were on guard, half sleeping. Suddenly there was an earthquake. A fearful radiance flashed in and around the sepulcher. The watch heard a man's voice talking to some women who had just arrived, saying that Yeshu had risen. Most of the guards were so panicked that they fled. Some, with more courage, cautiously looked inside the tomb after the women had left. The saw only grave clothes."

Pilate was seriously disturbed. The story corroborated the women's. He asked Malchus, "Then why did Caiaphas write me about a stolen body, sleeping guards?"

"Because this is now the official story. The chief priests met with the scribes and elders to decide what to do. They concluded that Yeshu removed himself from the grave by some fearfully occult necromancy, a sorcerer's trick of some kind, inspired by Satan. But if they allowed the guards' story to become public knowledge, even if they gave a demonic explanation for it, the people would say Yeshu was indeed the Messiah. Everyone would flock to his cause until Roman legions would finally have to put down the movement. They couldn't have that, so they had the guards claim that Yeshu's followers stole the body while they were sleeping."

For some time Pilate looked at Malchus without really seeing him. Then he clapped him on the shoulder, "I appreciate your honesty."

"If my Lord Caiaphas learns anything of this, I am undone, of course."

"Your story will not be divulged."

And then, while dismissing him, Pilate said, "One more thing, Malchus. Don't feel you have to answer this, but just why were you so candid with me? You were, after all, compromising your own master."

The servant smiled. "Because I now have a higher master, Excellency. Yeshu Hannosri healed me, and so I believe the other reports about him must be true also. I merely wanted you to know the truth."

"He healed *you*? How?"

Malchus related the incident of his severed ear while Pilate watched him skeptically. "Are you *sure* it was cut off, Malchus?"

"It was on the ground. . . ."

"And now, I suppose, you believe he actually . . . *rose* from the dead?"

"Yes, Excellency."

"Good day, Malchus."

More of the inexplicable. Pilate furrowed his brow. Because of the ear story and the servant's new faith, he questioned the reliability of Malchus' statements in their discussion. No, the man wasn't necessarily coloring the facts, but what if he, too, were under a spell of some kind? In that case, would he ever learn the truth about the bizarre events of the past weekend?

Pilate arranged to leave Jerusalem in short order, delegating to the Antonia commandant the task of maintaining law and order during the remaining days of the Pesach.

He wanted to escape the extravagant fanaticism of the city, that Holy Utopia where otherwise respectable men and women dreamed dreams and conjured up visions. Procula, however, wished she might have had a further talk with Joanna, or better still, with some of the disciples of the man her husband had sent to the cross. It was not to be. Procula had to leave Jerusalem, but she carried with her a treasury of indelible impressions she would never shake off. Nor would she try.

Chapter 21

IN CAESAREA, Pilate was surprised to find that much of the populace knew of the events in Jerusalem during the recent Passover. He had hoped the news would not penetrate the other world represented at his capital, but returning Jewish pilgrims carried back every incident, every rumor. He was concerned that reports of his role during that festival week could damage his prestige as governor. Strangely, this was not the case. Most Jews appreciated his deferring to the Sanhedrin, while those who sympathized with Jesus' cause looked back at his crucifixion only through the happy lens of the resurrection. And the large gentile element at Caesarea was not interested in what had transpired at Jerusalem, regarding Jesus only as a curiosity.

Pilate wanted to forget the entire episode, and in a way it was easy to do. The news and the rumors from Rome were certainly important enough to refocus his attention on the political puzzle there. After the fall of Sejanus, most Romans had confidently expected the party of Agrippina to stage a major comeback, beginning with her return from exile. But the inscrutable Tiberius had not recalled his daughter-in-law. Though her eldest son had died, there were hopes that Drusus, her second son, might now be released from his subterranean prison in the Palatine palace to assume the role of heir apparent.

Fresh news arriving in the port of Caesarea canceled that expectation for Procula, who had always sympathized with Agrippina. The distraught Drusus, all hope of release

258

exhausted, had begun to curse Tiberius. His blasts were carefully recorded by his guards, and later read to the Senate. No more meals were brought to Drusus' cell. The hapless youth spent the final eight days of his life chewing the stuffing out of his mattress in a delirious quest for nourishment.

Mother Agrippina fared little better. Crushed by the loss of her second son, she starved herself to death on the isle of Pandateria. By a quirk of fate, she died the same day on which her archenemy Sejanus had been executed two years earlier. Hardly saddend by these tidings, Tiberius boasted to the Senate that at least Agrippina had not been strangled or thrown down the Stairs of Mourning, as would have befitted her treason and masculine ambition. The conscript fathers thanked the princeps for his mercy.

To Pilate and Procula, it was a clear revelation that Tiberius had always been suspicious of Agrippina and her brood. While Sejanus had played on this suspicion for his own advancement, the emperor's mistrust lingered on even after the prefect had been swept away. But there was a last son of Agrippina to whom the aging princeps showed some favor, Gaius, the youngest. He was called Caligula, which meant "Little Boots," or "Bootsie," a nickname conferred on him by the troops of his father Germanicus when, as a small boy, he strutted about in his own little soldier's uniform, complete with miniature boots. Tiberius had sheltered Caligula from the schemes of Sejanus by keeping him at Capri. Shrewdly, the youth avoided showing any grief at the destruction of his mother and brothers lest he be sent their way. Instead, he carefully aped the moods and fancies of the princeps, answering his every whim. Rome sensed that a grooming process was underway, and that Tiberius' teen-age understudy on Capri would likely succeed him. Caligula now celebrated his marriage to the daughter of a senator, and, like all higher officials in the Empire, the prefect of Judea was careful to honor the heir apparent with a present, a large and handsomely wrought silver urn from Phoenicia.

Occasionally Pilate thought back to the events in Jerusalem. Despite all his arguments before Procula in defense of his conduct, a nagging twinge of conscience told him that he had not played a hero's role in the Jewish capital, and that either an innocent man had gone to the cross from his tribunal, or someone guilty of religious indiscretions had been punished too severely. He cursed his removing the *jus gladii* from the Sanhedrin. If he hadn't, the case of Jesus of Nazareth would never have crossed his tribunal. Damn Sejanus! Damn his needling pressure!

Pilate wanted to forget. But events seemed to conspire to prevent his forgetting. Jerusalem was a hotbed of rumor. There were reports that the risen Jesus had been sighted on a mountain in Galilee, by the shore of the Sea of Tiberias, around the suburbs of Jerusalem. Later accounts even had it that he had soared into the heavens, leaving the earth at the Mount of Olives.

But the stories which both amused and yet alarmed Pilate concerned the resiliency of Jesus' adherents. Inexplicably, instead of running off to Galilee and hiding, his disciples were braving the ire of the Sanhedrin and remaining in Jerusalem. And they weren't being very quiet about it either. The tribune at the Antonia wrote that on a Jewish holiday called Pentecost, he had led a squad of men to control a crowd which had gathered round the house where Jesus' followers were staying. They were addressing the people in a dozen different languages, so that all visiting pilgrims would be able to understand. Some thought it was gibberish and jeered, "They're all drunk!" That was when the impressive hulk of a man, Peter, smiled good-naturedly and replied, "No . . . we haven't been drinking. It's only nine o'clock in the morning!" That brought a laugh which Peter used to launch into some kind of moving oratory, the tribune wrote, for afterward about 3000 of the crowd joined Peter's cause. Pilate might be interested in a phrase from Peter's address: "By the deliberate plan of God, you used pagan gentiles to crucify Jesus of Nazareth. But God restored him to life again, and made him both Lord and Messiah."

Pilate replied by return courier that the tribune was to keep the movement under close surveillance. The fact that 3000 should suddenly wish to join the following of someone who had been crucified seven weeks earlier was both incredible and ominous. Any seditious preaching or any resort to arms was to be reported at once. As to Peter's statement that it was by their god's determination that the Jews used Pilate and his Roman auxiliaries for the execution, he could make no sense of it. Why should the Hebrew god want Romans to do the dirty work?

The tribune's next report stated that there was nothing undercover about the movement. The leaders taught the people openly in the temple. One afternoon, two of them healed a lifelong cripple who was a fixture at one of the temple gates. When the worshipers saw him dancing around the precincts for joy, they ran up to the disciples in amazement. Again it was Peter who preached a powerful message and several thousand more joined their cause. He said nothing treasonable. He didn't even mention Rome except to tell the people that they had repudiated the innocent Jesus when Pilate wanted to release him. At least they had the story straight, the tribune commented, and apparently they bore no deep grudge against the prefect. But the captain of the temple guard arrested the two disciples and threw them into prison. Next day, the Sanhedrin heard their case, but finally let them off with a warning, since they could hardly condemn men who had just healed a cripple.

When the commandant's third report arrived, Pilate was beginning to wish the man were not so faithful a correspondent, since this message would probably contain more of the inexplicable. He was not disappointed. Jerusalem now reverberated with interest in the risen Jesus, the tribune wrote, and the wonders of healing the disciples were performing in his name. Townspeople were actually carrying the beds of their sick into the streets so that the disciples might cure them. Again the religious establishment tried to check the movement by arresting its leaders, but they escaped from prison and resumed their teaching in the temple. At another hearing before the Sanhedrin, they were ordered to stop their missionizing. They refused, claiming, "We must obey God rather than men." A motion was introduced to condemn them to death, but it was defeated when Rabbi Gamaliel advised leaving them alone. The movement was either of human or divine origin, he argued. If human, it would collapse of itself, as had the causes of all pseudo-Messiahs before Yeshu Hannosri; but if divine, it would be irresistible, for who could fight God? The Sanhedrin had the disciples flogged and then discharged with a warning. Nevertheless, they were carrying on and winning more converts. But no, the tribune wrote, nothing they preached seemed politically dangerous. On the other hand, if the prefect wished them detained for questioning he would arrest them.

Pilate wondered what to do about this "Jewish subsect in-the-making," as he now styled the Jesus-inspired movement. Arrest the nucleus of leaders? No. No, for the same reason that the Sanhedrin probably took no action. One religio-political trial had been quite enough at this time for both the Jewish and the Roman hierarchy. No, because the disciples seemed innocent of charges which would concern Rome, though the rate at which they were attracting adherents was disturbing. No, since it was even a little gratifying to see how a dead man could inspire this kind of loyalty. No, because he couldn't care less if the Jews, who were already fractured into various competing groups and parties, should now spawn an additional tiny and insignificant offshoot, call them Jesusians, Nazarenes, Messians, or whatever. They would linger a short time, he confidently predicted, and then die out.

Procula was unabashedly happy to learn that her husband had no plans to arrest Jesus' followers. She fairly thrived on reports about what the disciples were doing.

But the distance from Jerusalem and the time since the Passover tended to blur for Pilate the inexplicable events which had once so troubled him. Perhaps the contagious religiosity of the city had temporarily addled his wits. From cool and dispassionate Caesarea, he wondered why he became so involved in the fate of one solitary and inscrutable Jew. But time was banishing it all from memory.

Then, as if in Hades' own conspiracy to remind him, came a letter from the least-expected source Pilate could possibly imagine: Thrasyllus, Tiberius' court astrologer on Capri.

Tiberius Claudius Thrasyllus to Pontius Pilatus, greeting. If you are in health, it is well. I also and the princeps are well.

Seven years have passed since our fateful luncheon at The Grotto. At that time you promised me a small favor, Prefect, but it was never done. I refer to the star or comet which hovered over Judea almost forty years ago. You were to consult the priests in Jerusalem about it and report to me.

What reminded me to inquire about this was the strange celestial event which occurred in the afternoon of the Friday following the Calends of April. A great darkness moved across the horizon from the southeastern Mediterranean and blackened our sky for several hours. Since it seemed to approach from your direction and from Egypt, please consult any local astrologer for an explanation. The phenomenon has upset my astrological calculations ever since that time. The princeps is also concerned. May I hear from you before another seven years elapse? Farewell.

Pilate knew that the uncanny darkness at the time of the crucifixion had covered all of Palestine, but he was absolutely astounded that it had also penetrated as far as Rome.

He had always disliked Thrasyllus, and the astrologer knew it, which is why he carefully included the remark about the emperor sharing his concern. Whether it was true or not Pilate could not afford to guess, but it was common knowledge that Tiberius now spent much time on his astrological hobby in the uppermost of his lavish villas on Capri, where he had fashioned an occult observatory. Too, Thrasyllus' granddaughter had married the new praetorian prefect Macro. The letter would have to be answered.

After consulting Caesarea's one astrologer, Pilate replied to Thrasyllus, apologizing that he had not written sooner. Yes, he had learned a little about the star. Gratus, his predecessor, told him it had attracted some eastern magi to Jerusalem who were looking for a king of the Jews, but they had been referred to a nearby town instead. If he wanted more details, he could consult Gratus in Rome, since the Jerusalem priests remembered little of the event. As to the darkness, it had indeed engulfed Judea at the stated time, but the local astrologer simply could not explain it. An earth tremor had accompanied the darkness, but the event remained a total mystery.

Pilate thought of mentioning the coincidence of the darkness with the crucifixion of another "king of the Jews," but he rejected the idea. With his astrologer's mind, Thrasyllus would surely belabor the coincidence.

The question of whether he ought to submit to Tiberius a special, detailed report on the crucifixion of Jesus had occurred to Pilate. It would demonstrate both his obedience to the imperial directive that he honor Jewish laws, and also his loyalty in crucifying someone who dared call himself king while Tiberius lived. On the other hand, in his now-metaphysical frame of mind, the princeps might become unduly interested in a religious luminary who had called himself a son of God, and he might even criticize Pilate for condemning him. Conversely, in a paranoid twist, Tiberius might suspect a great eastern conspiracy against him and punish Pilate for not rounding up and crucifying the entire following of the would-be king, rather than just the ringleader. Better to let sleeping dogs lie.

Legally, of course, he would have to include some notice of Jesus' execution in his official *acta* or annual report which he submitted to Tiberius. When he drew this up at the close of the year 33, the following extracts appeared in Pilate's *acta* under the section entitled, "Judiciary Acts":

... ages 38 and 41, respectively.

Both highway robbers, convicted of theft and murder perpetrated between Jericho and Jerusalem on March 26, A.V.C. 786. *Accusatores:* five eyewitnesses among Galilean pilgrims attending the Passover festival in Jerusalem. Tried on April 2; sentenced, crucified, and died on April 3, A.V.C. 786, in Jerusalem.

IESVS BAR-ABBAS, age 45

Son of a rabbi; resistance leader. Accused of murder and insurrection, but released prior to trial, as requested by the Great Sanhedrin and the citizens of Jerusalem by reason of the annual Passover amnesty, April 3, A.V.C. 786, in Jerusalem.

IESVS NAZARENVS, age 36

Galilean teacher, "prophet," and pseudo-Messiah. Case was remanded to the jurisdiction of the tetrarch Herod Antipas, who waived his authority and returned the defendant for Roman trial. Convicted of capital blasphemy by the Great Sanhedrin, with verdict endorsed by the prefect. Also convicted of constructive treason for claiming to be *"Rex Iudaeorum."* *Accusatores:* Joseph Caiaphas, high priest, and the Great Sanhedrin. Tried, sentenced, crucified, and died on April 3, A.V.C. 786, in Jerusalem.

During the early months of 34, domestic affairs seemed to be running smoothly in Palestine. Pilate's truce with the Herodian tetrarchs was holding rather well, and there was no threatening correspondence from Rome. But death now staged a dramatic interruption in cutting down the popular tetrarch Philip, who had married his dancing niece Salome. Since Philip left no children, Herod Antipas was hoping the emperor might award his tetrarchy to him, which would double the lands under his control. But instead, Philip's territory was attached to the province of Syria.

The time had come for Pilate to see if either his Syrian or Egyptian fences needed mending. To the north, the four Roman legions in Syria stood especially high in Tiberius' favor, since they alone had not hung images of Sejanus among their military standards, and the emperor had rewarded them handsomely for this prudent gesture. The recently arrived commander of these now-elite forces, Pomponius Flaccus, represented a new quantum of power on Pilate's horizon, since for the first time in his experience, Syria was not ruled by an absentee governor. He planned to pay Flaccus a visit during the spring of 35, but fate seemed to cherish a vacant post for Syria. Flaccus suddenly died before Pilate could make the trip.

On the southern frontier, he stayed in close touch with Avillius Flaccus, the prefect of Egypt, where the people were astir about a resurrection story of another kind. After a heroic absence of many centuries, the wondrous phoenix had been sighted again, that remarkable bird which supposedly lived hundreds of years, then died and virtually came to life again in its one offspring, which also lived for centuries. On a more serious level, Flaccus warned Pilate of possible anti-Roman developments among the peoples of the Near East. On a scouting trip up the Nile, he had discovered caches of contraband arms which were to be used in a planned insurrection. He could not know what the situation was in Judea, but he advised Pilate to be on his guard.

Yet, in pleasant contrast to the turmoil two years earlier, Judea seemed quite serene. In fact, Pilate had only one altercation with the Sanhedrin. It concerned a follower of Jesus named Stephen, whose brilliance in preaching the new faith had led to his trial for blasphemy before the Sanhedrin. His defense was so bold that he was pulled outside the walls of Jerusalem and stoned to death. When Pilate learned of it in Caesarea, he dispatched a caustic note to Caiaphas which protested the stoning as contrary to Roman law and warned against any such incidents in the future. Apologetically, the high priest promised he would try to prevent anything similar from happening again, though he did reserve the Sanhedrin's right to counteract the growing movement of the Nazarene.

It was another of the items which reminded Pilate of that fateful Passover, but in this case he merely felt vindicated. "See, Procula," he contended, "if I hadn't been in Jerusalem for that Passover, they would have stoned Jesus in precisely the same way as this Stephen and called it a mob action which could not be prevented."

Her answer was unbending. "But you *were* in Jerusalem."

A shock in Pilate's private life at Caesarea was what he called the "spiritual defection" of Cornelius. Responding to his wife's genuine Judaism, the centurion had had their first child, a boy, circumcised. And now he himself became a near-convert to the Jewish faith. Indulging a traditional Roman prejudice, Pilate found it difficult to accept Cornelius' new religious allegiance. The centurion tried to explain that he was not a full proselyte; he just admired and shared the Jewish belief in one God. He claimed it was a magnificent substitute for the gods and goddesses of Roman paganism which Pilate himself despised. But his interest in Judaism should in no way affect their close friendship, Cornelius insisted.

But it did. With regret, Pilate noticed the beginnings of a change in their relationship. The old camaraderie had waned when Cornelius became a family man, which was understandable. But beyond this was the man's new religiosity: he attended worship in the local synagogue and soon began contributing to its support. He was even known to pray privately on occasion. It was all very un-Roman, a bitter disappointment to Pilate. On the other hand, the Jewish community in Caesarea was pleased that a highly placed Roman in the provincial capital should follow their faith, even if he had not become a full proselyte. This might well diminish future friction between Pilate and the Jews.

But there was less chance of such abrasions now. The Sanhedrin, in full alarm at the growth of the Nazarene movement, had no time for any further tilts with Pilate. A general persecution against the sect was instituted, a house-by-house search for adherents of Jesus, who now fled Jerusalem and scattered across the country districts of Palestine. An ardent young student of Gamaliel named Saul was serving as zealous inquisitor in ferreting out any who remained and packing them off to prison. Finally, only the disciples stayed in Jerusalem, and even they left periodically to spread the rapidly growing new faith.

Pilate had no time to plumb the theological niceties of

the movement, nor did he concern himself with any of the journeying apostles. His total attention was now claimed by the arrival of the new governor of Syria, Lucius Vitellius, fresh from his consulship at Rome. He had had a highly successful administration, and Tiberius placed such great confidence in Vitellius that he came armed with an extraordinary command to settle all affairs in the turbulent Roman East, not just in his appointed province of Syria.

The Near East was in turmoil because the Parthian Empire, that perennial dagger in Rome's eastern flank, was now making a renewed twist. Convinced that Tiberius was an unpopular old man who would do nothing to oppose him, King Artabanus III of Parthia moved to control Armenia, which was Rome's protectorate. But by building disaffection inside Parthia and allying with her enemies, Tiberius resisted. The capable Vitellius was dispatched to carry out this policy, and his intrigues with leading Parthian magnates to replace Artabanus so rattled the king that he was ready to talk terms. Vitellius marched his Syrian legions to the banks of the Euphrates and negotiated a settlement with Artabanus in the middle of a specially constructed bridge spanning the river. They agreed that Rome would recognize Artabanus in Parthia, while he would recognize Rome's control of Armenia. It was an astute diplomatic coup for Vitellius, who had triumphed without shedding a drop of Roman blood or spending a needless sesterce.

And Pontius Pilate had watched it all happen with a good deal of chagrin, because Vitellius' assistant at the negotiations was none other than the sometime foe-and-friend, Herod Antipas. Friends they might be, ever since the reconciliation in Jerusalem, but rivals they would remain, and each had sought an opportunity to pay court to Vitellius upon his arrival in Syria. Antipas had won—handsomely. Vitellius had taken the tetrarch with him to the Euphrates parley because he could speak Aramaic, the diplomatic language of the entire Near East. And Antipas made the most of this foray into international affairs. He entertained the negotiating parties at a sumptuous banquet in a pavilion pitched on the bridge itself, and immediately afterward wrote Tiberius a glowing account of the whole affair. While this annoyed Vitellius, whose official report to the princeps arrived later as old news, Antipas' stock was never higher in Rome.

Just when Herod Antipas was looking his best, events in Samaria were daubing an unflattering portrait of Pilate. Samaria comprised the northern third of his province, a hilly country peopled by halfbreed Israelites of mixed Semitic stock. The Jews despised these neighboring cousins, and were despised by them, not merely because of racial but also religious differences. Pilate had paid scant attention to the Samaritans, but when rumbles developed among them, he turned to his advisers for a briefing.

The Samaritans, he was told, recognized only the five books of Moses as true Scripture, banning all the other Hebrew prophets from their canon. They had even erected a rival temple to counter Jerusalem's on Mount Gerizim, which lay south of their capital, Sebaste, but a Jewish prince had destroyed the temple a century and a half ago, and it was never rebuilt. Mount Gerizim, however, remained sacred to the Samaritans, so holy in fact that an unscrupulous demagogue who specialized in mendacity was now using the mountain as his prime prop in a mass religious confidence game. For weeks he had been advertising himself as the long-awaited Messianic *Taheb* or "Restorer," and many credulous Samaritans believed that he was truly the prophet Moses had predicted when he had said, "The Lord your God will raise up for you a prophet like me from your midst, from your brethren: him you shall heed."

And the people were certainly paying heed to the counterfeit holy man. Fresh information reaching Caesarea told of a mass movement developing under his aegis. As proof for his claims, the would-be Second Moses now promised to perform the gesture expected of the Samaritan Messiah: he would lead them up Mount Gerizim and unearth the sacred vessels from the Ark of the Covenant which Moses had secretly concealed in a cave somewhere in the mount. After that, Pilate's council advised, the Samaritan masses would probably hail the man as the Restorer and inaugurate his rule by rebuilding their temple and fortifying Gerizim. In Samaritan beliefs, it would be the beginning of the millennium, when the holy mount, which had once been the site of the Garden of Eden, so they taught, would again constitute Paradise.

The tragic deception in all this was not merely that the imposter himself had most likely hidden bogus vessels in a spot on the mountain where he would "discover" them, but that the people did not catch the glaring error in Samaritan belief itself. Not only had Moses never hidden anything on Mount Gerizim, he had never even set foot in Palestine west of the Jordan. Pilate recalled that item from Antipas' travelogue at the Dead Sea.

But sober historical fact could never stand in the way of the promised spectacular. A date for the great event was finally announced, and the multitudes were to assemble at the village of Tirathana near the base of Gerizim. The men were to bring weapons, for the ministry of the Restorer also had military implications. Many Samaritans believed he would conquer eleven nations and eventually triumph over the whole world.

Since Mount Gerizim was only thirty miles from Caesarea, Pilate learned the date almost as soon as the Samaritans. He had planned to send only an auxiliary guard to police the situation and, if necessary, prevent the people from being exploited. But when he learned of the call to arms, he drastically revised his plans, for Gerizim lay astride the major north-south highway of central Palestine, the shortest route from Jerusalem to Galilee. With the imposter's Messianic claims, anything might be possible from an armed crowd.

Marshaling two detachments of heavily armed infantry and half his cavalry, Pilate set out for Samaria's holy mountain. His auxiliaries included men from the Italian Cohort in the unlikely event that, if it came to blows, his Samaritan auxiliaries might lose heart at having to battle their brother Samaritans. His cavalry squadron, the *Ala I Gemina Sebastenorum*, "First Wing of Sebastenians," was totally Samaritan.

The gravity of the situation was underscored by the pseudo-prophet's call for weapons, the first potential armed resistance Pilate faced in his almost ten years as prefect of Judea. Many threatening multitudes had gathered in Judea during this time, but they had never been armed. Coupled with the Egyptian prefect's warning of growing anti-Roman sentiment supported by secret caches of weapons, Pilate's concern mounted. Incipient insurrection had to be crushed at its birth, or his five cohorts would never be able to control it. Calling to Vitellius for emergency help would hardly be an appropriate overture to their first meeting.

Pilate and his troops arrived late in the evening before the day of the projected climb of Mount Gerizim. He saw that it would be strategically foolish to attempt a blockade

of Tirathana, the village where the Samaritans were en-
camped, so he had his men bivouac secretly along the path
which would be used for the ascent.

The next day, an enthusiastic horde surged out of the village and headed for the lower reaches of Gerizim, the one
mountain which, they swore, had kept its peak dry in the
Great Flood, the holy hill toward which all pious Samaritans faced in prayer. But soon they found their route
blocked by ranks of infantry, with cavalry moving in on
their flanks.

Pilate had his herald trumpet the throng to attention.
Then he called out to the Samaritans: "If you are merely
on a religious pilgrimage to the top of your sacred mountain, why do you need weapons? Lay down your arms!"

Loud protests and grumbling answered him, then hissing
and jeers. One spokesman shouted, "We won't leave our-
selves defenseless, Prefect! If we throw down our weapons,
your men will attack us."

"No harm will come to you if you lay down your arms.
But it's treasonable to assemble a crowd of this size fully
armed. You have an illegal army here."

There was a short pause, then a yell from the Samaritan
ranks: "And this illegal army shall be victorious! Under the
guidance of our Holy Restorer, no harm can come to us.
Fellow Samaritans, drive these pagans off our sacred
mountain!"

A lusty war whoop followed, and the battle was on. The
Roman troops were taken by surprise, since they had not
really expected resistance, and the center line of Pilate's
outnumbered infantry bent into a concave crescent from
the onslaught. He himself was gashed on the cheek by a
flailing Samaritan sword, and barely managed to beat off
his attacker. It was his first pitched battle as prefect of
Judea.

The Samaritans fought with blazing religious enthusiasm
on their own holy ground. Though cut down steadily, they
advanced rank after rank. The hills re-echoed the strident
clang of swords smashing on shields, the triumphant yell of
men driving javelins into their mark, the shrieks of the
wounded.

Wheezing in the whirling dust, Pilate quickly checked
the position of his forces, then signaled his infantry to
counterattack while his herald trumpeted the cavalry to
swoop down from the sides. The Roman forces soon re-

gained control. The horse closed in on the Samaritan flanks and pressed them hard. Fortunately, women and children in the multitude had fled the scene, and now some of the men joined them. But the Samaritan core continued fighting surprisingly well, and troops fell on both sides. Finally, however, the professional discipline of the auxiliaries made the difference. Although outnumbered by the Samaritans, they now put their motley army to flight and then chased down the fugitives. Some escaped, but many more were taken prisoner.

Outraged at the resistance and smarting from his own wound, Pilate declared martial law and set up a military tribunal shortly after the battle. The ringleaders of the armed rebellion he sentenced to death, as well as several who were most influential in the religious hoax, including the pseudo-Restorer himself. Since crucifixion would take too long, they resorted to simple field execution by sword. The uprising was quelled entirely.

Pilate hoped the Samaritans would eventually appreciate his liberating them from belief in an obviously false Messiah who was trying to deceive them. Unlike Judea's "king of the Jews," this one was truly guilty. Leaving a tribune with one cohort to police the area, he returned to Caesarea in triumph.

It was late in November of 36. After the Samaritan tumult, things had gone better for Pilate. Judea was again peaceful enough to warrant his planning a trip with Procula to Greece and the Aegean islands in the new year. She needed the change; so did he. There were no quarrels with the Jews. In fact, Caiaphas had commended him for his handling of the Samaritan challenge. Even the chronic neighboring rivalry with Herod Antipas seemed to swing once again in Pilate's favor, despite the tetrarch's coup at the Euphrates. Earlier that month, Antipas was ignominiously defeated in a war with King Aretas, who had finally launched his long-expected attack against the man who had divorced his daughter and insulted their royal house.

While savoring this development, Pilate was informed that a special envoy named Marcellus waited to see him with an important message from the governor of Syria. As he was shown into Pilate's office, Marcellus gave a smart Roman salute, clenched hand on chest. Pilate returned it. Then he was handed Vitellius' letter. While slitting the seals, he assumed it was an invitation to a state visit in Antioch, for which he had been angling in order to meet the powerful Vitellius. Then he read:

Lucius Vitellius, *proconsul Suriae*, to Pontius Pilatus, *praefectus Iudaeae*, greeting.

The Council of Samaria has formally accused you of a needless massacre of their countrymen at Mount Gerizim in your province. They have sworn to me that the gathering intended no sedition or rebellion against Rome, but assembled at Tirathana only as refugees from your violence. Members of the Council have reaffirmed their allegiance to the princeps.

By authority of his imperial majesty, Tiberius Caesar Augustus, and as his special commissioner for eastern affairs, I herewith suspend you from your duties as *praefectus Iudaeae*, effective immediately, and cite you to return to Rome as soon as possible in order to give the emperor your account of the affair at Mount Gerizim in defense against charges brought against you by the Council of Samaria. A Samaritan delegation will serve as *accusatores* at your arraignment in Rome.

Marcellus, my associate who delivers this message, will serve as acting prefect of Judea during your absence. You will be kind enough to spend the next week in familiarizing Marcellus with the functions of your office. Late in December, I will arrive in Judea to assist him, as well as to review affairs in your province. I trust you will not delay your return to Rome, and that a guard will not prove necessary to assist in that return. Farewell.

Pilate felt a cramping pressure at the pit of his stomach, and his heart thumped in a mad cadence as his nerves caught fire. The letter spelled the end of his governorship, perhaps the end of his career, but for the moment he had only one thought: to maintain a Stoic calm in front of the man appointed to succeed him. Was it grim Roman efficiency or cruel calculation which had led Vitellius to notify him of his suspension in this embarrassing manner?

Pilate stared at his successor, who somewhat nervously avoided his eyes. "I need not tell you, Marcellus, that the proconsul is grossly mistaken in his opinion of the Samaritans," he said with studied serenity, "and that his conduct in this discharge is extraordinary."

A patrician-looking man, somewhat Pilate's junior, Marcellus straightened and replied, "Extraordinary? The princeps will decide that. . . ."

Pilate reread the message hurriedly, then commented, "For example, this passage about the Samaritans assembling at Tirathana 'only as refugees from my violence.' That's a bald lie, their own perjury to explain the embarrassing fact that they were fully armed, all of them."

Marcellus said nothing.

Pilate continued his case. "And what would *you* do, Marcellus, if you had to face an armed rebellion of thousands of your subjects astride the main highway in your province? Cheer them on?"

"Are you certain it was a rebellion, Prefect? Perhaps diplomacy might have won the day. But all this is beside the point. I'm not here to review your case but to assume your command. Will you show me where my aides are to be quartered?"

Late that night, Cornelius filled Pilate in on the background of Vitellius' action; he had wormed the information out of one of Marcellus' aides after a long evening of wining the man in Caesarea's finest tavern. The Council of Samaria, the Samaritan analogue to the Jewish Sanhedrin, was so furious at Pilate's field executions that members of the Council had traveled to Antioch to present their case to Vitellius, formally denouncing Pilate "for the slaughter of innocent Samaritan victims." Under normal circumstances, Cornelius continued, Vitellius should have summoned Pilate to Antioch to hear his side of it before deciding guilt in the matter, but he did not do so for several reasons. Tiberius had alerted Vitellius to "keep an eye on Pontius Pilatus, who might be outliving his usefulness in Judea." Also, on the trip to the Euphrates, Herod Antipas had been dropping gentle hints that his rival governor did not understand the Jews nearly as well as—well, he for one. Even though Vitellius knew Antipas well enough to surmise what motivated these comments, he deduced that there was no smoke without some fire. And finally, since Pilate could appeal his decision to the emperor anyway, Vitellius decided not to hear his defense. Instead, he had dismissed the Samaritan embassy with a promise of redress for their grievances, and dispatched his friend Marcellus to Caesarea.

Pilate embraced Cornelius in gratitude. The centurion

had risked his whole future in the new Judean administration in order to get vital information—for a friend.

The week which followed was one which Pilate wished might have been deleted from his life, as he tried later to obscure it from memory. There was the galling task of closing a decade of administration in a few days, and in a climate of dishonor. Perfunctorily Pilate groomed Marcellus, and presumptuously Marcellus learned. Because of the legal cloud hovering over him, Pilate discouraged any social amenities by his friends in Caesarea to honor his departure.

Procula was shocked by the abrupt nature of the suspension, but she adapted rapidly to the new circumstances. Though very apprehensive about the future hearing before Tiberius, she reminded her husband that they both had been anxious to return to Rome. For him it had been ten years.

But this was scant consolation for Pilate. What galled him as much as Vitellius' arbitrary action in the affair was his own ironical miscalculation. In his later administration, Pilate's one fear had been that the Jews would complain about him to Tiberius and cause his recall. Now it had happened, but not because of Jews. Curiously, the despised Samaritans had done what the Jews only threatened to do. Who would have thought that their ignored, clannish, half-breed relatives would have unseated him? Pilate knew very little about the Samaritans other than that they made decent auxiliary troops. As part of his defense, which he was already framing, he would use the fact that his auxiliaries fought loyally against their racial brothers.

It was the matter of his defense which led Pilate to leave Judea as soon as possible. He wanted to hurry to Rome, since it would be to his advantage to catch the ear of the princeps before it was filled with Samaritan deception, he explained to Procula. It would require another terrible overland journey for her—the Mediterranean was closed to distance shipping in December—but they resolved to outrace the Samaritans.

Shortly before their departure, the disturbing news came like a Parthian shot. During a visit to Jerusalem, Vitellius granted a Jewish request to regain custody of the high priest's garments, pending Tiberius' approval. Jerusalemites greeted that bit of diplomacy with wild enthusiasm. The proconsul also announced that the emperor had ordered his Syrian legions to fight King Aretas in behalf of Herod Antipas. Now Pilate had to leave not only in dishonor, but with the knowledge that his rival had finally triumphed. With Antipas this high in the graces of the princeps, the future looked ominous for Pontius Pilate.

Cornelius had loyally volunteered to accompany his prefect back to Rome, but Pilate asked him to remain instead and communicate any future information which would aid his case, should any arise. After a final review of his auxiliaries, Pilate formally transferred command to Marcellus. His troops urged him to hurry back to Judea, but Pilate merely smiled gratefully. That night, Cornelius and his wife hosted Pilate and Procula at a small gathering of their closest friends on the eve of their departure.

Early the next morning, they set out on the road to Rome via Antioch in a caravan of four heavy carriages, accompanied by members of their personal staff. For Pilate, as for Palestine, it was the passing of an era.

Chapter 22

THE RETURN journey could not have been taken at a worse time. Late December lay almost at the center of *mare clausum*, the November 10 to March 10 period of closed sea, when none but the foolhardy would risk a voyage on the treacherous winter Mediterranean. Even the largest merchantmen making emergency runs during these months resorted to risky coasting passages from port to port, but prevailing northwestern gales often delayed them for weeks. There was only one reliable option for anyone who had to get to Rome quickly at this time, the land journey across Asis Minor and Greece.

Not that this route was more comfortable. Land travel stopped almost as completely as voyages during the winter because this was the rainy season, when the Anatolian plateau became a sea of mud, and the famed mountain pass at the Cilician Gates could be snowed shut for days. Even if the route were passable, howling blasts of north wind chilled warm-blooded Mediterranean types.

Yet Vitellius' letter of accusation would be in the emperor's hands before the year was out, for the imperial post took a maximum of forty days between Syria and Rome. Pilate, therefore, had had no choice but to use the land route despite its hazards and discomforts.

Every twenty-five miles or so, the Roman highway north was punctuated by a series of *mansiones*, halting stations with overnight accommodations, and between each of these were two *mutationes*, changing stations for relays of fresh horses. In this way, the imperial post could speed its messages by exchanging horses each 8⅓ miles. Whenever Pilate's entourage needed lodging or fresh horses, he simply produced his *diploma,* an official letter of introduction which the Roman government provided its traveling magistrates in order to facilitate their journeys. It also exempted Pilate's party from any of the numerous road taxes, tolls, customs, and frontier duties.

The trip to Antioch was uneventful, but as they rounded the corner of the Mediterranean into Asia Minor, a fierce sleet storm tore down on them from the Taurus Mountain range, ripping open the canvas covers on one of their carriages. Emergency patchwork failed to repair the damage as they limped and skidded into Tarsus, the eastern port of entry to the Cilician Gates. Here they halted for several days, waiting for word that the pass was cleared of snow. They used the time to provision themselves and have the tarpaulin mended.

Just before resuming their journey, aides reported that the man who presented the bill for repairing the carriage canvas insisted on speaking to Pilate. They brought in a youngish, bearded fellow who looked like a Jew but dressed like a Roman. He stared at Pilate for several moments with a curious expression, the kind of glance someone might assume in observing a strange animal species at the zoo. Then, raising his finger and pointing directly at Pilate's nose, he said, "You, Prefect, have committed the most heinous crime in history."

"What crime, wretch?" Pilate glowered.

"The greatest atrocity of which a human being is capable, Excellency: crucifying the Son of God." He paused to let his words register. "But you were driven to it and can be forgiven . . . even for this."

Pilate was startled at the reference, intrigued that a man 500 miles from Jerusalem should know about the Passover which he had all but forgotten in his present difficulties. "Who are you?" he demanded.

"One closely related to you in guilt, for once I also persecuted followers of Jesus. My name is Saul. I am a Pharisee, formerly a student of the Rabbi Gamaliel in Jerusalem, and now a tentmaker here in Tarsus until my time has come to teach the gentiles about the Christ."

Impatient to resume his journey, Pilate scowled at Saul and said, "Enough of your effrontery. I should have you thrown into jail for addressing a Roman magistrate in this manner."

"That won't be necessary, Excellency. I, too, am a Roman citizen, and under the jurisdiction of the Proconsul Vitellius." That statement, of course, neutralized Pilate's threat. Saul continued, "I wanted to speak with you, because you, of all people, should know the truth of what happened in Jerusalem three years ago."

"Then tell me," Pilate sneered. "Who stole the body, and how did they succeed with guards camped at the tomb?" The same elusive puzzle had never really been solved.

"It *wasn't* a grave theft. Yeshu returned to life. He rose from the dead."

"Then you're just another devotee of the Jesus cult," Pilate shrugged.

But Saul insisted, "No, Prefect, not just another devotee. Once I hated the Nazarene and everything he stood for. You condemned only *one* innocent man, but I was so misguided in my zeal that I arrested *many* innocent followers of Yeshu in the name of the Sanhedrin."

"*You* were the one responsible for Caiaphas' drive against them?"

"Yes, in part. Did you know about the stoning of a man called Stephen?"

"The lynching?"

"Yes. Well, I helped organize it."

"Then why are you now defending Jesus? Why do you call him 'Son of God'?"

"Because I saw him. . . ."

"So did I. So what."

"I saw him a year *after* you crucified him."

"You're mad."

"First hear my story, Prefect, then judge. Some time after the martyrdom of Stephen, I was traveling to Damascus in order to root out the followers of Yeshu there. But on the way, an overpowering event occurred. . . ."

The story of the conversion of the man who would one day be known as St. Paul made little impression on Pilate. But Procula, who was listening unobtrusively, was deeply interested and added this to the store of information about Jesus which she had continued accumulating. What particularly struck her were Saul's closing comments. Both Pilate and he had been part of God's higher design for the human race, he tried to explain. What took place that Passover had cosmic significance. All history would turn on that event, Saul predicted. Someday Pilate would understand.

But he understood only that the whole conversation was verging too metaphysical for his tastes. He suggested that Saul take his money and be off. "If I, too, see Jesus on the road to Rome, I'll begin to believe your story." Pilate thought it a generous jocularity under the circumstances.

"Just remember," Saul urged, "when the staggering realization of whom you crucified finally dawns on you, *don't* commit suicide, like Ish-Kerioth, the man who betrayed him. You can be forgiven. *I* was!"

Pilate had dreaded his coming confrontation with Tiberius. But now he had one small consolation. In Rome, at least, he would escape the flaming religious fanaticism of the East.

Snow in the nearly mile-high pass of the Cilician Gates had melted enough to enable Pilate's party to proceed. For forty miles they wound their way upward toward the Gates, a series of sharp defiles which notched the otherwise impregnable Taurus barrier. Near the summit, the pass tapered down to a precipitous narrows, where melted snow water gushed across the roadway. Here Pilate halted his entourage to remind them that Cyrus, Xerxes, Alexander the Great, and Caesar had all marched through the very gap in which they were now pausing. Procula was shivering. She wondered if Pilate might postpone his lecture until that evening?

They continued along the route used by the Roman imperial post, since it alone remained open at all seasons. Leading northwest across Asia Minor on the old Persian King's Highway, then via a short ship run to Philippi, the route continued west through Greece on the Via Egnatia to the Adriatic, where there was ferry service to Brundisium in Italy. The distance from Caesarea to Rome along this route was about 2000 miles, and allowing the average carriage travel time of twenty-five miles per day, the total trip would require about eighty days.

The rest of the journey was a wearying succession of starting at dawn, traveling in the morning and early afternoon, halting at twilight. Evenings were spent either at the imperial *mansiones* or, occasionally, at public inns, where the best quarters were reserved for the Roman governor and his staff. Since the highway was virtually deserted during the winter, horses or accommodations posed no problem. Despite the constant cold drizzle which dogged their caravan, the journey was not as dreadful as Pilate and Procula had imagined, particularly since the inns were good, and the old cities of Sardis and Pergamum surprisingly impressive.

By the end of February, 37, they finally reached the port of Dyrrachium on the Adriatic, where they boarded a ferry for the passage across the narrows to Brundisium on the Italian mainland. Here Pilate sought out the praetorian commandant at the port to get the latest news from Rome and Capri. The tribune, newly arrived from the capital to relieve a colleague, was indeed full of news.

Tidings from Capri were not good. Tiberius' mood had worsened over the last months, ever since the death of his friend and adviser Cocceius Nerva. Apparently, Nerva was so disenchanted with the direction of Roman government that he starved himself to death on Capri, despite Tiberius' pleading at his bedside. Then, when Thrasyllus the astrologer also died, the princeps spent more time back on the mainland at villas of friends. . . . But no, he had not returned to Rome. Yes, the senatorial trials, executions, suicides, and exiles were still continuing, the commandant assured Pilate, though not as many as in previous years. And yes, several of the suits still harked back to the Sejanian conspiracy. For example, Trio, the ex-consul, was finally implicated. He drew up a testament which taunted Tiberius for senility and for shirking imperial duties by his exile on Capri—after which, of course, he slit open his veins and died.

News of the still tempestuous judiciary climate at Rome was hardly consoling to a governor returning in disgrace to face a hearing before the emperor, and Pilate left Brundisium in severe depression. He had hoped that the more than five years which had elapsed since the fall of Sejanus would have blunted Tiberius' resentment. Apparently, time had not healed.

Procula tried to cheer him as they traveled up the Appian Way, but inwardly she was as concerned as he. Their anxiety focused not on the accuracy of the Samaritan charges, but on the prospect of appearing before Tiberius in his present mood. They reviewed his chances, now in deadly earnest, since the long journey was ending and the confrontation would probably take place shortly.

If the princeps restricted the hearing solely to the Samaritan indictment, Pilate felt he could clear himself. Before leaving Caesarea, he had taken depositions from all the officers who had accompanied him on the expedition to Mount Gerizim, and these testified to the dangerous nature of the tumult, the fact that the Samaritans were armed, and, above all, that they refused to lay down their weapons. In any of Rome's provinces, this would spell treason. Pilate's role in the field executions which followed, while perhaps less defensible, was not more than what other Roman prefects would have done in a similar situation.

But *would* Tiberius limit his hearing to the Samaritan affair alone? In his present mood, he might easily use it as a wedge with which to pry open the Pandora's Box of all Pilate's administrative troubles. And if he chose to resurrect the Jewish complaints and probe his past relationship with Sejanus, then there was added danger. And even if Pilate were to make a good defense of his administration, he might achieve little if the seventy-seven-year-old princeps were approaching the illogic of senility. Pilate's mood took on blacker hue.

One recent precedent caused him special anxiety. Pomponius Labeo, who had been a provincial prefect like Pilate, was arraigned on charges of maladministration in the Balkans. Shorn immediately of the title "Caesar's friend," Labeo slashed his wrists and bled to death rather than face trial. Suicide was very popular, for if a man were tried and condemned he forfeited his estate and was debarred from private burial. But if he passed sentence on himself by self-destruction, his will was respected and the body interred.

Ever since he heard the grim report, Pilate had trouble shaking it from consciousness, for there were alarming parallels in his case. For the first time now, the possibility had at least to be considered. If he were to commit suicide rather than trusting the dubious mercies of Tiberius, Procula would inherit his estate untouched and could resume her place in Roman society without disgrace. Her own grandfather had taken his life by swallowing gypsum to permanently soothe his stomach pains, but the suicide had not tarnished his reputation or the family's.

As they traveled northward up the Italian boot, a feeling of utter dejection swept Pilate. Fear of the princeps was being replaced with a sense of total futility at having dedicated the best decade in his life to govern a province from which he was now returning under a cloud. Life was a tedious exercise in frustration, a training ground for meaninglessness, an arena without significance. Perhaps suicide was not only a viable option, but the proper one. Even something of nobility, a sacrifice for the security of Procula.

They now reached Caudium, where Pilate's aged relatives rejoiced to see them again. But it was a reunion sobered by news of what lay ahead for Pilate. He himself put on a front of unconcern for his family's benefit and shared no dark thoughts with them or Procula. Inwardly, however, he was struggling with a personal battle of decision. Before landing in Italy, he had given no thought to self-destruction, but after the dismal reports of Tiberius' temperament and the pessimistic calculation of his own future, he was less surprised at the arguments he could muster in its favor.

Pilate spent no more than a week at Caudium, lest he jeopardize his case for failing to announce his arrival. Generally, the "three-month rule" applied to returning governors. Once their successors arrived, ex-prefects were to leave their provinces at once and not delay their return to Rome longer than three months. His time was nearly up.

He decided that Procula should stay in the security of Caudium. In case anything happened to him, the Pontii were to conduct her safely to the Proculeii in Rome. Despite Procula's remonstrances, he insisted on facing his fate alone. They kissed very tenderly, very emotionally at parting, a bittersweet reminder that their love had not really suffered through the ten and a half years of their marriage.

Without her knowledge, Pilate had deposited his last will and testament with the municipal magistrate of Caudium. Everything was now arranged to suit either alternative: confrontation with the princeps, or a lonely suicide.

Soon after he left Caudium, however, that issue was resolved. Pilate finally made up his mind. A sense of personal dignity and a hope bound up with his love for Procula decided the matter. He would fight for his honor; he would face the princeps.

Tiberius was no longer near Rome, he had learned, but sojourning in a villa at Misenum on the Bay of Naples. And the bay was nearby, just thirty miles west of Caudium across the Apennines. With one aide and several large bundles of documents, he made the short trip on the Ides of

March in 37 A.D. After a day of rugged travel, the familiar view unfolded despite the blustery gray weather: the majesty of Mount Vesuvius to the left, Neapolis before them, and the port of Puteoli further west. Since leaving that harbor a decade earlier, Pilate had now come full circle.

Just around the bend of the bay's shoreline beyond Puteoli, the promontory of Misenum pointed its slim finger toward Capri. The jewel ringing that finger was the palatial villa where Tiberius was staying. As they drew up to the gates of the mansion, his aide informed the captain of a praetorian squad at the entrance, *"Pontius Pilatus, praefectus Iudaeae voluit colloqui cum Naevio Sertorio Macrone, praefecto praetorio."* His contact for arranging an audience with Tiberius would be the prefect of the Praetorian Guard, Naevius Sertorius Macro, the man who had cleverly baited the trap which snared his predecessor Sejanus.

One of the guards delivered the message. They waited. Suddenly a dozen couriers streaked out of the villa, mounted their horses, and took off in a furious gallop toward Puteoli. Pilate and his aide looked astonished. Inside the mansion, a welling sound of excitement now reached the level of a general din. Then wild cheering broke out. Baffled, Pilate asked the guards, "What's happening?"

"I don't know," replied one of them. "Unless the doctor's announced that the princeps is recovering—"

"He's ill?"

"Of course. Haven't you heard? Hard breathing all week . . . fever. He wouldn't see a doctor though."

Just then a wildly jubilant group poured out of the villa, waving their arms and cheering a tall, slender youth with broad forehead and hollow eyes. Though balding at the crown, the rest of his body was hirsute. He was smiling broadly at the acclaim.

"LONG LIVE GAIUS CAESAR!" the people cried while clustering about Caligula, trying to kiss his hand. "The tyrant is dead! The shade of Tiberius be damned! LONG LIVE GAIUS CAESAR!"

Caligula was beaming, acknowledging the adulation with both hairy arms raised. He pointed to Tiberius' signet ring on his left hand, and the people raised a triumphant shout.

A troop of praetorians marched into the courtyard with the thud of measured steps and then snapped to attention. A blistering trumpet call sounded. Squaring themselves into ranks, they extended their arms in a stiff salute and cried, *"Hail Caesar! Hail Caesar! Hail Caesar!"* again and again.

Scarcely trusting his eyes or ears, Pilate could hardly absorb the news. Tiberius was dead. The focus of his anxieties, dead. The man who threatened his life and fortunes, dead. He luxuriated in relief at the incredible turn of events. No confrontation with an angry emperor! Probably a quashing of Vitellius' indictment against him, as Caligula's new regime began with clean slates. The tension which had been building ever since his citation to Rome now dissolved in a flood of joy. "Hail Caesar. *Hail Caesar!"* he joined in.

The praetorian prefect found Pilate in that properly patriotic pose. "You're Pontius Pilate, aren't you?" asked Macro.

"Yes, worthy Macro. Congratulations on the new princeps."

"Coincidence that you should arrive just as Tiberius died. He was rather angry at you after reading Vitellius' report."

"I am prepared at any time to offer a full defense of my conduct."

"It's impossible," Macro said, "to decide on any hearing now, or even if there will be a hearing."

"Certainly." Pilate noticed that the prefect was extremely nervous.

"You'll be in Rome?" Macro inquired.

"Yes."

"I'll discuss it with the new princeps after he has taken office. We'll let you know."

"Vale, my Prefect." They exchanged salutes.

Pilate went in to pay his respects to the body of the dead Tiberius. His relief confirmed by the unforgettable image of the waxen corpse being prepared for state funeral, he hurried back to Caudium in a triumphant mood.

Procula wept for joy at the news. Together they finished the final leg of their journey to Rome, where they were feted at a second glad reception at the home of her aging but elated parents, the Gaius Proculeii.

Chapter 23

TIBERIUS WAS dead, and Rome broke into a carnival atmosphere at the news. People rushed into the Forum shouting, "Hook his body down the Stairs of Mourning!" Some openly thanked the goddess Roma for having delivered her city from the last feeble grasp of the tyrant. Others implored Mother Earth to allow his shade no rest until it had descended to its proper domicile of the damned. Though one of Rome's ablest administrators, Tiberius had sacrificed his popularity by parsimony, his long self-exile on Capri, and, above all, by the dangerous legal climate.

This is why the Senate and the Roman People united to pin their hopes on the popular prince Gaius Caligula. His father Germanicus had been both saint and martyr in the cult of the Roman state; his mother Agrippina and his two brothers had been persecuted and killed. "Little Boots" was the last member of a family nearly extincted by a fate from which they had deserved far better, in the popular mind. Therefore when Caligula escorted the body of Tiberius from Misenum to Rome, the roadsides were framed with decorated altars blazing with sacred torches. Rome had become a mother, lavishing her vast maternal instincts on a new hero-son.

Technically, Tiberius' will had named Caligula co-regent with Gemellus, another younger grandson. But the Senate disregarded that testament in the name of Caligula's obvious popularity and now unanimously conferred full and absolute power on him. For Roman livestock it was some-

285

thing of an unparalleled tragedy; more than 160,000 animals were sacrificed over the next weeks to implore an auspicious reign for Caligula.

Whether or not in answer to such prayers, the new princeps began very well indeed. With proper reverence, he eulogized Tiberius at a magnificent state funeral in Rome, and when the flaming pyre had consumed the body, he carried the ashes to the circular mausoleum of Augustus. He did the same for the remains of his mother and brothers, crossing over to the islands of exile and personally reposing their urns in the same tomb as that of the man who had banished them. He renamed the month of September "Germanicus," an added filial touch.

Caligula revived republican-style elections, granted more authority to the Senate, and even recirculated republican writings which had been suppressed under Tiberius. Of paramount interest to Pilate was Caligula's policy of recalling exiles who had been banished and dismissing indictments against all who were awaiting trial on political charges. He also publicly burned documents relating to former suits and warned informers that their field day was over. Quite naturally, the Romans greeted these policies with unrestrained enthusiasm.

Further enhancing this popularity, Caligula canceled certain taxes while extending government generosity in staging free public shows, races, and gladiatorial combats. He also took a renewed interest in the equestrians, a class Tiberius had largely ignored. And so the day came when the Gaius Proculeii, the Pontius Pilati, and other prominent equestrian families in Rome were invited by the young emperor to a lavish banquet in his Palatine palace. It was here that Macro formally introduced Pilate to Caligula for the first time.

Said the princeps, "Oh yes, Pontius Pilate. I would like to speak to you sometime soon concerning Judea."

"I stand at your disposal, Princeps," replied Pilate.

This was the extent of their brief exchange, but it was enough to churn Pilate's emotions. He had hoped that with the new regime there would be no review of his case. And yet, if Pilate wished to advance in Roman government, and he still did, then the cloud on his record would necessarily have to be dispelled before he gained higher office. And since the youthful Caligula seemed a fair and rational sort, unlike Tiberius, the latter prospect grew more attractive.

Pilate decided to clean his slate. After getting his papers in order, he consulted with his second cousin, Gaius Pontius Nigrinus, who was one of the consuls for the year, and then planned to ask Macro to institute a hearing before the emperor at his early convenience.

But Caligula and Macro anticipated him by several days, since the Samaritan delegation, delayed by the change of government, had now arrived. Pilate cursed his luck for not having seized the initiative a bit earlier. It would have looked handsomer if he as the defendant had called for his own trial. He was summoned to the Palatine early in June of 37 to answer the charges against him.

The hearing before Caligula took place in a glittering and pillared hall of the Palatine palace overlooking the Forum directly to the north. Pilate had not brought counsel with him, since his ten years on the bench were more than enough schooling in Roman law. At first, Pontius Nigrinus had volunteered to accompany him to the hearing, but on second thought they both decided against it. As consul, Nigrinus would have been preceded by ten lictors, which the young Caligula might have misunderstood as attempted intimidation. It would also have enlarged the scope of a hearing Pilate wished contained. The only person he brought along was one defense witness, the tribune of Judea's Italian Cohort, who was in Rome on furlough.

What surprised Pilate was the small number in the Samaritan delegation, just four, and the fact that Caligula had someone else sitting with him on the dais, obviously an important friend, judging from the purple splashing about his costume. He had a Semitic look about him, incongruous with the Romans in the room, but akin to the four Samaritans. Or were there five? An erect and distinguished-looking man in rich attire now joined them.

The prefect Macro introduced the various principals at the hearing. The man on the tribunal with the emperor was called Agrippa; the fifth person in the Samaritan delegation he presented as "Thallus, the renowned historian." He was Tiberius' affluent and scholarly freedman who, Pilate suddenly recalled, was of *Samaritan* origin. So the prosecution had a friend at court indeed!

Caligula opened the proceedings by pointing out that since the province of Judea was of imperial, not senatorial, rank, there could be no appeal from his tribunal to the Roman Senate. Both parties agreed.

The Samaritans then formally indicted Pilate for excessive cruelty, assault and battery, massacre, illegal executions, and religious persecution.

"Pontius Pilatus, rise to face your accusers," Caligula directed. "How do you plead?"

"*Not guilty* on all counts, Excellency."

Evidence was then taken from the prosecution. Three of the Samaritans had been present at what they termed the "Mount Gerizim Massacre" and showed Caligula scars from wounds suffered in the battle. In essence, they stated that theirs had been a peaceful gathering, solely for religious purposes. Weapons were brought along only for defense against highwaymen. Pilate erred brutally in executing fourteen of their leaders after wounding and killing others in battle. He should not have interfered with their religious observances in the first place. He was careless about Jewish religious practices as well, and they listed the familiar episodes.

Thallus then submitted a further document, Vitellius' formal explanation to Tiberius of why he had ordered Pilate's suspension. Caligula directed that it be read aloud. Listening carefully and making occasional notes, Pilate was disturbed at how much extra material Vitellius had included concerning the various frictions, imbroglios, and riots which had broken out under his administration in Judea. Genuine concern throbbed inside him for the first time. He who had presided over countless cases in the past was now on the other side of the bench. The judge was being judged.

Thallus was conducting himself brilliantly as prosecutor for the Samaritans, and both Caligula and his friend Agrippa started to stare at Pilate with all the fascination of two hawks eying a common prey. Pilate continued scribbling notes with his stylus and nervously rechecking the order of his depositions. Once he leaned over to confer with the tribune from the Italian Cohort.

When Thallus had finished, Caligula called for evidence for the defense. Pilate began by countering the formal indictments. "The charges of 'excessive cruelty,' 'assault and battery,' and 'massacre' cannot stand," he argued, "for Rome could bring a countersuit against the Samaritans on precisely the same grounds. This was military combat, a formal, pitched battle between two Roman cohorts and a *de facto* Samaritan army, since the insurgents had many more weapons than would ever have been needed against highwaymen. Every man was armed. Granted, a few defensive weapons against brigands would have been acceptable as they came *separately* to the village of Tirathana. But after they had united into a multitude of thousands, why did they remain armed? Why, if this were a religious procession? It would be ridiculous to assume that bandits would have tried to attack a throng of that size.

"In this connection, I submit for your examination my letter of suspension from the proconsul Vitellius. You will note a *different* reason stated here for the Samaritans being armed." Pilate showed Caligula the sentence: "They have sworn to me that the gathering . . . assembled at Tirathana only as refugees from your violence." Then he resumed, "The plaintiffs knew that this was a hastily contrived lie at the time. They assembled at Tirathana certainly not as refugees from my violence, but as a staging area for their ascent of Mount Gerizim. So now they have altered the indictment. I submit that this represents the way they have handled truth in their entire version of the episode.

"Now, as to the remaining charges, just as there was no religious persecution on my part, so also there were no illegal executions. With many of our Roman auxiliaries wounded, dying, and some dead, I naturally meted out appropriate punishment to the leaders of what was clearly a treasonable insurrection against imperial authority. Under martial law they were judged and executed. Any Roman magistrate in these circumstances would have acted in a similar fashion."

As witness for the defense, Pilate now had his tribune give a detailed account of what transpired at Mount Gerizim. His testimony showed the Samaritans in a substantially different light from their own claims as a peace-loving folk bent only on a religious quest. Finally, Pilate laid his depositions before Caligula, which further supported the tribune's version and testified to the military conquests expected of the Samaritan "Restorer." The princeps and his friend spent some minutes reading through them. Then Caligula called for the summations.

Thallus sought to rebut Pilate's arguments, stressing particularly that the leaders of a Samaritan religious gathering should not have been massacred with that kind of un-Roman barbarity. He also leaned heavily on Pilate's previous troubles in Judea. Finally he suggested, "Exile, no, death itself is not too great a punishment for one who has so shamefully abused his public trust in a province of imperial Rome."

Shuddering inwardly, but also angry at Thallus' request, Pilate countered in his summary by pointing out that he was not presently on trial for any problems with the Jews, but that he would gladly broaden his defense in that respect should the princeps be willing. "But a martial-law execution of the chief seditionists in a thwarted rebellion is certainly within the prerogatives of a Roman provincial governor." Pilate went on to cite examples of similar executions in other Roman provinces at various times in history.

"Finally, as to my alleged troubles with the Jews, not a prefect assigned to Judea has returned without insisting that these are a most difficult people to govern. The province is undergarrisoned, underestimated, and misunderstood in Rome. In this situation, a provincial governor *must* halt incipient insurrection immediately, particularly when it breaks out on the major arterial highway of his land. Despite these difficulties, the emperor Tiberius continued me in office for ten years, which he certainly would not have done had my administration been inadequate. You recall his concern for good provincial government. As to my occasions of friction with the Jews, these are minor compared to the riots which periodically flare up between *Samaritans* and Jews."

It was a telling point, so Pilate concluded, "Excellency, I rest my case." He sat down, confident that Caligula, as one Roman official to another, would appreciate his arguments and acquit him. He still did not understand what the man named Agrippa was doing on the emperor's tribunal.

Caligula retired for a few minutes with Agrippa. Pilate was nervous, but optimistic. The tribune smiled and patted him on the shoulders.

Then the emperor returned. While asking Pilate to stand for the judgment, he had a peculiar smile on his face which faded rapidly. Fastening hollow gray eyes on the defendant, he announced, "Pontius Pilate, I absolve you of the charges of massacre, illegal executions, and religious persecution. . . . But I find you guilty of assault and battery, and of excessive cruelty."

Pilate's jaw sagged open in astonishment.

Caligula continued, "A provincial governor who knew

the art of diplomacy would have been able to find some recourse other than bloodshed and execution. You might at
least have let the proconsul Vitellius hear their case."

Pilate remained stupefied, incredulous. Caligula was
showing political naïveté. "But Excellency," he blurted,
"our history is full of instances where insurrection was
dealt with exactly as I handled it. Innocent Roman lives
were lost to rebellious—"

"You *dare* interrupt me during sentencing?" Caligula
glared.

Pilate curbed his tongue and lowered his eyes to the
highly polished, tessellated floor. The throbbing of his heart
caused a welling, rhythmic pressure in his eardrums. He
felt nauseated. Chilly sweat broke out and trickled down
his spine.

"Tell me, Pilate," Caligula smirked. "Can you imagine
what being hurled from the Tarpeian Rock would be like?
Or being decapitated in the Tullianum and having your
body hooked down the Stairs of Mourning? Like Sejanus?"

Pilate's eyes flashed about in horror. He saw that the Samaritans were smiling in eager anticipation.

"Well, you probably deserve such a fate, but in our gracious charity during this inauguration of our reign, we sentence you merely to confiscation of your entire estate and
exile for life. . . . You have three weeks to leave Italy—not
a day longer. Perhaps . . . yes, perhaps Vienne in Gaul
might be appropriate."

Pilate's thoughts wrestled in helpless inner turmoil. Caligula's charity, a *small* consolation. . . . It didn't make sense.
Trials for people *far* guiltier than he had been dismissed.
. . . What would Procula do now? Slowly he raised his eyes
to the young princeps and saw only unbending resolve in
the contemptuous cast of his countenance.

Caligula dismissed the Samaritan delegation with vague
promises of compensation from Marullus, the new provincial governor whom he would shortly dispatch to Palestine.
At the same time he warned them that Rome would tolerate no further armed meetings of any kind.

Agrippa walked over to Pilate, who was still anchored to
the spot where he had been sentenced. "What's the matter,
Prefect?" he asked. "You feel you're innocent, do you?
What does that matter? Haven't *you* ever condemned an
innocent man?"

Pilate was instructed to remain where he was until Caligula and Agrippa had conducted the Samaritan delegation out of the palace. The tribune offered his sympathies and excused himself. Pilate slumped into a couch and propped his chin on his left hand. The gold ring which had conferred friend-of-Caesar status on him cut into his jaw. He pulled it off his finger and flung it out a window toward the Forum below.

Perhaps he should have been thinking of how best to break the news to Procula. He might have considered some kind of final appeal to the mercies of Caligula. Conceivably, he could have philosophized on the fragile bubble of contrarieties which is human existence. Or he might simply have succumbed to despair. Strangely, Pilate himself thought, he did none of these things. He merely reflected on Agrippa's last remark to him and about the event it conjured up. Had he never condemned an innocent man? So this is how the prophet Jesus must have felt? No. Pilate had made a solid defense; Jesus had not. But no matter. They were both condemned. Where was justice? What is truth?

Caligula, Agrippa, and Macro returned, the last carefully closing the door behind them, so that only the four were now in the colonnaded hall.

"Well now, Pilate," the emperor smiled. "Don't look so crestfallen. Our little pantomime is over. No, you're not going into exile, and we won't take a solitary sesterce from your treasures. Ahaha! You stare at me? Certainly. I would too, under the circumstances." He nudged Agrippa and Macro, both of whom were quaking with laughter at what they all found a tremendous joke.

"I suppose we do owe you an explanation, Pilate," Caligula continued, in what he knew was a diabolical understatement. "Tomorrow the four Samaritans are leaving for Puteoli, well satisfied that they've succeeded in their mission of vengeance against you. It was a long trip for them, so the least we could do, for appearance's sake, was to give you a severe sentence. This way I'll be very popular with my new subjects in Samaria . . . even if, regrettably, it was at your expense. I must confess, Prefect, if I'd been at that mountain and faced that rebel army, I'd have taken the same measures."

"I doubt it," Agrippa smiled. "You'd have executed a good deal more than fourteen!"

Caligula let out a roar of laughter, nodding his head and

slapping Agrippa's back. Then he looked at Pilate and said, "There, there, man. I do believe you're shedding a tear. Put your emotions in order, Prefect. Though it must be quite an ordeal to pass from the horror of threatened death, to the ignominy of exile, to full acquittal—all within a quarter of an hour."

"But Excellency," said Pilate with mounting elation, "what about Thallus? He's not returning to Samaria. . . ."

"Oh, he's party to the plot. While he deplores your bloodshed, he's glad you killed the false prophet. Of course, you can't return to Palestine . . . or become famous in Rome, for that matter. That would ruin it all. Ahaha! Certainly you didn't hope to be reinstated as prefect of Judea?"

"Oh, no. *No*, Princeps! Quite on the contrary. Ten years is enough for anyone there."

"And if the Samaritans should ever learn that you're still at large here in Rome, we'll claim that you were recalled from exile for good behavior, or some such excuse. Anyway, by that time their tempers will have cooled too. Join us for lunch, Pilate."

It was a simple luncheon on the Palatine. Its sybaritic luxury was limited to a mere eight courses and only four changes in wine. All the while, it seemed, the thin lips of Caligula, sticky with an exquisite vintage, were drawn into the same, inscrutable smile.

Between one of the middle courses, he emitted a long belch. Then, apropos of nothing, he asked, "Did you and Procula enjoy your trip up the Nile? Ha. Hahaha! And I can also tell you the exact length of your aqueduct from the Judean hills into Jerusalem . . . the number of pillars in your Tiberiéum in Caesarea." Caligula continued to supply other minute details from Pilate's administration in Judea which, of course, astounded him.

"Now how could I possibly know these items?" the princeps inquired, indulging in his favorite game, playing with people. "Do you *really* know who my friend Agrippa is, Pilate?"

"Not a descendant of the great Marcus Agrippa?"

"No, but named in his honor," Agrippa smiled. "My full name is Julius Herod Agrippa."

"Oh, the grandson of Herod the Great? The brother of Herodias, wife of Antipas?"

"The same."

"I've certainly heard of you, but I don't believe we'd ever met in Palestine."

"No. I've been in Rome much of the time."

For all his forty-seven years, Agrippa was still ruggedly handsome; more so, Pilate thought, than his painted sister Herodias was beautiful.

"Agrippa's life story thus far makes the wanderings of Ulysses seem positively boring by comparison," Caligula interjected. "He was brought up at the court of Tiberius as companion to his son Drusus, the one Sejanus poisoned. Then he sailed to Palestine—I still think it was to escape your creditors, Agrippa. There he got so depressed at leaving Mother Rome that he contemplated suicide. But his dear sister Herodias invited him to Galilee, where she got him some small government job to tide him over. What was it again, Agrippa?"

"*Agoranomos,* superintendent of the market at Tiberias."

"But you know these Herodians; they never get along. Once he and Herod Antipas got drunk at a banquet and started trading exquisite insults, so naturally Agrippa had to leave Galilee. Now Pomponius Flaccus had just arrived as our new governor in Syria, and, would you believe it, Flaccus turned out to be Agrippa's old comrade from Rome! So it was up to Antioch for our wandering friend here. But alas! The people of Damascus hired him to lobby in their behalf with Flaccus, who took that unkindly. So once again Agrippa played bankrupt vagabond. But, knowing that only Rome could improve his fate, he borrowed more money and sailed back to Italy. When he landed, my grandfather Tiberius first had him pay off old debts in Rome, then welcomed him back to court life on Capri, where he's spent the last year tutoring me. Agrippa is now my closest friend. And do you know who loaned him the funds to pay off his debts? Our rich friend and sage whom you just met, the Samaritan Thallus!"

"An amazing tale," said Pilate.

"Oh, but it's not finished yet," said Caligula. "I almost lost my Agrippa. In one false move he nearly ruined the game. One day he and I were out driving on Capri, and, thinking no one could hear us, he said, 'You know, Gaius, I wish to God Tiberius would soon go off the stage and leave the government to you. You're so much more worthy of it.' I smiled, but *thank Jupiter*, I said nothing! Because the chariot driver overheard us."

"The damnable Eutychus," Agrippa muttered.

"Well, he told Tiberius about the comment one afternoon when he was being carried around his hippodrome in a litter. Grandfather pointed to Agrippa in a rage and told Macro, 'Arrest that man.' Macro, who hadn't heard the charge, was bewildered, not knowing whom to arrest. When the litter rounded the track a second time, Grandfather was nettled to see Agrippa still standing there. '*Him*, Macro, seize *him!*' he said. 'Whom?' asked Macro. 'Agrippa, you dunce.' "

"It was a long six months in prison, Gaius," Agrippa commented. "But the worst of it was not knowing it would be just six months until Tiberius died. For a while, I think, he had in mind to have me pitched off the cliffs of Capri."

"Why not? You'd committed *maiestas*, you know. But then came the great day at Misenum. Macro told me you were there, Pilate."

"Yes, Princeps. I wanted him to arrange my hearing before Tiberius. I had no idea—"

"Yes, well, do you know what I did after Grandfather died?"

"You released Agrippa," Pilate humored.

"Not just released him. I welcomed him into the palace with open arms. I had his shaggy hair cut and presented him with a new wardrobe."

"*Far* more than that, dear friend," smiled Agrippa. "In a symbolism which must have drawn tears from the gods, you presented me with a chain of gold, equal in size to the iron fetters which had bound me in prison. And then you put a diadem on my head."

Pilate was becoming ill at the touching affection, but he dared do nothing more than smile agreeably. The power which the mature Agrippa exercised over the impressionable young emperor was ominous.

"You realize the significance of the diadem, Pilate?" asked Caligula.

"The symbol of royalty?"

"Exactly. I have the honor to present to you Herod Agrippa I, the new *king* of Gaulanitis, Trachonitis, and Batanea."

"Philip's former tetrarchy? I thought it was now part of Syria."

"*Was*, Pilate."

"My heartiest congratulations, King Agrippa."

Agrippa nodded briefly.

"Yes," Caligula added, "and we may well increase his territory. Rome has tried prefects in Judea . . . without a great deal of success. It may take a Jew, or a part Jew like Agrippa, to govern a nation of Jews. At any rate, if our new prefect Marullus doesn't work out, Agrippa will succeed him also in Judea. The last time that province was well governed was under his grandfather Herod the Great."

Pilate swallowed the insult—he had no choice—and then shifted the conversation. "Marullus is replacing Vitellius' man Marcellus?" he asked.

"Yes. Of course. Vitellius has tried to endear himself to the Jews by a whole series of changes, but I'm not sure of them. You know that he dismissed your friend Joseph Caiaphas from the high priesthood?"

It was news to Pilate. "What about Vitellius' war in Antipas' behalf against King Aretas?" he asked.

"*That* stopped the moment I acceded to the principate. Antipas is now Agrippa's *rival* in Palestine. I didn't want Roman legions used to support the competitor of my closest friend."

A gratifying morsel of information, thought Pilate.

By now they had finished lunch. Pilate was about to excuse himself from the palace when Caligula asked, point-blank, "Tell me, Pilate, do you think you have any future in Roman government? How and where would you like to serve the Empire next?"

"I'm at your disposal of course, Princeps. But I'd like to take an extended vacation before assuming any new post."

"I think you should. How old a man are you?"

"Almost fifty."

"You might consider retirement, then. No, I really don't think Rome can use your services in the future, Pilate. Certainly you did nothing worthy of exile or death, but Agrippa has given me a full report of your decade in Judea. There were many instances of tactlessness. Forethought, diplomacy, sensitivity, and skill were missing on numerous occasions. Of course, some things you did very well. Taxes were collected regularly; you kept the peace; Caesarea was well administered. The Tiberiéum, the aqueduct, and other constructions were well conceived. But you failed in other matters. The standards and the shields affairs were silly.

Perhaps Thallus was right about the Samaritans being pacified without bloodshed. Possibly such frictions were unavoidable and you couldn't help it. You're not a Jew—we Romans do have that handicap—and you did govern as well, I suppose, as any of our prefects so far. That much should be said."

Pilate cast a not-so-friendly glance at Agrippa, and Caligula caught it.

"No, Pilate. Don't think unkindly of Agrippa as some kind of spy who observed you the whole time. He admitted to me that he reflected the Jewish viewpoint in commenting on your administration. He also spoke in your behalf after the hearing this morning."

They reached the door of the palace. Caligula extended his hand and said, "So, Pontius Pilatus, your career for the state is concluded. Rome thanks you. And you'll receive the usual government pension, of course."

Pilate was trying to make as graceful an exit as possible under the circumstances when he saw Agrippa whisper something to Caligula. The emperor nodded his head.

"It's time for the baths," said Agrippa. "Might I accompany you, Pilate?"

The very last thing Pilate wanted to do that afternoon was to visit the baths with Herod Agrippa. But a king had made the request. He was in no position to refuse.

Their litter went several blocks north up the Via Lata, then west to the Baths of Agrippa. As they were deposited, Agrippa dropped the pleasantry, "I've always thought *these* baths especially well named."

Pilate ignored the bad humor.

"But Pilate, don't you think it a bit of irony that you, who have judged the Jews for so many years, should finally be judged by one? Gaius virtually gave me full sway in determining your fate. And even if you won't believe it, I could have given the princeps a worse accounting of your administration in Judea. I can show you letters from the Pharisees which pleaded for your exile."

"Why?" Pilate retorted angrily. "You know that would've been unjustified."

"Simply because the Pharisees reject any non-Jewish government. So if it could be demonstrated that a Roman is just not able to govern Jews, then the emperor might make another arrangement. You, of course, as the latest example, were dispensable in the interests of that cause."

"Do you share that viewpoint?"

"Partially. Which is why I had to expose some of your foibles. I concur in the thought that any Roman is *ipso facto* a poor governor of Jews. You just don't know enough about us to handle us correctly."

By this time they had stripped and were swimming about in a section of the cool bath reserved for Roman officials. Then they shifted to the warm mists of the *tepidarium* before moving on to the steamy vapors of the hot baths.

It all fell into place in Pilate's mind. Clearly, Agrippa was aiming at kingship over Judea. Soon, undoubtedly, he would supply evidence to show that Marullus, like Pilate, was inadequate as prefect, and then his good friend Caligula would enlarge his diadem to include Judea and Samaria as well.

"I think I understand the situation," said Pilate, "but tell me this: why didn't you go along with the Pharisees in requesting my exile?"

"Several reasons," Agrippa replied. "First, I value justice, and exile *would* have been too severe. You did try in Judea, Pilate. You yielded when you should have in the various quarrels with the Jews, and I think Antipas and my other uncles overreacted on those insignificant shields. But it was symptomatic that you didn't quite have the right touch."

Now they moved into the dry-heat room, where they lay on marble slabs while being scraped down with strigils. Agrippa looked carefully at Pilate and continued, "Another reason I didn't press for punishment in your case was this: the Arabs have an old proverb, 'My enemy's enemy is my friend.' Dear Herod Antipas may be both uncle and brother-in-law to me, but he remains my deadly political enemy. I'll never forgive his humiliating me. Now, Antipas and you didn't get along either, despite your half-hearted attempts at friendship. . . ."

It took Pilate only a moment's thought to ask, "When do you plan to indict Antipas before Caligula?"

"*Gaius*, Pilate," he laughed, "he insists on Gaius. Never call him 'Baby Boot' to his face."

"Before Gaius, then?"

"You're a bit ahead of me. But on the right track. If it

ever comes to that, I may need a witness here in Rome who can testify to Antipas' maladministration."

"And I could hardly provide that witness in exile."

"Exactly."

"Eventually, then, his territories would be added to yours, perhaps Judea as well—a restoration of your grandfather's kingdom."

"It's time for massage and the unguents."

When that process was completed and they had dressed, Agrippa warned, "I need not suggest that you keep this conversation confidential. If, for example, you were indiscreet enough to report any of our remarks to the princeps, I should deny them, accuse you of malicious lying, and do everything possible to secure your exile. You see, I plan to stay in Rome some months yet before taking over my new kingdom."

Pilate nodded.

As they parted outside the baths, Agrippa said, "Oh yes, Pilate, there *was* another reason I felt you had governed comparatively well. I'd nearly forgotten it. You handled one case in Judea masterfully, I thought: the blasphemy-treason trial of that Galilean, Yeshu Hannosri. Oh, I can see why you, as a Roman, were lenient at first, but, believe me, that kind of heresy had to be cut down at its source. Yes . . . absolutely. It was a good decision, Pilate—crucifixion. A good decision."

Chapter 24

Pilate returned home exhausted. His day on the Palatine, a lurching shuttle between hope and despair, had smothered his spirit. Whatever relief he gained in successfully defending himself was blighted by his dismissal from imperial service, even if the official explanation would be that Pilate had requested retirement. With wifely solicitude, Procula begged to be told everything, but Pilate put her off until the next morning. That night he looked up an old friend at the *Castra Praetoria,* and together they got quietly drunk.

Like a wounded organ trying to repair itself, Pilate's mind supplied rationalizations for his new status. Even if Caligula had offered him another prefecture away from Rome, he would not have accepted it, since he had been away from the city too long. Nor did he need such an office. His father-in-law Proculeius had invested his funds so shrewdly during the decade of his absence that by now Pilate could retire even without pension and still lead a life of comfortable opulence. As to the negative appraisal of his competence in Judea, someday Rome would appreciate his efforts there. And how accurate were the critical opinions of an unseasoned twenty-four-year-old trying to play at emperor, whose only source of information was a Herodian opportunist twice his age but biased against Pilate? And what extraordinarily bad taste, turning the imperial tribunal into a stage just to coddle the Samaritans.

When Procula finally heard the full report of the critical

hours before Caligula, she was too happy to bother consoling her husband. Privately, she had lived in mortal fear of the eventual hearing before the emperor. With that shadow removed, nothing else mattered, especially now that Rome would be their future home. Too independent to be a social climber, she was relieved that Pilate would now be anchored clear of the treacherous crosscurrents of Roman politics.

But adjusting to the role of spectator rather than actor proved very difficult for Pilate. He lived a week or two with his rationalizations, then grew tired of them. Personal candor compelled him to face reality and see there the figure of Pontius Pilatus—ex-prefect, pensioner, retired man, emeritus before his time. His idealistic goals had him rising to lofty heights in the Empire; his actual fate saw him pensioned out of government service.

"But for the few who achieve greatness," he told Procula, "every man arrives at that point in life where he must come to terms with the fact that history will pass him by. For those with little ambition, that point comes early, so they can adjust to it with the easy resiliency of youth. Yet I aspired; that point was postponed in my life. But now I've reached it. And I'm not young. Accepting that realization now is difficult, terribly difficult."

"Is it that important, Pilate, having history recognize you?"

"It is, I think. It's the only thing which ultimately gives life a larger dimension, the one factor which finally affords it some meaning. You will have existed for more generations than merely your own. You will have affected the future, perhaps altered it for the better."

"Why isn't this generation enough, Pilate? It certainly is for me."

"You're a woman, Procula."

"Which by definition excludes us from greatness," she jibed. "But your life is far from over. You're only fifty, and some of the greatest achievements in Roman politics and culture were fashioned by men older than you."

Pilate failed to relish such consolation. While he appreciated Procula's efforts, he resented the new circumstances which occasioned them.

Some weeks passed, and he began struggling more successfully with his problem of adjustment. But just when he was becoming reconciled to leaving the center stage of politics, something would remind him of his now-peripheral status and reopen the wound. At the end of August, for example, the Temple of the Divine Augustus was dedicated at Rome amid much pageantry. The hymn of consecration was sung by a mass choir of boys and girls from the noblest families. There was a public feast and two days of spectacles. There were horse races, gladiatorial combats which saw 800 bears and lions slaughtered, and finally a circuit of the hippodrome by Caligula himself, six horses drawing his triumphal chariot amid frenzied cheering by the adoring people of Rome. But even though his equestrian rank permitted him to sit in the lowest fourteen rows as spectator at these events, Pilate's name had been omitted from the list of official invitations. It symbolized his divorce from Roman public life.

A month later, Rome was shocked to learn that the emperor was almost at the point of death. Never in fully robust health, Caligula had suffered a complete nervous breakdown which, with other complications, made palace physicians despair of his life. All Rome was tormented with apprehension at losing the popular young princeps, who had reigned but six months. Temples were besieged with suppliants. Some threatened the gods. A commoner offered to exchange his own life for the emperor's if he recovered, while an equestrian swore he would fight in the arena as the lowest gladiator. Such devotion, of course, would not fail to impress the princeps if he survived.

Caligula did recover and was moved indeed. He called for the equestrian with gladiatorial ambitions and packed him off to the arena, where he had to battle and beg for his life. Then he located the poor pleb who had vowed to offer his life for the emperor's and inquired why the man was still alive. Caligula had him wreathed and garlanded as if for sacrifice, paraded through the city, and finally pitched to his death from the Tarpeian Rock.

Rome thought this conduct somewhat strange, but she would see far stranger antics from Caligula from now on. Apparently, the illness had unhinged his mind. One day, Pilate returned from the Forum where he had gathered the latest word on the princeps, and told Procula: "Rome had an emperor, now she has a monster."

Perhaps due to some faulty gene in the Julio-Claudian dynasty, the monster had been lurking in Caligula even be-

fore his breakdown, though his better qualities had usually
kept the beast well chained. Still, there had been earlier
symptoms, and Pilate began piecing the stories together.
On Capri he had shown definite traces of megalomania and
cruelty. His grandmother Antonia had also caught him at
incest with one of his sisters, and though later it was Antonia who saved his life by exposing Sejanus' conspiracy,
Caligula had not bothered to attend her funeral in early
May, merely viewing her flaming pyre from the comfort of
his dining room. His hearing on the Palatine showed Pilate
that even the emperor's better moods were capable of ca-
price. But after his illness, the benign part of Caligula succumbed to the new role he was creating for himself as Oriental despot.

The man had had no training to rule. Unlike Tiberius, he
had never commanded any armies, and had little experience in public office. Now, with the adoring world at his
feet, the young princeps' head was permanently turned, and
he became intoxicated with power. He began by lashing out
against those closest to him. His potential rival, the teen-
age Gemellus, was put to death because his breath smelled
of an antidote, Caligula claimed. The temerity of the fellow—assuming that the emperor was trying to poison him!
The luckless Gemellus had only taken cough medicine for
a chronic cold.

Macro, the praetorian prefect, made the mistake of continually reminding Caligula how much he owed to him, so
Macro and his wife and children were all forced to commit
suicide. The news staggered Pilate, since only a few months
earlier he had seen him basking in the princeps' favor.

Anything was permitted in the private life of the "Greatest and Best of Caesars," as he now liked to be styled. He
lived in habitual incest with his sisters, but was capable of
love beyond the family. At the wedding banquet of a
friend, he carried the bride away from the table to his own
palace, "divorcing" her a few days later. He recognized
Caesonia as his third wife only after she had borne him a
baby girl. Caligula said he was sure of the parentage, because the baby had a savage temper and regularly tried to
scratch out the eyes of children who played with her.

Pilate learned many of the grotesque stories first-hand,
since his old friend Cassius Chaerea was a praetorian tribune assigned to the Palatine. It was with Chaerea that Pilate had guzzled wine the night of his dismissal from gov-

ernment service. Lately, the tribune was spending many an evening at Pilate's home, reporting on Caligula with obviously loathing and congratulating Pilate on his lucky escape from immediate contact with "Crazy Boots," as he had slightly adjusted the emperor's name.

Predictably, Caligula soon showed contempt for the Senate. Interviews with senators were usually conducted with them trotting alongside his chariot, their togas flapping in the breeze until the business was concluded. Others played sycophant and waited on him hand and foot.

"Remember that I have the right to do anything to anybody," he once told Antonia, and his reign became a studied effort to demonstrate that claim. He now launched a program of private executions of senators and equestrians, which were carried out by graduated woundings "so that the victim may *feel* he is dying." Final decapitations often took place before Caligula while he was lunching. Procula was so horrified at such reports that Pilate now sent her out of the room whenever Cassius Chaerea arrived with his latest brace of stories.

The only way commoners escaped the imperial vengeance was by their sheer numbers. Once at the races, the rabble deliberately cheered the red faction rather than Caligula's beloved greens. "I wish the people had but a *single* neck," he growled. Then he ordered the awnings over the top edges of the hippodrome drawn back so that the plebes would bake in the sun for their perversity.

Caligula had now reached an ultimate stage of megalomania by laying serious claim to his own divinity. Julius Caesar and Augustus had been deified after their deaths, but this was taken seriously only in the East, where the idea of a ruler cult originated. Most practical Romans regarded their "deified" emperors only as quasi-saints. But Caligula insisted on a more literal interpretation, and he wanted his deity in this life where he could enjoy it. He now deigned to be worshiped personally in the Temple of Castor and Pollux at appointed hours, taking his place between the divine brothers. Later he erected a separate temple to his own godhead, which housed a lifesized statue of himself in gold. Each day, his priesthood dressed the statue in clothing identical to Caligula's own costume for the day. His favorite horse he appointed as high priest of his cult and enrolled it in the Senate. And since he was having so many god-to-god conversations with Jupiter, he had a special bridge constructed from his palace to the deity's temple on the Capitoline to facilitate their communication.

Pilate watched the moral deterioration of the emperor with a strange mixture of horror and consolation. Like any normal citizen, he was aghast at the enormities of the man who was supposed to symbolize Rome. But he no longer felt sorry for himself at being dismissed from government service. In the unfathomable irony of the times, that dismissal had been his salvation. The powerful Macro had gone the way of Sejanus, as had others in positions to which Pilate at one time aspired. Under the new Caligula, security could be found only in anonymity. Pilate thanked Fate for having permitted his hearing to take place *before* the princeps' breakdown. His one continuing prayer now was simply that Caligula should forget him. He and Procula made it a rule never to attend public or social functions at which the emperor might see them from any proximity.

Pilate's cousin, the ex-consul Pontius Nigrinus, could not find such refuge under the welcome blanket of privacy. He told Pilate that each banquet with Caligula was a personal crisis. Recently the princeps suddenly broke out laughing uproariously at a dinner party, and the new consuls who were reclining at his sides asked him what was so funny. "I just happened to think," Caligula explained, "just a nod of my head and both your throats would be cut on the spot. Aha! Ahahaha!"

In the summer of 38, the princeps finally let his close friend and adviser Agrippa return to Palestine in order to assume his kingdom. Agrippa had become rather odious in Rome as Caligula's "trainer-in-tyranny," though he was hardly responsible for his insanity. But Pilate was greatly relieved to have Agrippa out of Italy, for he represented Palestine to Caligula, and Palestine might remind him of a recent ex-prefect.

Letters from Cornelius in Caesarea kept Pilate and Procula well-informed on events in Judea. He was recently promoted to tribune, the ex-centurion reported happily, but something far more significant had happened to him, something too difficult to put into writing just now. Meanwhile, Pilate's good friends Herod Antipas and Herodias were en route to Rome, Cornelius added. Herodias, it seems, was so furiously jealous that her brother Agrippa should have left Palestine a homeless debtor and returned as a king that she had hounded her husband to seek a similar fortune in Rome. At first Antipas would have none of it, since he was mellowing in his old age, Cornelius wrote. But finally he succumbed to his wife's ambitious urgings and they were now going to appeal to Caligula to confer the title of king also on Antipas and extend his territories.

"The foolish sheep," Pilate chuckled to Procula. "They don't know the lion waiting for them in Rome, or the wolf who is now licking his chops in Palestine. How could Antipas play into Agrippa's hands like that?"

"And to think they used to call him The Fox," commented Procula, to keep the menagerie intact.

"Deliver us, Jupiter, from scheming and ambitious women!" Pilate prayed with mock solemnity.

"Just so Agrippa doesn't try to involve you before Caligula in any countermove to stop Antipas."

"I don't think he'll have to. Agrippa has the emperor's ear like no one else in the Empire."

Several months passed without any further news of Antipas' mission. Overcome by curiosity, Pilate went to see his friend Cassius Chaerea, who had just returned from a tour of duty guarding the emperor at Baiae, a luxurious spa on the Bay of Naples where Caligula had been taking the hot baths.

"Have I heard anything about the tetrarch of Galilee paying Caligula a visit?" Chaerea smiled. "Do you mean a Herod and a Herodias?"

"Yes. Herod Antipas."

"What a shambles! They arrived at Puteoli and caught the princeps while he was still at Baiae. Herod told his story, how he was more fit to be king than Agrippa, and all the time Caligula was reading Agrippa's long letter of indictment against his brother-in-law, which had just been delivered. It merely accused Herod of disloyalty, ineptitude, conspiracy with Sejanus, and treasonable alliance with the Parthians against Rome. As proof, Agrippa wrote, Herod's armories bulged with weapons and equipment enough for 70,000 troops."

"What!"

"Yes. That was Caligula's reaction. He asked Herod about the contents of his armory, and he was unable to deny the size of his arsenal. Then and there Caligula stripped him of his tetrarchy and all his property—"

"And awarded it all to Agrippa," supplied Pilate.

"Right. Then he condemned Herod to perpetual exile in Gaul."

"What about Herodias?"

"When Caligula learned that she was sister to his beloved Agrippa, he offered to let her keep her property and live in freedom apart from Herod."

"Which she did, of course."

"No. I thought she would, too. But she told the princeps, 'Loyalty to my husband prevents my accepting your kind offer. When I have shared his prosperity, it's not right that I should abandon him in adversity.' So now they're both in exile."

"Imagine, at the end, nobility in Herodias."

Caligula made another sweeping change in the East when he recalled Vitellius from his post as governor of Syria. Pilate thought it one of the emperor's few enlightened measures, since he had never forgiven Vitellius for the high-handed manner in which he suspended him from office. Because of his successes in the East, Vitellius had incurred Caligula's jealousy, and it was only by the most groveling tears and servility before the princeps that he was able to save his own life. Later, when Caligula asked the chastened ex-governor if he could see the Moon in bed with him, Vitellius replied with slavish tact, "No, Master. Only you gods are able to see one another."

But the lover of the immaterial Moon certainly knew how to spend very material cash. Caligula now grew as prodigal with the sesterce as Tiberius had been frugal. Chaerea disgustedly told Pilate of the worst example. The astrologer Thrasyllus had once predicted that Caligula had no more chance of becoming emperor than of driving a team of horses across the Gulf of Baiae. So, at vast expenditure, Caligula bridged the three and one-half miles of water between Puteoli and Baiae by lashing together a double line of merchant ships and heaping a roadbed of dirt across their decks. Then, mounted on his favorite steed and resplendent in the armor of Alexander the Great, Caligula rode back and forth across the new bridge to the compulsory cheers of throngs on both ends. The next day he repeated the trip in a chariot, followed by the Praetorian Guard. Having rescued the veracity of the dead Thrasyllus in this bizarre fashion, he ordered the bridge dismantled as a hazard to navigation.

"The damnable fool!" Chaerea swore at the end of his story. "What did Rome do to deserve such a maniac?" Pilate started giving some serious thought to the possibility of emigration.

The bridge, and such other necessary projects as a private navy of jeweled pleasure barges, squandered in one year the imperial treasury of 2,700,000,000 sesterces which Tiberius had patiently amassed during his entire administration. In order to replenish his funds, Caligula began pillaging the populace by various means, all illegal. Once he even resorted to auctioning off the furniture of Augustus and Tiberius at enforced astronomical bids. But it was Procula who heard the best story. At another palace sale, Caligula told his auctioneer not to overlook the "bidding" of a tired soul in the third row who kept nodding in his sleep. On awakening, the drowsy fellow learned that thirteen gladiators had been knocked down to him for a mere 9,000,000 sesterces.

Still there was not enough money. A whole cavalcade of new and unheard-of taxes was levied, and this kept the government half solvent. But his personal income suffered, so Caligula condemned to death some of the wealthiest Romans and seized their estates. Finally, he even opened a brothel in the palace itself, where the men of Rome could trade on credit—at high interest rates, of course. Roman statecraft had plunged to a new nadir in this, the 792nd year since the founding of the city.

In lucid moments, Caligula realized that his popularity was slipping. The time-hallowed method for a Roman emperor to regain favor with his subjects was foreign conquest. It was not for nothing that his father was named Germanicus; he, too, would march north and battle the Germans. In September of 39, Caligula crossed the Rhine with his legions and made several forays against Germanic tribes. What he really accomplished was the suppression of a conspiracy against him by the legate of Germany and his own brother-in-law. Both were executed.

Wintering in Gaul, Caligula dreamed of returning to Rome in glorious triumph to celebrate his victory over a foe at the very ends of the earth: he would invade Britain. In the spring of 40, he moved as far as the English Channel, but was too cowardly to cross it. Yet he had to have booty to parade at his forthcoming triumph, so he ordered his legionaries to gather sea shells from the channel shores and fill their helmets with these "spoils from the ocean." There was also the problem of captives: victories, even mythical victories, required prisoners. Caligula had the tallest Gauls dye their hair red to look like Germans so that they could be "captured" and then paraded in his Roman triumph.

Shortly after the emperor's return, Cassius Chaerea appeared at Pilate's door with a face draped in anxiety. "I'm sorry, old friend," he said, handing him a dreaded summons to the Palatine. "Hope it's nothing serious."

Once again Pilate tasted severe apprehension. "Any inkling what it's about?"

"No."

Pilate had hoped Caligula would by now have forgotten about his very existence; but, unfortunately, the unhinged brain of the princeps still had its memory intact.

When Pilate arrived at the palace and was ushered into Caligula's quarters, he found him stalking about the room in a rage, exchanging rapid-fire comments with his chamberlain, an Egyptian named Helicon, and his favorite actor, Apelles, a Greek.

Caligula shot a glance at Pilate and rasped, "Oh, it's you, Prefect. Yes. Once I told you that you didn't use enough diplomacy on the Jews. Now I tell you that you used too much! That hateful, rebellious, stiff-necked people have just committed treason and heresy and apostasy in Judea! Tell him, Apelles."

"You know that sleepy little town of Jamnia in Palestine?" the actor asked Pilate. "The one near the Mediterranean coast?"

"Yes," Pilate responded cautiously.

"The gentile citizens of Jamnia erected a brick altar to our emperor's divinity in honor of his recent victories in Germany. But the Jews in town promptly tore it down."

"Yes," Caligula snarled, "they overturned it, destroyed it completely! An altar erected to *me,* to my *divinity!*"

"Majesty," said Pilate, "isn't Herennius Capito our procurator there?"

"He's the one who just wrote me the horrible details. Here. Read his letter."

Pilate did as directed. Then it occurred to him why Apelles was there. The actor came from Ascalon, which lay very near Jamnia. He and Helicon had probably filled the emperor with additional anti-Semitism to feed his flaming ire at Capito's letter.

"Now," Caligula continued, "as former prefect of Judea, tell me what I should do to *punish* the Jews for this atrocity, this unbelievable sacrilege. Helicon here and Apelles have made their suggestions. Let's hear yours."

Despite the extreme danger, Pilate could not resist asking, "Excellency, might it not be advisable to consult King Agrippa? I understand he's presently in Rome."

Caligula glared at Pilate with his vacuous gray eyes. Then he snapped, "At times like this I rejoice in the fact that my dear Agrippa is only one-quarter Jew and three-quarters Idumaean. I might discuss this with him later if I feel he can give me an objective answer. I'm not sure he can. But don't evade my question! I'm talking to you, Pilate, not Agrippa. You. What would you do to chastise the Jews for this horrendous act?"

"First I would try to identify the perpetrators."

"Dolt! The perpetrators were Jews!"

"Yes, but *which* Jews? Capito should find those guilty and punish them. After that he should warn the leaders of the synagogue in Jamnia against any further attempts on the altar and assess them the cost of its reconstruction. Several Roman auxiliaries might also be stationed there to guard the sacred precincts."

"That's *all* you would do?"

"It would seem to be an effective—"

"That's all you would do?" he screamed. "No wonder the Jews rode roughshod over you in Judea!"

Pilate shuddered at the change which had come over the princeps since their last meeting. Caligula was unable to remain in one place or keep his eyes fixed at anything for longer than a few moments. He romped about his private quarters like a claustrophobic tiger.

"Well, Pusillanimous Pilate, I'll tell you what your emperor and god is going to do. Helicon and Apelles here think it's a fine idea. I'm going to have a colossal *statue of myself* erected in Palestine. And *where* do you suppose?"

"In Jamnia, Majesty?"

"No, Fool! In Jerusalem itself. Ahahaha! What do you think of *that?* And more than Jerusalem," he simpered. "The statue to my divinity will be erected . . . in what they call the Holy of Holies, in the Jewish *temple itself! That* should teach them."

Pilate was now certain that Caligula was insane. Jews, hypersensitive to images, now tolerating Caligula's statue in their *temple?* It would be an unthinkably appalling violation of their most cardinal laws against idolatry, Pilate knew, and would render the entire temple useless for future worship. No ritual purification could eliminate such a desecration. He recalled a little contest staged by his troops after the Jews had protested their standards. The best answer was sought to the question, "What is the most unholy combination of things that can be done to offend a Jew?" The winning reply was this: have an uncircumcised gentile sell blood sausage from a strangled pig on the Sabbath Day in the forbidden courts of the temple. A Samaritan had concocted it, a unique combination of dreadful violations of Hebrew law. But now there was a new winner: Caligula's plan made the Samaritan's look pious by comparison.

As diplomatically as he could, Pilate explained to Caligula how the statue scheme would represent the ultimate abomination for Judaism, the supreme sacrilege; that the people would never, under any circumstances, tolerate it. He had to tell the truth; otherwise, when Caligula's plan miscarried later on, it would be the worse for him. But now, when he saw the imperial eyes widening in rage, he quickly shifted to another tack. "You should know, Majesty, that the Judeans may be a recalcitrant people, but not a day passes without public sacrifices being offered up at their temple in *your* behalf." Pilate labored the point, for he thought it might be the one hope of sidetracking the emperor from his fantastic intention.

Caligula glowered at Pilate, his lips quivering. All color drained from his face. For some moments he was unable to speak but for assorted animal-like noises. Pilate was terrified.

Finally, Caligula violently cleared his throat and found his tongue. "I . . . didn't . . . ask . . . for . . . your . . . objections, Pilate. Only your suggestions, but you have no suggestions worth anything." He walked over and locked his eyes onto Pilate's, their faces just inches apart. "Now I want to know just one more thing from you. Concentrate, Peculiar Pilate, you may yet furnish me *one* normal answer. . . . What will *really* happen when my statue is erected? You see, Petronius will come down from Syria with two legions to do the job, so there's no question about whether or not the statue will go up. But how long will it take the Jews to learn their lesson and accept my deity?"

Pilate now realized his life was at stake. He guarded every syllable: "If you order the statue erected, Majesty, it will certainly be erected."

"That's better, Pilate," Caligula smirked. "The Jews will allow it, then?"

"Of course. They'd have to. How could women and children halt your legions?"

Caligula scowled. "What about the men?"

"They would all have been killed or taken prisoner in defending the purity of their temple."

"You mean their silly belief in one god is *that* strong? No race is so fanatic about religion. When 10,000 Roman legionaries arrive, watch how quickly they change their minds! You are a fool, Pilate, and you've given me nothing but foolish answers. *Guards! Guards!*" he cried, clapping his hands as several praetorians came into view. "Arrest this man! Seize him!"

Frigid perspiration broke out on Pilate's brow. He suddenly gambled all on the precarious assumption that Caligula's fury was a matter of the moment, that if he could stall a bit he might yet surmount the crisis.

"Majesty," Pilate smiled serenely, "I thought you and Jupiter Capitoline were on close terms."

"We are."

"Well, last night the great Olympian Father of the Gods came to me in my sleep and told me that you, his brother, would summon me to the palace today, and that if I spoke frankly, you would be better served than if I merely told you what you wanted to hear."

Only a lunatic, at best a fanatic, would have believed the story, but it was enough to make Caligula pause. In that hesitation, Pilate continued his dangerous gambit. "Since I am merely a mortal, Divinity, indulge the fact that I cannot see into the future with your prophetic eye. If your statue stands in the Jerusalem temple, the mistaken opinion of one, Pontius Pilatus, will be the necessary foil against which your sovereign wisdom will shine all the brighter."

"Yes. That makes sense," he said slowly. "At last you've come to your wits. Guards . . . dismissed. But don't leave

Rome, Pilate. The day my statue is dedicated in Jerusalem, I'll want you at a corresponding ceremony in my temple here at Rome. There you will deliver a public testimony about your error and my divine omniscience."

"I look forward to that day, Excellency," Pilate lied, as he bowed deeply and left the palace.

It was the first time in his life that he had been driven to absolute sycophancy. It was nauseating, dishonest, and humiliating; but necessary in humoring a madman. Small wonder Vitellius had stooped to the same expedient. Probably only Agrippa might yet stop the insane plan of the princeps, and even he might not succeed. The gods knew, Pilate had tried.

But Caligula did not bother consulting Agrippa. The tribune Chaerea kept Pilate very closely informed of the emperor's next moves, since he might be involved again at any time. Caligula now commanded Publius Petronius, the new governor of Syria, to make and erect his statue. It was to be larger than life-size and plated with gold. He was to use the Syrian legions to overcome any Jewish resistance.

Disgusted that the Roman military should be used for such purposes, Petronius nevertheless complied. He ordered the statue constructed at Sidon and then advanced with two legions to the borders of Palestine.

Cornelius wrote Pilate what happened next. Understandably frantic at the projected monstrosity of sacrilege, the Jewish populace went on an agricultural strike in protest. A delegation of Jewish leaders met with Petronius, respectfully imploring him not to execute Caligula's plan. They would sooner die, all of them, than tolerate idolatry and blasphemy on this scale. Petronius agreed to temporize. His troops would spend the winter in camp before proceeding, and he planned to write the artisans in Sidon to take their time on the statue.

After additional conferences with the Jews, Petronius realized the impossibility of Caligula's scheme, so he did a very heroic thing. At the risk of his life, he wrote the emperor of the enormous difficulties which would be caused by execution of his orders and wondered if they might not be rescinded.

Caligula, meanwhile, was unable to keep the joyful news to himself. Like a boy anxious to open a gift before his birthday, he could not resist telling his dear Agrippa about the object lesson he was planning for Jerusalem. When he heard the staggering news, Agrippa actually fainted and had to be carried home in a litter.

Later, Agrippa consulted with Philo, the famed Jewish philosopher who was in Rome at the time to represent the Jewish case in race riots which had broken out in Alexandria. Together they sent a long memorandum to Caligula which explained Hebrew theology in relation to the emperor's plan. Included was a prominent reference to Pontius Pilate, pointing out that if the Jews had objected to Pilate's shields, which had only his and Tiberius' names inscribed on them, how much greater would be their protest against an idol.

But the memorandum was long and philosophical. Apparently it failed to impress Caligula. King Agrippa got much further by entertaining the princeps at one of the most lavish banquets even he had ever attended. Tongues wagged about its courses, its sumptuousness, above all, its wines. Cassius Chaerea was on duty with his guards that night, so he could give Pilate an eye-witness account.

When Caligula had drunk well and Agrippa had toasted him to proper excess, the emperor countered graciously by suggesting that the king ask a favor of him.

"No, Magnificent Friend," Agrippa replied modestly. "I seek no personal advantage. You've already conferred on me far more honors than I deserve."

"No, Esteemed King and Colleague, but you must request something . . . anything which will contribute to your happiness."

His imperial quarry properly cornered, Agrippa sprang his very risky trap. He pleaded with the emperor to countermand his orders about the statue.

Pilate quickly saw it as a reiteration of Salome requesting the head of John the Baptizer from Herod Antipas. Like the tetrarch, Caligula was embarrassed and sorry he had left himself open. Like the tetrarch, the emperor could not go back on his word before the friends who were banqueting with him. Like the tetrarch, he granted the wish. The statue project was allowed to lapse.

Shortly afterward, Petronius' letter arrived with the identical request. It could not have come at a worse time. Caligula was pouting over Agrippa's trick and Petronius seemed a convenient scapegoat. He sent him orders to commit suicide. He also secretly arranged that another statue for Jerusalem be constructed in Rome.

Gaius Caligula planned to visit Egypt, the only land which really understood how a ruler could be god incarnate. But before making the trip, he wanted to be sure no conspiracy developed in Rome behind his back. In two secret notebooks entitled "The Sword" and "The Dagger," signifying public execution or private assassination, he began listing names of the chief patricians and equestrians who were to be slain before he sailed. Chaerea found out about them; how, he would not tell his friend Pilate.

But the princeps did so need a change of scene. An insomniac for much of his life, he rarely slept more than three hours in twenty-four. A typical night would find him wandering among the colonnades of his palace, calling for Dawn to show herself. Once he summoned three ex-consuls to the Palatine at midnight. Arriving in mortal fear of their lives, they were seated below a stage on which Caligula suddenly burst out in a solo dance, accompanied by flutes and clogs.

Nor were theatrics limited to evenings. In the daytime he sometimes dressed in lion's skin and carried a club to indicate that his versatile deity was that day incarnated as Hercules. By dusk he might be clutching a trident to reveal himself as Neptune. Wigged and dressed as a maiden set for the hunt, the divine transvestite was now Diana. But his favorite pose was with golden beard and wooden thunderbolt in his right hand. Who but Jupiter? He had even contrived a "thunder-and-lightning machine" which would rumble and flash in competition with Jupiter's own natural reverberations, of which he was terrified.

Rome could tolerate this farce no longer, for the humor in it had been lost in the general atmosphere of terror. Romans of every class were being exterminated like so many pests. Each magistrate now considered himself a doomed man, and wondered only when the tyrant would cut him down. A well-knit conspiracy was launched. The praetorian prefects—Caligula had created two of them in hopes of diluting their power—their staff of tribunes, and some in the imperial court were part of it. But the principal role was claimed by Pilate's old-school, no-nonsense comrade, Cassius Chaerea, who was a republican at heart. The praetorian tribune cut so masculine a figure that the puny and effeminate Caligula, begrudging him his physique, loved to taunt him with womanliness. Whenever Chaerea asked for the day's password, Caligula would suggest: "Venus," or

"Love," or "Fertility," and the like. And when an amenity required him to kiss the princeps' hand, Caligula would extend it, but then draw back all fingers except the middle one, an obscene gesture which has stood the test of time.

On the night of January 23 in the year A.D. 41, Chaerea paid Pilate a hasty visit. "This is *absolutely secret*," he whispered, "but do you want to see history being made before your eyes?"

"Certainly. But what do you mean?" He noticed that Chaerea was very nervous and continually looked around to see if he were being overheard.

"Come with me to the Palatine tomorrow morning," he murmured.

"To the *Palatine?* Too dangerous for me."

"Don't worry. The praetorians will keep you out of sight and we control the whole palace security."

Pilate knew he should refuse the invitation and he was about to refuse. But once Chaerea's intentions registered in his mind he was unable to refuse. That night he could barely sleep, and Procula asked what was the matter. "Indigestion," he fibbed.

Early the next morning, he and Chaerea went to the Palatine. As a precaution, Pilate was wearing an old praetorian uniform whose helmet covered his face fairly well. About 10:00 A.M. they walked over to the palace theater where Caligula was attending a dramatic spectacle. Chaerea seemed to be communicating with scattered pairs of eyes solely by using his own. Staying in a dark alcove at the rear of the theater, Pilate cringed a bit when he saw the theme of the pantomime: a robber chieftain being crucified. Soon the stage was saturated with great quantities of artificial blood, a deadly omen to portent-seeking Romans. At the close of the mime, Caligula stood up and delighted his guests with the announcement that he himself would make his public debut on the stage that evening. Then he left for lunch via a covered passageway which connected the theater with the rest of the palace.

Pilate watched him walking through the lengthy portico. Suddenly Cassius Chaerea and another praetorian tribune named Sabinus loomed up in his path.

"May we have the day's password, Princeps?" asked Sabinus.

"Well, let's see . . . How about 'Cupid' in *your* honor,

gentle Chaerea," said Caligula, a sickly sweet smile stretching his gaunt features. "No, on second thought, we'll make it Jupiter.' "

"So be it!" cried Chaerea, as he yanked out his sword. "As god of sudden death, may he assist yours!" He plunged the sword into Caligula's neck.

"Guards!" he screamed, a rivulet of blood pouring from the gash.

Sabinus dirked him in the breast. Caligula yelled in pain, his knees starting to bend. Praetorians and magistrates in on the plot now came running toward Caligula from both ends of the portico, brandishing bared daggers. They clustered about the falling emperor to share in the honor of his assassination.

Too late the litter bearers and members of his German bodyguard came dashing to his rescue. Caligula was dead, his body torn by some thirty wounds.

Pilate quickly blended into the crowd and escaped the scene, as Chaerea had insisted, for there was danger from Caligula's bodyguards. He had now seen what he came to see. And he luxuriated in a flood of relief.

Caligula's corpse was hauled outside where it was spat upon and ridiculed by the rejoicing populace. His statues were toppled. Cries of "Liberty!" "Restore the Republic!" rent the air. It was a tyrant's typical end.

News of such a death spread faster than normal communications. Across the Mediterranean in Syria, Petronius learned the glad news almost a month *before* Caligula's letter ordering his suicide arrived, since the ship carrying it had been delayed three months by storms. Now he could read the death command in laughter rather than terror. He was saved. In Jerusalem, the temple reverberated with thanksgiving to God for having delivered his people from the tyrant and his statue. The Jews were saved. Those senators and equestrians who now read their own black-listed names in the confiscated notebooks "The Dagger" and "The Sword" were saved.

But no one was more jubilant than Pilate and Procula. The madman who for nearly four years had represented a standing threat to his freedom if not his life, was no more. With tears of happy gratitude he embraced his friend Chaerea. Pilate was saved.

Chaerea produced "The Dagger" notebook and showed

Pilate one of the most recent entries in the list of prominent equestrians. It read:

Pontius Pilatus?

Chapter 25

UNDERSTANDABLY, PILATE had long since developed republican inclinations. His decade of trying to please the irascible Tiberius, followed by four fearful years under Caligula had buried his erstwhile monarchism. Many an evening discussing politics with Cassius Chaerea had aided in the republicanization of Pontius Pilate, and he now took pride in his kinship to Pontius Aquila, the conspirator against Caesar.

Just after the assassination, Pilate did what lobbying he could among his equestrian and senatorial friends to urge a restoration of the Republic. And now his and many other personal efforts seemed rewarded. The Senate convened in extraordinary session to declare the end of the Roman Empire, the near century which had witnessed the rule of Caesar, Augustus, Tiberius, and now, by far the worst, Caligula. In its place, the conscript fathers voted to revive democracy and restore the Roman Republic.

Pilate was present as guest of the Senate through the influence of his now-important friend, Cassius Chaerea, Rome's man of the hour. When the tribune-hero asked the triumphant consuls for the new watchword, they replied "Liberty," to the wild cheering of the senators. The glorious day of political freedom had dawned.

Meanwhile, unknown to Chaerea, Pilate, or any of the republicans, fate was calling to center stage the forgotten man of Roman politics, Caligula's Uncle Claudius, who had spent the fifty years of his life, not really waiting in the wings, but acting out a ludicrous sideshow of his own. Spindly-legged and wobbly from a childhood infantile paralysis, Claudius had other handicaps, including mental blocks and a speech defect which made him stammer and appear simple-minded. Tiberius had named his nephew "Clau-Clau-Claudius" and given him no serious consideration as his successor, since the imperial family thought him merely a biological embarrassment. Caligula had treated him as court buffoon, a role Claudius was only too happy to play, for otherwise he would have been put to death as a rival to the throne. But, in fact, Claudius was no fool. His personal impediments had driven him into the seclusion of scholarly pursuits, and, tutored by the great Livy, he wrote important works on Etruscan and Carthaginian history, as well as Roman law.

Claudius thought he himself would not survive Caligula's assassination. During the bloody turmoil that day, he had fled into the palace and hid. Later, when the praetorians were ransacking the place, they chanced to notice two feet sticking out beneath a curtain in an upstairs alcove. The feet, of course, belonged to Claudius, who expected instant death. Instead, the troops whisked him off to the *Castra Praetoria* and hailed him as the new emperor. The guards were supported by many in the populace who feared that a democratic republic would only return Rome to bloody civil war.

But the Senate would not back down at a time of unparalleled opportunity. The conscript fathers dispatched two tribunes to the *Castra*, who advised Claudius not to assume the principate but yield to the Senate, which would stop him by military force if he had not learned his lesson from Caligula's fate. Claudius wavered, but since he was safe with the praetorians, he temporized for the moment.

Enter King Herod Agrippa, adventurer, opportunist, fisher-in-troubled-waters, and now alterer-of-Roman-history. When he learned that Claudius was being detained at the *Castra Praetoria*, he hurried over to join him at the camp. Both the same age, Claudius and Agrippa had been educated together at the palace school.

Claudius was at the point of yielding to the Senate, when Agrippa arrived and urged him *not* to let power slip from his hands. "History is summoning you, beloved Claudius," he said. "The blood of the Caesars pulses in your veins and must not be frustrated. You were born to rule. What will future ages say of a Claudius who was too selfish to guide Rome with his moderation and wisdom?" Claudius promised to think about it.

After Agrippa left the *Castra,* he received a summons from the Senate. Quickly perfuming his hair as if he had just been called away from a banquet instead of visiting Claudius, he appeared before the senators. They requested his advice, as a visiting sovereign, on the present constitutional crisis. Shrewdly, Agrippa appeared pro-Senate, but argued that the Urban Cohorts, on whom the fathers were relying in the coming showdown with Claudius, were no match for the praetorians. "Instead of declaring civil war," he urged, "why not send a delegation to Claudius and negotiate your differences?" The Senate agreed. Naturally, Agrippa was one of the ambassadors dispatched to the Praetorian Camp.

Before Claudius met with the delegation, Agrippa got his ear privately. He reported the Senate's confusion and urged him to stand his ground, with diplomacy. Then Agrippa joined the rest of the delegation to echo the Senate's line. Claudius delivered a handsome reply, promising that he would be princeps in name only, and would fully involve the Senate in governing Rome. Having experienced the terror of life under his nephew, he could never be a tyrant.

At dawn the next day, the Senate met to hear the reply. Again Pilate was present, this time as a member of Chaerea's committee to restore the Republic. Unlike many of their fellow praetorians, Chaerea, Sabinus, and others refused to consider Claudius, and now they strove to firm up the Senate in its resolve to restore the Republic. Pilate darted between benches in the chamber, trying to hold communications together among republican senators.

But their cause faced an ominous development. The Urban Cohorts on which the Senate was relying grew restless and impatient. Finally they demanded that the Senate choose a chief executive, yes, a princeps. Several candidates other than Claudius were discussed, with little enthusiasm. The more realistic senators, seeing what was inevitable, got up from their benches and hastened out of the chamber to be the first to congratulate Claudius on his increasingly obvious accession.

In dejection, Pilate watched Chaerea hurry to the rostrum to remind the senators that they had just dispatched one tyrant, and should not create another. Barely 100 senators were left in the chamber—the full body numbered some 600—and the Urban Cohorts now raised their standards and marched off to swear allegiance to Claudius. With no military support, the republican cause collapsed. Slowly, mournfully, the remaining conscript fathers rose and filed out of the Senate chamber.

Pilate walked over to Cassius Chaerea. In their mutual depression, no words were possible. The restored Roman Republic had lasted barely forty-eight hours. Pilate clasped his friend's shoulder and they finally left the Senate hall. As the last to leave, they were, in a sense, the last two citizens of the "Second Roman Republic."

Claudius, with Agrippa at his side, was borne in triumph over to the Palatine, hailed by plaudits from the fickle Roman masses. As one of his first official acts, the now-emperor Claudius rewarded the man who was so instrumental in raising him to empire. In a speech before the Senate, he bestowed the rank of consul on Agrippa, and then announced: "Finally, beloved Friend, we name you king not only of those territories which you now hold, but also of Judea as well. We have recalled the prefect Marullus. You will recognize that you are now king over all the lands formerly ruled by your grandfather Herod the Great."

Agrippa expressed profound gratitude to Claudius and the Senate, promising that Judea would be a most loyal ally of Rome. He then returned in triumph to Palestine, where the Jews welcomed him with an enthusiasm unparalleled since the days of the Maccabean princes. His first act after arriving in Jerusalem was to offer sacrifices of thanksgiving and dedicate to the temple the golden chain which Caligula had given him.

From his home near the Proculeius mansion, Pilate surveyed these developments with less the dispassion of a spectator and more the involvement of a citizen. It was not jealousy at Agrippa's phenomenal success which haunted him so much as the apparent destruction of the republican cause. Claudius might well have yielded to a restored senatorial republic had this foreign opportunist not tutored him to empire. An alien king had changed the course of Roman history. He suspected the Republic would never have another chance.

And Pilate lost a close friend in the case of Cassius Chaerea. Everyone in Rome, including the new emperor, agreed that Chaerea was a hero, that his tyrannicide had been a splendid deed for the state. But, in the grotesque political calculation of the time, the hero had to die. Claudius put it this way: "I am pleased that Caligula is gone. I am displeased that a princeps has been assassinated." As an ominous precedent, it could not go unpunished. A deterrent for Claudius' own safety was necessary. Chaerea would have to be sacrificed. The Senate agreed.

The tribune bore his fate with Stoic dignity, but Pilate wept for his friend as he accompanied him to the place of execution.

"Come off it, Pilate. Rome needs a 'martyr' about now anyway," he quipped. "I was prepared for this when I killed the tyrant."

"But the state needs you, Chaerea."

"Sorry. In the words of Cato, 'I don't want to survive Liberty.' "

The tribune Lupus, a fellow conspirator, was also being marched out to execution, but he broke down in tears.

"Stop it, Lupus!" Chaerea remonstrated. "Put on your thick skin and play the wolf!" It was a pun on *lupus*, Latin for wolf.

A large crowd had gathered at the place of execution. Chaerea looked down at the executioner, a smaller man than he, and said, "Tell me, lad. Are you an old hand at this sort of thing, or is this the first time you've held a sword?"

"I've had a little practice," he admitted. "Remember, I also worked for Caligula."

"There's a good chap. But do me a favor—Pilate, can I borrow that sword for the last time?" Chaerea had given him the sword with which he had dispatched Caligula.

"Here, lad. Use this one."

"Why?"

"It has sentimental attachment. So long, Pilate. See you in the Elysian Fields. And you, Lupus, if I hear one yelp out of you, I'll haunt you to Hades and back. See how easily it's done now. Lay on, lad. It's a privilege to die for the *Republic!*"

Chaerea bared his neck. It was severed in one blow. Lupus, who could not match that brand of courage, stuck his neck out gingerly. His execution required several strokes.

A revulsion at these unnecessary deaths swept Rome almost immediately. In remorse, Claudius tried to undo what had been done by releasing and restoring to office Chaerea's fellow conspirator Sabinus, who was scheduled to die. But Sabinus thought his survival would be a breach of loyalty to his dead comrades, so he killed himself.

The progress from martyrdom to canonization was rapid. The Roman people showered gifts on the relatives of the dead conspirators and sacrificed to their shades, pleading with them to be gracious rather than vengeful at the gross public ingratitude.

To the consummate relief of Rome and the entire Empire, Claudius soon proved to be a decent and surprisingly able emperor, as finally even Pilate had to admit. Grandiloquently named Tiberius Claudius Caesar Augustus Germanicus, the one-time court jester collaborated well with the Senate, as he had promised, and made that body more representative. He abolished the universally detested charge of *maiestas* to avoid any future legal reigns of terror. He introduced much-needed centralization and administrative efficiency in the imperial government. His program of public works improved Rome's water supply and laced the provinces with highways and canals. Ostia, at the mouth of the Tiber, was reclaimed as port of Rome, which spared travelers the 140-mile trip south to Puteoli. Claudius' foreign policy was similarly successful, and two years after his accession, he made a swift conquest of Britain. From that victory, his legions were able to bring more than sea shells back to Rome in triumph.

Above all, under Claudius, Rome no longer seemed to thrust its politics to the center of world attention. Life in the Mediterranean could flow back into normal channels. So could Pilate's.

Perhaps for the first time in their marriage, Pilate and Procula knew serenity. Two-thirds of their wedded life thus far had been spent under the strain of provincial administration in Judea, the last third in the hell of uncertainty under Caligula. Pilate's civil pension and the income from his holdings provided them a very comfortable life, particularly since Rome was enjoying increased economic prosperity. There was no expense for rearing children, a blight in their marriage to which they had become reconciled by now.

Yet Pilate had trouble adapting to leisure. With time on

his hands, the thought of standing for public office haunted him. There was no upper age limit for Roman magistrates and he thought himself still in his late prime. He was even tempted to apply to Claudius for a position in his expanding civil service, perhaps in the department governing the provinces. The princeps needed trained officials—he was resorting to freedmen to fill many important posts in his growing bureaucracy—and Pilate could easily dispel any cloud over his record by appealing to the fact that it was Caligula who had retired him. The way from such an appointment into Claudius' cabinet itself would be short.

But Procula did everything possible to pierce Pilate's projections. "What if Claudius should suddenly get ill and transform himself into a monster? The inclination seems to run in the family. Then he'd strike out against those nearest him. Have done with the government, Pilate."

"But Vitellius returned to politics and seems to be doing well."

"Only by fawning and toadying. That's not for you. And remember that Agrippa, who is a favorite of Claudius, could still block your career."

"Why? He's off in Palestine with all his ambitions fulfilled."

But Pilate was not really arguing with conviction. He was simply trying to reserve future alternatives for himself. Everyone must live with a few goals, a little hope, some objective for existence.

Procula made it her responsibility to keep their day as full as possible. Aside from gladiatorial shows, which they loathed and avoided, there were the races, the theater, and many social engagements. Of greater interest to Pilate were the lectures of visiting Greek philosophers, or public readings by Roman authors of the Silver Age. He now read more than ever. And he was even able to gratify his political susceptibilities by regular visits to the Senate, where, as an ex-officeholder, he had the perennial privilege of observing. Periodically, various officials in Claudius' bureaucracy consulted him on Eastern affairs, since Pilate was considered a resource person for questions affecting Syria and Palestine.

Once Claudius himself called Pilate to the Palatine for a conference. It concerned, of all people, King Herod Agrippa. Claudius laid before Pilate a map of Jerusalem and studied it for some moments.

At close range, Pilate found the princeps quite dignified in appearance. He was tall, pleasant featured, and crowned with a luxurious crop of white hair which became him. He had a slight halt to his gait, an occasional tic in his head, but he was hardly the physical and social cripple of popular repute. Rumor, apparently, had exaggerated Claudius' garden variety of handicaps.

"Now, Pilate, some disturbing information has reached us about Jerusalem," he said, with only a soft slur in his elocution. "Our friend Herod Agrippa is erecting fortifications along the northern boundary of the city." He traced his finger along the general path of the new construction which he had marked in on the map lying before them. "You should know the city, Pilate. Does this new wall have any, shall we say, military implications?"

"Possibly, Princeps," he admitted. "But the question is one of motivation. Which enemy would Agrippa wish to hold off? Certainly not the Rome which gave him his throne. Parthia? Only a remote possibility. And Aretas of Arabia is dead now." Pilate studied the map further. "So I'd gather that Agrippa is building this new wall merely to enclose the northern suburbs, an area running from the execution hill, Golgotha, here in the west," he pointed, "to beyond the Tower Antonia in the East.

"*Probably* that's his motivation," Pilate continued. "But from the dimensions of the wall which you cited, there's no question but that Jerusalem will be much stronger in the event of siege. Should it ever revolt, it would now be harder for Rome to retake the city."

"That seems a fair estimate of the situation," said Claudius. "And it corresponds to my thinking. Do you have any recommendations?"

"You know Agrippa far better than I, Princeps. Undoubtedly he's loyal to Rome. At the same time, it might be well to have the governor of Syria make inquiries."

"He already has. It was Marsus who first alerted me to the wall. He's even more concerned than you. At any rate, I'm going to write Agrippa to proceed no further on the north wall. Its present height may stand, but not a foot higher. It was good of you to come, Pilate. We may well need your advice in the future."

"I'm always at your service, Princeps."

With that the audience ended and Pilate left the palace. The news about Agrippa was rather interesting, he thought. Was militaristic ambition rearing its grisly head in Palestine? Or was the wall just an innocent example of normal Herodian construction mania? Was Claudius having second thoughts about abandoning Roman control of Judea? Or harboring qualms about his beloved Agrippa? The endless fascination of politics!

But even more striking was the realization that for the first time in years, it was possible for Pontius Pilate to leave the Palatine without extreme depression or gnawing uncertainty. Rome was returning to respectability.

Chapter 26

THE PONTIUS Pilati now spent much of the warmer half of each year at a seaside villa near Antium on sunny Mediterranean coastlands about thirty-five miles south of Rome. The country estate was one of several owned by Procula's father, who was disposing of his properties before death claimed him in extreme old age.

The salubrious climate and natural beauty around Antium revived Pilate's spirit and helped inter the morbid memories of Sejanus, Tiberius, and Caligula, who occasionally still haunted his dreams.

He had aged physically. There were fissures setting in on each side of his nose, crow's-feet flanking his eyes, and a rather well-corrugated brow. His receding hairline now reached across much of his scalp, leaving an island of graying thatch in the center. Pilate ascribed it to Rome's political terror. Procula called it normal, male-pattern baldness.

She was only in her late thirties—it was not yet a question of aging with her. Procula's maturing countenance still retained its youthful beauty and formed a progressive contrast with that of her husband. She chuckled at his ire the first time an innkeeper at Antium inquired whether he and his daughter wished to order dinner. Though motherhood was denied her, Procula felt fulfilled and, for the first time in their marriage, a genuinely happy woman. She no longer had to plot to keep her husband out of trouble.

Fulfillment, however, remained a problem for Pilate. After a busy administrative career, retirement freighted too much time to his address. Whenever they went to Antium, he took along a young library of scrolls to read. A deepening interest in philosophy now seized him. He suggested to Procula that they finally take their long-planned, always-interrupted tour of Greece and the Aegean. It would enable him to sit in the lectures of the ranking philosophers of the · day and explore with them a question he had once asked— he forgot under what circumstances—and which now seemed of growing significance to him: What is truth?

A monopoly on truth was confidently proclaimed by every philosophical school in the Empire, and by each religious cult—and just as confidently contradicted by all the rest. Pilate feared it might be a frustrating search, this quest for truth. Perhaps, he thought, the philosopher Nausiphanes was right after all when he taught, "The one thing certain is that nothing is certain."

One day, while Pilate was walking along the Mediterranean shore "in dialogue with my soul," as he described his sandy peregrinations, someone in a military tunic came running along the beach toward him.

"Stop, Pontius Pilatus," he cried, "I've come to arrest you! Claudius wants to see you in chains!" But the man was smiling.

"Cornelius!" Pilate beamed. "I thought you'd never return. Did you bring along your wife and family?"

"Yes. They're inside the villa visiting with Procula. We're five now: two boys and a girl. . . . And I've been transferred to the *Castra Praetoria.*"

"Congratulations, Tribune, also on the promotion."

"Thanks, Prefect."

"But why didn't you return to Rome before this? Surely the Italian Cohort didn't stay on in Caesarea after Herod Agrippa became king."

"Oh, no. Everything Roman moved out of Palestine, from the prefect of Judea down to the gilded Roman eagles. Agrippa kept the Sebastenian auxiliaries, but our cohort was transferred to the legions in Syria. I just returned from there. . . . But I wager the Italian Cohort will move back to Caesarea in short order now."

"Why?"

"Haven't you heard? Agrippa is dead."

"What?"

"Yes. Happened shortly after the Passover this year."

"After only three years as king of Judea? How did it happen? Assassination?"

"No. It was all very strange. He was in Caesarea, presiding over festive games in honor of Claudius. On the second day of the spectacles, he entered the theater at daybreak and delivered his address, wearing a garment woven entirely of spun silver. It caught the rays of the rising sun and glittered so radiantly that some of the credulous and the flatterers actually started hailing him as a deity. 'This is a god speaking, not a man!' they cried."

"And what did Agrippa say to *that*," Pilate smirked, "admit it?"

"He said nothing. And that was his downfall, he claimed. He should have condemned the blasphemous flattery. Feeling an intense stab of pain in his heart and stomach, he staggered and said, 'An immortal god am I? No, just a mortal man on his way to the grave. God wills it. I must accept.' They carried him back to the palace—your home for ten years. After five days of horrible pain, Agrippa died."

"Incredible! Who'll govern Palestine now?"

"His son, Agrippa the Younger, is here in Rome getting his education at the palace school. I understand Claudius at first thought of appointing him king, but his advisers suggested that the lad would have a terrible time of it since he's only seventeen. So the princeps is set to appoint Cuspius Fadus as procurator of Judea. Once again, it seems, Rome will govern Judea directly."

"Fadus as *procurator?*"

"Yes. Prefects of Judea are to be called procurators from now on. Same job, different title." He hesitated, then added, "I just happened to recall. Maybe I shouldn't tell you this after all the trouble you had with the Jews regarding images, but Agrippa sinned in this respect more than you ever thought of doing. The coinage which he minted outside of Jerusalem was stamped with his own *image*. And he even had *statues* of his daughters sculptured and set up in the forum at Caesarea. Yet the Pharisees loved him."

"But for me they staged riots, demonstrations, protests, letters." Pilate shrugged his shoulders. "Well, that's a closed chapter. . . . So, Cornelius, tell me more about yourself: how's my favorite Jew?"

"Fine. But I'm a Christian now."

The word Christian had no significance whatever for Pilate. "Oh," he said, "I see Procula waving us in for dinner. Come on, Cornelius. You can't imagine how the sea adds an edge to the appetite."

Back at the villa, Pilate was delighted to see the rest of Cornelius' family, particularly the younger boy, who had been named Pilatus in his honor.

"First of all, I categorically insist," said Pilate, with contrived bombast, "you folks have to spend some time with us. At least a week. It's been so long."

The Cornelii protested, only out of courtesy, and then gladly gave in.

Several hours later, after a tasty seafood dinner, Pilate began once more to speculate about the sudden death of Herod Agrippa.

"I have my own reasons for despising that man," commented Cornelius.

"Oh? Why?"

Cornelius looked at his hosts, then knowingly at his wife. Finally he took a long breath and said, "Because Agrippa executed James-ben-Zebedee and would have done the same to Simon Peter if he hadn't escaped from prison."

"And who might they be?" Pilate wondered.

"James and Peter? Two of the leading disciples of Jesus the Christ."

Pilate paused and pondered. "Jesus the Christ?"

"Yes. Don't you remember? The one you sentenced at the Passover. . . . It must be eleven years ago now."

Pilate searched his memory. "No . . . or . . . yes," he finally said. "Galilean. Came from Nazareth, correct? Yes, I remember now. That old puzzle! But what's your interest in his disciples?"

Again Cornelius assumed the expression of one who had a long story to tell and knew the telling must come shortly, but who was apprehensive about his hearers' reaction. Finally he declared, "Pilate, I—our whole family—are Christians."

"Are what? Didn't you use that term before?"

"Christians. Yes, I did. The followers of Jesus the Messiah—the Christos—are now called Christians."

For some moments Pilate stared blankly at Cornelius.

"It's quite a story. If you'll listen," Cornelius continued, "I'll—"

"*You?*" Pilate blurted. "You're *members* of that Jewish cult?"

"Yes."

"But didn't that sect die out long ago?"

"No. On the contrary."

"But Caiaphas and the Sanhedrin had all but hounded them out of existence, hadn't they?"

"They didn't succeed. The Christians have organized themselves into congregations in each major town in Palestine. Now they're spreading as far as Alexandria, Damascus, Antioch, and beyond. There are isolated households even in Rome which are Christian."

"But what does Agrippa have to do with it?"

"Agrippa thought the whole movement was subversive—he had hoped that you had put an end to Jewish Messianism by crucifying Jesus—so he was determined to root out the ringleaders. The outspoken and courageous James was first. He was beheaded. When Agrippa saw how this pleased the priests, he went on to arrest Peter, the leader of the disciples. But although he was under constant guard at the Antonia, Peter escaped prison in the dead of night and Agrippa never caught him again."

Pilate started nodding his head toward the close of Cornelius' statement and said, "He's the one, then."

"The one what?"

"Peter. He's the one who must have engineered the grave robbery."

"What grave robbery?"

"Stealing the body of Jesus from under the noses of the guards. A clever fellow this Peter, an escape artist evidently."

"Pilate, Peter was chained between two guards. If somehow he escaped them, he would have had to get beyond the bars of his cell. If he got out of the cell, he would have had to go through four squads of sentries and two separate guard posts. You know how the Antonia is laid out. Then there'd be the wall and the iron gate, always barred at night. How could he have escaped through all that?"

"Well, how did he then?"

"The same way that Jesus' sepulcher was empty on Sunday morning."

"How?"

"By divine intervention. Just as Jesus most assuredly rose from the dead."

Pilate studied his friend for some time with a quizzical expression. Finally he shook his head and said, "Do you *really* believe that, Cornelius? A solid, sensible citizen like yourself?"

"I do."

"But I thought you were a good Jew."

"I never became a full proselyte. But even if I had it wouldn't have made any difference. My wife is Jewish and Christian at the same time. So are my children. So, in fact, are most members of the Christian congregations."

An element of strain had intruded in the dinner-table conversation, so the women quietly retired while Cornelius and Pilate continued their discussion.

"I can't believe how credulous you are, Cornelius. I, your friend, put a man to death, and now you believe that man has come back to life and is the object of your faith. Yet you still consider me your friend?"

"Yes, of course."

Pilate shook his head in dismay. Then he asked, "When did you go beyond Judaism to join this . . . this cult? An why do Peter and James, if those are the names, mean something special to you?"

"I was converted to Christianity by Peter."

"When? How?"

"It was in a mid-afternoon, shortly after you left Caesarea, that I had a terribly realistic perception or vision—now don't scoff, Pilate: this thing happened." Cornelius was glaring in earnest. "I was instructed in this perception to send to Joppa for a man named Simon Peter, who was staying at the seaside home of another Simon, a tanner by trade. Naturally, after this vision passed, I questioned the reality of the whole experience. But obviously I had to check on its validity. I sent two servants and my orderly off to Joppa. They came back with Peter, who was staying at precisely the address indicated in the perception."

By now Pilate wished Cornelius would either suppress his new fanaticism or leave him in peace. Only visionaries had visions. Only enthusiasts were so enthusiastic. He wondered how to terminate the conversation with any shred of decency.

"I don't trust visions any more than you do, Pilate, especially since our late, crazed emperor used to specialize in them," Cornelius chuckled. "But hear me out. I most solemnly swear to you as a friend and as a Roman that I had not previously known the location of this Simon Peter. You see, I didn't believe the perception either. I was just testing out my sanity in sending for the man. When he arrived, I couldn't help but recognize the intervention of a higher power. Wouldn't you have?"

Pilate shifted uneasily in his couch and replied, "If what you say is precisely what happened, there may be an explanation. Perhaps you had already heard that Peter was in that area but *forgot* you'd heard he was. Or it might—"

"Explanations!" Cornelius erupted. "Excuses! An old habit of yours! I brought you eyewitness reports about Jesus' healings and the phenomenon of raising the dead, and you only opened your bag of logical tricks and came up with some threadbare explanation which was far more fantastic than the event it was supposed to explain. Even though I wasn't in Jerusalem at the time of Jesus' crucifixion and resurrection—would that you'd taken me along—from even *your* reports of what happened I was far more impressed with the facts, even your version of the facts, than the explanations for them which you volunteered."

"But every effect *must* have its *natural cause!*" Pilate bellowed.

"Every effect must have its cause," Cornelius corrected. "And the cause in these cases is Jesus the Christ, the power of God-become-man."

At this point Cornelius ventured his core explanation of Christianity. The universe, he explained, was created by God, but its perfection was violated by man. Instead of condemning humanity, the Creator-God sent an extension of himself—his Son—into the world in the form of a man, Jesus of Nazareth, who atoned for human disobedience by suffering, dying, and rising again for all mankind. Through faith in him, sinful men are forgiven, despite their unworthiness, and gain everlasting life. Cornelius elaborated on this theme, using the thinking and language of the Roman military.

Pilate said nothing. He reflected for some time, then went down to the cellar of his villa to fetch more wine. After pouring two large goblets and handing one to Cornelius, he asked, "Where did you learn all this?"

"From Peter. Let me finish that story. Before my men met him, Peter had had a similar perception indicating that *I* would be sending for *him*. So he came without further ado, bringing along six members of the Christian congregation at Joppa. I invited some of my closer Roman friends and my wife's Jewish relatives to meet Peter, and we had quite a conference."

"I can imagine," Pilate observed, his comment only barely disguising his skepticism.

Cornelius ignored the tone and continued. "Peter is a most impressive man, and held us spellbound for several hours. He was exuberant about what he called 'the universal faith.' His visit proved that Christianity was to become more than a special brand of Judaism: now gentiles were to be welcomed into the faith as well as Jews. 'Truly, God shows no partiality,' he said, 'but in every nation anyone who is god-fearing and does what is right is acceptable to him.' "

Pilate continued sipping his wine carefully.

"When Peter finished, we found his message so convincing and the faith so magnificent that we asked to join the movement. Peter welcomed and baptized us."

"You mean everyone at your gathering? The Romans too?"

"Everyone. My wife, our children, the Jewish relatives, and Roman friends. Peter stayed on with us for about a week, teaching us more of the faith and filling in details about Jesus' life which I hadn't known. In leaving, he told me, 'You, Centurion, are the first in what will be a great army of gentile converts to the faith. Since you were selected for this honor, battle nobly for tho Christ."

Pilate felt Cornelius' eyes boring in on him. He took a long quaff from his goblet and said, "I believe in your sincerity, Cornelius. I also believe we've discussed this enough for one day."

They moved on to politics, a far more congenial theme, thought Pilate, and they downed additional flagons of wine. Finally the household and the guests retired for the night.

In bed, just one or two comments from Procula told Pilate that the women had been discussing the same matters as the men. Before dropping off to sleep, he wondered when the Jesus phenomenon would finally leave him in peace . . . all but forgotten in recent years, and now revived.

The next day, Cornelius was careful not to mention Christianity to Pilate. He realized he had administered a concentrated dose of religion to an unsuspecting and unwilling patient, and there was risk of undesirable reactions. And the faith was not a medicine.

But it was the factor which had altered Cornelius' life, and therefore, also his relationship with Pilate. It had to be discussed, and, surprisingly, it was Pilate who broached the matter that evening.

On balance, he had received so much additional information about Christianity that the movement strangely intrigued him. Not that he had a moment's sympathy for the new faith. He saw that Cornelius was indirectly but unabashedly trying to convert him, a prospect Pilate found too bizarre for further thought. But, after all, he had unwittingly served as midwife at the birth of what evidently was becoming a new religion—a rare enough situation—and so he felt something of an obstetrician's responsibility for it.

There was also the undercurrent of the mysterious, the occult, the inexplicable which had attended the entire career of the man whom he had crucified but whose memory clung. Pilate had at least a philosopher's interest in this phenomenon. As Cornelius related new details of the life of Jesus of Nazareth, many additional supernatural incursions studded the story, establishing the Christ in a metaphysical dimension.

The next morning, they discussed the philosophical presuppositions of religion itself, and here there was less argument. Long ago, Pilate had abandoned Greco-Roman polytheism and now admitted, "If I *were* a religious man, Cornelius, I think I'd join Plato and Aristotle, or even Cicero and Vergil, for that matter, and be a monotheist. Aristotle's First Cause, his argument that creation intuits a creator, commends itself to reason. A single deity seems the only intelligent recourse. Now to that extent the Jews were right, and I can see why you and my Procula found interest in the system. Why even our learned Varro confessed his belief in one god, the soul of the universe, who may also be identified as the god of the Jews, he wrote. But believing that this one god revealed himself in the man I crucified . . . that goes beyond reason."

Somewhere Pilate hoped to find the key which would unlock and expose the mystery of the new faith, the chink which would disprove it, something in one of Cornelius' stories about the Galilean which would refute his claims. Instead, the new data supplied by his friend seemed to forge links which connected facts Pilate already knew. For example, there was the unresolved question of the star over Judea and the baby rumored to be king of the Jews. When he learned that this was the infant Jesus of Nazareth who had *not* been killed, he was stupefied. Jesus, then, had carried the title "king of the Jews" from Bethlehem to Golgotha, thirty-six years later!

Now Pilate grew aroused and defensive. "Tell me this, Cornelius, don't you really believe Jesus was son of god in the figurative sense in which all men are supposedly sons of a creating god?"

"No, friend. Jesus came from the essence of God."

"Then you believe this as an inspiring religious myth, don't you?"

"No. As history. As event. As fact. Just as Jesus rose from the dead in reality and not in myth."

Cornelius had touched the most sensitive nerve in Pilate's memory of the Nazarene affair. Pilate had never settled the question of the missing body. Pressing his hands to the sides of his head, he said, "But if what you say were true, then *I would have executed deity!*"

"The human expression of deity," Cornelius responded gently.

"Then why didn't your god burn me with a thunderbolt the moment I condemned his son to the cross? Yes!" Pilate brightened, "Why was no curse placed on me? As I sat on my tribunal that day, I had a faint recollection that this situation had occurred once before somewhere, but until now I couldn't recall it. Yes, the *Curse of Pentheus* . . . from Greek mythology."

"The Pentheus story?"

"It's best told in a tragedy by Euripides. Pentheus was king of Thebes. One day, the god Bacchus, or Dionysus as the Greeks call him, came to Thebes for a celebration.—Now notice the amazing parallels in this story, Cornelius.—Dionysus was welcomed into town by women who were singing and waving garlands and branches of ivy. But Pentheus, who had no idea the stranger was an offspring of Zeus, a son of god, ordered him arrested. Dionysus was then led before Pentheus by a band of soldiers, who said their prisoner had not tried to resist arrest.—Sound familiar, Cornelius?—But word came that the maiden followers of the stranger, who were also imprisoned, had shaken off their fetters and escaped into the mountains . . . a great wonder!

"Now Pentheus threatened Dionysus, but he responded gently that the king would not be able to keep him in prison. 'God will set me free,' the son of god claimed. But Pentheus didn't recognize his divinity and ordered him bound and scourged. Then Dionysus arranged a special curse for the king. While he hurried off into the mountains to chase down the Theban women, the god maddened Pentheus' own mother and sisters who were also out in the hills. They saw Pentheus only as a mountain lion and tore him limb from limb in their frenzy. But at the last moment, Dionysus opened all eyes. Pentheus knew he was paying with his life for having punished a god, and the women saw their atrocity."

"Oh, Pilate. Comparing a wild bacchanal to the Palm Sunday crowds? The god of drink to Jesus? You as Pentheus? The women as the disciples?"

"The point of comparison is merely that if your Jesus is a deity, a human judge unknowingly condemned a god in both instances. In the Greek myth, the judge was dismantled. *Why* didn't some similar catastrophic punishment fall on me? After all, I would have committed the most horrendous crime possible: executing divinity. I'd be a godkiller!"

"But Pilate—"

"A cosmic crime! In the name of my sanity, I *must* believe that Jesus was perhaps innocent, a good man—but thoroughly mortal like everyone else."

"Unless, of course, you're mistaken. But to answer your question, Pilate, it happened by a higher design, according to which *both* Jews and gentiles were to be responsible for . . . for this final sacrifice. Just as all classes joined in condemning the Christos, so, by divine reflex, his death and resurrection atoned for all classes, all races. You, then, also took part in making the faith universal, Peter told me. Your unwitting error is forgivable, like any other sin, even if that error was spectacular, extraordinary. Peter was insistent on that point and told me to tell you about it if I ever saw you in Rome. So, again, you didn't know it, but you were one of God's instruments in the drama of salvation."

Pilate was going to comment that he didn't like being used without his knowledge, but he canceled the thought as petty. Finally he said, "It's just too much to absorb, Cornelius. The implications for me personally . . . would be staggering."

For several moments the tribune reflected, then said, "I know, Pilate, I know. . . . Well, friend, we've abused your hospitality long enough. I must report to Rome. From now on I'll be at the *Castra,* so we must get together again. But don't worry: no more sermons." He laughed, then added with a wink, "But I will be around to help answer any questions you might have."

"And maybe I won't ask any," Pilate smiled, clapping him on the shoulder. "But you're a good man, Cornelius."

He and Procula bade the Cornelii farewell.

In the days following their visit, Pilate suspected from Procula's random comments that she had more than a smoldering interest in Christianity. He was sure of it when they returned to Rome that fall. He discovered that she had started attending meetings for Christian worship at the home of a couple named Aquila and Priscilla. Cornelius and his family, together with a small group of Roman Christians also gathered here regularly for this purpose.

But Procula did not invite her husband to join them. She had learned never to try to push Pilate into anything. Meanwhile, she began to pray for him. For her, the visit of the Cornelii at Antium was the latest milestone in a journey to faith which had begun years before in Judea.

However, conversion to a belief centering in the man he had crucified was a grotesque hurdle for Pontius Pilate. If only Jesus had told him more that Friday. He might have released him. But in that case, what would have happened to Christianity?

Pilate did sense one strong, personal argument in favor of the faith: if Jesus were not divine, Pilate's own life and career would ultimately prove insignificant, meaningless. History would truly pass him by. But if the Christians were right, his lifework would take on profound dimension indeed. Yet was that, in itself, a sufficient motive for accepting the faith? Was it honest?

Epilogue

PILATE COULD never know it—he would have been astounded to know it—but, apparently insignificant ex-prefect that he was, his would eventually be the most familiar name in all of Roman history. For uncounted masses in future ages, who knew little about a Caesar or Augustus or even Nero, would still confess in The Creed: "I believe in Jesus Christ . . . who . . . suffered under Pontius Pilate."

Many would remember Pilate only in horror from that clause as the man who killed Christ. They would invent the most terrifying, and certainly imaginative, punishments for him: torture, exile, insanity, compulsive hand-washing, suicide, drowning, decapitation, being swallowed by the earth, and even that ancient punishment for parricide—being sewn up in an ox-skin with a cock, a viper, and a monkey, and pitched into a river. Medieval legends would add the familiar stories of his restless corpse, accompanied by squads of demons, disrupting localities from Vienne in France to Mt. Pilatus in Switzerland, causing storms, earthquake, and other havoc.

On the basis of the earliest sources, however, it is clear that nothing of the sort ever happened to Pilate, let alone his corpse. The early Christian church understood "suffered under Pontius Pilate" not in the sense of blame so much as for purposes of historical documentation and chronology. Much subsequent Lenten preaching to the contrary, one of the earliest church fathers claimed that Pilate "was already a Christian in his conscience." Greek Orthodoxy canonized his wife. To this day, October 27 is Saint Procula's Day in their calendar, while the Ethiopian church recognizes June 25 as "Saint Pilate and Saint Procula's Day."

Sinner or saint, cosmic blunderer or expedient functionary, Roman prefect or instrument of the Divine, Pontius Pilate—beyond any debate—would become one of the very controversial figures in history.

Historical Note

ALL MAJOR episodes in this book are historical and have been documented in the Notes below. Aside from the familiar role of Pilate at the trial and crucifixion of Jesus, such principal events as his involvement in the standards affair, the aqueduct construction and riot, the episode of the golden shields, the clash with the Samaritans, and his recall are all attested by ancient sources, notably Josephus and Philo. Archaeology has supplied additional data conerning his construction of the Tiberiéum and the coinage he minted in Judea.

As for coinage, there is no evidence that Pilate issued any coins during his first years in Judea. But in 29 A.D., he minted bronze quadrans pieces embossed with the *simpulum*, a sacred ladle used for Roman sacrifices. Since the *simpulum* was widely used on coinage throughout the Empire, this may have been a small attempt on Pilate's part to Romanize Judea. Later, in 30-31 A.D., perhaps under pressure from Sejanus, Pilate issued the coin shown below featuring a *lituus*, the curving, spiral-headed staff symbolizing the priestly-prophetic office of the Roman augur. Thoroughly embedded in Rome's past—this crosier was used in consecrating the early kings of Rome—the *lituus* motif was in general vogue on imperial coins at that time. Pilate's using a symbol freighted with such a Roman mystique on quadrans pieces minted in Judea appears to be a further Romanizing pledge of provincial allegiance to Tiberius and the Empire.

Left: The *lituus* is at the center of the obverse, and the lettering is Greek: "TIBERIOU KAISAROS," ("of Tiberius Caesar"). *Right:* In the left fringe of the reverse are berries, while "LIZ" within the wreath indicates the "17th" year of Tiberius' reign, i.e., 30-31 A.D.

Paradoxically, the pagan Pontius Pilate embossed what would shortly become a Christian symbol on his coins, since the *lituus* would be re-used as the crosier or bishop's crook, the symbol of episcopal office to the present day.

This novel's portrayal of the politics, Roman and Judean, in which Pilate was engulfed is absolutely authentic. Some of the connective material, however, was contrived, but done so on the basis of probabilities with no violation of known historical facts. Because of missing evidence, some relationships were necessarily presumed. The true family gens of Procula is unknown, and even her name comes only from a very early tradition, the *Acta Pilati* in the so-called *Gospel of Nicodemus*. Procula's is the *only* proper name in this book not attested by an original primary source, but no other name for her is known, and Procula is most probably accurate. Since the name "Claudia Procula" derives from a late tradition, "Claudia" is discarded.

The precise relationship of Pontius Pilate to the various Pontii cited in these pages is presumptive, but members of the gens Pontius would indeed be related, and the ancestral home of the Pontii was Samnium. Nothing is known of Pilate's parents. His presence at the collapse of The Grotto is merely assumed, though his advancement through Sejanus' efforts is demonstrable. Even if the letters cited in these pages are not authentic, as such, the correspondence itself and the sentiments expressed are highly probable. Indeed, some of the phrases in the letters are direct citations from the sources.

Pilate's trip to Machaerus with Antipas is possible, but not documented. His contact with Cornelius is highly probable, since both were Roman officers in Caesarea at the same time. It is not known if Pilate ever conversed with Saul (St. Paul), Herod Agrippa, or Caligula. Finally, his friendship with Cassius Chaerea is based only on the inference that Pilate did rise in office through the Praetorian Guard, where he would have known Chaerea as a fellow tribune.

As indicated, there is an interesting divergence of opinion concerning the fate of Pontius Pilate. Aside from Tiberius' dying before he could hear his case, the original source tells us nothing. The traditional negative view that Pilate committed suicide has been common ever since the church historian Eusebius. In his *Ecclesiastical History,* Eusebius wrote:

> ... tradition relates that ... Pilate, he of the Saviour's time, in the days of Gaius ... fell into such great calamity that he was forced to become his own slayer and to punish himself with his own hand, for the penalty of God, as it seems, followed hard after him. Those who record the Olympiads of the Greeks with the annals of events relate this.
>
> (ii, 7. Kirsopp Lake's translation in
> *Loeb Classical Library*)

However, no extant records, Greek or otherwise, confirm this statement, and Eusebius himself calls it tradition. Indeed, in his *Chronicon* Eusebius cites "the Roman historians" rather than the Greek as his source for the same statement, indicating that he had trouble documenting Pilate's presumed suicide (ed. Migne, XIX, 538). Moreover, Eusebius' motivation in recording the tradition of Pilate's suicide is less that of a critical historian and more that of an apologist and moralist in describing divine vengeance as overtaking Pilate. Finally, Eusebius was writing in the fourth century A.D., and there is considerably earlier evidence than this.

When the noted pagan philosopher Celsus wrote his *Logos Alethes* ("True Word") in 178 A.D., one of the arguments he used against Christianity was the fact that, unlike King Pentheus, Pilate *suffered nothing* for having condemned alleged divinity. In 248 A.D., the early church father Origen published his refutation *Kata Kelsou* ("Against Celsus"), but against Celsus' argument concerning Pilate's fate Origen replied only that the Jews, not Pilate, were responsible for the crucifixion (ii, 34). Clearly, there was no church tradition of Pilate's suicide, execution, or punishment in the second or third centuries.

Earlier still, Tacitus, who mentioned Pilate in his famed passage about the Christians (*Annals,* XV, 44) published in 117 A.D., as well as Josephus, make no reference either. Probably most illuminating is the testimony of a contemporary of Pilate who despised him, the Jewish philosopher Philo. In his *Embassy to Gaius,* which reports his famed mission of 39-40 A.D., Pilate is castigated (xxxviii), but no mention is made of any subsequent suicide or any punishment inflicted on him by Caligula, who certainly either decided Pilate's case or dismissed it. Though this is an argument from silence, the silence is eloquent, since on other occasions Philo took keen delight in recording the punishments of people he scorned, as witness his *In Flaccum* ("Against Flaccus," xviii, 146 ff.).

This raises the final question of whether a reasonable rather than hostile portrait of Pontius Pilate is possible. For the past seventeen centuries, Pilate has had an unusually bad press, and most tend to cloister him next to Judas Iscariot in mind and memory. This view seems unjustified, both by the practice of the early church in its crucial first three centuries, and, more importantly, by the sources themselves. Aside from scattered references in ancient authors, the chief primary sources for Pilate are: Flavius Josephus in his *Jewish Antiquities* and *Jewish Wars;* Philo in his *Embassy to Gaius;* and the New Testament Gospels, Matthew, Mark, Luke, and John. Of these seven writings, one is hostile to Pilate, while the other six range from slightly critical to favorable. Philo, the hostile source, has Herod Agrippa write Caligula (in the memorandum cited on page 314 above) of ". . . the briberies; the insults, the robberies, the outrages and wanton injuries, the executions without trial constantly repeated, the ceaseless and supremely grievous cruelty" of Pilate (xxxviii. F. H. Colson's translation in *Loeb Classical Library*). Nothing in any of the other sources on Pilate corroborates this judgment, and it is doubtful that Tiberius, even with his predilection for keeping his governors at their posts for long terms, would have allowed Pilate a whole decade of administration in Judea if he were such a wretch.

The dissonant source must therefore be examined, and the context may explain Philo's censure. The Jewish philosopher despised foreign administration of Judea, and in the above citation he seemed to be unloading his holy ire at the loss of Judean independence on the man who represented Rome in Palestine before his beloved Agrippa was made king. Since his account was published after Caligula's death, he was writing for the benefit of the emperor Claudius, and it would therefore be in the interest of his cause to portray the previous Roman administration of Judea in the worst possible light so that the Jewish homeland would not be returned to provincial status. Accordingly, we look, not for clear history from Philo in this connection, but heavily colored emotion and lyricism, rhetoric and exaggeration. As Stewart Perowne aptly comments on Philo's reference to Pilate (in *The Later Herods,* Abingdon Press, Nashville, 1958): "This may be dismissed as just the sort of stuff that is traditional in a region where words have never been regarded as necessarily a reflection of fact, but are held to possess a being of their own, independent and free. The idea is as old as Homer. . . . To call Philo's rhapsody lying would be a mistake: he was merely conforming to a conception of language which is not that of the modern west." (p. 50). This opinion is largely shared by other commentators, in works cited in the Notes.

Therefore with Josephus recording Pilate's humanity as well as his blunders, and the New Testament casting him virtually as Jesus' lawyer for the defense before capitulation to popular pressure, a more balanced portrait of Pontius Pilate is possible, even if he is hardly the saint the Ethiopians would make of him.

Notes

Though Pilate used to delight the morbid imagination in the Middle Ages, there is very little modern scholarship on his life or career. The study by Gustav Adolf Müller, *Pontius Pilatus, der fünfte Prokurator von Judäa und Richter Jesu von Nazareth* (Stuttgart, 1888) is ably corrected and supplemented by Hermann Peter, "Pontius Pilatus, der Römische Landpfleger in Judäa," *Neue Jahrbücher*, I (1907), 1–40. A fair estimate of Pilate and an excellent investigation of his aqueduct to Jerusalem is provided by Frank Morison, *And Pilate Said . . .* (New York: Charles Scribner's Sons, 1940). Periodical literature concerning Pilate is cited in the notes below. The few historical novels on Pilate have been of minimal historical or literary value.

CHAPTER 1

(Pages 9–20)

TIBERIUS AND SEJANUS: This and following sketches of Roman politics as of 26 A.D. are drawn from Tacitus, *Annals*, iv, 1-54; Suetonius, *Tiberius*, i–xxxviii; and Dio Cassius, *Roman History* (hereafter merely "Dio Cassius"), lvii.

THE PONTII: For a catalogue of the prominent members of Pilate's gens, see the article "Pontius" in Georg Wissowa, ed., *Paulys Real-Encyclopädie der classischen Altertumswissenschaft* (Stuttgart: Metzlersche and Druckenmüller Verlag, 1953 ff.).

THE FULVIA SCANDAL: Josephus, *Jewish Antiquities* (hereafter *Antiq.*) xviii, 3, 5.

PILATE'S SALARY: A stipend of 100,000 sesterces for the prefect of Judea is posited by Otto Hirschfeld, *Die Kaiserlichen Ver-*

waltungsbeamten bis auf Diocletian, 2nd. ed. (Berlin: 1905), pp. 436 f.; and by H. G. Pflaum, *Les Procurateurs Equestres sous Le Haut-Empire Romain* (Paris: A. Maisonneuve, 1950), pp. 150 f. Cp. also Dio Cassius, liii, 15, 3–6. Because of the chronic inflation of the American dollar, it becomes very difficult to assign a meaningful value to the sesterce in current terms. The suggested salary of $20,000, for example, would have a far greater buying-power in imperial Rome.

L. AELIUS LAMIA: Tacitus, *Annals,* iv, 13; vi, 27, and Dio Cassius, lviii, 19.

CHAPTER 2

(Pages 21–34)

GAIUS PROCULEIUS: Dio Cassius, li, 2; liii, 24; liv, 3; Horace, *Carmina,* ii, 2; Pliny, *Natural History,* xxxvi, 183; Plutarch, *Antony,* lxxvii, 7; Quintilian, *Institutio Oratoria,* ix, 3, 68; and Tacitus, *Annals,* iv, 40. While Proculeius is accurately portrayed in the text, his relationship to the wife of Pilate is necessarily only assumed in the absense of other evidence.

THE DEBATE ON GOVERNORS' WIVES: Tacitus, *Annals,* iii, 33–34.

HEROD AS MESSIAH: Hermann Vogelstein, *History of Jews in Rome* (Philadelphia: Jewish Publication Society of America, 1940), pp. 28 f.

ANNIUS RUFUS: Josephus, *Antiq.,* xviii, 2, 2.

THE ASS IMAGE: Rome's information about Judaism was astonishingly inaccurate, considering the fact that a Jewish community had existed in Rome ever since the second century B.C., which grew when Pompey returned with Judean captives in 61 B.C. In a short time, Roman Jews were supposedly so numerous that Cicero once told a jury he would have to speak softly so that the many Jews present would not be able to hear. While this was merely a lawyer's stratagem, Jews were taking part in public affairs, and Romans should have understood them better. The abhorrent misinformation about the Exodus and the ass image, for example, should have been corrected by Pompey's experience, and yet the great historian Tacitus, writing as late as 110 A.D., would record the same tired calumny as gospel in his *Histories,* v, 3 ff.

CHAPTER 3

(Pages 35–48)

GAIUS PONTIUS: Livy, *Ab Urbe Condita Libri,* ix, 1 ff.

PONTIUS TELESINUS: Velleius Paterculus, *Historia Romana,* ii, 27, 2.

AEMILIUS RECTUS: Dio Cassius, lvii, 10, 5.

THRASYLLUS: Tacitus, *Annals*, vi, 20–21; Suetonius, *Tiberius*, xiv. Thrasyllus was referring to the Great Conjunction of planets in 7 B.C., which appears only once in eight centuries.

PONTIUS AQUILA: Suetonius, *Divus Iulius*, lxxviii; Appian, *Roman History—The Civil Wars*, xi, 16 (113); and Dio Cassius, xlvi, 38, 40.

TIBERIUS' ENTOURAGE AND THE COLLAPSE OF THE GROTTO: Tacitus, *Annals*, iv, 57–59; Suetonius, *Tiberius*, xxxix- xl. A description of the modern excavation of the grotto at Sperlonga is given in Paul MacKendrick, *The Mute Stones Speak* (New York: St. Martin's Press, 1960), pp. 173–78. Later emperors tried to reclaim the grotto, but it was not really used again until World War II, when it served as an ammunition cache. The great cavern was first excavated in the summer of 1957, in connection with road improvements along the Italian west coast, when ruins of the pool and much statuary were discovered.

CHAPTER 4

(Pages 49–57)

"CAESAR'S FRIENDS": Suetonius, *Tiberius*, xlvi. It was Pilate's status as *amicus Caesaris* which was threatened during Jesus' trial. Cp. John 19:12 and Ernst Bammel, "Philos tou Kaisaros," *Theologische Literaturzeitung*, 77 (April, 1952) 206–10.

PROCULEIUS AND CLEOPATRA: see the first note under Chapter 2, above.

ANTIPATER AND CAESAR: Josephus, *Antiq.*, xiv, 8.

CHAPTER 5

(Pages 58–67)

CAESAREA: This description of the harbor and the city is based on Josephus, *Antiq.*, xv, 9, 6; and *Jewish Wars* (hereafter *Wars*), i, 21, 5–8.

VALERIUS GRATUS: Josephus, *Antiq.*, xviii, 2, 2.

"HEROD'S PIG": Macrobius, *Saturnalia*, ii, 4.

HEROD AND ROME: Josephus, *Antiq.*, xiv, 14 and xv, 6; *Wars*, i, 14 and 20.

HEROD'S DEATH: Josephus, *Antiq.*, xvii, 6–8.

HEROD AND THE MAGI: Matthew 2:1–12.

"YOU MUST NOT PUT A FOREIGNER . . ." Deuteronomy 17:15.

MEMBERS OF THE SANHEDRIN: Besides the New Testament, reference to CAIAPHAS, ELEAZAR, JONATHAN, and BEN-PHABI is found in Josephus, *Antiq.*, xviii, 2, 2, and 4, 3. Additional information on Ishmael ben-Phabi comes from *Pesahim* 57a (Babylonian *Talmud*) and *Yoma* 35b. ALEXANDER: Acts 4:6; Josephus, *Antiq.*, xviii, 6, 3. ANANIAS BEN-NEBEDEUS: Acts 24:1; Josephus, *Antiq.*, xx, 5, 2. The Babylonian *Talmud* also calls him Johanan ben Narbai or Nidbai, and charges him with gluttony in *Pesahim* 57a. Cp. also *Kerithoth* 28b. HELCIAS (or Helkias): Josephus, *Antiq.*, xx, 8, 11. GAMALIEL: Acts 5:34–39; 22:3 and *passim* in the *Mishnah* and *Talmud*. JOCHANAN BEN-ZAKAI: *Sotah* 27b ff.; 40a; 49b; *Gittin* 56a; and *passim* in *Mishnah* and *Talmud*.

CHAPTER 6

(Pages 68–84)

COHORS AUGUSTA SEBASTENORUM: presumed from Acts 27:1, and named in *Corpus inscriptionum Latinarum*, vi, No. 3508.

". . . NOT MAKE YOURSELVES A GRAVEN IMAGE": Exodus 20:4–5, the classic restriction against idolatry.

RELIGIOUS SIGNIFICANCE OF ENSIGNS: see Josephus, *Wars*, vi, 6, 1 for an instance of Roman soldiers sacrificing to their standards in Jerusalem after the fall of the city.

"GOD IS OUR REFUGE. . . .": Psalm 46:1–2, 6, 9–11.

JEWISH PAINTING AND SCULPTURE: Vogelstein, *op. cit.*, pp. 35 ff., cites instances in Mesopotamia and Rome.

HEROD AND THE GOLDEN EAGLE: Josephus, *Antiq.*, xvii, 6, 3.

THE AFFAIR OF THE STANDARDS: Josephus, *Antiq.*, xviii, 3, 1; *Wars*, ii, 9, 2–3. Eusebius, *Ecclesiastical History*, ii, 5, 7 ff., is just a reflection of Josephus. A modern scholarly interpretation of this incident is provided by Carl H. Kraeling, "The Episode of the Roman Standards at Jerusalem," *Harvard Theological Review*, XXXV (October, 1942), 263–89.

CHAPTER 7

(Pages 85–97)

CAESAREA: Josephus, *Antiq.*, xv, 9, 6; *Wars*, i, 21, 7.

PILATE'S TIBERIÉUM INSCRIPTION: Probably in tribute to Tiberius, Pilate used Latin at a time and place where Greek would ordinarily have been used. Originally embedded in the Tiberiéum, the inscribed stone was reused—long after Pilate's time—in constructing a theater, among whose ruins it was found by the Italian archaeologists. Unfortunately, some of the facing of the inscription had been chipped away, leaving only the lettering shown to the left. To the right is the suggested reconstruction:

```
—STIBERIÉVM      [CAESARIEN]S. (IBVS)TIBERIÉVM
—TIVSPILATVS              [PON]TIVSPILATVS
—ECTVSIVDAE             [PRAEF]ECTVSIVDA[EA]E
—E                              [D]É[DIT]
```

See Antonio Frova, "L'Iscrizione di Ponzio Pilato a Cesarea," *Rendiconti Istituto Lombardo* (Accademia di Scienze e Lettere), 95 (1961), 419–34.

Of great importance is the inscription's reference to Pilate as "prefect," which corrects the title of "procurator" usually ascribed to him, based on anachronisms in Josephus (*Wars*, ii, 9, 2) and Tacitus (*Annals*, xv, 44). During the reigns of Augustus and Tiberius, governors of Judea were called prefects. Claudius first changed their title to procurator. The New Testament very accurately refrains from calling Pilate procurator, using the Greek for governor instead.

Frova conjectures that the Tiberiéum might have been a "piazza porticata" near the theater of Herod, possibly a kind of "porticus post scaenam." The Pilate inscription at Caesarea is also discussed by B. Lifshitz, "Inscriptions latines de Césarée," *Latomus*, XXII (1963), 783; and by Attilio Degrassi, "Sull'Iscrizione di Ponzio Pilato," *Rendiconti dell'Accademia Nazionale dei Lincei*, Classe di Scienze morali, storiche e filologiche, XIX (Marzo-Aprile, 1964), 59–65, who suggests "[Dis Augusti]s" instead of Frova's "[Caesarien]s." in the first line. While it is possible that Pilate might have dedicated the Tiberiéum to the "divine Augustans" (i e., Augustus and Livia), as Degrassi admits, Livia was not officially consecrated until 42 A.D., and even allowing for such an eastern-style anticipatory gesture as this, it would seem unlikely that Pilate, knowing Tiberius' attitude toward his mother and step-father, would have made such a dedication. Frova's original suggestion, then, seems most appropriate.

ARCHELAUS: Josephus, *Antiq.*, xvii, 13, 1–5; Matthew 2:22.

PHILIP: Josephus, *Antiq.*, xviii, 4, 6. Philip was the first Jewish ruler to impress the effigy of any human being on his coins. For his coinage, see Emil Schürer, *A History of the Jewish People in the Time of Jesus Christ* (Edinburgh: T. & T. Clark, 1900), I, ii, p. 15.

TIBERIAS: Josephus, *Antiq.*, xviii, 2, 3.

MARRYING A BROTHER'S WIFE: prohibited in Leviticus 20:21.

ANTIPAS' DIVORCE AND ARETAS: Josephus, *Antiq.*, xviii, 5, 1.

CHAPTER 8

(Pages 98–111)

HEROD AND JERUSALEM: Josephus, *Antiq.*, xv, 8, 1 ff.; xvii, 10, 2.

TEMPLE NOTICE PROHIBITING GENTILES: Josephus, *Antiq.*, xv, 11, 5; *Wars*, vi, 2, 4. Archaeologists have discovered two notices with this inscription at Jerusalem.

HEZEKIAH'S TUNNEL: II Chronicles 32:2–4, 30. Cp. also II Kings 20:20, and, for David and the Jebusites, II Samuel 5:6 ff. The cited Siloam inscription is authentic. It was since chiseled out of the rock wall near the tunnel entrance and is now in the Turkish Museum of the Ancient Orient in Istanbul. Gihon has continued its small but steady flow down to the present day, and people can still wade through Hezekiah's tunnel, probably the only Biblical site which is entirely extant.

JEWISH TAX APPEAL UNDER GRATUS: Tacitus, *Annals,* ii, 42.

USE OF SHEKALIM: Surplus from the half-shekel temple dues is discussed in *Shekalim,* iv, 2, and the citation in the text is translated by Herbert Danby, *The Mishnah* (London: Oxford, 1938), p. 155. See also the discussion by E. Mary Smallwood, ed., Philo Judaeus, *Legatio ad Gaium* (Leiden: E. J. Brill, 1961), p. 301. The Jewish traditional laws grouped under the rubric *Shekalim* would later constitute a tractate and be incorporated into the *Mishnah,* the collection of Jewish sacred traditions.

THE JERUSALEM AQUEDUCT: Josephus, *Antiq.*, xviii, 3, 2; *Wars,* ii, 9, 4. Nothing in the sources indicates Pilate's negotiations with the Judean authorities prior to construction of the aqueduct, but it would seem obvious that such an enterprise, involving massive building operations in the vicinity of the temple, could not possibly have been undertaken without at least tacit approval of the temple authorities. Nor could Pilate have seized the temple treasury to finance construction of the aqueduct, as a cursory reading of Josephus might seem to indicate. For gentiles to enter the temple, where the sacred treasure was stored, would have been impossible—short of war between Rome and Judea—and seizing the sacred treasury would have elicited an immediate embassy from the Jews to Tiberius, which would have demanded Pilate's recall. He must, therefore, have had some cooperation from the temple authorities. The subsequent popular outcry was, apparently, just that: a protest of the people, not the authorities, who may even have warned Pilate in advance of the approaching demonstration, see Josephus, *Wars,* ii, 9, 4.

CHAPTER 9

(Pages 112–122)

PACUVIUS: Tacitus, *Annals*, ii, 79; Seneca, *Epistulae Morales*, xii, 8.

THE AQUEDUCT RIOT: Josephus, *Wars*, ii, 9, 4. Cp. also *Antiq.*, xviii, 3, 2. For further discussion of Pilate and the water system of Jerusalem, see Frank Morison, *And Pilate Said.* . . . (New York: Scribner's, 1940), pp. 105 ff., to which this portrayal of the aqueduct episode is indebted.

VOLESUS MESSALA: Seneca, *De Ira*, ii, 5, 5.

VARUS: Josephus, *Antiq.*, xvii, 10, 10. ALEXANDER JANNAEUS: *Antiq.*, xiii, 14, 2.

CHAPTER 10

(Pages 123–131)

JOHN THE BAPTIZER: Matthew 3:1 ff.; Mark 1:2 ff.; Luke 3:1 ff.; John 1:19 ff.

EVENTS AT ROME IN 29–30 A.D.: Suetonius, *Tiberius*, liv; *Gaius Caligula*, vii; Tacitus, *Annals*, iv, 68–70; v, 3 ff.; vi, 23; Dio Cassius lviii, 1, 1 ff.; 2, 7; 3, 8 ff. Pliny, *Natural History*, viii, 145. Besides Caligula, Tiberius had a natural grandson, Gemellus, but he was only ten at this time—too young for serious consideration as successor.

SEJANUS AND THE JEWS: Philo, *De Legatione ad Gaium*, xxiii, 159 ff.; *In Flaccum*, i, 1 ff. Cp. Eusebius, *Ecclesiastical History*, ii, 5.

CAPITAL PUNISHMENT AND THE SANHEDRIN: In *Shabbath* 15a of the Babylonian *Talmud*, the following statement is germane: "Forty years before the destruction of the Temple, the Sanhedrin went into exile and took its seat in the Trade Halls. . . . They did not adjudicate in capital cases." (Trans. by H. Freedman in *Shabbath*, Moed I, *The Babylonian Talmud* [London: Soncino Press, 1938] who explains that the Sanhedrin left their Chamber of Hewn Stone in the temple at this time for another place on the temple mount [p. 63].) Since the temple was destroyed in 70 A.D., "forty years before the destruction of the Temple" would be 30 A.D., or under Pilate's administration. Moreover, *Sanhedrin* 18a and 24b of the Palestinian *Talmud* (the *Yerushalmi*) states: "Capital punishment was abolished forty years before the destruction of the Temple." (Trans. by M. Movsky.) See also Ethelbert Stauffer, *Jerusalem und Rom im Zeitalter Jesu Christi* (Bern: Francke Verlag, 1957), p. 121. Also, by the same author, *Jesus and His Story*, (New York:

Alfred A. Knopf, 1960), p. 72. However, Schürer, *op. cit.* II, i, p. 188, suggests that the date for the withdrawal of this right from the Sanhedrin, i.e., 30 A.D., need not be considered precise, since the *jus gladii* may have been suspended when Judea became a Roman province rather than first under Pilate's administration. Nevertheless, a literal reading of the sources would indeed point to 30 A.D.

THE SANHEDRIN VACATES HALL OF HEWN STONE: *Shabbath, loc. cit.* (above).

CHAPTER 11

(Pages 132–145)

THE ESSENES: Josephus, *Wars*, ii, 8, 2 ff. The Essene monastery was recently excavated at Khirbet Qumran. Its library included the famed "Dead Sea Scrolls" found in nearby caves during the spring of 1947.

DEAD SEA GASES: Strabo: *Geographica*, xvi, 2, 42; Genesis 18:20 ff.

HEROD AT CALLIRRHOE: Josephus, *Antiq.*, xvii, 6, 5; *Wars*, i, 33, 5.

"TIBERIUS ONLY AN ISLAND POTENTATE": Dio Cassius, lviii, 5, 1.

THE EXECUTION OF JOHN: Mark 6:17 ff.; cp. also Matthew 14:3 ff., and Josephus, *Antiq.*, xviii, 5, 2. Pilate's presence on this occasion is only presumed.

MACHAERUS: now called *Tell Mukawir* by the Arabs, the citadel remains a huge, trapezoidal mound, dead as the Sea over which it towers. Buried within it are the ruins of Antipas' citadel, but they have never been excavated.

CHAPTER 12

(Pages 146–155)

SALOME AND PHILIP: Josephus, *Antiq.*, xviii, 5, 4.

GAIUS GALERIUS: Seneca, *ad Helviam*, xix, 4–6; Pliny, *Natural History*, xix, 3.

SEJANUS AND LIVILLA: Although Zonaras' epitome of Dio Cassius, lviii, 3, states that it was Livilla's daughter Julia to whom Sejanus was engaged, Frank B. Marsh, *The Reign of Tiberius* (New York: Barnes and Noble, 1959), p. 192, and other scholars would seem to be correct in assuming that the lady in question was indeed Livilla, not Julia, the error intruding via Zonaras.

CORNELIUS AND THE ITALIAN COHORT: Acts 10:1. For the identity and full name of the *Cohors II Italica*, see the article "Cohors" in *Paulys Realencyclopädie*, VII, pp. 304 ff. There is some debate over whether the Italian Cohort could have been in Judea prior to Vespasian, but also scholarly support for the implication in Acts that this cohort and Cornelius must have been in Caesarea at least by ca. 35–36 A.D., if not earlier.

THE GALILEAN VICTIMS: Luke 13:1–3. This incident is not further explained in the New Testament. While this may have been a cruel action on the part of Pilate and is used by some in building a case against him, it need not have been. In commenting on the episode, Jesus did not fault Pilate, and, by the context of the Siloam tower collapse, the implication is probable that this also may have been an accident involving the innocent. Cp. also Kraeling, *op cit.*, p. 288, who points out that Pilate might not have had anything to do with the event, since everything perpetrated by Roman auxiliaries in Palestine would be ascribed to him.

CHAPTER 13

(Pages 156–166)

MEMMIUS REGULUS: Although Tiberius and Sejanus were consuls for the year 21, they had appointed Regulus and Fulcinius Trio to succeed them as *consules suffecti* ("substitute consuls") later that year, a common practice. See Tacitus, *Annals*, v, 11.

THE FALL OF SEJANUS: The chief source is Dio Cassius, lviii, 9 ff., since the relevant passages in books v and vi of Tacitus' *Annals* are lost. See also Suetonius. *Tiberius*, lxv, and Seneca, *De Trunquillitate Animi*, xi, 11. For the FATE OF SEJANUS' CHILDREN, See Tacitus, *Annals*, v (vi), 9; Dio Cassius, lviii, 11.

ANTONIA: Josephus, *Antiq.*, xviii, 6, 6, is the sole source on Antonia's crucial role in unmasking Sejanus.

SOURCES FOR THE SEJANIAN CONSPIRACY: Tacitus, *Annals*, iv, 1 to vi, 2; Suetonius, *Tiberius*, lxi, lxv; Dio Cassius, lvii, 19 to lviii, 16.

CHAPTER 14

(Pages 167–176)

POMPONIUS FLACCUS: Tacitus, *Annals*, vi, 27.

A. AVILLIUS FLACCUS: Dio Cassius, lviii, 19, 6; Philo, *In Flaccum*, i, 1 ff.

CESSATION OF LITUUS COINS: No crosier coins of Pilate dated after 31 A.D. have been discovered. On Pilate's coinage, see "Historical Note" above and Ethelbert Stauffer, "Zur Münzprägung und Judenpolitik des Pontius Pilatus," *La Nouvelle Clio*, I and II (1949–1950) 495–514, although Stauffer is unduly severe with Pilate. Such conclusions of his as "Dieser Mann [Pilatus] war unter den vielen schlimmen Prokuratoren Judaeas mit Abstand der schlimmste" (p. 511) simply contradict the facts, especially when Pilate is compared with such later procurators as Cumanus or Florus. See also P. L. Hedley, "Pilate's Arrival in Judea," *The Journal of Theological Studies,* XXXV (1934), 56–57; E. Mary Smallwood, "Some Notes on the Jews under Tiberius," *Latomus,* XV (Juillet–Septembre, 1956), 314–29; A. Kindler, "More Dates on the Coins of the Procurators," *Israel Exploration Journal,* VI (1956), 54–57; and B. Oestreicher, "A New Interpretation of Dates on the Coins of the Procurators," *Israel Exploration Journal,* IX (1959), 193–95.

TIBERIUS' LETTER TO PILATE: This is a paraphrase of Tiberius' sentiments at this time regarding the Jews, according to Philo, *De Legatione ad Gaium,* xxiv, 160 ff. The exact date is presumed, though the year 32 would be accurate.

ZADOK: *Gitten 56a* (Babylonian *Talmud*).

NUMA AND THE SHIELDS: Plutarch, *Numa,* xiii; Horace, *Carmina,* i, 37, 2; Quintilian, *Institutio Oratoria,* i, 6, 40; Ovid, *Fasti,* iii, 259 ff.

JEWISH SHIELDS IN ALEXANDRIA: Philo, *De Legatione ad Gaium,* xx, 133.

THE INCIDENT OF THE GOLDEN SHIELDS: Philo, *op. cit.,* xxxviii, 299–305. Some authorities have suggested that this is merely Philo's version of the standards episode reported by Josephus, as F. H. Colson in *Loeb Classical Library, Philo,* X, 151. But the incidents are too different in too many details to give this suggestion credence. What is questionable is Philo's extreme bias against Pilate in reporting this event. In fairness to Pilate, it should be stated that Josephus, our most competent and complete source on Pilate apart from the New Testament, omits this episode entirely.

Philo's reference to Pilate's dedicating the shields "in Herod's palace in the holy city" (*De Legatione,* xxxviii, 299), which he further identifies as "the house of the governors" (*op cit.,* xxxix, 306) should end the long—and unnecessary—debate over whether Pilate and Procula stayed at the Tower Antonia or the Herodian palace during their visits to Jerusalem. It is further unlikely that Procula would have been subjected to quarters in a military barracks.

For further discussion, see my article "The Episode of the Golden Roman Shields at Jerusalem," *The Harvard Theological Review,* 62 (January 1969), 109–121.

CHAPTER 15

(Pages 177–190)

FEEDING THE 5000: Matthew 14:13 ff.; Mark 6:31 ff.; Luke 9:11 ff.; John 6:1 ff.

EVENTS AT ROME IN 32 A.D.: Tacitus, *Annals*, vi, 1 ff. GALLIO: History would remember not him, but his son Gallio, before whose tribunal St. Paul would later stand in Greece and be acquitted (Acts 18:12 ff.). For the father, see *Annals*, vi, 3.

TIBERIUS' LETTER: Philo, *loc. cit.* Philo mentions, but does not quote, the very threatening letter Tiberius sent to Pilate.

ANIMAL IMAGES OF ANTIPAS' PALACE: Josephus, *Vita*, xii.

SIMON MAGUS: Acts 8:9 ff.

BAR-ABBAS: Some ancient NT manuscripts at Matthew 27:16–17 include the full name "Jesus Bar-Abbas," while others cite only "Bar-Abbas."

JESUS AT THE TEMPLE: John 10:22–39.

LAZARUS: John 11:17 ff.

CAIAPHAS AND THE SANHEDRIN: John 11:47–53.

THE SANHEDRAL PROCLAMATION: But for the caption and the last sentence, this proclamation is verbatim from the rabbinical tradition on "Yeshu Hannosri" in *Sanhedrin* 43a, The Babylonian *Talmud*, trans. by Jacob Shachter (London: Soncino Press, 1935), Nezikin V, p. 281. The last sentence of the notice is derived from what is undoubtedly the NT version of this proclamation in John 11:57.

CHAPTER 16

(Pages 191–203)

EVENTS AT ROME IN 32–33 A.D.: Dio Cassius, lviii, 18–21 ff.; Tacitus, *Annals*, vi, 15–19.

PALM SUNDAY: Matthew 21:1 ff.; Mark 11:1 ff.; Luke 19:28 ff.; John 12:12 ff.

THE CONVERSION OF ZACCHAEUS: Luke 19:2 ff.

JESUS CLEANSING THE TEMPLE: Matthew 21:12 ff.; Mark 11:15–19; Luke 19:45–48; John 2:13. The Fourth Gospel, however, places this incident earlier in Jesus' ministry, while the Synoptics assign it to Holy Week.

JESUS' DIALOGUES WITH OPPONENTS: Matthew 21:23–23:39; Mark 11:27–12:40; Luke 20:1–47.

WHO WOULD ARREST JESUS? The Synoptic Gospels credit the Jewish temple guard with the arrest of Jesus and make no reference whatever to any involvement by the Roman military.

In John 18:3 and 12, the arrest is made by Jewish police and a *"speira"* (a "band," presumably Roman, *or* the temple guard"), which is led by a *"chiliarchos"* ("tribune" *or* "commander" of the temple guard). With this indefinite language, the Synoptics' parallel citation of only the Jewish police, the absence of the term "Roman" even in John, and Pilate's apparent surprise Good Friday morning that the case was coming to his tribunal, it seems unlikely that he committed Roman auxiliaries to make a religious arrest when the temple guard was entirely competent for this purpose. So also Kraeling, *op. cit.,* p. 266: "That Roman soldiers had anything at all to do with the capture of Jesus is extremely doubtful."

THE LAST SUPPER: Matthew 26:17 ff.; Mark 14:12 ff.; Luke 22:7 ff.; John 13:1 ff.

CHAPTER 17

(Pages 204–211)

TWO WITNESSES NECESSARY FOR PROSECUTION: Deuteronomy 19:15.

A BROKEN LEG ON THE SABBATH: *Shabbath (Mishnah),* xxii, 6.

THE ARREST AND RELIGIOUS TRIAL OF JESUS: Matthew 26:47 ff.; Mark 14:43 ff.; Luke 22:47 ff.; John 18:1 ff. For the judicial procedure of the Sanhedrin, see the *Mishnah* tractate *Sanhedrin,* iv, I to v, 5. A list of further irregularities at the Sanhedral hearing is provided by A. Taylor Innes, *The Trial of Jesus Christ* (Edinburgh, 1905), pp. 55–59. Indeed, because of the various irregularities in this case, scholars still argue over whether there was in fact any formal Jewish trial at all before Caiaphas, or simply an informal hearing, a grand-jury action to prepare for the final and determinative Roman trial.
PROCEDURE FOR STONING: *Sanhedrin,* vi, 1–4.

CHAPTER 18

(Pages 212–236)

THE DATE OF THE CRUCIFIXION: This is clearly of decisive importance to any consideration of Pilate's role at the trial of Jesus. Briefly, the years 29, 30, or 33 A.D. are most commonly proposed in the vast scholarly literature on this question, but the earlier datings seem to raise more problems than they solve. The most precisely given "anchor date" in the Gospels is Luke 3:1–2, where it is stated that John the Baptist began his public ministry "in the fifteenth year of the reign of Tiberius Caesar," i.e., 28–29 A.D. Allowing a half to one full year for John's independent ministry and three to three and one-half for Jesus' would seem to require 32–33 A.D. (The usual explanation that Tiberius shared a co-regency with Augustus from 12 A.D. so that the fifteenth year of Tiberius could fall as early as 26 founders on the facts of Roman history: the princeps never dated his reign from a time when the great Augustus was still alive, nor do our sources for this era, Tacitus, Suetonius, or Dio. Moreover, coinage in the Tiberian era dates his reign only from the death of Augustus.)

There is also this evidence from Roman history. The indirect threat of the prosecution at the trial of Jesus to appeal to Caesar against Pilate would not have been likely before the fall of the anti-Semite Sejanus in October of 31, and Tiberius' pro-Jewish policy which would have entertained such an appeal did not begin until after that time. Therefore the Passover of 32 or 33 would seem the best options for dating the Crucifixion. April 3, 33, is the preferable date, because it best answers the requirements for Nisan 14 falling on a Friday in the Jewish calendar. A brilliant discussion in support of 33 A.D., involving also astronomical calculation, is provided by Richard W. Husband, *The Prosecution of Jesus* (Princeton, 1916), pp. 34–69. A. D. Doyle posits the very probable thesis that the four sons of Herod complained about the golden shields—*after* the fall of Sejanus—at the Passover of 32 when they would naturally be together in Jerusalem, with the Crucifixion thus taking place a year later. See his "Pilate's Career and the Date of the Crucifixion," *The Journal of Theological Studies*, XLII (1941), 190–93. The 33 A.D. dating is favored also by *Cambridge Ancient History*, X, 649; J. K. Fotheringham, "The Evidence of Astronomy and Technical Chronology for the Date of the Crucifixion." *The Journal of Theological Studies*, XXXV (1934), 146–62; *et al.*

Finally, there is the direct patristic evidence of Eusebius. In his *Chronicon*, ii (ed. Migne, XIX, 535), he stated that Christ suffered "in the 19th year of the reign of Tiberius," i.e., 33 A.D., and he cites Phlegon's reference to the abnormal solar eclipse (see below) as taking place in the "fourth year of the 202nd Olympiad," which extended from July 1, 32, to June 30, 33 A.D. Since Christ was crucified at the time of the Passover, i.e., spring, 33 would be the year.

For further discussion, see my article, "Sejanus, Pilate, and the Date of the Crucifixion," *Church History*, XXXVII (March, 1968), 3–13.

ROMAN PENALTIES FOR SEDITION: Justinian, *Corpus Iuris Civilis, Digestae*, xlviii, 8, iii, 4–5.

THE CHARGE OF SORCERY: While the New Testament does not cite sorcery as a particular charge raised against Jesus, this indictment is plausibly mentioned in the *Acta Pilati*, i, and specifically in the early rabbinical traditions concerning "Yeshu Hannosri" in *Sanhedrin* 43a (Babylonian *Talmud*).

ANTIPAS "THAT FOX": Luke 13:32.

THE HEARING BEFORE HEROD ANTIPAS: Luke 23:6–12. CHUZA: Luke 8:3.

MANAEN: Acts 13:1, though the NT does not mention whether or not Chuza and Manaen accompanied Antipas to Jerusalem at this time. But since his wife Joanna was definitely there for this Passover (Luke 24:10), it is more than probable that Chuza was there as well.

THREE OPPORTUNITIES GIVEN THE DEFENSELESS: see A. N. Sherwin-White, *Roman Society and Roman Law in the New Testament* (Oxford, 1963), p. 25.

THE ROMAN TRIAL AND CRUCIFIXION OF JESUS: Matthew 27; Mark 15; Luke 23; and John 18:28–19:42. For legal aspects, see also Sherwin-White, *op. cit.*, pp. 22 ff., and A. H. M. Jones, *Studies in Roman Government and Law* (Oxford, 1960).

CHAPTER 19

(Pages 237–246)

"THE INNOCENT MAN": Plato, *The Republic,* ii, 5. The "innocent" or "just" man (*ho dikaios*) was the term used by both Plato and Pilate's wife.

"SANHEDRIN . . . A SLAUGHTERHOUSE": or "destructive tribunal," according to *Makkoth* 7a (Babylonian *Talmud*). Other rabbis said "once in *seventy* years."

THE GUARD AT THE TOMB: There is some controversy as to whether the Jewish temple police or Pilate's Roman auxiliaries were used to guard the sepulcher. The Greek of Matthew 27:65 cites Pilate's statement simply as: "You have a guard," though grammatically this could also be translated, "You may have a guard." But the first interpretation seems preferable, since the watch reported the empty tomb directly to the chief priests rather than Pilate (Matthew 28:11), which the temple police would certainly have done. Pilate's auxiliaries would clearly have reported to him, and only to him. Tertullian, *Apologeticus,* xxi, 20, also speaks of a Jewish military guard at the tomb.

THE FULL MOON: This was rather a time for lunar, not solar, eclipse. In point of fact, on the evening of Friday, April 3, A.D. 33, a partial eclipse of the moon *did* take place, which would have been visible in Jerusalem for some minutes after sundown. See Fotheringham, *loc. cit.*

CHAPTER 20

(Pages 247–257)

JESUS SPEARED: John 19:34. The phenomenon of separated blood and water flowing from Jesus' body has led some pathologists to conclude that the lance had most likely penetrated the pericardium, liberating extravasated blood which had separated into its two constituents of red cells and plasma, possibly indicating a heart previously ruptured from intense agony.

THE RESURRECTION ACCOUNTS: Matthew 28; Mark 16; Luke 24; John 20–21; I Corinthians 15:4 ff. Malchus' role in this chapter is only assumed. Several Jewish writings acknowledged that the tomb was empty on Sunday morning; see the discussion on the *Toledoth Jeshu* in Samuel Krauss. *Das Leben Jesu nach jüdischen Quellen* (Berlin: S. Calvary, 1902), pp. 45, 58 ff.

CHAPTER 21

(Pages 258–275)

EVENTS AT ROME IN 33 A.D.: Tacitus, *Annals*, vi, 20 ff.

ACTIVITIES OF THE DISCIPLES: Acts 1–5.

THE DARKNESS AT THE CRUCIFIXION: This phenomenon evidently was visible in Rome, Athens, and other Mediterranean cities. According to Tertullian, *Apologeticus*, xxi, 20, it was a "cosmic" or "world event." Phlegon, a Greek author from Caria writing a chronology soon after 137 A.D., reported that in the fourth year of the 202nd Olympiad (i.e., 33 A.D.) there was "the greatest eclipse of the sun," and that "it became night in the sixth hour of the day [i.e., noon] so that stars even appeared in the heavens. There was a great earthquake in Bithynia, and many thing were overturned in Nicaea."—Fragment from the 13th book of Phlegon, *Olympiades he Chronika*, ed. by Otto Keller, *Rerum Naturalium Scriptores Graeci Minores*, I (Leipzig: Teubner, 1877), p. 101. Trans. mine.

GRANDDAUGHTER OF THRASYLLUS: Ennia Thrasylla married Sertorius, Macro, Dio Cassius, lvii, 28.

THE ACTA: Pilate's official *acta* have never been found, and these "excerpts" are merely a fractional attempt at reconstruction. The so-called *Acta Pilati* from the *Gospel of Nicodemus* is an early apocryphal writing with gross historical inaccuracies and fantasy, and therefore not a reliable source, though a little of its evidence is valuable. Eusebius stated that the "Acts of Pilate" which circulated under the pagan emperor Maximian in his campaign to subvert Christianity were forgeries which foundered on the impossible date assigned the crucifixion: 21 A.D. (*Ecclesi-*

astical History, i, 9). They have never been found. Counterforgeries of "Acts of Pilate" by Christians in the fourth century A.D. are of no greater value, and they have not been found. Noteworthy support for possible Acts of Pilate is provided by Justin Martyr, *Apology*, xxxv and xlviii (". . . that these things did happen you can ascertain from the Acts of Pontius Pilate. . . .") and the early Latin church father Tertullian, who, in two famous passages from his *Apology*, stated:

> It was in the age of Tiberius, then, that the Christian name went out into the world, and he referred to the Senate the news which he had received from Syria Palestine, which had revealed the truth of Christ's divinity; he did this exercising his prerogative in giving it his endorsement. The Senate had not approved beforehand and so rejected it. Caesar held to his opinion and threatened danger to accusers of the Christians. (*Apologeticus*, v, 2).

> This whole story of Christ was reported to Caesar (at the time it was Tiberius) by Pilate, himself in his secret heart already a Christian. (*Apologeticus*, xxi, 24, both T. R. Glover's translations in *Loeb Classical Library*.)

While this may be succulent source material for a historical novelist, it cannot, in honesty, be used in a documented historical novel. Although so early an authority as Tertullian (born ca. 150 A.D.) must be heard with respect, his account of Pilate's report to Tiberius would seem an inaccurate presumption on his part, or a less than critical use of interpolated documents. The cited passages do not ring true for several reasons. If Pilate did write his emperor about "the truth of Christ's divinity," he would also have had to admit to the colossal blunder of crucifying him. In his present probationary position, Pilate could not have afforded such an advertising of error. Even less likely would have been Tiberius' favorable attitude toward the divinity of Christ, since he detested deification of himself or anyone else. Nor would the Senate have rejected something which the emperor favored.

THE SYRIAN LEGIONS: In Rome's military, only the Syrian legions had not displayed Sejanus' image in their standards, according to Suetonius, *Tiberius*, xlviii.

POMPONIUS FLACCUS: Tacitus, *Annals*, vi, 27. Although Tacitus cites Flaccus' death among the events of 33 A.D., he does not follow a strict chronological order in every case, and other evidence indicates that Flaccus did not die until 35 A.D., see Schürer, *op. cit.*, I, 1, pp. 363 ff.

THE PHOENIX: Tacitus, *Annals*, vi, 28. AVILLIUS FLACCUS: Philo, *In Flaccum*, xi, 92.

STEPHEN AND THE PERSECUTION: Acts 6–8.

VITELLIUS: Tacitus, *Annals*, vi, 32. Josephus, *Antiq.*, xviii, 4, 4–5, is accurate in placing this event in the reign of Tiberius rather than of Caligula, as is erroneously done by Suetonius, *Gaius Caligula*, xiv, 3, and Dio Cassius, lix, 27, 3.

THE MOSAIC PROPHECY: Deuteronomy 18:15.

THE TAHEB AND SAMARITAN ESCHATOLOGY: Cp. John MacDonald, *The Theology of the Samaritans* (London: SCM Press 1964), pp. 361 ff. James A. Montgomery, *The Samaritans* (Philadelphia: Winston, 1907) is still of value, cp. pp. 86, 234 ff. The military responsibilities of the *Taheb* grew in Samaritan beliefs in the early centuries A.D.

THE SAMARITAN INSURRECTION: Josephus, *Antiq.* xviii, 4, 1–2.

CAIAPHAS COMMENDS PILATE: This is merely an assumption, but it is based on a preferable and logical reading of "Samaritans" instead of the variant "Jews" in the text of Josephus, *Antiq.*, xviii, 4, 2, as those who accused Pilate, as well as on the great traditional hostility between Jews and Samaritans.

MARCELLUS AND PILATE'S DISMISSAL: Josephus, *loc, cit.*

VITELLIUS' VISIT TO JERUSALEM: Josephus, *Antiq.*, xv, 11, 4: xviii, 5, 1.

PILATE'S DEPARTURE: Josephus, *Antiq.*, xviii, 4, 2–3. A late December, 36, departure for Pilate is plausibly suggested by E. Mary Smallwood, "The Date of the Dismissal of Pontius Pilate from Judaea," *The Journal of Jewish Studies*, V (1954), 12–21.

CHAPTER 22

(Pages 276–281)

TRAVEL IN THE ROMAN EMPIRE: A. M. Ramsay, "The Speed of the Roman Imperial Post," *Journal of Roman Studies*, XV (1925), 60–74. Also W. M. Ramsay, "Roads and Travel (in NT)," in Hastings' *A Dictionary of the Bible*, V (1927), 375–402.

THE CONVERSION OF SAUL: Acts 9:1–30. Any conversation between Pilate and Saul is pure conjecture, of course, but there is a strong probability that they were both in Tarsus at the end of 36 or the beginning of 37, Pilate on his overland return trip to Rome, and Saul in his Cilician silent years after his first visit to Jerusalem in 35/36 (Galations 1:18, 21). For the determination of Pauline chronology in this connection, see Jack Finegan, *Handbook of Biblical Chronology* (Princeton, 1964), p. 321.

EVENTS AT ROME IN 34–37 A.D.: Tacitus, *Annals*, vi, 28–49. POMPONIUS LABEO: *Annals*, vi, 29.

THE "THREE-MONTH RULE": Dio Cassius, liii, 15, 6.

DEATH OF TIBERIUS: Tacitus, *Annals*, vi, 50; Suetonius, *Tiberius*, lxxiii; Dio Cassius, lviii, 28. That Tiberius died before Pilate reached Rome is stated by Josephus, *Antiq.*, xviii, 4, 2. Tacitus and Seutonius suggest that Macro and/or Caligula may have accelerated the death of Tiberius by smothering him under pillows, or administering a slow poison.

CHAPTER 23

(Pages 285–299)

REACTION TO TIBERIUS' DEATH: Suetonius, *Tiberius*, lxxv. However, some later historians, notably Theodor Mommsen, would rank Tiberius among Rome's finest emperors.

CALIGULA'S EARLY PRINCIPATE: Tacitus, *Annals*, vi, 45–51; Suetonius, *Gaius Caligula*, i–xvi; Dio Cassius, lix, 1–9.

GAIUS PONTIUS NIGRINUS: Suetonius, *Tiberius*, lxxiii; Dio Cassius, lviii, 27. Some relationship between Pilate and the consul Nigrinus—if not specifically "second cousin"—is assumed from their common gens name.

THALLUS: "Thallus" is the emendation made by most scholars at the difficult passage of Josephus, *Antiq.*, xviii, 6, 4, where the Greek would read "another" rather than "Thallus."

PILATE'S DEFENSE: Subsequent events within Samaria itself make Pilate's apparently harsh conduct in this episode seem almost lenient by comparison. Some years later, Vespasian's commander Cerealis slaughtered 11,600 Samaritans on Mount Gerizim, according to Josephus, *Wars*, iii, 7, 32.

HEROD AGRIPPA: The story of Agrippa forms its own novelette in the pages of Josephus. Cp. *Antiq.*, xviii, 6, and *Wars*, ii, 9, 5–6.

CHAPTER 24

(Pages 300–318)

THE FATE OF ANTIPAS AND HERODIAS: Josephus, *Antiq.*, xviii, 7. In his *Wars*, ii, 9, 6, Josephus cites Spain rather than Gaul as the place of exile, which is not a large discrepancy since this Lugdunum was not the modern Lyons in France, but Lugdunum Convenarum near the Pyrenees and the Spanish border.

VITELLIUS' SYCOPHANCY: Dio Cassius, lix, 27, 4–6.

THE LATER CALIGULA: Suetonius, *Gaius Caligula*, i–xlii; Dio Cassius, lix. While the anti-imperial bias of Suetonius must be taken into account, his negative portrait of Gaius is supported by the version of Dio Cassius. Caligula was apparently a victim of megalomania and other mental disorders. Unfortunately, the record of Tacitus is lost for the entire reign of Gaius.

xlvii; Dio Cassius, lix, 25, 2 ff. Some scholars question the truth of the seashell and false-prisoner stories.

AGRIPPA'S LETTER TO CALIGULA: Philo, *De Legatione ad Gaium*, xxxviii.

AGRIPPA'S BANQUET: Josephus, *Antiq.*, xviii, 8. Josephus makes no mention of the letter cited by Philo.

SOURCES FOR THE REIGN OF CALIGULA: Suetonius, *Gaius Caligula;* Dio Cassius, lix; Josephus, *Antiq.*, xviii, 6–8 to xix, 1; *Wars*, ii, 9–10; Philo, *In Flaccum; De Legatione ad Gaium.*

CHAPTER 25

(Pages 319–327)

AGRIPPA AND CLAUDIUS: Josephus, *Antiq.*, xix, 2–5; *Wars*, ii, 11, 1–6.

THE EARLY REIGN OF CLAUDIUS: Josephus, *loc. cit.;* Suetonius, *Divus Claudius*, x–xii; xlii; Dio Cassius, lx, 1–8.

AGRIPPA AND THE NORTH WALL OF JERUSALEM: Josephus, *Antiq.*, xix, 7, 2.

CHAPTER 26

(Pages 328–339)

PILATE CHILDLESS? Whether he and Procula did or did not have children is not known. No mention of any is made in the sources.

NAUSIPHANES: cited by Seneca, *Epistulae Morales*, lxxviii, 45: "*Hoc unum certum est nihil esse certi.*"

DEATH OF AGRIPPA: Josephus, *Antiq.*, xix, 8, 2; Acts 12:20 23.

AGRIPPA'S COINAGE AND STATUES: Josephus, *Antiq.*, xix, 9.

AGRIPPA, JAMES, AND PETER: Acts 12:1 ff.

PETER'S VISIT TO CORNELIUS: Acts 10:1–11:18.

PENTHEUS AND DIONYSUS: Euripides, *The Bacchae.*

PROCULA, AQUILA, AND PRISCILLA: According to a very early tradition, Pilate's wife became a Christian, see Origen, *Commentarii in Matthaeum*, 121–22 (ed. Migne, XIII, 918). Probably the earliest Christian congregation at Rome met in the home of Aquila and Priscilla, presumably on the Aventine Hill. See Acts 18:1 ff.; I Corinthians 16:19 ff.; Romans 16:3 ff.

EPILOGUE

(Page 340)

THE PILATE LEGENDS: For a summary of these, see Morison, *op. cit.*, pp. 231–41.

"A CHRISTIAN IN HIS CONSCIENCE": Tertullian, *Apologeticus*, xxi, 24: *"ipse iam pro sua conscientia Christianus."*